STAR WARS

THE NEW JEDI ORDER

EDGE OF VICTORY II
REBIRTH

D0714720

Also by Greg Keyes

The Chosen of the Changeleing
    THE WATERBORN
    THE BLACK GOD

The Age of Unreason
    NEWTON'S CANNON
    A CALCULUS OF ANGELS
    EMPIRE OF UNREASON

The Psi Corps Trilogy
    BABYLON 5: DARK GENESIS
    BABYLON 5: DEADLY RELATIONS
    BABYLON 5: FINAL RECKONING

Star Wars-The New Jedi Order
    EDGE OF VICTORY 1: CONQUEST
    EDGE OF VICTORY 2: REBIRTH
    THE FINAL PROPHECY

STAR WARS

THE NEW JEDI ORDER

EDGE OF VICTORY II
REBIRTH

GREG KEYES

arrow books

Published in the United Kingdom in 2001 by
Arrow Books

7 9 10 8

First published in the United Kingdom in 2001 by Arrow

Arrow Books
The Random House Group Limited
20 Vauxhall Bridge Road, London SW1V 2SA

Addresses for companies within the Random House Group Limited can be
found at: www.randomhouse.co.uk/offices.htm

The Random House Group Limited Reg. No. 954009
www.randomhouse.co.uk

www.starwars.com

www.starwarskids.com

A CIP catalogue record for this book
is available from the British Library

ISBN 9780099410447

The Random House Group Limited supports The Forest
Stewardship Council (FSC), the leading international forest certification
organisation. All our titles that are printed on Greenpeace approved
FSC certified paper carry the FSC logo. Our paper procurement
policy can be found at www.rbooks.co.uk/environment

Printed and bound in Great Britain by
CPI Antony Rowe, Chippenham, Wiltshire

For Gina Matthiesen

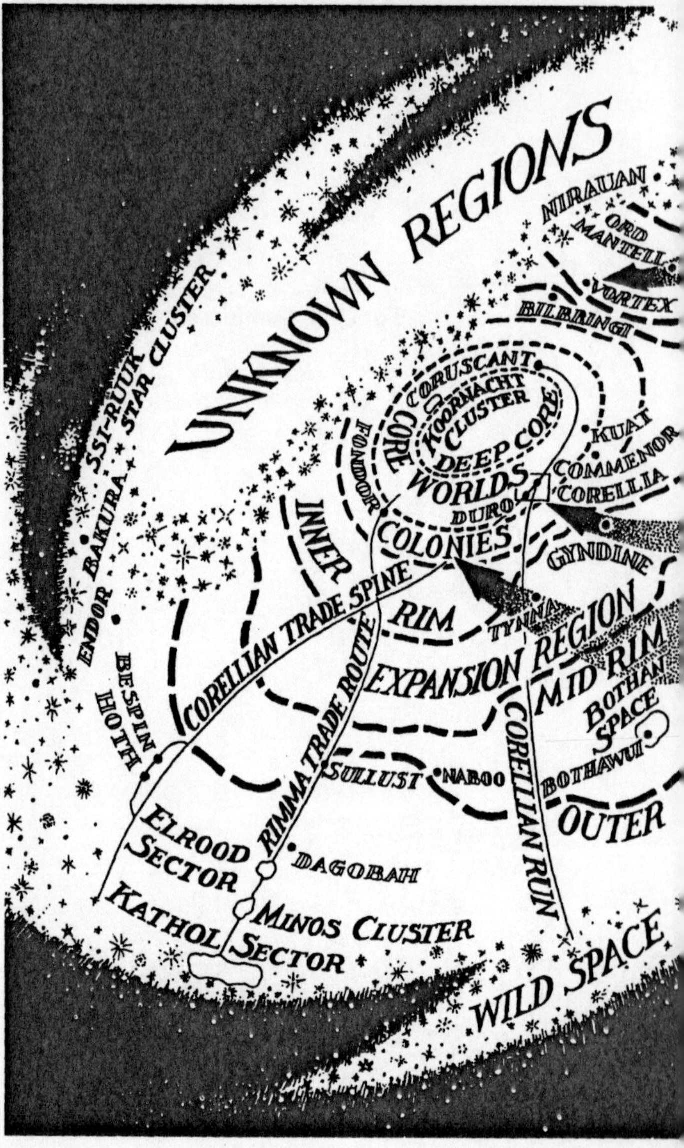
UNKNOWN REGIONS
SSI-RUUK STAR CLUSTER
BAKURA
ENDOR
BESPIN
HOTH
NIRAUAN
ORD MANTELL
VORTEX
BILBRINGI
CORUSCANT
KOORNACHT CLUSTER
CORE
DEEP CORE
FONDOR
WORLDS
KUAT
COMMENOR
CORELLIA
DURO
INNER
COLONIES
GYNDINE
CORELLIAN TRADE SPINE
RIM
TYNNA
EXPANSION REGION
MID RIM
BOTHAN SPACE
RIMMA TRADE ROUTE
CORELLIAN RUN
SULLUST
NABOO
BOTHAWUI
OUTER
ELROOD SECTOR
DAGOBAH
KATHOL SECTOR
MINOS CLUSTER
WILD SPACE

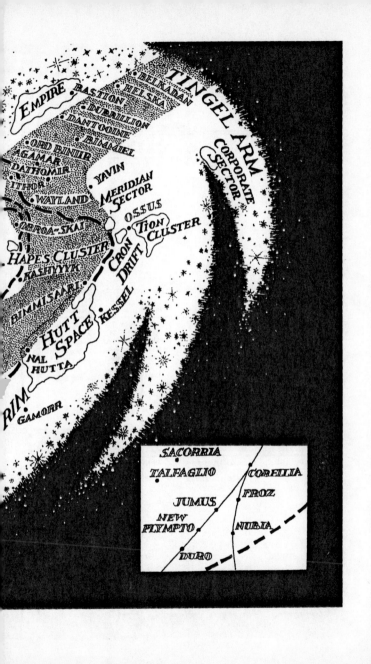

STAR WARS: THE NOVELS

44 YEARS BEFORE
STAR WARS: A New Hope

Jedi Apprentice Series

32 YEARS BEFORE
STAR WARS: A New Hope

Star Wars:
Episode I
The Phantom Menace

22 YEARS BEFORE
STAR WARS: A New Hope

Star Wars:
Episode II

20 YEARS BEFORE
STAR WARS: A New Hope

Star Wars:
Episode III

3 YEARS AFTER
STAR WARS: A New Hope

Star Wars:
Episode V
The Empire Strikes Back
Tales of the Bounty
Hunters

3.5 YEARS AFTER
STAR WARS: A New Hope

Shadows of the Empire

4 YEARS AFTER
STAR WARS: A New Hope

Star Wars: Episode VI
Return of the Jedi
Tales from Jabba's Palace
THE BOUNTY HUNTER WARS:
The Mandalorian Armor
Slave Ship
Hard Merchandise

The Truce at Bakura

6.5–7.5 YEARS AFTER
STAR WARS: A New Hope

X-Wing: Rogue Squadron
X-Wing: Wedge's Gamble
X-Wing: The Krytos Trap
X-Wing: The Bacta War
X-Wing: Wraith Squadron
X-Wing: Iron Fist
X-Wing: Solo Command

14 YEARS AFTER
STAR WARS: A New Hope

The Crystal Star

16–17 YEARS AFTER
STAR WARS: A New Hope

THE BLACK FLEET CRISIS
TRILOGY:
Before the Storm
Shield of Lies
Tyrant's Test

17 YEARS AFTER
STAR WARS: A New Hope

The New Rebellion

18 YEARS AFTER
STAR WARS: A New Hope

THE CORELLIAN TRILOGY:
Ambush at Corellia
Assault at Selonia
Showdown at Centerpoint

— What Happened When?

10–0 YEARS BEFORE
STAR WARS: A New Hope

THE HAN SOLO TRILOGY:
The Paradise Snare
The Hutt Gambit
Rebel Dawn

APPROX. 5–2 YRS. BEFORE
STAR WARS: A New Hope

THE ADVENTURES OF LANDO
CALRISSIAN:
Lando Calrissian and the Mind-
harp of Sharu
Lando Calrissian and the
Flamewind of Oseon
Lando Calrissian and the Star-
cave of ThonBoka

THE HAN SOLO ADVENTURES:
Han Solo at Stars' End
Han Solo's Revenge
Han Solo and the Lost Legacy

STAR WARS:
Episode IV
A New Hope

0–3 YEARS AFTER
STAR WARS: A New Hope

Tales from the
Mos Eisley Cantina
Splinter of the Mind's Eye

8 YEARS AFTER
STAR WARS: A New Hope

The Courtship of Princess
Leia

9 YEARS AFTER
STAR WARS: A New Hope

THE THRAWN TRILOGY:
Heir to the Empire
Dark Force Rising
The Last Command
X-Wing Isard's Revenge

11 YEARS AFTER
STAR WARS: A New Hope

THE JEDI ACADEMY TRILOGY:
Jedi Search
Dark Apprentice
Champions of the Force
I, Jedi

12–13 YEARS AFTER
STAR WARS: A New Hope

Children of the Jedi
Darksaber
Planet of Twilight
X-Wing: Starfighters of
Adumar

19 YEARS AFTER
STAR WARS: A New Hope

THE HAND OF THRAWN
DUOLOGY:
Specter of the Past
Vision of the Future

22 YEARS AFTER
STAR WARS: A New Hope

JUNIOR JEDI KNIGHTS:
The Golden Globe
Lyric's World
Promises
Anakin's Quest
Vader's Fortress
Kenobi's Blade

23–24 YEARS AFTER
STAR WARS: A New Hope

YOUNG JEDI KNIGHTS:
Heirs of the Force
Shadow Academy
The Lost Ones
Lightsabers
The Darkest Knight
Jedi Under Siege
Shards of Alderaan
Diversity Alliance
Delusions of Grandeur
Jedi Bounty
The Emperor's Plague
Return to Ord Mantell
Trouble on Cloud City
Crisis at Crystal Reef

25 YEARS AFTER
STAR WARS: A New Hope

THE NEW JEDI ORDER:
Vector Prime
Dark Tide I: Onslaught
Dark Tide II: Ruin
Agents of Chaos I:
Hero's Trial
Agents of Chaos II:
Jedi Eclipse
Balance Point
Edge of Victory I:
Conquest
Edge of Victory II:
Rebirth

The author would like to thank the following people:

The Flying Rat Toli club, for support during a dark time.

Shelly Shapiro and Sue Rostoni for timely help, advice, and hard work at every stage of the process. My fellow authors—Troy Denning, Jim Luceno, Elaine Cunningham, and Mike Stackpole for helping me try and get things right. Thanks also to Michael Kogge, Colette Russen, Kathleen O'Shea, Deanna Hoak, Ben Harper, Leland Chee, Chris Cerasi, Enrique Guerrero, Eelia Goldsmith Hendersheid, Helen Keier, and Dan Wallace. And again, to Kris Boldis for his support. It's been a blast, everyone!

DRAMATIS PERSONAE

Anakin Solo; Jedi Knight (male human)
Booster Terrik; captain, *Errant Venture* (male human)
Cilghal; Jedi healer (female Mon Calamari)
Corran Horn; Jedi Knight (male human)
Colonel Gavin Darklighter; Rogue Squadron (male human)
Han Solo; captain, *Millennium Falcon* (male human)
Jacen Solo; Jedi Knight (male human)
Jaina Solo; Jedi Knight (female human)
Kae Kwaad; master shaper (male Yuuzhan Vong)
Kam Solusar; Jedi Master (male human)
Kyp Durron; Jedi Master (male human)
Leia Organa Solo; former New Republic diplomat (female human)
Luke Skywalker; Jedi Master (male human)
Mara Jade Skywalker; Jedi Master (female human)
Nen Yim; shaper adept (female Yuuzhan Vong)
Nom Anor; executor (male Yuuzhan Vong)
Onimi; Supreme Overlord Shimrra's jester (male Yuuzhan Vong)
Qurang Lah; warleader (male Yuuzhan Vong)
Tahiri Veila; Jedi student (female human)
Talon Karrde; independent information broker (male human)
Traest Kre'fey; admiral (male Bothan)
Tsavong Lah; warmaster (male Yuuzhan Vong)
Vergere; familiar to the deceased Yuuzhan Vong priestess, Elan (female Fosh)

PROLOGUE

Blood, drifting in starlight.

That was the first thing Jacen Solo saw when he opened his eyes. It had beaded into what looked, in the dim, like polished black pearls reflecting the ancient starlight filtering through the transparisteel a meter or so away. He noted absently that the spheroids were all spinning in the same direction.

He was spinning, too, very slowly, through the little nebula of blood. Even in the negligible illumination he could tell he was only a few centimeters from a wall.

From the ache in his leg and skull, he had a good idea where the blood was coming from. It was cold, too, but the air seemed stuffy.

What was going on?

Outside the window, something large and irregular moved to block the stars, and he remembered.

Tsavong Lah, warmaster of the Yuuzhan Vong, clicked the obsidian-sharp talons of his new foot against the living coral of his command chamber floor and considered it in the pale light of the mycoluminescent walls.

He might have had the foot the cursed *Jeedai* took from him replaced with a clone of his own, but that would have been not only dishonorable but personally unsatisfying. That an infidel had taken something from him was bad enough; to pretend that the wound had never happened was unthinkable.

But a hobbling warmaster would lose respect, especially if he had not made the sacrifice himself.

The pain was fading, and feeling was coming into his new foot as the nerves learned their way. The four armored digits of a vua'sa now made up half his stride.

The choice was an homage to the most ancient traditions of his office. The first warmaster created by Yun-Yuuzhan had not been a Yuuzhan Vong, but a living weapon-beast he named vua'sa. A Yuuzhan Vong challenged the vua'sa to single combat, triumphed, and took its place. Even now, Vua was a popular name among the warrior caste.

Tsavong Lah had bade the shapers grow him a vua'sa. Though the creature had been extinct since the ancestral home planet was lost, its pattern still existed in the deeps of shaper memory-qahsa. They had made it; he had fought it and triumphed, despite having to fight on one foot. Now Tsavong Lah knew the gods still deemed him worthy of his station.

And from the cooling corpse of the vua'sa, he had a new foot.

"Warmaster."

Tsavong recognized the voice of his aide, Selong Lian, but did not look up from the examination of his prize.

"Speak."

"Someone petitions for words with you."

"Not my expected appointment?"

"No, Warmaster. It is the deception-sect priestess Ngaaluh."

Tsavong Lah growled in the back of his throat. Worshipers of Yun-Harla had failed the Yuuzhan Vong of late. Still, the sect was powerful, and Supreme Overlord Shimrra continued to favor the antics of those who worshiped the Trickster goddess. And since Yun-Harla oversaw the elevation of warriors and had possibly aided him in his fight with the vua'sa, he perhaps owed the goddess a favor, as well.

"Let me hear her words," he said.

A moment later, the priestess entered. She was slender, her back-sloping forehead narrower than most, the bluish sacs beneath her eyes mere crescents. She wore a ceremonial robe of living tissue grown to resemble a flayed skin.

"Warmaster," she said, crossing her arms in salute. "I am greatly honored."

"Your message," he snapped impatiently. "I have other business waiting. Harrar sent you?"

"Yes, Warmaster."

"Speak, then."

"The priestess Elan, who died to further the conquest of the infidels—"

"Who failed her task," Tsavong Lah reminded.

"Just so, Warmaster. She failed, but died nevertheless in the cause of the glorious Yuuzhan Vong. The priestess Elan had a familiar, a sentient creature named Vergere."

"I am aware of that. Did it not die with its mistress?"

"No, Warmaster. That is what I have come to tell you. It managed to escape the infidels and make its way back to us."

"Did it."

"Yes, Warmaster. She has communicated to us much of interest concerning the infidels, things she learned in their custody. Much more she knows and will not tell except to you, Tsavong Lah."

"You suspect an infidel trick? An attempt to assassinate me, perhaps?"

"We do not entirely trust her, Warmaster, but determined to bring you her words so you might decide how to treat her."

Tsavong Lah inclined his heavily scarred features. "It is good you did so. She must be interrogated and examined by the haar vhinic, of course. Afterward, have her brought to my ship, but keep her far from me. Tell her I will need further proof of both her intelligence and intentions before she may stand before me."

"It will be done, Warmaster."

He gave the priestess the sign of dismissal, and she immediately departed. Good. A priestess who knew her station.

His aide immediately took her place at the red-flanged receiving portal. "Qurang Lah has arrived, Warmaster," he said. "And the executor, Nom Anor."

"They will see me, now," Tsavong Lah pronounced.

Qurang Lah was his crèche-brother, a less elevated version of himself. His face was cut in deep hatch marks, and the gash of Domain Lah, while not as deep as the war-master's ear-to-ear cut, was still a clear marker of his lineage.

"*Belek tiu*, Warmaster." Qurang Lah saluted with crossed arms, as did the much slighter executor by his side. "Command me."

Tsavong Lah nodded at his crèche-brother, but fixed his gaze on Nom Anor. The executor's one real eye and the venomous plaeryin bol that occupied his other socket stared unblinking back at him.

"Executor," Tsavong Lah rumbled. "I have taken your latest suggestions under advisement. You are certain they are ripe for conquest?"

"The hinges of their fortress are weakened, Warmaster," Nom Anor replied. "I have seen to it personally. The battle will be a quick one, the victory easily secured."

"I have heard this from you before," the warmaster said. He turned his attention to the warrior. "Qurang Lah. You have been briefed in the matter. Have you anything to say?"

Qurang Lah revealed his sharpened teeth. "Conquest is always desirable," he said. "However, this seems a foolish time to move. The infidels tremble before us; they fear to counterattack; they dare dream our bloody path ended with Duro and that we might be satisfied to live in the same galaxy with abomination-using vermin. This is to our advantage; the shipwomb produces their doom, but it must be given time. At this moment, our fleet is thinly scattered, more thinly than the infidels know. One misstep now, before the shipwomb again swells our fleet, could be costly indeed."

"There will be no cost," Nom Anor asserted. "And the moment to strike *is* now. If we wait longer, the *Jeedai* will have more time to act."

"The Jeedai." Tsavong Lah snarled. "Tell me, Nom Anor. With all of your infidel contacts and all your self-proclaimed expertise in manipulating them, why have you been unable to bring me the one Jeedai I desire above all others—Jacen Solo?"

Nom Anor did not flinch. "That is a most difficult task, as you know, Warmaster," he admitted. "Certain elements among the *Jeedai* and their allies have gone rogue. They no longer answer to the senate, or any other body where we have allies. That is my point; when you told the infidels that we would cease our conquest if the *Jeedai* were delivered up to us, it was a brilliant strategy. It gave us time to build our force and secure our territories. It gave us many *Jeedai*. But Jacen is kin to Skywalker, the master of them all. He is the son of Leia Organa Solo and Han Solo, both worthy opponents who have managed to vanish for the time being. I have strategies that will uncover them; even now, a plan unfolds regarding Skywalker and his mate Mara and that will bring the others running, Jacen included."

"And this place you wish to feel the talons of our might? This involves the *Jeedai*?"

"It does not, Warmaster. But it will throw their senate into desperate confusion. It will give us the leverage we need to end the *Jeedai* threat forever. As of now, the government of the New Republic still refuses to make it policy to outlaw the *Jeedai*. In one stroke I can change that, as well as build us a new fortress overlooking the Core. But the time is now; if we wait, we will lose our opportunity."

"Nom Anor has counseled us ill before," Qurang Lah said.

"This is too true," the warmaster returned. "But it chafes me not to strike, to pretend quiescence so long. The number of *Jeedai* the weak-kneed infidels have given us has declined lately. We were humiliated at Yavin Four. There must be atonement, and Yun-Yuuzhan craves the scent of blood."

"If you wish it, Warmaster," Qurang Lah said, "I shall lead my fleet. I never shrink from battle when my duty calls."

"*Hurr,*" Tsavong Lah murmured, considering. "Nom Anor, you will implement your plan. Qurang Lah will command the Yuuzhan Vong forces, and you will advise him how to proceed. If your advice is again flawed, there will be a more serious reckoning. If it is good, as you assure me it will be, you will atone for your recent mistakes. Do you understand?"

"I understand, Warmaster. I will not fail."

"See you do not. Qurang Lah, have you anything else to say?"

"I have not, Warmaster. My duty is clear now." He snapped the salute. "*Belek tiu*. The infidels will fall before us. Their ships shall burn like falling stars. As I speak it, it is already done."

PART ONE

THRESHOLD

ONE

"You've had worse ideas, Luke," Mara Jade Skywalker reluctantly admitted, nodding her head back so the sunlight fell on her face and her deep red-gold tresses trailed behind her. Posed that way, eyes closed, framed against the blue line of the sea, her beauty closed Luke's throat for a moment.

Mara's green eyes opened, and she looked at him with a sort of wistful fondness before arching a cynical brow.

"Getting all fatherly on me again?"

"No," he said softly. "Just thinking how ridiculously lucky I am."

"Hey. I'm the one with the hormone swings. You aren't trying to one-up me, are you?" But she took his hand and gave it a squeeze. "Come on," she said. "Let's walk a bit more."

"You sure you're up to it?"

"What, you want to carry me? Of course I'm up to it. I'm pregnant, not hamstrung. You think it would be better for our kid if I spent all day lying around sucking on oorp?"

"I just thought you wanted to relax."

"Absolutely. And this is relaxing. Us, all alone, on a beautiful island. Well, sort of an island. Come on."

The beach was warm beneath Luke's bare feet. He had been reluctant to agree to going shoeless, but Mara had insisted that's what one did on a beach. He found, to his surprise, that it reminded him pleasantly of his boyhood on Tatooine. Back then, in the relative cool of early evening—one of those rare periods when both blazing suns were nearly set—sometimes he would take his shoes off and feel the still-warm sand between his toes. Not when Uncle Owen was looking, of course, because the old man would launch into an explanation of what shoes were for in the first place, about the valuable moisture Luke was losing though his soles.

For an instant, he could almost hear his uncle's voice and smell Aunt Beru's giju stew. He had an urge to put his shoes back on.

Owen and Beru Larses had been the first personal casualties in Luke Skywalker's battle against the Empire. He wondered if they had known why they died.

He missed them. Anakin Skywalker may have been his father, but the Larses had been his parents.

"I wonder how Han and Leia are doing?" Mara wondered aloud, interrupting his reverie.

"I'm sure they're fine. They've only been gone a few days."

"I wonder if Jacen should have gone with them?"

"Why not? He's proven himself capable often enough. And they're his parents. Besides, with half the galaxy after him, it's better he stay on the move."

"Right. I only meant it makes things worse for Jaina. It's hard on her, doing nothing, knowing her brother is out fighting the fight."

"I know. But Rogue Squadron will probably call her up pretty soon."

"Sure," Mara replied. "Sure they will." She sounded far from convinced.

"You don't think so?" Luke asked.

"No. I think they would like to, but her Jedi training makes her too much of a political liability right now."

"When did the Rogues ever care about politics? Has someone said this to you?"

"Not in so many words, but I hear things, and I'm trained to listen to the words behind the words. I hope I'm wrong, for Jaina's sake."

Her feelings brushed Luke in the Force, running a troubled harmony to her assertion.

"Mara," Luke said, "my love, while I'll believe you when you say picking up parasites on a strange beach is relaxing—"

"Nonsense. This sand is as sterile as an isolation lab. It's perfectly safe to walk barefoot. And you like the feel of it."

"If you say so. But I forbid any more talk about politics, Jedi, the war, the Yuuzhan Vong, anything like that. We're out here for you to relax, to forget all of that for a day or so. Just a day."

She narrowed her eyes at him. "You're the one who thinks the whole universe will collapse unless you're there to keep it spinning."

"I'm not pregnant."

"Say something like *that* again, and I'll make you wish you were," she said, a bit sharply. "And by the way, if we do this again, it's your turn."

"We'll play sabacc for it," Luke responded, trying to keep a straight face but failing. He kissed her, and she kissed him back, hard.

They continued along the strand, past a rambling stand of crawling slii, all knotted roots and giant gauzy leaves. Waves were beginning to lap on the beach, as they hadn't earlier, which meant they were on the bow side of the "island."

It wasn't an island at all, of course, but a carefully land-scaped park atop a floating mass of polymer cells filled with inert gas. A hundred or so of them cruised the artificial western sea of Coruscant, pleasure craft built by rich merchants during the grand, high days of the Old Republic. The Emperor had discouraged such frivolity, and most had been docked for decades and fallen into disrepair. Still, many were in good enough shape to refurbish, and in the youth of the New Republic, a few sharp businessmen had purchased some and made them commercial successes. One such person, not surprisingly, had been Lando Calrissian, a long-time friend of Luke's. He had offered Luke use of the craft whenever he wished it. It had taken Luke a long time to call in the offer.

He was glad he had done it—Mara seemed to be enjoying it. But she was right, of course. With everything that was happening now, it was hard not to think of it as a waste of time.

But some feelings could *not* be trusted. Mara was showing now, her belly gloriously rounded around their son, and she was suffering from all of the physical discomforts any woman did in that situation. Nothing in her training as an assassin, smuggler, or Jedi Knight had prepared her for this compromised state, and despite her obvious love for their unborn child, Luke knew physical weakness grated on her. Her comment about Jaina might just as well have been about herself.

And there were other worries, too, and a pocket paradise wasn't likely to help her forget them, but at least they could take a few deep breaths and pretend they were on some distant, uninhabited world, rather than in the thick of the biggest mess since before the Empire had been defeated.

No, strike that. The Empire had threatened to extinguish liberty and freedom, to bring the dark side of the Force to ascendance. The enemy they faced now threatened extinction in a much more literal and ubiquitous sense.

So Luke walked with his wife as evening fell, pretending not to be thinking of these things, knowing she could feel he was anyway.

"What will we name him?" Mara asked at last. The sun had vanished in a lens on the horizon, and now Coruscant began to shatter the illusion of pristine nature. The distant shores glowed in a solid mass, and the sky remained deep red on the horizon. Only near zenith did it resemble the night sky of most moonless planets, but even there was a baroque embroidery of light as aircars and starships followed their carefully assigned paths, some coming home, some leaving home, some merely arriving at another port.

A million little lights, each with a story, each a spark of significance in the Force that flowed from them, around them, through them.

No illusion, here. All was nature. All was beauty, if you had eyes willing to see it.

"I don't know." He sighed. "I don't even know where to start."

"It's just a name," she said.

"You would think. But everyone seems to believe it's important. Since we went public with the news, you wouldn't believe how many suggestions I've gotten, and from the strangest places."

Mara stopped walking, and her face reflected a sudden profound astonishment. "You're afraid," she said.

He nodded. "I guess I am. I guess I don't think it's 'just a name,' not when it comes to people like us. Look at Anakin. Leia named him after our father, a gesture to the person who became Darth Vader, as a recognition that he overcame the dark side and died a good man. It was her reconciliation with him, and a sign to the galaxy that the scars of war could heal. That we could forgive and move on. But for Anakin, it's been a trial. When he was little, he always feared he would walk the same dark path his grandfather did. It was just a name, but it was a real burden to place on his shoulders. It may be years before we learn the full consequences of that decision."

"For all that I admire your sister, she is a politician, and she thinks like one. That's been good for the galaxy, not so good for her children."

"Exactly," Luke said reluctantly. "And whether I like it or not, Mara, because of who we are, our child will inherit part of our burden. I'm just afraid of placing an extra one on his shoulders. Suppose I named him Obi-Wan, as a salute to my old Master? Would he think that means I want him to grow up to be a Jedi? Would he think he had to live up to Ben's reputation? Would he feel his choices in life constrained?"

"I see you've thought a lot about this."

"I guess I have."

"Notice how quickly this takes us back to the things you said we weren't supposed to talk about?"

"Oh. Right."

"Luke, this is who we are," Mara said, stroking his shoulder lightly. "We can't deny it, even alone on an island." She dipped her foot in the wavelets lapping onto the beach. Luke closed his eyes and felt the wind on his face.

"Maybe not," he admitted.

"And so what?" Mara said, playfully kicking a little water on the cuff of his pants. But then her face grew serious again. "There is one *very* important thing I want to say, now, before another second passes," she informed him.

"What's that?"

"I'm really hungry. Really, really hungry. If I don't eat right away, I'm going to salt you in seawater and gobble you up."

"You'd be dissapointed," Luke said. "It's fresh water. Come on. The pavilion isn't far. There should be food waiting."

Luke and Mara ate outside at a table of polished yellow Selonian marble while the blossoms around them chimed a quiet music and released fragrances to complement each course. Luke felt ridiculously pampered and a little guilty, but managed to relax somewhat into the mood.

But the mood was broken during the intermezzo, when the pavilion's protocol droid interrupted them.

"Master Skywalker," it said, "an aircar is approaching and requesting admittance through the security perimeter."

"You have the signal?"

"Most assuredly."

"Transfer to the holostation on the table."

"As you wish, sir."

A hologram of a man's face appeared above the remains of their meal. It was human, very long, with aristocratic features.

"Kenth Hamner," Luke said, a sense of foreboding pricking up his scalp. "To what do we owe this pleasure?"

The retired colonel smiled briefly. "Nothing important. Just a visit from an old friend. May I come aboard?"

That's what his words said. His expression, somehow, conveyed something altogether different.

"Of course. Link to the ship's computer, and it will land you somewhere appropriate. I hope you like grilled nylog."

"One of my favorites. I'll see you soon."

A few moments later, Hamner appeared from one of the

several trails leading to the pavilion, accompanied by the droid.

"You two make me wish I was young again," Hamner said, smiling, looking them over.

"We're not so young, and you're not so old," Mara replied.

Hamner offered her a short bow from the waist. "Mara, you're looking lovely as ever. And my deepest congratulations on your upcoming event."

"Thank you, Kenth," Mara returned graciously.

"Have a seat," Luke said. "May I have the droid bring you something?"

"A cold drink of a mildly stimulating beverage perhaps? Surprise me."

Luke sent the droid off with those rather vague instructions and then turned to Hamner, who was now seated.

"You didn't come here just to congratulate us, did you?"

Hamner nodded sadly. "No. I came to give you a heads-up. Borsk Fey'lya has managed to secure an order for your arrest. The warrant will be served about six standard hours from now."

TWO

Somewhere between the Corellian Trade Spine and the Kathol sector, the Star Destroyer *Errant Venture* dropped out of hyperspace, reoriented its massive wedge-shaped frame, and resumed lightspeed. An uninformed observer would have had less than a minute to wonder what a Star Destroyer was doing in such an out-of-the-way part of space and why it was painted red.

Deep in the Destroyer's belly, Anakin Solo hardly noticed the transition, so intent was he on what he was doing. He stood quickly into narrow profile, the point of his lightsaber aiming toward the deck, pommel level with his forehead and pointed at the ceiling. With two quick twists of his wrist, he deflected a pair of stun bolts from the remote whirring around him. He flipped the lightsaber to an identical position behind his back to catch the blast from a second remote, then dropped into a crouch, his luminescent weapon whipping up to high guard. A leaping somersault carried him over the sudden coordinated flurry of shots from the two flying spheres. By the time his feet touched the deck, he was weaving a complex set of parries that sent reddish bolts hissing against the walls.

He was in the rhythm, now, and his blue eyes sparkled like electron arcs as the stinging rays came faster, more often, better timed. After a few minutes of this, sweat was plastering his brown hair to his head and soaking his dark Jedi robes, but none of the painful though harmless attacks had found their mark.

He was warmed up, now.

"Halt," he commanded. Immediately the spheres became stationary and quiescent.

He deactivated his lightsaber and set it aside. From a wall cabinet, Anakin removed another lightsaber, thumbed it on, took a few deep breaths, calmed his racing pulse. It was quiet in the storage compartment he'd converted into his training space. Quiet and spare and off-white. A motley trio of droids regarded him with unblinking eyes. Even the most casual observer could see they had been cobbled together from spare parts, though the central chassis of each was that of a rather common worker drone. They did not look particularly dangerous, until one examined what they held in their hands—wicked-looking staffs, sharp on one end, spoon-shaped on the other. They looked remarkably like snakes, an impression enhanced by the fact that they undulated now and then.

Anakin blew out another breath and nodded at the droids.

"Begin sequence one," he said.

The droids flashed into motion, their spindly frames moving with eye-daunting speed, two flanking him on either side, one driving straight toward him. Anakin backpedaled and parried, dropped, and swept the legs out from under the droid on his right. The other two were attacking, one staff spearing at his neck, the other gone suddenly flexible, flicking around his rising parry toward his back. Anakin stepped forward a centimeter and felt the wind from the vicious whip-over as it came up short of his spine.

That's it, he thought. *I'm learning the range. The smallest movement possible to prevent the attack from landing is the best.*

He dropped the high parry into a riposte. The droid, suddenly too close to him, tried to retreat but stopped instantly, deactivated when Anakin's weapon touched its torso.

The downed droid was back up by then, and Anakin found himself circling, holding them at the very outside of his guard and in his field of vision. That kept them off him, and he could probably do that forever. He wouldn't win the fight that way, though, so he gave them a rhythm to follow and let them try to break it.

One of the staffs suddenly spit a stream of liquid at him. He twisted his body to avoid it, again allowing only a centimeter for the miss. At the same moment, the other droid broke tempo and leapt in deep.

Anakin parried, but the staff wrapped around his wrist. He felt a distinct and painful electric shock. The other droid was an instant behind, leveling a blow at Anakin's skull.

Somewhere a blaster shrieked, and the droid suddenly didn't have a weapon—or the arm that held it.

"Halt!" Anakin shouted, and hurled himself away as the staff instantly released his hand. He came down in a fighting posture.

A dark-haired man with a blaster stood in the doorway. He had a beard liberally tinseled with silver and wore green robes the same shade as his eyes. He held the blaster up in a nonthreatening way, as if surrendering.

"Why did you do that?" Anakin asked, trying to suppress the anger suddenly boiling up. He had worked hard on that droid.

"You're welcome," Corran Horn said, holstering his weapon.

"Those are training droids. They wouldn't have hurt me."

"Oh no? Are those training amphistaffs they're holding? If he'd hit you with it . . ."

"He wouldn't have. They're programmed to arrest their blows the second the staff touches my skin. And yes, they are training amphistaffs. They aren't real."

Corran's eyes widened in surprise. "How did you manage that? Why didn't your lightsaber cut through them?"

"It's not a lightsaber."

Corran's expression was almost worth the damage to the droid.

"It's just a blade-shaped force field, a weak one," Anakin explained. "Wouldn't cut anything. The things my droids have act like amphistaffs and move like them, but they just spit dye and deliver a shock when they hit. They only weigh a kilogram or so."

"I guess I ruined your droid for no good reason, then," Corran said.

Anakin's anger was entirely mastered now. It was something he had been working on. "It's okay. I built it; I can fix it. I've got nothing but time."

"I'm just curious," Corran said, eyeing the droids. "Booster has a couple of duelist elites in storage. Why not use one of them to train with?"

Anakin deactivated the "weapon" and returned it to the cabinet. "Duelist elites don't move like Yuuzhan Vong warriors. The droids I built do."

"I wondered what you've been puttering at for the last few weeks."

Anakin nodded. "I don't want to lose my edge. You saw what happened—the one you shot had me."

"Practice is fine," Corran said. "I just wish you had informed me of what you were doing. Might have saved me a skipped heartbeat and you a droid."

"Right. I forgot," Anakin said.

Corran nodded again, this time with a more thoughtful look in his eye. "You didn't notice me coming. That's not good. You have to learn to extend your sphere of responsibility beyond the immediate battle."

"I know," Anakin replied. "I wasn't using the Force. I'm training to fight without it."

"Because the Yuuzhan Vong can't be sensed in the Force, I assume."

Anakin nodded. "Of course. The Force is a wonderful tool—"

"The Force isn't merely a tool, Anakin," Corran admonished. "It's much more than that."

"I know," Anakin said, a bit peevishly. "But among other things it is a tool, and for fighting the Yuuzhan Vong, it's just not the right tool for the job, no more than a hydrospanner is what you would use to calibrate the input feed of an astromech."

Corran cocked his head skeptically. "I can't precisely dispute that, but it's not because it isn't wrong."

Anakin shrugged. "Try it like this, then. All Jedi training

involves the Force, even combat training. Sensing blows and blaster bolts before they happen, that sort of thing. Shoving our enemies around telekinetically—"

"With some exceptions," Corran dryly reminded him.

"Right. So you should know what I mean. What do you think of Jedi who can't win a fight without resorting to telekinesis? For that matter, you were CorSec long before you were Jedi. You should be able to see that the Force has become as much of a crutch for us as anything. The Yuuzhan Vong prove that."

"Sounding a little like your brother. Are you abandoning the Force?"

Anakin's eyebrows arched up. "Of course not. I'll use it when it works. When I was being hunted by the Yuuzhan Vong on Yavin Four, I discovered ways to use the Force against them. I looked for the holes in the Force around me. I listened to the voices of the jungle and felt the fear of its creatures when the Yuuzhan Vong warriors passed near."

"And you learned to sense the Yuuzhan Vong themselves," Corran pointed out.

"Not with the Force, though. With the lambent I used to rebuild my lightsaber."

"How can you be sure? I've never believed the Yuuzhan Vong don't exist in the Force. They *must*. Everything does. We just don't know how to do it. You attuned yourself to a piece of Vong biotech and now you can sense them. Can you be sure you haven't found where they live in the Force?"

"Maybe I did make some sort of metalinkage, but if I did I think it's more of a translation from one to another. I can't be sure. All I know is, I can use it. But if I lose my lightsaber, or it's destroyed, or the lambent dies—I still want to be able to fight them."

Corran placed a hand on Anakin's shoulder. "Anakin, I understand you've been through a lot. The Yuuzhan Vong have taken much that was precious from you. I'll always be grateful for what you did for my children, and so I'm telling you this as a friend. You need to control your emotions. You can't allow yourself to hate."

Anakin shook his head. "I don't hate the Yuuzhan Vong, Corran. My time with them helped me to understand them. More than ever, I think they must be stopped, but I promise you, I do not hate them. I can fight them without anger."

"I hope what you say is true, but anger is a quick-change artist and a trickster. More often than not, you don't see it for what it is."

"Thanks," Anakin said. "I appreciate the advice."

Corran again looked slightly skeptical. Then he motioned toward the droids. "These droids were a good idea. I'd be happy to help you repair that one."

"That's okay. Like I said, I have plenty of time on my hands."

Corran smiled. "Getting a little deck fever?"

"I'm ready to get back out there, if that's what you mean. But Tahiri still needs me."

"You're a good friend to her, Anakin."

"I haven't been. I'm trying to be."

"Tahiri won't get over her ordeal in a few months. She needs more time. I think she'll understand if you have to go."

Anakin dropped his gaze from Corran's. "I promised her I would stay a while, and that's what I'm going to do. But it's hard, knowing what's going on out there. Knowing my friends and family are fighting while I'm here doing nothing."

"But you aren't doing nothing; you just said it yourself. You're still a part of the defensive effort. Protecting the Jedi students is important. Jumping randomly around the galaxy is probably the safest thing we can do, but there's no telling when the Yuuzhan Vong or one of their sympathizers will pick up our trail. If they do, we'll need everyone we can get."

"I guess so. I'm just so *restless*."

"You are," Corran agreed. "I've noticed you've been kind of itchy. That's why I was looking for you, in fact."

"Really? What for?"

"We need supplies. Obviously, if we're trying to keep our location secret we can't take the only red Star Destroyer in the galaxy into an inhabited system. I was going to take one of the transports out. I thought you might like to go. Hopefully it will be a boring trip, but—"

"Yes," Anakin said. "I'll do it."

"Good. I could use a copilot. I'll meet you in the docking bay tomorrow, say after morning meal?"

"Great. Thanks, Corran."

"No problem. See you then."

THREE

Jacen watched the ship approach as if in a dream. It remained a black presence against the stars—it had no running lights. *It must be in the shadow of the* Millennium Falcon, he thought.

The Force told him there was nothing there at all.

It gradually moved from the umbra into the distant orange light of the nameless star a parsec below them, and now he could see details. Distances were deceiving in space—he couldn't tell how large it was. It was spicular, like two cones with their bases pushed together. Where the cones met, three finned, heartlike structures projected. These Jacen recognized as dovin basals, living creatures that bent space, time, and gravity around themselves. There could be no doubt it was a Yuuzhan Vong ship, for it was made—rather, grown—from the same yorik coral Jacen had seen so many times already. Its surface was roughened by numerous small welts, as if the ship had contracted Bakuran fever bumps.

When he realized the bumps were coralskippers, the Yuuzhan Vong equivalent of starfighters, he suddenly grasped the scale. The thing was the size of a Dreadnaught.

And it was coming for them. It was almost certainly what had yanked them so brutally out of hyperspace.

Jacen snapped out of his fog of confusion and pushed away from the bulkhead. He was in the dorsal gunner's turret. He'd been sitting there in contemplation before the sudden terrifying jolt. His head was bleeding, but not critically, so far as he could tell.

He pulled himself quickly along the rungs of the ladder

into the main cabin. He fought the feeling of falling; it had been a while since he had done any zero-g training.

"Mom! Dad!" His voice rang in the silent ship. A primitive part of him cringed at the sound, warning him that the predator outside would hear him. It couldn't, of course, not through the vacuum, but human instincts were older than space travel.

He got no answer. Frantic now, he pushed himself through the darkness to the cockpit.

He found them there, and for a heart-stopping moment thought they were dead, so still were they in the Force. But both were breathing.

"Dad!" He gently shook his father's shoulder, but got no more than a reflexive response. Still gently, fear overcoming reluctance, he probed a little in the Force, suggesting the older man awake.

Han Solo stirred. "Huh? Whzzat!" Then he jerked fully alert, saw Jacen, and pulled back his fist.

"It's me, Dad!" Jacen said. Next to him, his mother began to stir, too. He couldn't feel anything seriously wrong with either of them. They had both been strapped in their crash couches.

"Jacen?" Han murmured. "What's going on? What happened?"

"I was hoping you knew. As near as I can tell, we've been interdicted by a Yuuzhan Vong ship. It's out there right now. I don't think we have much time."

Han rubbed his eyes and looked at the control panel, where a few feeble lights were still clinging to life. He let out a long, low whistle.

"That's not good," he said.

"Han? Jacen?" Leia Organa Solo sat straighter in the crash couch. "What's happening?"

"The usual," Han replied, flipping switches. A few more indicators came on. "Power system's off-line, artificial gravity off-line, emergency life support on its last legs, big ship full of bad guys outside."

"A really big ship," Jacen added.

"Just like old times." Leia sighed.

"Hey, I told you it would be like a second honeymoon."
Han's voice dropped lower and grew more serious. "You all
right?"

"I'm fine," Leia said. "I'm wondering what made us
black out."

"Probably the same thing that fried the power couplings," Han remarked. Then his eyes widened. "Oh, no."

"I told you it was big," Jacen said, as their lateral drift
brought the Yuuzhan Vong ship into view.

"Do something, Han," Leia said. "Do something *now*."

"I'm doing, I'm doing," he muttered, working at the controls. "But unless someone wants to get out and push . . ."

"Why aren't *they* doing anything?" Leia wondered.

"They probably think we're dead in space," Han replied.
"They may be right."

"Yes, but—" She stopped. Two of the coralskippers had
detached from the larger vessel and were coming toward
the *Falcon*.

Han unbuckled himself. "Take my seat, Jacen. I had a
shielded power core installed, but the couplings have to be
changed."

"I'll do it."

"You don't know the *Falcon* well enough. You two stay
up here. The second I give you power, go, and I mean, *go*."

"We're too close. They'll snatch us with their dovin
basals."

"They'll snatch us for sure if we sit here."

He kicked back through the doorway and was gone,
swallowed by the darkness beyond.

The coralskippers continued to approach, in no apparent
hurry.

"Mom, look," Jacen said, pointing. Against the starfield
were some brighter sparks, drifting in a nebulous lens.

"What is it?"

"Something reflecting the light from the primary. A bunch
of somethings."

"Ships," Leia said. "Other ships they've interdicted."

"Uh-huh. Must be a dozen or more."

"Well." She sighed. "I guess we found out something

useful on this trip. This isn't a safe route to smuggle Jedi through."

A series of curses drifted from somewhere in the back of the ship.

"Han?" Leia shouted.

"Nothing. Hit my head," the answer came back.

Another few moments of rummaging about, and then another, more colorful set of curses.

"It's going to take at least half an hour," Han called.

"We don't have that," Leia whispered. "They'll be boarding us any minute. If they even bother, and don't just cut us to pieces."

"They'll bother," Jacen said. "The Yuuzhan Vong hate to waste good slaves and sacrifices. I guess we'd better get ready to meet them." He unclipped the lightsaber from his belt. Leia unbuckled herself and drew her own weapon.

"You let me deal with this, Mom. You're still favoring that leg."

"Don't worry about me. I was doing this before you were born."

Jacen was about to lodge another protest when he saw the expression on her face. She wouldn't be budged.

As they passed the lounge, a growl that made Jacen's hair stand on end prompted him to ignite the cold green glow of his lightsaber. Two sets of black eyes blinked at the light.

"Lady Vader," one snarled. "We fail you."

"You failed no one, Adarakh," Leia told her Noghri bodyguards. "Something put us all out."

"Your enemies are about, Lady Vader?" the second Noghri, a female—Meewalh—asked.

"They are. Adarakh, you're with me. Meewalh, you help Jacen."

"No," Jacen said. "Mom, you need them more than I do. You know it."

"The first-son speaks right, Lady Vader," Meewalh agreed.

Leia's eyes flashed at the insubordination. "We don't have time to argue about this."

That was confirmed a heartbeat later when something

bumped against the hull, followed by a second, similar impact.

"What's that?" Han called up.

"Just get us some power," Leia called back. "Fine. Both of you, with me. Jacen, watch yourself. None of this not-using-the-Force nonsense."

"I'm over that, Mom."

She kissed Jacen quickly on the cheek. "Watch out for my boy." Then she pushed toward the cargo lifter, where the first impact seemed to have been. The Noghri went silently after her, as nimble in free-fall as on foot.

Jacen shifted the grip on his lightsaber and found a hand-hold to steady his weightless body as he tried to figure out where the second boarder was.

Within seconds, something began gnashing and grinding against the outer bulkheads, enabling him to locate it in the lounge. Moving slowly, he flattened as best he could against what would be the ceiling if the gravity came back on.

Must be grutchins, he thought. Yuuzhan Vong technology was all biologically based. They used modified insectoid creatures to hull ships. There would be fumes from the acid, then, and maybe worse, but there was no time to seek vac suits. If the Yuuzhan Vong were simply going to open the ship to space, they'd all had it. But if the enemy wanted the Solos dead, they would have blasted them while the ship was powered down, since they had, at best, contempt for nonliving tech and no use for the *Falcon* whatsoever. Knowing the Yuuzhan Vong, they were eager for live captives, not freeze-dried corpses.

Jacen calmed his mind and waited.

Not much later, a hole appeared in the wall. As predicted, an acrid, choking stench came through, but not the feared explosive decompression of the cabin. Jacen stayed out of visual range until something poked its head through an opening wide enough for a human to step through.

Jacen flicked on his lightsaber.

Something like a huge beetle was revealed in the viridian light of his blade. Jacen drove his point into its eye before it could even twitch. For what seemed a long moment, the energy blade refused to penetrate beyond the first few centimeters. The creature yanked its head back and forth violently, but Jacen kept the point on until, finally, with a sputter, it pushed in. The beetle spasmed and died.

Jacen came off the ceiling and, avoiding the steaming edge of the hole, hurled himself through the breach.

A flexible coupling had attached itself to the outside of the ship. It was about twenty meters long. Halfway down its length a Yuuzhan Vong warrior pulled himself along by means of a series of knobs protruding from the sides. Jacen kicked against the projections nearest him, accelerating toward the Vong.

His enemy was humanoid, with black hair plaited and knotted behind his head. His forehead sloped sharply down to dark eyes above swollen purplish sacs and an almost flat nose. He wore the characteristic vonduun crab armor and carried an amphistaff coiled around one wrist. A savage grin appeared on his scarred and tattooed face, and he duplicated Jacen's move. The amphistaff straightened, pointing at the young Jedi like a lance.

When they were only about four meters apart, the staff spit something at him. If past experience was a guide, it was almost certainly poison.

Jacen reached for the whirling droplets in the Force, but it felt as if he were reaching through syrup. He stopped it within a few centimeters of his face, at the same time kicking the tube wall obliquely so that he hurled up to the top of it. The warrior passed beneath him, running face-first into the suspended toxin. Grimly, not looking back, Jacen pulled out of the tumble his maneuver had resulted in and propelled himself toward the open hatch beyond. Behind him, the warrior stifled a hoarse cry.

The coralskipper wasn't big, but it was big enough for two. He could see the second warrior, just poking his head out. This time, there was no aerial joust; the Yuuzhan Vong waited for him, feet braced against something behind him, his amphistaff in guard position.

They met in a stir of blows that killed Jacen's momentum and set him bouncing around the coupling, trying to reorient. The Yuuzhan Vong didn't budge, but continued to strike at Jacen in a measured, conservative way. Jacen found he had to fight one-handed and use the other to anchor himself. He kept his lightsaber extended and his movements small. The next time the Yuuzhan Vong struck, Jacen nailed him in the back of the hand. The warrior grunted and released the staff. With a snarl, he launched himself at Jacen.

The sudden attack took the young Jedi by surprise. The warrior managed to get his wrist in a lock, and the two went tumbling back through the tube. Too late, Jacen realized his lightsaber was still on, slicing through the wall of the coupling like tissue.

Needles were suddenly under his skin, trying to push themselves out. Desperate, Jacen brought his elbow up beneath the Yuuzhan Vong's jaw. He felt teeth clack together, and his opponent let go. The slit, now five meters long, yawned into space, and the warrior floated right through. A moment later, the body of the first warrior followed him.

Black spots dancing before his eyes, Jacen managed to grab one of the knobs, but the slit was only a meter away and the pressure of an atmosphere was pushing him toward it. He was going to black out, and he knew it. Grimly, he flicked off his lightsaber and hooked it into his belt, then reached with his other hand and started pulling himself against the wind. His strength was fading fast, however, and even if he made it, it would only be a matter of time before the *Millennium Falcon* was empty of atmosphere.

But he wasn't going to make it. He had failed, not just himself, but his mother and father, as well.

He reached once again in the Force, trying to pull his mass back toward the *Falcon*. He managed the connection, but space had seeped into his head, and darkness with it.

He went out, so far as he could tell, for only a second. Wind was still whistling by, but it had faded to a thin shriek, and in the spots still dancing before his eyes he saw what had saved him. The coupling—alive like all Yuuzhan Vong technology—was sealing itself. As he watched, the last few centimeters of the tear zipped themselves together.

Mom! He could feel the hammering of her pulse behind him, and pain in her not-quite-healed legs.

He propelled himself back into the *Millennium Falcon,* pushing himself madly toward the cargo lift area.

It took him an instant to sort out that that battle was over, too. The Noghri were still dismembering one of the Yuuzhan Vong boarders. The second floated near Leia; his head was drifting a few meters away. Han seemed to have just come in, brandishing a blaster.

"Jacen?"

"Got both of 'em," he acknowledged grimly.

"Great. Leia, you keep watch. Let us know if they send anything else our way. Jacen, you check out those skips and figure out some way we can accelerate without opening ourselves to space."

Right, Jacen thought. The minute the drive went on, the coralskippers would exert their inertia. At some point acceleration would make them massive enough to tear the couplings, no matter how strong they were.

"I'm on it, Dad. And hang on before you engage the drive. I have another idea."

"Always thinking. That's my boy."

FOUR

Nen Yim pushed up through the clear membrane and stroked the pale, feathery coils of the ship's brain, the rikyam, with her shaper's hand. She trembled, her specialized fingers twitching. Once those digits had been the legs of a crustaceanlike creature, bred for no other purpose but to be hands to shapers. Its animal origins were still obvious; her fingers—narrower, slimmer, and stronger than those of the average Yuuzhan Vong—protruded from beneath a dark, flexible carapace that now served as the back of her hand. Two of the "fingers" ended in pincers; another had a retractable blade. All were studded with small, raised sensory nodes that tasted anything they touched. Nen Yim's training as a shaper required that she know by taste all elements and more than four thousand compounds and their variants. She had known the quick, nervous flavor of cobalt with those fingers, savored the pungency of carbon tetrachloride, wondered at the complex and endless variations of amino acids.

And now she trembled, for the scent here was morbid.

"The rikyam is dying," she murmured to the novice at her side. "It is more than half dead."

The novice—a young man named Suung Aruh—twitched the tendrils of his headdress in dismay.

"How can that be?" he asked.

"How can it be?" Nen Yim repeated, anger creeping into her voice. "Look around you, Novice. The luminescent mycogens that once sheathed our halls in light now cling in sickly patches. The capillaries of the maw luur are clotted with dead or mutated recham forteps. The *Baanu Miir* worldship is dying, Initiate. Why should the brain be any different?"

"I'm sorry, Adept," Suung said, his tendrils knotted in genuflection. "Only . . . what is to be done? Will a new rik-yam be grown?"

Nen Yim narrowed her eyes. "Under whom were you trained before my arrival?"

"I—the old master, Tih Qiqah."

"I see. He was the only master shaper here?"

"Yes, Adept."

"And where are his adepts?"

"He trained no adepts in his last year, Adept Nen Yim."

"Nor did he really train any initiates, it seems. What did you do for him?"

"I . . ." His mortification deepened.

"Yes?"

"I told him stories."

"Stories?"

"Crèche-tales, but with adult overtones. He insisted."

"He used you merely to amuse himself? As personal servants?"

"Essentially, Adept."

Nen Yim closed her eyes. "I am assigned to a dying ship. At the mere rank of adept, I am the highest member of my caste, and I haven't even a trained initiate."

"I have heard," Suung said, "that the lack is due to the need for shapers in the battle against the infidels."

"Of course," Nen Yim replied. "Only the senile, inept, and disgraced remain to tend the worldships."

"Yes, Adept," Suung said.

"Aren't you going to ask which I am?" Nen Yim snarled.

The novice hesitated. "I know you were once part of one of the holy programs," he said cautiously.

"Yes. A program that failed. My master failed. I failed. We failed the Yuuzhan Vong. The honor of death was denied me, and I have been sent here to do what I can for our glorious people." *Sent?* she thought in her cloistered mind. *Exiled.*

Suung made no answer, but waited for her to continue.

"Your training begins now, Initiate," Nen Yim said. "For I have need of you. To answer your question, no, we cannot grow a new rikyam for the ship. Or, rather, we could, but it would do the ship no good."

She glanced around. The inner torus of the worldship was sharply curved in floor and ceiling, the color of old bone, illuminated only by the lambents the two shapers carried with them. She looked back up at the rikyam, or what she could see of it. Its numberless coils of neurons grew in the still center of the ship, where neither up nor down existed—unlike the more affluent worldships, the *Baanu Miir* got its gravity from spin, not dovin basals, which had to be fed. Encased in multiple layers of coral-laced shell perforated by osmotic membranes, the brain could be accessed from the inner torus of the ship, where only shapers were allowed. Here, where the ship's spin only imparted a vague rumor of artificial gravity, the membrane could be exposed by stroking a dilating valve in the shell. Only the hand of a shaper could pass through the membrane to the nerve curls within.

"This ship is almost a thousand years old," she told Suung. "The organisms that make it up have come and gone, but the brain has always been here. It has managed the integration of this ship's functions for all of those years, developing outrider ganglia where they were needed, shaping the ship in its own unique way. It is for this reason that our worldships live so well, for so very long. But when the brain sickens, the ship sickens. Things can be done, but ultimately the ship, like all things, must embrace death. Our duty, Novice, is to keep this ship from that desired embrace for as long as possible, until new worldships can be grown or planets settled. In the case of this ship, we must await the former; *Baanu Miir* could never stand the strain of faster-than-light travel. It would take us decades or centuries to reach a habitable world."

"Couldn't the habitants be transferred to a new world on swifter, smaller vessels?" Suung asked.

Nen Yim smiled tightly. "Perhaps when the galaxy has

been cleansed of infidels and the warriors no longer need every vessel available to carry on their war."

"Is there anything to be done now, Adept Nen Yim?" Suung asked. He had a certain eagerness in his voice that amused and even slightly heartened her. It wasn't Suung Aruh's fault he knew nothing.

"Go to the qahsa, Initiate, where the knowledge and history of our people are kept. There you will find the protocols of shaping. Your scent and name will give you access to them. You will memorize the first two hundred and recite them to me tomorrow. You should be able to recall them by name, by indications, by applications. Do you understand?"

His tendrils scarcely managed the genuflection, so disarrayed with excitement had they become. "Yes, Adept. It shall be done."

"Go now and leave me to contemplate this matter."

"Yes, Adept."

A moment later, she was alone in the inner torus. Even so, she looked about furtively before peeling down the front of the living oozhith that clung to her body and served to cover most of it from sight. Beneath the oozhith, clinging to her belly, was a film-flat creature. It retained the vestigial eyes of its fishlike ancestor but otherwise resembled an olive-and-black mottled pouch, which was more or less what it was— a very special sort of container.

She reached back through the osmotic membrane to touch the fractal coils of the rikyam again. With the pincer on her smallest finger, she clipped off four discrete pieces of the brain and placed them in the pouch. The material closed lovingly around the coils, lubricating them with oxygen-rich fluids that would keep them healthy until she reached her laboratory and a more permanent way of keeping the neurons alive.

She took a deep breath, contemplating the enormity of what she was about to do. The shapers were guided and strictured by the protocols, the thousands of techniques and applications given them by the gods in the misty past. To experiment, to try to invent new protocols, was heresy of the first order.

Nen Yim was a heretic. Her master, Mezhan Kwaad, had been as well, before the *Jeedai* child Tahiri took her brilliant head from her neck. Together Nen Yim and she had dared to formulate hypotheses and test them. With her death, Mezhan Kwaad had absorbed most of the blame for both the heresy and the failure. Even so, Nen Yim had been spared only because shapers were already too scarce.

Baanu Miir was dying, as a single glance at its decaying chambers made clear her first day within it. For a brain this ill, no protocol she knew would serve, and as an adept she could not access the mysteries beyond the fifth cortex of the qahsa. She would have to make her own protocol, despite already being tainted with heresy, despite the fact that she was certainly being watched.

Her first duty was not to the calcified shaper codes, but to her people. The gods—if they existed at all—must understand that. If the worldship failed, twelve thousand Yuuzhan Vong would die—not in glorious battle or sacrifice, but smothered in carbon dioxide or frozen by the chill of space. She was not going to let that happen, even if it meant this would be her last shaping and her last act in this life.

She replaced the pouch-creature on her abdomen and rolled the oozhith back over it, feeling the tiny cilia of the garment digging into her pores and resuming their symbiotic relationship with her flesh. Then she left the dying brain and returned through dim and opalescent chambers and corridors to her laboratory suite.

FIVE

"Arrest us?" Mara asked Hamner as the droid set his drink down. Her voice was radium at absolute zero, and Luke shivered. It was the voice of the woman who had once tried to kill him and very nearly succeeded.

"What's the charge?" Luke asked.

"Fey'lya has evidence that you were behind the unsanctioned military action at Yavin Four a few months ago," Hamner said. "That opens you to a variety of charges, I'm afraid, especially since as chief of state he expressly forbade you to engage in any such activity."

"What evidence?" Luke asked.

"The Yuuzhan Vong released a prisoner taken on Yavin Four," Hamner said. "Fey'lya's calling it a 'hopeful sign of goodwill.' The prisoner testified that Jedi were involved with and in fact led an unprovoked attack against the Yuuzhan Vong in a neutral system. He claims to have been a part of that force, which he asserts was led by Talon Karrde. He further maintains that Karrde had frequent communication with you, and that he witnessed those communications."

Mara's eyes had narrowed to slits. "It's a lie. None of Karrde's people would talk. It must be one of the Yuuzhan Vong's Peace Brigade collaborators, coached in what to say."

"But it *is* true, at the bottom of it all?" Hamner said.

Luke nodded tersely. "Yes. After the Yuuzhan Vong warmaster offered to stop with the worlds he had already conquered so long as all of the Jedi were turned over to him, I realized the students at the Jedi academy were in danger. I asked Talon Karrde to evacuate them. When he arrived, the

Peace Brigade was already there, trying to capture the students and turn them over to the Yuuzhan Vong as a peace offering. Karrde wouldn't let them do that. I pleaded with Fey'lya to send New Republic military. He wouldn't. So, yes, I sanctioned his effort and sent what help I could. What do you think I should have done?"

Hamner's long face nodded thoughtfully. "I don't blame you. I only wish you had contacted me."

"You weren't around at the time. I talked to Wedge, but it was out of his hands."

"But their witness is a liar," Mara interjected. "We can prove that."

"And become liars ourselves?" Luke replied. "He's lying about who he is and what he saw, maybe, but most of his accusations are true, if a bit distorted."

Hamner knotted his fingers together. "There's more, anyway. Internal security went back over the records of starship comings and goings in that period. Of course, they already knew Anakin Solo had faked a clearance, but they also discovered you had had a visit from Shada D'ukal, one of Karrde's top people. The transponder ID she used to land on Coruscant was a forgery. Finally, it's clear Jacen and Jaina Solo also left for parts unknown, also circumventing planetary security—in your ship, Mara."

"Again, Kenth, what would you have done?" Mara asked accusingly. "We couldn't leave our students to the Yuuzhan Vong just because the New Republic was too cowardly to act."

"And again, Mara, I'm not arguing with you. I'm just telling you what they have."

"I knew this was going to come out eventually," Luke murmured. "I had thought it might be overlooked."

"The days when Fey'lya might have overlooked Jedi activities are long gone," Kenth said. "It's hard enough for him to hold back the tide of representatives who demand he acquiesce to Tsavong Lah's conditions."

"You aren't saying Fey'lya is on *our* side," Mara said incredulously.

"Mara, whatever else you might think of him, Fey'lya

isn't ready to throw all of the Jedi to the rancors. That's part of the reason he's taking this tack—damage control. By appearing to act against Luke, he can maintain a moderate position regarding more extreme anti-Jedi sentiment."

Luke nodded as if to himself, then directed his gaze at Hamner. "What's your opinion here?"

"Luke, I don't think you'll be brought to trial, or any such thing. The arrest will be a house arrest. You'll be expected to make a general statement to the Jedi to stop any unsanctioned activity. Other than that, you won't suffer any hardship."

"The Jedi are being hunted all over the galaxy. I'm expected to tell them not to fight back?"

"I'm telling you how it is."

Luke locked his hands behind his back. "Kenth, I'm sorry," he said. "I can't do that. I'll try to keep my people out the way of the military, but other than that—well, the Jedi have a mission older than the New Republic."

Something snapped into place in Luke's mind as he said that, solidified a thought as only a spoken word can. He suddenly realized that he meant what he had said with all of his heart and being. What had kept him from admitting it earlier? When had he confused the Jedi ethic with government at large? Why had he been apologizing for so long? Because he feared estrangement from the republic he had helped to build? But they were the ones doing the pushing, not him. Not the Jedi—not even Kyp and the other renegades. Luke might disagree with them in philosophical particulars, but not in the broad strokes—the Jedi were supposed to be helping people, working to bring justice and balance.

"That's why I wanted you to know in time to do something about it if you want to," Hamner replied. He paused, as if considering his next words very carefully. "I don't think Fey'lya imagines you will stand for it, either."

"You mean he thinks we'll run and further implicate ourselves."

"Not exactly. He wants to be able to say you're out of his

reach and no longer his responsibility. To 'pick you out of his fur,' as the Bothans say."

"Oh," Mara said. "He wants us out there, all right, in case he needs us one day, but until then he's perfectly willing to turn his back on us."

"Something like that," Hamner replied. "No move has yet been made to impound your ships."

"He wants me in exile," Luke concluded.

"Yes."

Luke sighed. "I was afraid this time would come. I had hoped it wouldn't. But here we are."

"Yes, here we are," Mara snarled. "Fey'lya had better pray I don't—" Her impassioned diatribe halted in its birth, and a look of profound fear moved across her face. Luke had never seen anything like it on her features before. It was more terrible than he could ever imagine at that moment.

"Ah!" Mara said, in a tiny voice.

"Mara?"

"Something's wrong," she said weakly, her face draining of color. "Something is *really* wrong." She wrapped her arms around her belly and clenched her eyes shut.

Luke sprang from his seat. "Get an MD droid, now," he yelled toward the droid.

In the Force, he felt Mara slipping away.

"Hold on, love," he said. "Please hold on."

SIX

Anakin was busy underneath the supply transport *Lucre*, micro-adjusting the repulsor pads, when a pinkish pair of bare feet appeared. He couldn't see the person the feet belonged to, but he knew who it was immediately.

"Hi, Tahiri," he called.

"Hi yourself," the indignant reply came. Knees squatted down onto the feet, then a pair of hands braced against the floor, and finally green eyes surrounded by a cloud of golden hair appeared. "Come out from under there, Anakin Solo."

"Sure. Just let me finish up."

"Finish up what? You have some reason to be tinkering with this ship?"

Uh-oh. Anakin sighed and pushed himself out from underneath the transport.

"I was going to tell you," he protested.

"I'm sure. When, just before you smoked jets out of here?"

"Tahiri, I'll be back. Corran and I are going for supplies, that's all."

She was staring down into his face now. He could bump her nose with his own by raising up a few centimeters. Her eyes were huge, and not all green, but striated yellow and brown along her iris rims. Had they always been like that?

She punched him in the shoulder, hard. "You could have told me yesterday."

"Ow!" He pushed farther away and sat up. "What was that for?"

"What do you think?" She straightened, too, and the rest of her face came into focus. Her forehead was etched by three nasty vertical scars, like crouching white worms. The

Yuuzhan Vong had tried to make her into one of their own. The scars were the most superficial reminders of the process.

"Look, I know I promised you I wouldn't leave you yet, but this won't take long. I'm getting jumpy."

"So what? Who cares? Didn't it ever occur to you how I might feel?"

"I thought I *had* considered that," Anakin speculated. "Come on, Tahiri. What's really the matter?"

She pursed her lips. In the background, Fiver whirred and bleeped happily at his task of preparing the ship, with a strident note or two aimed at Corran's astromech, Whistler. Across the broad bay, one of Terrik's men cursed as something clanged against the ground. The pain of an insulted thumb wisped by the two Jedi.

"They don't like me here," Tahiri said softly. "They all act like my skin is about to split open and a krayt dragon will step out."

"You're imagining things," Anakin soothed. "Everyone understands you've been through a rough time."

"No. No one understands it at all. Except you. Maybe not even you. They're either afraid of me or repelled."

Anakin tried a sentence or two in his head, didn't like the sound of them, and tried another.

"Have you thought about having those scars removed?" he asked. "Booster's MD droid could do it."

Oops. Anakin realized he should have replayed that one a few times before speaking, too. He saw Tahiri was about to erupt into a full-out verbal assault, and he braced for it.

Wrong again. Her face calmed, and she shook her head. "I paid for them," she said. "I won't give them up."

"Maybe that's what worries people," Anakin said softly.

"Let them worry, then. I don't care."

"But you just—"

"Hush. You don't understand anything after all."

"I don't understand what you're asking me to do. You want me to stay here with you?"

"No, dummy," Tahiri said. "I want you to take me with you."

"Oh." He felt a profound confusion, and suddenly a lot of his father's complaints about women made more sense.

Or less, as the case might be. Tahiri had been his best friend for five years, since she was nine and he was eleven. They had a strong bond in the Force, and were together far more powerful than either was alone. The Jedi Master Ikrit had seen this long ago, and lately had been proven correct. Due to this bond, Anakin and Tahiri could communicate at a level far beyond language.

So why did he spend more than half of his time bewildered in any conversation with her?

"You're sure you're ready for that?" he asked.

"For what? It's just a supply run, right? Minimal danger? Nowhere near Yuuzhan Vong space?"

"Right," Anakin said cautiously. "But there's always danger."

"Especially when you don't trust everyone on your ship."

Anakin's eyebrows dropped. "Okay, now *you're* being dumb. You know I trust you."

"Really? I almost killed you back on Yavin Four, you know."

"I know. And I know that wasn't really you."

"No?" Tahiri's face went curiously blank. "I'm not sure. Sometimes I don't know who I am anymore."

Anakin put his hand on her shoulder. "I do," he said. "You aren't the same as you were before the Yuuzhan Vong captured you. Neither am I. But you're still Tahiri."

"Whatever that means."

"If you want to go with us, I'll talk to Corran. I honestly didn't think you would want to get out so early."

Tahiri shook her head emphatically. "I've spent enough time crying and curled up in a ball. You think you're the only one the walls are closing in on? Whoever I am, I'm not going to figure it out moping around here." Her voice took on a softer, pleading note. "Let me go with you, Anakin."

He mussed her hair, the way he had done a hundred times. It suddenly seemed too familiar, and he felt his face warm. "Okay," he said. "Next time, just ask, though. You don't always have to come after me like I've done something wrong. We don't have to fight *everything* out."

She smiled. "Sorry. You never mean to do anything wrong. But most times it just turns out that way."

SEVEN

R2-D2 tootled and bleeped as he went about the task Jacen had assigned him. The little droid had extended his linkage and repair arms into one of the compact missiles floating near the narrow trash-exhaust tube. In the faint light of the glow stick, the squat, domed cylinder of the little droid looked very much the antique he was.

A clumsy clank sounded behind Jacen as C-3PO struggled with weightlessness.

"Oh dear," C-3PO said excitedly. "I wasn't built for this, you know. Zero gravity confuses my circuits."

"Just hang on to something," Jacen muttered. "When Dad gets the power back on, we'll have gravity again. Just make sure you're on the floor and not the ceiling when that happens."

"Good heavens. Who can tell the difference? I'm going to need a good overhaul when this is all over. This *will* be all over soon, won't it, Master Jacen?"

"One way or the other."

"I almost wish you had left me deactivated."

"Just be thankful you've got good surge overload circuits, or you might have been deactivated permanently." He closed the panel on the final missile. "Well, that will either work or it won't," he said philosophically.

"I don't understand," C-3PO said. "What will work or won't?"

R2-D2 whistled something vaguely condescending and derisive.

"Well, of *course* I shouldn't be expected to understand, you little trash sweeper," C-3PO retorted indignantly. "I'm a protocol droid, not a metal-grubbing screw turner. Oh! No offense to you, Master Jacen."

"None taken. I wish someone a little better at this than I were here—Anakin, for instance. If I've made a mistake, I may well blow us out of the sky."

"Oh, no!"

"Okay, time for your part, Threepio. I need you to cycle this lock manually."

"But, Master Jacen, all of the air will evacuate."

"True. But I won't be here—I'll be on the other side of the outer pressure lock. The vacuum won't hurt you."

"I suppose not. But *why*, Master Jacen?"

"I need you to take each of these missiles to the end of the dump vent and give them a good shove in the direction of that Yuuzhan Vong interdictor."

"Me, handle a concussion missile?"

"If it's any comfort, if it exploded it wouldn't make any difference to you if you were holding it or a meter away, like you are now. There still wouldn't be enough of you left to plate a spoon with."

"But—but—what if I fall out of the ship?"

Jacen smiled thinly. "Don't," he said. "Once all the missiles are away, you and Artoo seal the vent up, cycle the lock again, and get back inside. I'll keep in touch by comm."

"Master Jacen, I am a *protocol* droid!"

"And I would rather be meditating. C'mon, Threepio. You've done more dangerous things than this before."

"Not willingly, Master Jacen!"

Jacen slapped the droid on his metal back. "Show me what you're made of, Threepio."

"I will gladly submit to an internal inspection," C-3PO said.

"You know what I mean. Go."

"Yes, sir." The droid had a noticeable quaver in his voice.

Jacen pushed out, plugged in a portable power source, and cycled the inner lock. It closed under protest, its hydraulics used to a more robust diet of electrons.

He made his way to where his mother was keeping watch from the cockpit.

"All quiet?" he asked.

"For now. Surely they must know something has gone wrong, though."

"Maybe, maybe not. We don't know what their procedures are in situations like this. Yuuzhan Vong warriors are proud—maybe they're giving these first guys every chance to deal with the situation before sending reinforcements. Maybe they're so confident we can't get away they aren't really paying attention. We're about to see how closely they're watching, anyway. I just sent some concussion missiles floating their way. With any luck, they'll think it's flotsam until it's too late." He concentrated briefly. "There. The first is away."

C-3PO was slow. It was a good five minutes before he got the next one out. The third took even longer. Jacen didn't stay to watch. He went down and finished welding auxiliary plating over the holes the Yuuzhan Vong had cut into their ship. It was too thin to have a good chance of holding, but it was all they had at the moment that might do. It would at least give them a few minutes. If worse came to worst—and neither this nor his other plan worked—they could always seal off the cockpit or put on vac suits. Of course, then they had to find a habitable planet or space station, fast.

His father came drifting up from beneath. "Are we ready?" he asked.

"As we'll be," Jacen replied.

"Let's go forward and give it a try, then," Han said. "The Yuuzhan Vong won't wait on us forever."

When they rejoined Leia in the cockpit, however, the enemy ship was still quiet.

Jacen activated the intercom. "How's it going, Threepio?"

"Dreadful, sir. I have two more to go."

"More coralskippers detaching," Leia observed suddenly.

"Negative, Threepio," Jacen said. "Get out of there, now."

"With pleasure, sir."

"Ready, everyone?" Han asked.

"Go," Leia replied.

Han worked his fingers across the instruments, and with a sudden snap, gravity reasserted itself. Jacen's stomach settled back where it was supposed to be, and he felt a wave of dizziness.

"Hang on." Han engaged maneuvering thrusters, and the *Falcon* began spinning like a coin on its side.

Jacen craned for visibility. Below and above, at the extreme edge of his vision, he could make out the coralskippers, still stationary. The living couplings were cinched in the middle, like balloons twisted and tied, and they were still twisting.

"Four times around is going to have to be good enough. Where are your missiles?"

"The first one is ready to go."

"Good thing I had the launchers reinstalled, I guess. Send the detonation signal on three. One, two—"

Jacen held his breath as he keyed the signal on three and blew it out when the distant concussion missile became a small white nova. At the same moment, Han kicked space with the ion drive, and they were *going,* as only the *Millennium Falcon* could go. The attached coralskippers whipped out behind them like braids, and Jacen couldn't see them anymore.

"They're trying to get a lock with their dovin basals," Leia reported.

"Jacen!"

"Yes, sir!" Jacen sent another signal, and the remaining missiles surged to life, burning their propellant cores and hurling their noses at the Yuuzhan Vong ship. Gravitic anomalies appeared and sucked all but one in, but the fourth impacted in a brilliant display.

"They blinked!" Leia whooped. "They missed their lock. Han, get us out of here!"

"What do you think I'm doing?"

The ship suddenly shuddered and yawed.

"What was that? What hit us?" Han demanded, just as it happened again.

"The coralskippers tearing loose," Jacen replied. "And

speaking of coralskippers, there are a couple headed our way. I'm going down to the turbolaser."

"Forget it. If those patches go, I want you up here. We'll outrun the skips."

"They're gaining."

"As soon as we're out of the interdictor's mass shadow, I'm going to lightspeed."

Jacen considered. "They'll catch us before that. I'm going down."

"Jacen—"

He left his father's protest behind him.

C-3PO was just returning to the safe, enclosed ship when the acceleration slapped him against the side of the waste chute. The last missile, which he had been pushing ahead of him back into the ship, suddenly tripled its weight and, as the vector of the force changed, went hurtling out into open space. It banged against C-3PO as it went by, and with a soundless cry of terror he realized he was going to follow it. Clawing desperately, he managed a handhold on the lock mechanism, but his golden legs dangled out into open space. Looking between them, he saw the stars churn around his feet.

"Artoo!" he broadcast frantically.

His digits were slipping.

Well, he thought to himself. *This hasn't turned out to be a good day at all. If only I had stayed on Coruscant with Master Luke.*

EIGHT

Mara had slipped into unconsciousness by the time the island's MD-10 medical droid had been activated. Luke gripped her hand as she lay on the grass near their table. Around them the cool air was fragrant with night perfumes and the gentle music of insects. Kenth Hamner stood by, restless but silent.

Luke summoned Master Yoda's voice. *A Jedi knows not fear.*

It helped, a little, but the fear didn't lurk far under the skin. He couldn't lose Mara, not now. Not ever.

He tried to push that away, as well. There was danger in thoughts like that. And yet the harder he tried, the more difficult it was, and all of his Jedi training seemed suddenly pale before the force of unfamiliar emotions.

Hang in there, Mara. I love you.

He felt her stir. She was in pain, but the Force told him she was still strong. And yet beneath that vitality was the undeniable feeling of *wrongness*. Not like when she had been so terribly ill with her Yuuzhan Vong–created disease, exactly. Could the organism have mutated again? Had her long, hopeful remission ended?

He watched, taut, as the medical droid dispassionately checked her vitals, using sensors to probe into his wife's body.

In the midst of it, her eyes fluttered open again, and he saw his own helpless fear reflected there.

"It's okay," he said. "It'll be okay. What happened?"

"It's the baby," she said. "It's our baby. Luke, I can't—"

"And you won't," he promised firmly. "It's going to be fine."

The MD droid reached a diagnosis a moment later.

"Toxic shock reaction in the placenta," it burred. "Indicates four cc's of cardinex."

"Do it," Luke commanded.

He watched as the hypo delivered the dosage. Within seconds, Mara's breathing calmed and her color began to return.

"What caused it?" Luke demanded of the droid.

"Unknown chemical agent."

"Poison?"

"Negative. Placental reaction unusual. The substance is not otherwise toxic. Substance is complex saline compound, partial analysis . . ." It listed a sequence of chemicals.

"Vergere's tears," Mara said softly. She tried to sit up.

"Just hang on. Stay down for a minute."

"I'm feeling better. Let me up, Skywalker."

"Tears?" Kenth Hamner said, confused.

"The Yuuzhan Vong infected me with some sort of biotic weapon," Mara explained. "It tried pretty hard to kill me. It would have, too, except that that creature with the Yuuzhan Vong assassin—"

"The one who pretended to defect?"

"Elan. Yes. She had a sort of pet or familiar who gave Han a vial of her tears—or at least that's what she said they were. She told him I should take them, and it felt right to me, so I did. My disease went into remission."

Hamner's long face looked thoughtful. "And you think the tears caused what just happened to you?"

"Let's not jump to conclusions," Luke protested.

"I ran out of the tears a few months ago," Mara said. "I've been taking a synthesized version. Luke, it's killing our son."

"You can't know that," Luke said. "The MD droid isn't equipped to do the kind of analysis that would prove that."

"I know," Mara said shakily.

Her certainty felt like ferrocrete. Luke sat down, pushing his fingers back through his hair, trying to think. He nearly jumped at the sound of a distant sonic boom—probably just some hotshot pilot practicing atmospheric maneuvers over the sea.

"I can have you at a medical facility in ten minutes," Hamner told Mara.

"No!" Mara nearly shouted. "Then we'd lose our chance to escape Fey'lya."

"Mara, we don't have a choice," Luke said.

She sat up again. This time Luke didn't try to stop her. "We do," she insisted. "I won't have my child born under house arrest. If I don't take the tears, I should be fine. Isn't that right, Emdee?"

The droid whirred and nodded. "Present danger has passed. Avoidance of the substance will prevent recurrence."

"What if it wasn't the tears at all?" Luke said, exasperation escaping with his words.

"It is," Mara replied. "I know it is."

"Then there was something wrong with the synthetic drug. If we're to synthesize a new one, we need to be here, on Coruscant."

"If we stay, they'll button us in so tight we'll never be able to escape. We'll be at their mercy, and what then? Suppose Fey'lya changes his mind and decides to give us to the Yuuzhan Vong? We'll be trapped, and how am I supposed to fight in this condition? Or worse, with an infant? Luke, it's time. You know it; I know it. So we have do this."

Luke closed his eyes and searched the back of his lids for options. He found none.

"Okay," he said finally. "Kenth, if you could be so kind as to take us to our apartments."

"Absolutely," Hamner said. "I am at your command."

In moments they were airborne. So far as Luke could tell, Mara was fine now. He himself was shaken to the core.

He activated the comm unit and placed two calls—one to Cilghal, the Mon Calamari Jedi healer, the other to Ism Oolos, a Ho'Din physician of great renown. Both agreed to meet him at their apartments. A third call—to the Ithorian Tomla El—revealed the healer was offplanet, working to aid refugees from his destroyed homeworld.

Hamner deposited them on the landing area of their roof.

Cilghal was already there, and the reptilian Ism Oolos arrived shortly thereafter.

Luke and Mara thanked Hamner. The liaison wished them luck and departed.

"You pack, Skywalker," Mara said, once they were inside. "We have to be gone in two hours."

"A thorough examination will take much longer than that," Oolos complained. "Some analyses I must do in my laboratory, to be certain of my results."

"You have to think of your child now," Cilghal agreed softly.

"No one needs to remind me of that," Mara said gruffly. "Get on with it."

Meanwhile, Luke reluctantly began preparation for their flight, but each step he took in that direction felt heavier. Coruscant had the best medical facilities in the galaxy. How could he deny his wife and child that?

He could feel Cilghal, concentrating, reading Mara in the Force, trying to glean information from its generation and interaction in her cells. He caught glimpses of Oolos taking skin and blood samples and sonic readings and feeding the data into his medical datapad.

Mara gave them an hour, then cut them off. Luke stopped what he was doing and came back into the room.

"Conclusions?" Mara asked.

Oolos sighed. "The MD droid was correct. The synthesized tears are having an unforeseen effect on the placenta. The actual attack was triggered by stress, but continuing to take them might well lead to the death of the child."

Cilghal nodded her bulbous head in agreement. "I concur," the Mon Calamarian said.

"Can you resynthesize them?" Luke asked. "Reconfigure the substance so it won't have that effect?"

Oolos clasped his scaled hands together. "We still do not know why the original tears worked," he said, a note of apology in his voice. "We were able to duplicate them without ever really comprehending them."

"Something must be different, though," Luke said, "or this wouldn't be happening."

"Unfortunately," Oolos replied, "I do not believe that to be true. The nature of cell reproduction in a fetus is quite unlike the normal cellular processes in an adult human. The 'tears' caused Mara's cells to mimic that process in some ways, hence her regeneration. The Yuuzhan Vong disease is still in her cells, you understand; her cells have merely been given the power to keep it in check and control whatever damage it causes."

"I still don't understand the problem."

"The problem is, the substance somehow does not recognize true fetal development as a part of the normal functioning of a human body. It thus tries to make adjustments to the developmental process, treating the child almost as it would an illness. In turn, Mara's natural immune system resists and rejects such modifications. Over time, the residue of this conflict has built up enough to cause toxic shock. According to her cellular history, this buildup began with the pregnancy, and only now reached dangerous levels."

"I was taking the real tears in the first months," Mara said.

"Precisely," the healer concurred. "The very qualities that allow the tears to remit your illness are a danger to your fetus."

"But my child is well?"

"I cannot feel that the child has yet suffered any damage from the process," Cilghal answered.

"I believe Jedi Cilghal to be correct," Oolos said.

"But Mara's in her final month," Luke said. "If it took eight months for the toxins to build up—"

"She has reached tolerance saturation," Oolos said. "Her body will flush those chemicals over the course of years, but in the next month she will remain at the danger level. It is unlikely that mere stress will provoke another attack, but a single taste of the tears could bring on a much more violent reaction than that she experienced today."

"Is there any way to flush these poisons artificially?" Mara asked.

"Yes."

"Without risk to my child?"

The Ho'Din scientist lowered the spines on his head. "No. The risk would be measurable."

"Well, let's add this to the 'what I already knew' category," Mara said. "I'll stop taking the tears until our son is born. Then I'll start taking them again."

"We could induce delivery now," Cilghal said.

Mara frowned. "That feels wrong. Cilghal, do you really recommend that?"

"I do," Oolos said.

Cilghal seemed reluctant. "I don't recommend it," she said at last. "Logically, it is the thing to do, and yet when I look down that path, I see deep shadows."

"And if I carry to term, without taking the tears?"

"Shadows there, too, and pain—but also hope."

Mara sat up and turned her gaze to Luke. "We ready to go?" she asked.

"I—Mara—"

"Don't even start. Our baby is healthy, and he'll stay healthy, I promise you that. We'll get through this, no matter where we are. We have to go. Let's *go*."

"May I accompany you?" Cilghal asked.

"Of course," Mara replied.

"Sadly, I cannot make the same offer," Oolos told them. "My responsibilities to my patients and the New Republic are too great to set aside. I wish I could convince you to remain near, but I surmise I cannot. I wish you only the best, the four of you. I will do what I can to improve the substance, based upon what I know. It would be prudent for you to check with me from time to time."

"Thank you," Luke told the healer. "Thanks for everything."

Jaina rolled her X-wing into the night-shadow of Coruscant, reveling in the feel of the stick in her hand, the shifting crush of acceleration. She felt like shouting out loud, and did. It was good to fly again! This was the best she had felt in a long time.

For months she had been forced out of the cockpit by damaged eyes, and even after they were healed, Rogue

Squadron had shown a marked reluctance to recall her. It had unfolded to her gradually, sickeningly, that given her Jedi status and her involvement in the rescue at Yavin 4, they really didn't want her back. She had gone from being their golden child to their ugly little liability. Only today Colonel Darklighter—the very man who had asked her to join the squadron—had suggested she extend her leave of absence indefinitely.

She didn't care right now. Coruscant was rushing below, a universe of stars turned inside out. She was one with the X-wing. Tomorrow she would hurt. Not today.

She aimed her ship's nose away from the planet and its multitude of satellites, out toward the stars, and wondered where her family was. Anakin was skipping around the galaxy with Booster Terrik, watching over his friend Tahiri. Her twin Jacen was with her mother and father, trying to set up Uncle Luke's "great river"—a series of routes and safe houses designed to help Jedi escape the Yuuzhan Vong and their collaborationist shills. She had stayed behind, assuming Rogue Squadron would recall her any day.

Well, another day, another mistake. She briefly considered chucking it all and heading out, perhaps to find the *Millennium Falcon* and the greater part of her family.

But she had to stick it out. Rogue Squadron was worth fighting for, and eventually they would recall her. How could they afford anyone sitting out now?

Of course, the Yuuzhan Vong had been relatively quiet since Yavin 4—since Duro, as far as the idiot government was concerned. But that couldn't last. Any thought that it could—that the enemy could be appeased by any number of sacrifices and concessions—was wishful thinking of a nearly criminal sort.

Her joy of flying was leaking out of her, swallowed by the sort of mental entropy that seemed to come with growing older. She considered going back, but if she had to sulk out here or down there, she might as well do it out here.

She was still fighting the downward emotional spiral when the comm demanded attention.

It was Aunt Mara, and she sounded more troubled than Jaina felt.

"Jaina, where are you?" Mara asked.

"Just out. What's the matter?"

"We're taking the *Jade Shadow* up. Meet me, will you? It's important." She ticked off a list of coordinates.

"Sure," Jaina replied. "Laying that course now."

"And Jaina—keep your eyes open. Trust no one."

"Mara, what—?"

"We'll discuss it when we rendezvous."

Great, Jaina thought. *What else could be going wrong?* But it could be almost anything, including some possibilities too terrible even to contemplate.

Luke and Mara decided not to risk being seen boarding the *Jade Shadow.* They made their way with an occasional pass of the hand and a suggestion backed by the Force. Some wouldn't remember them at all; others would not be able to recall their faces, though both were well known.

Taking off was a little trickier, but Mara hadn't lost her knack, managing to secure a launch authority using a fake transponder ID and then filing a flight plan to orbit. As Luke watched Coruscant dwindle, he felt, oddly, a strange elation, a kind of freedom he hadn't known he missed. He glanced over at Mara.

"How are you feeling?"

"Fine, now. I contacted Jaina. She'll meet us in orbit." She eased the angle of their climb and glanced at Luke. "This is the right thing to do, you know."

"I'm still not sure."

"It's done, now. Where are we going, by the way?"

"We'll find Booster first," he decided. "I've arranged a way for us to contact him. He'll have some of the medical facilities you need, at least. After that—the Jedi need a haven, a base to operate from. I've already done preliminary searching. That will have to wait, though. Your health is our first priority right now."

She nodded. "I *am* going off the drug."

"And risk your illness coming back, full-blown?"

She pursed her lips. "That's a risk, but right now it looks like the lesser of two." She made a face at her instruments. "By the way," she said, "looks like your first priority has been bumped back. I've got planetary security hailing us and at least four ships on an intercept course."

Luke opened to the hail and activated the visual communications array.

"*Jade Shadow*, this is planetary security." The screen showed a pale gold Bothan male. "You must return to ground immediately. Slave yourselves to us for escort."

Luke smiled tightly. "This is Luke Skywalker of the *Jade Shadow*. We're outward bound and not prepared to turn back."

The Bothan looked extremely uncomfortable. "I have my orders, Master Skywalker. Please help me carry them out with minimum fuss."

"I'm sorry for the inconvenience, Captain, but we aren't returning to ground."

"I'm authorized to use force, Master Skywalker."

"This ship will defend itself," Luke replied reluctantly. "Let us go, Captain."

"I'm sorry. I can't."

Luke shrugged. "Then we really have nothing else to discuss." He switched off the comm.

"Can we outrun them?" he asked Mara.

"It'll be tight." She eyed her instruments again. "Probably not. They must have been on to us almost from the beginning. Two of the ships are coming in from a high orbit."

"Right. Waiting for us. I was more than half expecting that."

"So much for Fey'lya wanting us to escape."

"They have to make an effort," Luke replied. "As efforts go, this isn't a big one."

"No, but maybe sufficient," Mara replied. "We'll at least have to fight them, which won't make us look any better."

Within moments the approaching ships were in sight.

"Military-grade shields," Mara remarked. "Hang on, Skywalker."

A moment later she began to fire.

If we weren't outlaws before, we are now, Luke thought. *How could it have come to this?*

Jaina couldn't believe what she was seeing. The *Jade Shadow* was under fire from four security interceptors. What was going on?

Not that it mattered. She powered up her weapons and dived in, ignoring the hails from the security ships but sending her own signal to the *Shadow*. It was Uncle Luke who answered.

"You two look like you could use a hand," she said. "What did you do to irk the sky cops?"

"Stay out of this, Jaina," Luke told her.

"Yeah, right. That'll happen." She was close enough to fire now, and fire she did, rolling between the trailing interceptor and spearing it with her lasers as she went past. The heavy shield took the shots easily, but she achieved the desired effect; the interceptor had noticed her now. It tried to lock on to her tail, but she was having none of that. Leaning on the stick, she circled tight and planetward. A few lucky shots grazed her shields, but they had a long way to go before they could bring her down. She nosed back up and had her pursuer in her sights again. She held the beak-to-beak collision course long enough to put a few more into its shields, then yawed starboard, missing the oncoming craft by a few meters. She eyed her proton torpedoes speculatively. She could take them out with those, but she still wasn't sure what was going on here, and it was probably a bad idea to kill someone in Coruscant's security force. For all she knew, it might even be a friend of hers. That meant she needed to cripple, not kill.

Both ships turned tight, trying once again to pick up the other's tail. Jaina had the more maneuverable ship and soon found herself flying up the interceptor's exhaust. She stuttered laser fire, following her opponents' attempts to shake her, until finally their shields failed. She cut the drive off as neatly as a gardener pruning a tree, then came around to disable their weapons.

By this time, the *Jade Shadow* only had two pursuers left,

and one of them was in bad shape. She wished she could have seen what tricks Mara had pulled out of her sleeve to achieve that. The *Shadow*'s shields were starting to get a little shaky, but between the two of them, Jaina was certain the remaining interceptors didn't have a chance.

A moment later, a cloud of blips appeared on her long-range sensors. Twelve starfighters, maybe more. And the *Jade Shadow* was flying right into them.

NINE

C-3PO yelped as he lost his handhold, but at the same instant something fastened onto his wrist.

"Artoo! Thank the maker!"

The ship made another violent turn, and C-3PO felt his insides try to escape into space through the soles of his metal feet. R2-D2 lurched forward, but only so far. C-3PO noticed with relief that his companion had secured himself with a cable of some sort.

"Clever Artoo! Don't let go of me!"

Jacen swung around in the laser turret, tracing lines of deadly light through the vacuum, walking them across the nearest coralskipper. Points of absolute darkness swallowed most of the beams before they could strike home, but a fluorescent puff of vaporized coral told him at least one had gotten through. The skip sloughed off starboard, but there were plenty more to take its place. Jacen grimly continued his deadly conversation with them, and they answered with volcanic gobs of plasma.

"Shields are failing," Han's voice crackled over the comm. "Jacen, how's it going down there?"

"Still here, Dad," he replied, swinging his seat to follow a skip so near he could have thrown a rock and hit it.

"We're out of the mass shadow in one minute," Leia said.

Something in the ship shrieked, and the inertial compensators failed. The g's they were pulling tried to smash Jacen into the ceiling. He managed to get his hands up in time to keep his skull from being crushed, but the force of impact stunned him momentarily. The dampeners went back on-line, and artificial gravity dropped him back roughly into his seat.

"That's it for the shields," his father husked.

Groggily, Jacen grabbed the trigger grips as a series of shudders ran through the *Falcon*.

"Go! Now!" Leia cried.

For an instant nothing happened. Then the stars were gone, and Jacen sagged in his couch.

"It was terrible, just terrible," C-3PO went on. "If it weren't for Artoo I would be just space flotsam. Master Jacen, I *told* you I wasn't suited for that sort of thing."

"You did just fine, Threepio. You saved us. Thanks."

"Oh. Well, I suppose . . . you're quite welcome."

"Right. So run some diagnostics on yourself. Relax."

"Do you think we've really escaped them?"

Han stepped into the cabin and answered that. "We left on a pretty messy vector. Even *I'm* not exactly sure where we're headed. We'll drop out soon and get our bearings, but I'm willing to bet we're not being followed. One thing is sure—we'll need repairs."

"The outer bulkheads?" Jacen asked.

"Like you figured. The coupling tore, but I was able to fix it before our patches gave way. Kinda spoils the look, though. It's gonna have to go."

Leia entered and lowered herself onto one of the couches. Jacen noticed she was favoring her right leg more than she had the day before. Her Noghri bodyguards stood silently nearby.

"What did they hit us with?" she asked.

"Something we haven't seen yet," Jacen said. "It may just be a side effect of their interdiction device."

"Or a powerful electromagnetic pulse. It shut our systems down, but didn't really do a lot of damage to them."

"It shut *us* down, too," Leia pointed out.

"Yeah. It did at that," Han allowed.

"So now what?" Leia asked.

"Now? Well, now we know the inner Corellian Run is hotter than novashine."

"For now. Maybe they shift those things around. How many interdictors can they have?"

"Well, I don't know," Han said, shrugging his shoulders. "They *grow* the things, remember?"

"There's that famous Solo charm," Leia remarked. "I wondered where it had gone."

Han opened his mouth to retort, but Jacen stepped in. "That interdictor had been there for a while. Remember the other ships we saw?"

Leia nodded. "True. I'd forgotten that."

"This is nuts," Han opined. "This whole thing. Luke's 'great river.' "

Leia frowned. "Look, we've had some setbacks, but—"

"Setbacks?" Han's brows tried to jump off his head. "Did you just say 'setbacks'? We had to shoot our way out of the meeting on Ryloth because your 'contacts' turned out to be Peace Brigade—"

"Oh, like your 'good friends' on Bimmisaari? The ones who wanted to decorate their speeder with our heads?"

"As a matter of fact," Han blustered, "things were going just great on Bimmisaari until you . . ."

They continued bickering, and Jacen listened with mixed emotions. On the one hand, it reminded him of old times, at least insofar as he could remember. They had always been like this, right up until the day Chewbacca died. Then— then they almost stopped talking at all. That silence had been one of the worst things Jacen had ever experienced. Now, they sounded like their old selves, but there was something brittle about it sometimes. As if some of the good nature at the base of it had evaporated. As though if the wrong thing got said, something might break.

Still, it was better than the silence.

As Han had guessed, it took a while to get their bearings and calculate a series of jumps that would take them on to their destination, the cluster of black holes known collectively as the Maw. He picked his way carefully through the enormous gravity wells, his old recklessness submerged beneath several layers of responsibility that a younger Han Solo could never have comprehended.

A younger Han Solo had never really believed in death—or rather, had never believed it could touch him. The loss of Chewbacca had changed that forever. Whenever he thought of losing Leia or one of his children, it put liquid nitrogen in his veins.

As he went carefully through the maze of deadly tides, Han was at least confident that there were few beings in the galaxy who could follow him. If an uninformed Yuuzhan Vong ship was tailing them, the invaders were as good as destroyed.

Thus, it was several days before his barely repaired *Falcon* made its final approach to the secret base they had named simply Shelter. It was a patchwork construction, largely put together from the pieces of the infamous Maw installation, which in its own time—the days of the Empire—had been a top-secret weapons facility. The facility itself had been blown to bits by its erstwhile commander, Admiral Daala, but using the wreckage, along with modules imported from Kessel—and with the help of some well-heeled friends—Han and Leia had managed to facilitate the construction of a space station.

As a location, the Maw was just too good to abandon, especially when a safe house was needed.

"Not much to look at," Han muttered, watching the rough cylinder gain resolution and reveal its makeshift nature. The base of it was an asteroid fragment, but living modules, a power core, and a rudimentary defense system rose obviously from its surface.

"But it's something," Leia said, over his shoulder. "It's a start. I never thought you could have pulled together the alliance it would take to build it, but there it is. Good work, Captain Solo." Leia smiled and slipped her hand into Han's.

"I . . . Thanks. But look what happened when I was out here. Anakin was nearly killed on Yavin Four, and we didn't have the slightest idea of what was going on."

"Anakin is safe on the *Errant Venture,* as safe as he can

be anyway. Jaina's on Coruscant. Jacen's with us. I think we've done as well as we can, Han."

"Maybe. Well, let's see what they've done with the place."

Lando Calrissian met them in the functional if unappealing docking bay. Someone had given it a coat of yellow paint, covering the mismatched plating it was built of, which was an improvement over the last time Han had seen it.

"I like what you've done to the *Falcon*," Lando said easily, as they stepped down the landing ramp. "The mottled yellow patches against matte black. Very stylish."

"Yeah, well, I've always had an eye for the trendy," Han replied.

"And the beautiful," Lando remarked, switching his gaze to Leia. "You're more bewitching than ever."

"And you're as glib as always," Leia replied.

Lando smiled his famous smile and bowed slightly at the waist.

"The *Falcon*—" Han began.

Lando waved his hand. "Think of it as done. We may not have much here, but we have what it takes to patch that old hunk of junk one more time, I think."

He scanned over their lived-in clothes and Jacen's bloodstains. "The same goes for the three of you. Visit the 'fresher and my MD droid, please. When you're done, I'd be pleased if you would join me in my stateroom for food and drinks, before we meet with the others who have come."

"The Hutt representative made it safely, then?" Leia asked.

"It was tight at times," Lando said, "but we got him here."

Han cleared his throat. "We can talk about that later," he said. "Jacen, Lando's right. You ought to have that cut looked at. And, Leia—"

"My legs are fine," she assured him.

"Why don't you let the medical droid take a look anyway? It certainly can't hurt."

"There's plenty of time," Lando said. "If you'll just follow me?"

To Han's relief, the MD droid didn't find much on Leia or Jacen to complain about, and so an hour later, freshened and in new clothes, the three of them followed one of Lando's droids to his stateroom. When the door opened, however, Han couldn't repress a grin.

"Why am I not surprised?" he asked.

"Welcome to my humble home away from home," Lando said. "Not up to my usual standards, I'll admit, but it's comfortable enough."

The chamber beyond might have been imported from one of Lando's casinos or luxury barges. The stone of the asteroid had been annealed, etched, and planished to resemble Naboo tile, and the floor was of finest polished Kashyyyk wood. The appointments were all old Coruscant—pre-Empire—comfortable, decadently upholstered in philfiber brocades.

"Have a seat. The droid will bring our drinks."

A shiny new SE-6 domestic sidled up and took their orders.

"Stimcaf," Leia said. "If I have to discuss anything, I want to be at least half awake."

"I have another theory on that," Han said. "I know you, Lando. Surely you have some Corellian whiskey around this dump."

"Only the best, Han, though the best isn't as good as it used to be."

"What is?"

"Besides us?" Lando said. "Not much."

Jacen ordered mineral water.

"Another sober fellow," Lando remarked. "But I think I'll join Han." He leveled his intelligent gaze at Jacen. "And you, young Jedi. How are things with you?"

"Very well, thanks," Jacen said politely.

"You've got a lot of your mother in you. Fortunate choice your genes made." He paused. "I understand you're hot property these days. I think you've even outdone the old man when it comes to the bounty you'd fetch."

"That's not funny, Lando," Han said.

Lando raised his eyebrows mildly. "I didn't say it was. Just making an observation. As you said, you know me."

"Only too well."

Lando made a wounded face, then brightened. "Ah, here are our drinks." He took his glass and raised it. "To the old times, and to better ones."

They drank. Han grimaced. "Boy, you weren't kidding. Whyren's Reserve this ain't."

"There have been better years, I'll grant you that." Lando's voice softened and became more serious. "I'm sorry I didn't make the funeral, Han. Some of my people got trapped near Obroa-skai when the Vong took it. I couldn't leave them hanging."

"I know," Han said, taking another drink. "I heard. That's what he would have wanted you to do."

"And you, Lando," Leia said. "How are things with you and Tendra?"

"Hey, we're making do. Losing Dubrillion wasn't a lot of fun, but I've managed to spread my assets out over the years. I've still got the operation on Kessel, though it's attracted some attention lately."

"Yuuzhan Vong?"

"Nah, just pirates and profiteers. And I've been approached by the Peace Brigade."

That got Han's attention. "Really?"

"I sent them packing. They didn't have the clout to back up their demands, and they knew it."

"Yes, but what did they want?" Leia asked.

Lando chuckled. "The usual. Help hunting down Jedi, though they must have known who they were dealing with. Mostly I think they wanted guards for one of their convoys."

"What sort of convoy?"

"It seems that the Brigade has expanded. They're not just in the business of hunting Jedi anymore—they've taken over the trade routes in Vong-occupied territory."

"They're *supplying* them?"

"And their subject populations. Sure. Somebody has to."

"Of all the vile . . ." Leia couldn't even finish, she was so disgusted.

They shifted to small talk. The whiskey was warming, and Han felt his shoulders relax a little.

"Well," Lando said, when their glasses were dry. "Our allies, such as they are, are waiting. We're probably as fashionably late as we can afford to be."

"Lead the way," Han replied.

Three beings awaited them in a conference room that evinced none of the luxury of Lando's suite—it was clinically spare. The most striking of the trio was a young Hutt, reclining with a bored expression and an impatient twitch in his thickly muscled tail. Next to him sat a human woman in her mid-thirties. Her skin was almost as dark as Lando's, her hair clipped and with severe bangs. She wore a formal business smock, black with a raised white collar. She looked serious, but the female Twi'lek another turn around the circular conference table looked positively grim.

"How thoughtful of you to finally show up," the Hutt remarked.

"Happy to be of service," Han replied, keeping his voice neutral. "And you'd be?"

"Bored," the Hutt replied.

Han frowned and raised his finger, but Lando cut in smoothly. "Han Solo, meet Bana. He's here on behalf of the Hutt resistance."

"And an investor in this . . . place," Bana added. "Despite which I've been ill treated. Kept in closed quarters for the journey. Very inhospitable."

"You understand our desire to keep the location of Shelter a secret," Lando said.

"I understand the insult involved. You imply I might sell the information? My people are fighting for their lives. There is no dealing with the Yuuzhan Vong, neither in goods nor information. They are a mad species, and such sensible things mean nothing to them." He drew his sluglike body straighter.

"No insult was intended," Leia soothed.

The Hutt cocked his head. "You are Princess Leia. You were present when my cousin Randa died."

"I was," Leia agreed. "He died bravely."

"This is Numa Rar," Lando continued, introducing the Twi'lek.

"It is an honor to meet you," the woman intoned, her pale blue head-tails twisting together.

Jacen spoke for the first time since entering the room. "I recognize you," he said to Numa Rar.

"Yes. I was a student of the late Daeshara'cor."

"You may have heard of the resistance on New Plympto, in the Corellian sector," Lando said. "Numa is a leader of that resistance."

He turned to the human woman. "Opeli Mors," he said. "A representative of the Jin'ri trade syndicate."

"Interesting," Han said. "I've never heard of that organization."

"Nor have I," Leia added.

Opeli Mors gave a brief, businesslike smile. "We are a relatively new concern. We formed to meet the needs of refugees soon after the fall of Duro. We welcome the opportunity to expand."

"War profiteers," Leia said.

"No business can operate without an income," Mors said. "Governments have the luxury of taxation. We do not."

"I know your type," Leia replied, her voice climbing several degrees with each word. "Profit is one thing. You people *gouge* until there's nothing left, then abandon your charges when they can no longer pay."

"Not true. We underwrite charity cases with monies we make from those who can afford our services. If we could operate on an entirely altruistic level, we would."

"I'll bet. What were your bosses before the invasion? Racketeers? Pirates?"

A slight line appeared on Mors's forehead. "I came here in good faith."

"Let's all just calm down," Jacen said, reprising the role

of mediator he had performed during the crisis at Duro. "Why don't we just get the preliminaries out of the way?"

"I've all but begged to move this along," Bana said.

"Mom?" Jacen said.

Leia was politic enough to know that her son was right. She nodded, sat, and folded her hands together.

"After the fall of Duro, Tsavong Lah, the Yuuzhan Vong warmaster, promised that if all of the Jedi in the galaxy were turned over to him, he would invade no more of our planets. A lot of people have taken him at his word."

"What concern is this of mine?" Bana asked.

"The Jedi protect even your kind, Hutt," Numa snarled suddenly.

"But if I see clearly where our friend is going with this, it's the Jedi who now need protecting."

"Not this Jedi," the Twi'lek replied. "I do not ask for rescue, only for help in my struggle."

"If you would let me continue?" Leia said mildly.

"Go on, please," Numa said, though she did not seem in the least chastened.

"Yes, we're trying to establish a network to get Jedi off worlds that are hostile to them to places where they can be safe. But Luke Skywalker's plan is much more comprehensive than that. We also want to be able to get Jedi *into* occupied systems—systems like yours, Bana."

"For what purpose?" Opeli Mors asked.

"To help where they are most needed. To connect with underground and intelligence networks. What we are after here is not a Jedi rescue network, merely one that lets Jedi move about in relative safety."

"And these Jedi—they would fight with my people against the Yuuzhan Vong?" Bana asked.

Leia and Jacen exchanged glances. Jacen cleared his throat. "Aggression, as such, is not the Jedi way. We would help, yes."

"Yes? You will run weapons to us? Supplies?"

"The network could be used for that, too," Han said. "As I see it, anyway."

"I should hope so," Bana replied. "The fortunes of our

family are not what they once were. When we spend money, we want a return."

Numa spoke again, dismissing the Hutt with a flick of her lekku. "I have heard, Jacen Solo, that you yourself attacked and humiliated the warmaster. Is this not aggression? Does not Kyp Durron even now take the fight to the enemy?"

"He did it to save my life," Leia said.

Jacen squared up his shoulders. "I don't agree with Kyp's tactics, nor does Master Skywalker."

"Then you would not agree with mine," Numa said. "Perhaps it was a mistake for me to come here."

Jacen studied her for a moment. "Your Master must have warned you of the dark side."

"Fear of the dark side is a luxury the people of New Plympto cannot afford. Will you help us or not?"

Anakin would agree with her, Jacen thought glumly.

"We will do what we can," he told her. "We will bring medical aid and food, help evacuate those who must leave. We will not come in as guerrillas. And avoiding the dark side is not a luxury. It is a necessity."

She did not reply to that, but in the Force Jacen felt her unrepentant.

"Mors?"

The woman stared at the table for a moment, then her gaze found Han's. "Personally, I would like to help," she said. "But my superiors—well. We could supply troops and ships, of course, of the sort experienced at the kind of activity you're planning, but—"

"But we'll have to pay," Leia said.

"Something, yes."

"Look," Han said. "The New Republic isn't in on this. They won't fund it."

"You built this station."

"Out of our own pockets," Lando said. "Even the Hutts contributed."

"Ah, but they stand to gain. Whatever our friend there may say, he knows your Jedi network is one of the slim hopes his people have for survival."

"You're in the same escape pod," Leia snapped. "You

think the Yuuzhan Vong will tolerate your business when they've conquered the entire galaxy?"

Mors shrugged. "Maybe. Maybe not. That's why I *have* been authorized to offer you the loan of one ship, at no charge. We'll consider it an investment."

Han nodded. "Well, that's something." He glanced around the table. "Why don't we see if we can find some *more* common ground?"

Han slouched into the kneading chair in the quarters Lando had provided. Though not as opulent as Lando's, they were more than comfortable.

"This isn't going to work," he muttered.

"Don't be defeatist," Leia said.

"I'm not. I'm being realistic. Somebody has to be, because your brother sure isn't."

"Don't start in on Luke again."

"Look, I'm glad he finally decided to *do* something," Han said, "but he could have chosen something doable. 'Make me a great river, Han, a stream to carry the endangered, the wounded, the weary to safety.' Very poetic. But how do we *pay* for it? Everyone in the room wants to take and take, but they don't want to give."

Leia's expression softened and she stroked her fingers on his cheek. He closed them in his own hand and kissed them.

He started to embrace her, but before he could complete it, she drew back from him a little, though gently.

"We *will* find the money, Han." And her eyes held a fire brighter even than that day on the Death Star when they first met. It burned through him like a blaster bolt. He nodded, and tugged her again, and this time she did not resist.

TEN

Nen Yim contemplated the mass of cells through an external maa'it, at a magnification of several hundred times their actual size, and for the first time in many cycles felt a minute amount of hope. She could not be certain, but she thought there were signs of regeneration; the mass had grown large and infinitesimally more massive. If so, her new protocol seemed to be working. Unfortunately, it would be some time before she could be sure, and though she was short of every resource imaginable, time was the commodity she had in least supply.

She noted the results in her portable memory-qahsa, then moved on to the next batch of trials. Before she could get a good start, however, her door burred softly, indicating a request for admittance to the shaping quarters. She moved to the villip on the wall and stroked it to life.

The face that appeared was the prefect Ona Shai, commander of the worldship. Her eyebrows had been cut into a series of vertical ridges, and one of her ears had been sacrificed to the gods.

"Prefect Shai," Nen Yim said. "What can I do for you?"

"I desire admittance, Adept."

Nen Yim dithered, inwardly. There was no time to hide her work, but then, no one else on the *Baanu Miir* was likely to comprehend what she was doing, much less recognize it as heresy.

"Please enter, Prefect."

A moment later the door burred a different tone, and Nen Yim opened it by exposing her wrist to its chemical sensor.

In person, the prefect was not particularly intimidating. Younger even than Nen Yim, she had been born with a slight stoop to her spine. Another degree of angle, and she would have been sent back to the gods at birth. She was habitually excitable and ill controlled, as was evident now.

"Adept," Ona said.

"Prefect."

For a moment the prefect stood there blankly, as if she had forgotten why she came. She passed a hand across her face, and her eyes wandered. She seemed almost in shock.

"Something has happened," she said at last. "It requires your attention."

"What, Prefect? What has occurred?"

"One-fourth of the population of the *Baanu Miir* is dead," the prefect said.

As Nen Yim stepped through the emergency membrane, she felt the vacuum-hardened ooglith cloaker tighten against her body, maintaining the pressure that kept her blood from boiling away into the airless chamber beyond.

The frozen bodies piled three and four deep on the floor hadn't been wearing cloakers. Nen Yim felt a tightness in her throat that had nothing to do with the hard-shelled variety of gnullith she had inserted there to pass the air from the lungworm coiled on her back.

They had time, she thought. *The air went out slowly, at first. They had time to reach this place, where the ship finally thought to seal itself off. Here they died, beating against a membrane they did not have the authority to permeate.*

"This is no way to die," she heard the prefect murmur over the tiny villips that pressed at their throats and ears.

"Death is always to be embraced," Sakanga, the warrior who completed their triad, reminded her. He was an ancient, almost mummylike man. Like the prefect, he was of the disgraced Domain Shai.

"Of course that is true," Ona said. "Of course."

"What happened here, Shaper?" the warrior asked, turning his attention to Nen Yim. "Meteor impact? Infidel attack?" He paused. "Sabotage?"

"It was not possible to tell," Nen Yim answered. "The rikyam's understanding was hazy. It is why I wished to come here, to seek evidence. The breach is at the end of this arm, that is all I know. Perhaps when I see it, I can say more."

"We should have a master on this ship," the prefect grumbled. "I do not demean you, Adept, but a worldship should have a master shaper on board."

"I quite agree," Nen Yim said. "A master is needed." *A master like my own, Mezhan Kwaad, not one of the mumbling dodderers who pass for them,* she finished silently.

They moved soundlessly through the carnage. Most of the bodies were slaves and Shamed Ones; in death, vacuum had mutilated them as they could not have been in life. Perhaps the gods would accept their final sacrifice, perhaps not. They were, at least, beyond caring.

The capillary platforms that would normally have taken them down the arm were as dead and frozen as the people who had once used them. The three were forced to descend by the bony spine with its intentionally runglike vertebrae. As they descended, their bodies grew gradually heavier with the illusion of gravity created by the ship's spin. Coming back up would be more onerous than descending. She wondered if the decrepit warrior would be able to manage it at all.

The chambers were jeweled with ice crystals, frozen in the act of boiling from and rupturing the soft inner walls. The once-pliant floor was as rigid as the yorik coral on the exterior of the ship, but much more dead.

They continued down, through progressively smaller chambers. They saw fewer dead down here, too, reinforcing Nen Yim's guess. The rupture had ended catastrophically, emptying the arm of air and life in a few tens of heartbeats, but it must have begun small.

Why had the rikyam given no alarm? Why hadn't the seals between each and every layer closed and hardened?

Eventually, they came to stars.

The arm curved toward the end, and "down" followed the anterior edge. Here objects weighed the most; the area had been reserved for the training of warriors originally, but since most able-bodied warriors had moved ahead of the slower worldships to the glory of battle, the tip had been transformed into a crèche, so that the children of the next generation would mature with thicker bones and more powerful muscles.

A futile hope for these children. Those who hadn't been hurled out into space regarded the stars they might have conquered with frozen eyes through a fifty-meter-long tear in the fabric of the hull.

Nen Yim shivered. The stars were decidedly *down*. If she were to fall, the spin of the ship would sling her irrevocably into trackless parsecs of nothing.

And yet it was glorious. As she watched, the disk of the galaxy spun into view, too enormous for even such a large gash to fully frame. The Core blazed, a white mass tinged blue, spreading into arms that gradually faded toward cooler stars. Technically, the *Baanu Miir* was already within the boundaries of that great lens, but even the nearest world was unreachably far from the *Baanu Miir*.

That became even more apparent as she examined the rupture. The edges of it were curled outward, revealing the tripartite nature of the hull. The outer shell was yorik coral, rigid metal-bearing nacelles wrapped around the hardy, energetic organisms that created and tended them. Below that were the sheared and frozen capillaries that carried nutrients and oxygen out to the arms and pumped waste products back for the maw luur to cycle and recycle, supplemented by the hydrogen atoms that the dovin basals pulled from surrounding space. There also were the muscles and tendons that could flex the great arm, contract it if need be, and here something had failed. When the rift occurred, the medial hull should have drawn together and been sealed by its own freezing. The outer hull would have replicated and closed the gap, and over time the dead, frozen cells should have been replaced by vibrant new ones. The soft, pliable inner hull would have healed as well, eventually leaving nothing more than a faint scar to remind of the disaster.

"What happened?" the warrior asked. "I don't understand this."

Nen Yim pointed to the rent mass of striated muscle.

"It tore itself," she said.

"What do you mean, it tore *itself*?" the prefect asked. "How can that be?"

"The muscles spasmed, as the muscles of your leg might after much exertion. They contracted and split the hull, then kept contracting, tearing it wider."

"That's impossible," the warrior grunted.

"No, only undesirable," Nen Yim replied. "The rikyam is supposed to monitor such fluctuations and moderate them."

"Then why didn't it?"

"My deduction? Because the rikyam's senses in this arm are dead. It is unaware that anything here exists. Very likely the impulse that ripped the hull was one of the few random impulses to enter here from the brain in many cycles."

"You're saying the rikyam itself did this?" Ona asked.

"Only indirectly. What you behold is the result of a ship-brain so far gone in senility that it is losing control of its motor functions."

"Then there is no hope," the prefect murmured.

The warrior glanced at the prefect in irritation. "What is this babble of hope? The Yuuzhan Vong were born to conquer and die. This is an obstacle, nothing more."

"Can you heal it?" Ona Shai asked Nen Yim.

"We can seal the rupture. The damage is crippling; the entire inner hull is dead. The medial hull will take many cycles to regenerate, assuming the maw luur still nourishes it. We can perhaps grow a ganglion to control the functions of this arm, but it will remain disconnected from the brain. Furthermore, it is probable that the rikyam is losing control of the other arms as well, if it hasn't already."

"You're saying we must abandon *Baanu Miir*." The prefect's voice was flat.

"Unless the rikyam can be regenerated. I am giving this all of my attention."

"See that you do. Meanwhile, a new worldship is being grown. I will petition that our people be transferred there. Yet many of the ships are failing; our chances are slim."

"Whatever our fate, we will meet it as befits the children of Yun-Yuuzhan." Sakanga gestured at the rim of the galaxy slipping from view. "Already we have warriors poised near that bright center. All of those worlds beneath us will be ours. Our sacrifices here will not be forgotten. It is not our place to complain."

"No," Nen Yim agreed. "But we will do what we must to ensure *Baanu Miir* provides another generation for that conquest. *I* will do what I must." *Though it will only earn me dishonor and death, I will do what I must.*

ELEVEN

Luke watched the blockade grow larger.

"Oh, boy," Mara said.

"No," Luke murmured, placing his hand on her shoulder. "Don't you see? They're no danger to us."

Jaina's voice crackled over the comm. "That's Rogue Squadron! I can't *believe* they would—"

She was interrupted by a hail that came simultaneously to the *Jade Shadow*.

Gavin Darklighter's image appeared on the *Shadow*'s display.

"*Jade Shadow*—it looks like you could use some help."

"This is unwise, Gavin," Luke responded carefully. "Those are Coruscant security forces pursuing us."

"I've explained their mistake to them," Gavin replied. "They won't trouble you again."

"They'll just send for more ships. This could really develop into a situation."

"Maybe the sort of situation the New Republic needs," Gavin replied. "First Corran, now you? Enough is enough. Fey'lya is selling us off to the Yuuzhan Vong a piece at a time."

"No, he's not. I have my disagreements with him, obviously, but he's trying to save the New Republic, in his own way. A civil war can only make us weaker."

"Not if we make it quick and painless. Not if we have real leadership when it's over, rather than the fractured, squabbling crowd that's got us sitting on our thumbs."

"You're referring to democracy," Luke replied. "Something we all fought very hard for. We can't throw it away simply because it becomes inconvenient. Gavin, we aren't having this conversation."

"Okay. I just wanted you to know you have support."

"And I appreciate it. But now is the time for you to flame out of this situation. If we go right now, we'll get a clear jump. Then you start talking your way out of this mess."

"You're sure you don't want an escort?"

"Positive."

Gavin nodded. "Understood. Take care. Mara, you too."

His face vanished from the screen, and Luke suddenly felt his fingers trembling.

"Luke?" Mara said, concern in her voice.

"That was too close," he said. "Too close. I won't be the excuse for a coup. Am I doing the right thing?"

"Absolutely. Let them arrest you, and you think this resistance won't come back up?"

"Did you know the squadron would do this?"

"I'd guessed it."

"And you think if we give up . . ."

"An attempted coup within a week, my guess. At the very least an extremely volatile situation. Skywalker, you were seeing clearly earlier. We have to go. For the New Republic's sake, for the Jedi's sake—and not least by a long shot, for the sake of ourselves and our son."

Jaina answered the private hail from Gavin Darklighter, trying to keep composed.

"Yes, Colonel," she said. "How may I help you?"

"Watch after Master Skywalker, Jaina. He needs you."

"I'll do my best, sir. Is that all?"

"No." Gavin's voice crackled. "I made a mistake not putting you back on duty once your vision was recovered. I let you down, and I'm sorry for that. I'd like you to consider yourself still a part of the Squadron."

"I appreciate that, Rogue Leader," she said quietly. "You understand that right now—"

"As I said. Master Skywalker needs you now. You're still on leave, as far as I'm concerned. Go, and may the Force be with you."

* * *

"Jaina, I need you to do something," Luke said. Coruscant was light-years behind them. There was room for an X-wing on the *Shadow,* but that space was already occupied by Luke's starfighter. Thus, they chatted over the comm. Mara and Luke had filled her in on the details of their flight from Coruscant, and Jaina in turn had explained her continued detachment from Rogue Squadron.

"Yes, Uncle Luke?"

"I need you to find Kyp Durron for me. I need to talk to him."

"He didn't have much good to say at the last meeting. Why should things be any different now?"

"Because things *are* different now," Luke replied. "Now I may have some things to say he might want to hear."

"Unless you're going to join him in guerrilla warfare against the Yuuzhan Vong, I doubt that," she replied.

"Be that as it may. It's imperative that the Jedi start drawing ourselves back together."

"If you ask me to find him, I'll find him," Jaina said. "I found Booster Terrik, didn't I?"

"This will be a lot easier than that, I should think," Luke replied. "I know exactly where Kyp is."

"How?"

"Kyp worries me. I took the liberty of placing a tracer on his ship."

"What? If the Yuuzhan Vong pick that up—"

"I didn't endanger Kyp. It's something new one of Karrde's people came up with to help us find each other without leaking our positions to the Yuuzhan Vong or their collaborators. Booster has one, too, so we'll be able to find the *Errant Venture* with relative ease. It's a fixed-signature signal, passed through relays and the HoloNet, and gives an off-read within a range from ten to fifty light-years. No one without the encryption key can use it to track him, in other words. At short range it sounds like engine noise, and if Kyp cuts his power to hide from sensors, it'll go off, too."

"Wow. Have I been fitted with one of those?"

"No, but the *Shadow* has, and I'll give you that encryption, too, along with Booster's."

"Sounds good. Where's Kyp now?"

"That's the disturbing thing. He's near Sernpidal."

A shiver feathered along Jaina's neck.

Sernpidal. Where Chewie had died. Sernpidal was as deep in Yuuzhan Vong territory as one could go.

This wouldn't be another little fetching mission. This could get very nasty indeed.

"That's a long way," she said. "I hope you have some extra juice over there for me."

"Plenty. We'll hook you up, and I'll transfer some supplies as well."

He grimaced, and she could tell that sending her off like this wasn't something he did without reservations.

"Thanks, Jaina," he said. "And may the Force be with you."

PART TWO

PASSAGE

TWELVE

"Oh!" Tahiri exclaimed, wrinkling her nose. "It *stinks*."

"Yep," Corran agreed. "Welcome to Eriadu."

Anakin agreed, as well, albeit silently. But it was a complex stink. If he imagined this stuff Eriaduans sucked in every day as a painting, an oily, bitter, hydrocarbon stench would be the canvas. Sulfury burnt yellow swirled over it, interspersed with starbursts of white ozone spangles and green chloride stars, all under a gray wash of something vaguely organic and ammoniac.

A light rain was falling. Anakin hoped it wouldn't burn his skin.

"Is Coruscant like this?" Tahiri asked. She had already forgotten the smell and was tracing with eager eyes the clunky but sky-reaching industrial buildings on all sides of the spaceport. Low leaden clouds dragged over the tallest structures, though the canopy opened in places to a more distant, pastel yellow sky.

"Not really," Anakin said. "For one thing, the buildings on Coruscant aren't this ugly."

"It's not ugly," Tahiri said. She sounded defensive. "It's *different*. I've never been on a world with this much . . . stuff."

"Well, Coruscant's got more 'stuff,' and now that I think about it, the lower levels make this look like a cloud city. But at least the air is clean. They don't muck it up like this."

"You mean this isn't natural, this smell?" Tahiri asked.

"Nope," Corran said. "They make things cheap and dirty here. The perfume you've noticed is one of the by-products. If they don't watch it, Eriadu will become another

Duro. Well, what Duro was before the Yuuzhan Vong got hold of it, anyway."

"I don't think you ought to go barefoot here, Tahiri," Anakin remarked.

Tahiri looked down at the grimy duracrete landing field and grimaced. "Maybe you're right."

Off to their right, a bulk freighter cut its underjets and settled on repulsorlifts.

"Okay," Corran said. "I'm going to arrange for the supplies we need. You two—"

"Stay and guard the ship, I bet," Anakin muttered.

"Right."

Tahiri's brow ruffled. "You mean I came all this way and don't even get to see the place?"

"No," Corran said. "When I get back, we'll go into town and find someplace to eat. We'll do a little exploring. But I don't want to stay long; there's no reason for anyone to double-check our transponder code, but if they do, we could run into a little trouble."

"Well . . . okay," Tahiri assented. She sat on the landing ramp, legs folded underneath her. Together she and Anakin watched Corran flag a ground transport and enter it. A few moments later, the blocky vehicle vanished from sight.

"Do you think people from here think clean worlds smell weird?" Tahiri asked.

"Probably. What did you think of Yavin Four, after all those years on Tatooine?"

"I thought it smelled weird," she concluded, after a bit of thought. "But in a good way. Mostly in a good way. I mean, part of it smelled like a kitchen midden or a 'fresher sump. But the blueleaf, and the flowers . . ." She trailed off, and her expression changed. "What do you think the Yuuzhan Vong did to Yavin Four after we left? Do you think they changed it, you know, like they did some of the other planets they captured?"

"I don't know," Anakin said. "I don't want to think about it." It had been hard enough to see the Great Temple where so much of his childhood had been spent destroyed. To imagine that the verdant jungle and all of its creatures were also gone was more than he was willing to put himself through without proof.

Tahiri's face stayed long.

"What?" Anakin asked, when she didn't say anything for a while.

"I lied a minute ago."

"Really? About what?"

She nodded at the cityscape. "I said it wasn't ugly. But part of me thinks it is."

"Well, *I* don't think it's all that attractive," Anakin replied.

"No," Tahiri said, her voice suddenly husky. "It's not like that. It's just that part of me sees this and thinks *abomination*."

"Oh."

The Yuuzhan Vong had done more to Tahiri than cut her face. They had implanted memories in her—of their language, of a childhood in a crèche, of growing up on a worldship.

"If you hadn't rescued me, Anakin, I would be one of them now. I wouldn't remember any other life."

"Part of you would have always known," Anakin disagreed. "There's something in you, Tahiri, that no one could ever change."

She shot him a startled frown. "You keep saying things like that. What do you mean? Is it good or bad? You mean I'm too stubborn, or what?"

"I mean you're too Tahiri," he said.

"Oh." She attempted a smile and half succeeded. "I guess I'll take that as a compliment, since you never give me any obvious ones."

Anakin felt his face warm. He and Tahiri had been best friends for a long time. Now that she was fourteen and he was sixteen, things were getting very confusing. It was like her eyes had changed colors, but they hadn't. They were just more interesting somehow.

She *had* cut her hair, right before they left for Eriadu— that had been a shock. She now wore it in a kind of bob, with wispy little bangs that tickled at her eyebrows.

She noticed his regard. "What? You don't like my hair?"

"It's fine. It's a nice cut. About the same length as my mom's is now."

"Anakin Solo—" Something inside her cut her sentence off short.

"Did you feel that?" she asked in a hushed voice.

And at the moment, he did. Something in the Force. Fear, panic, resolution, resignation, all bound up together.

"It's a Jedi," he murmured.

"A Jedi in trouble. Bad trouble." She uncoiled like a released spring. "Where are those shoes?"

"Tahiri, no. I'll go. Someone has to stay with the ship."

"You do it then. I'm going." She stood up and went into the ship. Anakin followed. She found a pair of walking slippers in her locker and put them on.

"Just wait a second. Let me figure this out."

"I don't need you to figure anything out for me. One of us is in trouble. I'm going to help."

She was already on her way out and down the landing ramp.

Repeating some of his father's more inventive expletives, Anakin hurriedly sealed the ship and ran after her.

He caught up with her at the customs-and-immigration line. She breezed past everyone else, but was stopped at the force gate, where a gray-haired official frowned down at her.

"You have to go to the back of the line."

"No, I don't," Tahiri said, passing her hand impatiently.

"You don't," the woman agreed. "But I need to see your identification."

"You don't care about that," Tahiri insisted.

"Never mind; don't bother," the official replied. "What's the purpose of your visit to Eriadu?"

"Nothing that would interest you. I have to get through, now!"

The woman shrugged. "Okay. Go on through." She dropped the force barrier, and Tahiri dashed past.

"Next."

"I'm with her," Anakin informed her. "You need to let me through, right now," he added.

"You need to be with her," the official said, dropping the force gate again, long enough for Anakin to get through.

Behind him, he heard the next person in line say, "Why don't you just let me through, as well?"

"Why would I do that?" the official wondered caustically.

Naturally, he'd lost sight of Tahiri, but he knew where she was going. The Jedi they were both feeling was in more distress than ever.

Anakin pushed his way through the rain-slickered portround crowd, through vendors and street performers, past long rows of cantinas and tapcafs and souvenir shops full of mostly fake lacy shellwork and grossly caricatured statuettes of Grand Moff Tarkin.

Three streets in, the crowd seemed to dissipate, and the grubby lanes were almost empty, except for the occasional six-legged rodent. Here the scent of hot metal was overpowering, though the streets were relatively cold and the rain had increased. And ahead of him somewhere, a Jedi's feet were slowing.

Anakin turned into a long cul-de-sac formed on the left by a chrome-facade skyscraper and on the right by the ribbed-steel wall of a ten-story-high heat sink, steaming in the rain. The end of the alley was the back of another building faced in blackened duraplast. A crowd of vagabonds was gathered, watching a murder about to happen.

The victim was a Jedi, a Rodian. He stood against the heat sink, trying to keep his lightsaber up. Five beings faced him—two with blasters, three with stun batons. All had just turned to face Tahiri, who was about six meters from them, arriving at a dead run, her lightsaber swirling bright patterns over her head.

Anakin saw all of this from a distance of fifty meters or so. He tried to coax his feet to lightspeed.

Taking advantage of Tahiri's distraction, the Rodian lurched forward. One of the men with a blaster shot him, and the descending screech of the bolt reverberated in the alley.

Tahiri's blade sheared through a stun baton, nearly taking the hand of the thickset woman wielding it. Anakin winced; Kam had been working with Tahiri on her lightsaber technique, and she was a quick learner, but still a novice.

Novice or not, the thugs with the stun batons backpedaled, drawing blasters instead of taking up the fight hand to hand. Tahiri pressed on, catching one of them and snipping the end of his weapon off. The next man back fired at her and missed. They started to encircle her.

Finally, Anakin arrived. He recognized the Rodian Jedi as Kelbis Nu. The man who had shot the Rodian saw him coming, took careful aim, and fired twice. Two bolts winged into the alley walls, courtesy of Anakin's lightsaber. He was running past the man, deftly slicing the blaster in half as he went, when he felt a gun pointing at him. He dropped and rolled as the bolt screamed over his head.

A person screamed, too—the man who had shot Kelbis Nu. The blast meant for Anakin had struck him high in the chest, and he fell, legs kicking.

Anakin came back to his feet and found Tahiri facing two men still armed with blasters and two unarmed. They looked uncertain.

It was only then that Anakin realized, by their patches and uniforms, that they were Peace Brigade.

The thugs started backing out of the alley in a small knot, blasters pointed defensively. Anakin stood about a meter to Tahiri's right and a little in front of her.

"Let's take 'em," she said. Her voice had a furious, cold quality to it that Anakin had heard twice; once when she was under the heaviest influence of her Yuuzhan Vong conditioning; once in a vision he'd had of her as a dark Jedi, her face mutilated by the scars and tattoos of a Yuuzhan Vong warmaster.

"No," Anakin said. "Let them go."

His generosity didn't stop the Peace Brigaders from taking a parting shot as they ducked around the corner.

"Jedi brats!" one of the men shouted. "Your days are numbered!"

When he was sure they weren't just hiding around the corner, waiting for his guard to drop, Anakin turned to survey the damage.

The Peace Brigader had stopped moving. Kelbis Nu was still alive—barely. His glassy eyes were looking beyond Anakin, but he reached up a hand.

"Ya . . . ," he said weakly.

"Tahiri, use your wrist comm. Try to find the local emergency channel." He took Nu's hand and pulsed strength from the Force into him. "Hold on for me," he said. "Help will be here soon."

"Ya—ya—ya . . . ," the Rodian gasped.

"Don't try to talk," Anakin told him. "Waste of strength."

Suddenly Kelbis Nu went still, his trembling ceased, and for the first time he seemed to actually see Anakin.

"*Yag'Dhul,*" he whispered, and behind that whisper was a stormwind of danger.

That was all. The Jedi's life left him with his last breath.

Tahiri was shouting at someone over her wrist comm.

"Never mind, Tahiri," Anakin said. "He's gone." Tears started in his eyes, but he battled them down.

"He can't be," Tahiri said. "I was going to save him."

"I'm sorry," Anakin said. "We got here too late."

Tahiri's shoulders began to twitch, and she made a sound like hiccuping as she fought to control her tears. Anakin watched her, wishing he could help, that he could make the grief go away, but there was nothing he could do. People died. You got used to it.

It still hurt.

"He said something at the end," Anakin told her, hoping to distract her.

"What?"

"The name of a planet, Yag'Dhul. It's not far from here, right where the Corellian Trade Spine and the Rimma Trade Route meet. And I felt . . . danger. Like he was trying to tell me something bad is happening there." He glanced down at the bodies. "C'mon. We'd better go."

"We have to do something," Tahiri said. "We can't just let those guys get away with it."

"We can't hunt them," Anakin said.

"Why not?"

"Because we're Jedi, not assassins."

"We could at least tell security or whoever enforces the law around here."

"We're supposed to be here anonymously, remember? If we draw attention to ourselves, we endanger the mission."

"Some mission. Getting supplies. This is more important. Anyway, we've already drawn attention to ourselves." She nodded at the crowd of vagrants drifting toward them, the curiosity of two dead bodies overcoming their fear of two live Jedi.

And as if to highlight her point, a trio of groundcars arrived at the end of the alley and disgorged armed, uniformed people.

"I guess we'll be talking to security after all." Anakin clipped his lightsaber to his belt and held up his hands to show they were empty.

The officers approached warily, led by a lanky, craggy-faced man with the fading remnants of a black eye. He looked down at the two bodies and back up at them. Then his eyes focused on their lightsabers—Tahiri still had hers in her hand.

He raised his gun. "Place your weapons on the ground," he said.

"We didn't do this," Tahiri exploded. "We were trying to help."

"Put it down, now, girlie."

"*Girlie?*"

"Do as he says, Tahiri," Anakin said, carefully detaching his weapon and placing it near his feet.

"Why?"

"Do it."

"It's good advice, kid," the officer said.

Radiating anger, Tahiri placed her lightsaber on the duracrete.

"Good. As officers of the judicials, it is now my duty to inform you that we are detaining you for questioning and possible prosecution."

"What? You're arresting us?" Tahiri said.

"Until we sort this out, yes."

"Ask the crowd. They saw what happened."

"We will; don't worry. There will be a thorough investigation. Make this easy on yourselves."

But words are only the shadows of thoughts, and behind the officer's words, Anakin felt something that suggested that this was going to be anything but easy.

THIRTEEN

By the time Jaina reached the vicinity of the Sernpidal system, her X-wing felt like a suit of clothes she'd been wearing for *way* too long.

In fact, her clothes felt that way, too, but more so.

Jedi meditation techniques and isometrics made the long hyperspace jumps bearable, but nothing could hide the fact that there was no room on an X-wing for a shower. Or room to stand up, to walk, to *run*.

That's not likely going to happen anytime soon, she chided herself. *So concentrate!*

She was near her goal now. Somewhere down there—or so the tracer told her—was Kyp Durron. Or his X-wing, at least.

Or merely the tracer beacon, if Kyp was more clever than Uncle Luke imagined. Jaina started sweeping with long-range sensors.

Kyp wasn't at Sernpidal anymore, but a system several very strange jumps away. The star at the bottom of the gravity pit was old, a white dwarf that at this distance was barely brighter than its much more distant, hotter cousins. It was wreathed with a lazy torus of nebulas ejected when the star collapsed into its present pale form. Jaina had appeared in the inner fringe of the gas cloud.

She punched up the stellar survey and found a brief entry more than two hundred years old. The star had a number but not a name. Six planets. The nearest to the sun was a lifeless rock; the next three were sheathed in frozen carbon dioxide and water ice. On the outer planets, the ice got more exotic: methane, ammonia, chlorine in various compounds. The largest planet, a gas giant, had picked up its own nebula from the outbound gases expelled from the parent star.

No known intelligent life in the system, no known life at all. No resources that couldn't be found more easily elsewhere, and no reason to come back.

But Kyp Durron had come here.

She followed the beacon in, dropping from above the plane of the elliptic. It took her to the fourth planet, a rock half the size of Coruscant that made Hoth seem like a hothouse. She tried not to fidget.

She hadn't expected to come in unnoticed, and she didn't. As she was making orbit a pair of X-wings rose up to meet her. One had the beacon in it.

A few moments later, she answered what turned out to be Kyp's hail.

"Amazing," he said. "Simply amazing. Jaina Solo, you continue to find ways to surprise me."

"Hello, Kyp."

"I'd ask you what could have possibly brought you to this place, but I almost don't want to know. If the Force guided you, it's almost too frightening."

"How so?"

"Because I was just about to come looking for you and Rogue Squadron," Kyp answered, sounding sardonic.

"Really."

"Yep. I've found something, Jaina—something I can't handle with my Dozen. Something that could strike a death blow to the New Republic if we don't deal with it now, while we can."

"What are you talking about?" Jaina asked.

"I'd rather tell you in person. Follow me in—we don't have much down there, but it's better than the cockpit of an X-wing."

Kyp and his followers had melted tunnels and caves through the water ice and sealed it, then sifted an oxygen-nitrogen mix from higher up, where the planet's atmosphere had condensed when its primary went cold.

"We keep it right at freezing in here," Kyp explained, "so our humble home doesn't melt." He handed her a parka. "You'll want that."

"To tell you the truth," Jaina said, "the cold feels good. Almost as good as it feels to stand up." Her legs were having a little trouble finding their stride in the lower gravity.

"Well, like I said, it's not much, but we like it," Kyp said.

"Kyp, what are you doing all the way out here? This whole sector must be crawling with Yuuzhan Vong."

"Oh, they aren't far, though you'd be surprised by their numbers, I think—but they aren't *here*. No worlds to colonize, no slaves to be had, no machines to be destroyed."

"Except you, your people, and your ships."

"Good point. But there are a lot of these played-out star systems near the Rim. This one isn't even particularly rich in ore because the star died with a whimper—no supernova to spew heavy metals all over the place. I don't see them looking here when all of their efforts are focused on the Core."

"You think they'll push toward the Core?"

Kyp rolled his eyes. "You're smarter than that, Jaina. The Yuuzhan Vong are taking a breath, that's all, hoping their collaborators will do some of the work for them. But they're building up everywhere. And what I've found out here—"

"Yes, you mentioned that."

"First things first, Jaina. Do you mind telling my why *you're* here? And, in all seriousness, give me a little hint as to how?"

"Master Skywalker sent me to talk to you."

"Really? He has something new to say?"

"He and Mara fled Coruscant after Borsk Fey'lya ordered their arrest."

Kyp blinked, and his brow creased.

"Come in here and sit down," he said. He ushered her into what was obviously his war room—a portable sensor sweep, a tactical display, and star charts were its furnishings. He pulled up a collapsible chair for Jaina and one for himself.

"That was uncommonly stupid," he murmured. "Even for Fey'lya. Do you think our chief of state is working with the Peace Brigade?"

"Master Skywalker doesn't think so. Neither do I."

"Huh," Kyp said dubiously. "So what is Master Skywalker doing now?"

"Aunt Mara's pregnant, you know. It's not long before her time comes. Uncle Luke's hiding out with Booster Terrik. He intends to find a planet to build a Jedi base on."

Kyp's eyes narrowed. "A base for what?"

"To operate from. A place where endangered Jedi can go, a place for them to strike from."

"Jaina," Kyp said, "choose your words carefully. What do you mean by 'strike'? Don't put words in the Master's mouth just because you think I want to hear them."

Jaina looked down at the floor. "No," she said, "he's still not advocating what you're doing. He's trying to build a network to pass people and information in and out of Yuuzhan Vong space. A system of places like this, and ships—"

"But no direct action. No bringing the fight home to the Yuuzhan Vong."

"Not exactly—not the way you mean. But, Kyp, he is doing something, and he needs your help."

Kyp shook his head. "I think he sent you out here to find out what I'm doing."

"Partly. But he also sent me to bring you back into the fold."

Kyp rubbed his jaw thoughtfully for a moment. "I don't object to what Master Skywalker is doing. I have my bolt-holes and contacts, but they're limited, scattered, one day at a time. I don't have the resources or the leisure to build and maintain a stable network. If Luke does, that's great. I wish he would take a more active hand, but this is more than I was starting to think he would do. He's right; I can be of help to him, in certain sectors. And I'll do it—I'll meet with him. But Jaina, I need something from you in return." He frowned. "Though this arrest business changes things." He mulled that over a bit and shrugged. "I'll lay it out for you anyway. I'm not on good terms with any of the military leaders. I need someone who is. Is that still you?"

Jaina thought back to her last encounter with Rogue Squadron. And Wedge Antilles, so far as she knew, was still on the side of the Jedi.

"They might listen to me," she allowed.

"Or your mother."

"What do you need, Kyp?" Jaina asked wearily.

He looked at her as if for the first time. "It can wait a few hours," he said. "Why don't you get cleaned up? We sank an old cargo tank to use as a warm room. There's a hot tub of water calling your name."

"That sounds really, really good," Jaina said. "That's not a proposition I'm prepared to refuse, anyway."

The rogue Jedi's eyes twinkled mischievously. "When you're done, we'll discuss what other propositions you might find interesting."

That did something tickly to Jaina's stomach. She tried to ignore it.

Clean and in a change of clothes, Jaina spent half an hour limbering up, enjoying the luxury of motion. Then she rejoined Kyp in the tactical room. A few more of his Dozen—plus however many now—were in evidence. They nodded at her when she entered.

"That better?" Kyp asked.

"A lot better," Jaina told him. "Solar diameters better. Parsecs better. So. What's up?"

"I like that," Kyp said. "You get to the point." He gestured for her to take a seat.

"Like I said earlier," he began, as she settled into the reinforced flimsiplast chair, "we've been mostly taking things day by day. Harassing Yuuzhan Vong convoys, providing aid to resistance movements, keeping our receivers tuned. The problem was, nothing we could ever do was enough. We were no more than ore mites, irritating the Vong. The other thing I realized was how little we really know about them. How many are there? Where do they come from? Are they *still* coming? So a few months ago I decided to spend some time on an extended recon. We began at the Rim, where they first entered, then visited Belkadan and Helska. It wasn't easy, but it wasn't as hard as I expected, either. I found a few answers. I found a lot more questions. But Sernpidal—Gavin Darklighter took Rogue Squadron to Sernpidal. After."

Jaina stiffened.

"Right," Kyp said. "You were with him, weren't you? What you saw was confidential, not something for crazy Kyp Durron to know. But when people see strange things, Jaina, they talk." He leaned forward on his elbows. "I've been known to accuse the New Republic and the Jedi of being slow to act, of having their priorities confused. Sometimes I've been right; maybe other times I've misstated the case. This time . . ."

He tapped on a holo display, and the Sernpidal system appeared. An adjustment, and a small section of it came into tight focus—a crescent of debris.

"The remains of Sernpidal."

Jaina suddenly felt her throat closing and tears welling behind her eyes. She'd thought she had a handle on this, on Chewbacca's death, but seeing the wreck of an entire planet, knowing somewhere in that jumble of rocks were the molecules that had once knit together into a person who had lived and loved, had held her when she was young—it stung. In some ways, Chewie had been a bigger part of her life than her own mother.

Kyp felt her grief and gave her the space of a few moments to adjust. Then he pointed to the holo.

"They did it to make ships," he said softly. "They grow the ships as they grow all of their tools. They feed the young ones on broken planets." He looked significantly at Jaina. "You knew this, right?"

She nodded.

"Right. Coralskippers, bigger ships, all of the things we've seen already. But then there's this."

He magnified yet again.

As they looked at the image, Kyp continued. "Gavin Darklighter saw the Yuuzhan Vong growing a ship the size of the Death Star. Why didn't anyone think that was a serious thing?"

The . . . thing . . . portrayed in the holograph was clearly a Yuuzhan Vong ship. It had the same organic look to it, and in color and alternating textures rough and smooth was much like the larger ships Jaina had already seen. But in form it was quite different.

It spidered across the sky, a huge, multilegged monster with each leg—or arm, or whatever—curving in the same direction, so the whole thing looked like a mad sculptor's attempt to portray a galaxy. It was beautiful and terrible, and it made her mouth dry to look at it.

"It didn't look like that before," Jaina said. "It was just an ovoid."

"What you and Gavin saw was hardly more than a seed," Kyp said. "That thing could swallow Death Stars for lunch. And no one has done *anything*."

"We've had our hands sort of full," she replied, aware that her voice was hushed. "How did you get this? Surely after Rogue Squadron's recon, the Yuuzhan Vong buttoned up the system."

"Oh, indeed they did," Kyp replied. "And for anyone besides someone trained as a pilot *and* a Jedi, I would say it was nearly impossible. But I'm the guy who guided your father through the Maw, using nothing but the most rudimentary command of the Force, and I've come a long way since then. Fluctuations in gravity are always squirreling little hyperspace entry points in and out of existence, spalled off larger ones. The Sernpidal system has been unstable since they destroyed the planet, which is how Darklighter got in. The Yuuzhan Vong have mostly corrected their earlier mistakes, but they can't cover all of them, especially those near the primary—and also when they're creating their own gravitic anomalies."

"Maybe because they think no one would be stupid enough to jump that close to a star?"

"Stupid or not, it worked. Despite that they very nearly

interdicted me. I lost a wingmate and made a jump out that nearly shredded me near a neutron star." He grinned again. "But it was worth it. I got a good, close look."

"You know what it is?"

"Yes. The whole thing isn't on-line yet, but they were putting some of its systems through trials while we were there."

"So what is it?"

"A gravitic weapon."

"Like a dovin basal?"

Kyp laughed. "Dovin basals, the big ones, can pull down a moon. They can generate anomalies that resemble quantum black holes. This thing could collapse a star."

"How do you know that's what it is? Why haven't we seen something like this before?"

"It's taken them a long time to grow it, Jaina. They couldn't grow one out there in the void between the galaxies, could they? And maybe not just any planet will do—maybe there was something special about Sernpidal. But remember, this was one of the first things they did when they began the invasion of our galaxy."

"There is some evidence they've been out on the Rim for at least fifty years," Jaina pointed out.

"I've seen a little evidence of that, too. But they weren't ready to invade, then. Blowing up a planet might have attracted someone's attention." He held up his hands. "I don't know. I only know one thing—that thing has to be stopped, now, before it's operational."

"I still don't understand how you can know what it is," Jaina said. "You've never been shy about jumping to conclusions."

Kyp tapped the holo console again. The view zoomed out.

"This is time lapse," he said softly. "Remember that Sernpidal was a hundred and fifteen thousand kilometers from its primary, which is still the approximate position of this weapon."

Jaina watched, at first not understanding what she was seeing. From the primary's corona, a small flare erupted, something she had seen happen on numerous occasions around numerous stars.

But the flare kept going, first a full solar diameter, then two. And as it grew longer, it gathered strength rather than diminishing, became a ribbon of superheated hydrogen and helium, dimming and cooling as it went but still clearly visible. In the artificial quickness of time lapse, it was only moments before the streamer reached the gigantic Yuuzhan Vong construction.

"Emperor's black bones," Jaina breathed.

"You see?" Kyp said. "Extrapolate. Only about an eighth of its systems seem to be 'alive,' yet it can generate a gravity well powerful enough and focused enough to pull enormous quantities of solar atmosphere over a hundred thousand kilometers. The dovin basal on Sernpidal pales to absolute insignificance next to that. Think of the size of the singularities it can create—big enough to swallow a ship? A *planet*? If we let them take that thing out, *nothing* can stop them."

Speechless, Jaina could only nod in horrified agreement.

FOURTEEN

"Oh, my goodness," C-3PO bleated as the *Falcon* dropped out of hyperspace with a sort of flat thud that sent them all a centimeter into the air. "It's another one of those terrible Yuuzhan Vong interdictors!"

"Relax, Threepio," Han said, his voice so dry he sounded almost bored. "The inertial dampeners are just being a little cranky, that's all. Lando's so-called technicians were a little less than thorough."

"More likely they didn't understand the extent to which this ship is put together with chewstim and wishful thinking," Leia joked. "No one else has *ever* been able to repair this thing except—"

She broke off, and Han knew why. The unfinished thought, *except you and Chewbacca,* was true. He and Chewie had made the *Falcon* galaxy-famous for doing the impossible, but it had almost always involved the Wookiee and him improvising circuits even as their shields were failing.

"You can say it," he told her.

"Look, Han," Leia said softly. "He can never be replaced—"

"No," he replied, more sharply than intended. "Not with Droma, not with you." His voice softened. "But he could never have replaced you, either, Leia. Let's leave it at that, huh? I like my new copilot just fine."

"Thank you. That means a lot to me."

"I mean, she's a little mouthy for my taste, and kinda snooty, but at least she's easy enough on the eyes—even with the new hairdo."

Leia's tender expression was metamorphosing into something less benign when the mass detector bleeped and C-3PO cried, "I told you! I absolutely told you!"

"Threepio," Han snapped, "have you ever been fired from a concussion missile tube?"

"No, sir. Of course, I *did* nearly fall out of the garbage-ejection tube a short time ago, which I must admit was terrifying, simply *terrifying*. I—"

"Threepio!" Han shouted.

C-3PO cocked his head and put one golden finger to the slit that implied his mouth. "Perhaps I should go see what Artoo is doing."

"Yes, do that."

Meanwhile, Leia had been analyzing whatever it was that had come out of hyperspace right behind them.

"It's a freighter," she said.

"A freighter? Here?" They were in occupied space, not far from Tynna.

Leia brought up the profile, revealing a blocky drive married to a long series of detachable storage pods headed up by a narrow habitation compartment. "Kuat Drive Yards *Marl*-class heavy freighter," Leia confirmed.

"Out *here*?" Han repeated incredulously. "She'll be easy pickings for the first Yuuzhan Vong ship she runs into. And where could she be going? Hutt space?"

"Maybe it's a relief vessel," Leia said. "Or a smuggler running weapons to the Hutts."

"That thing's got no legs," Han said. "Any smuggler worth his spice would know better."

"Well, there it is," Leia said.

"I can see that." He set his lips. "I just had an unpleasant thought."

Leia nodded grimly. "I just had the same thought."

"Yeah. Have they seen us yet?"

"I doubt it."

"Let's keep it that way. Run silent and let them pass. We'll see for sure where they're going."

"Why don't we just ask them?"

Han gave her a brief open-mouthed stare. "Boy, do you

have a lot to learn. Let me handle this, willya? I know what I'm doing."

"Right. I've heard that a time or two. I've usually had cause to regret it."

"At least you always *lived* to regret it, sweetheart."

When the *Falcon* powered down, Jacen was deep in meditation. He'd spent hours coaxing his wants, needs, and expectations into corners of his mind far from the conscious, surrendering himself into the silent flow of the Force.

He tuned out the sensations of the Force around him: his mother, the lesser voices of his father and the Noghri, the faint impressions of the droids and the ship itself. He wasn't searching for anything at all, merely trying to become a part of the living Force, detached from the particulars of it. Just to feel it ebbing and flowing through him, not even seeking understanding, for in seeking one often missed what was sought, or came to an understanding tainted by desire.

Desire, like fear and anger, had to be released.

For a brief moment he almost found that center he was searching for, the universe spreading out in its entirety, and in that instant he saw again a vision of the galaxy tipping, of a fundamental imbalance waiting to happen.

There, memory and desire betrayed him. He saw himself facing Warmaster Tsavong Lah, his mother bleeding at his feet. He saw his brother, Anakin, confident and cocky after his escape from Yavin 4. He saw himself, only days before, slaying the two living coralskippers and their pilots.

The death of one diminishes us all. Surely that had to be the case with the Yuuzhan Vong as well, though they didn't appear in the Force.

Which was impossible, if the Force was what the old Jedi Masters said it was.

He actually wished Anakin were here, so they could have one of their arguments. Anakin now held that what they knew as the Force was only a manifestation of something greater, more overarching, something Jedi could only glimpse. To Jacen that felt utterly wrong, and yet it was hard to dispute that it fit the facts as they stood now.

Anakin also thought of the Force as little more than an energy source, something with which the Jedi worked their wills. That also felt wrong, and yet Jacen now seriously questioned the opposing view, that the Force had a will of its own, and that the proper role of the Jedi was to understand that will and work through it.

Neither extreme felt right in Jacen's gut, and yet he had no answer of his own. He had abandoned his vow not to use the Force, but it had given him no more certainty about when or how it *ought* to be used, or what a Jedi *ought* to do. Again, Anakin's certainty was both enviable and worrisome. Anakin was determined to oppose evil, and just as determined that he could know what evil was, even without the Force to enlighten him.

Maybe Anakin was right. Jacen knew that he couldn't just stand by and do nothing. He had been given gifts and learned to use them, and it was incumbent on him that he find the proper way to do so. But how was he to judge? *Who* was he to judge?

Maybe he had been wrong to strike out on his own, to leave the apprenticeship of Master Skywalker. But somehow, he knew, Uncle Luke's path could not be his, no more than Anakin's could be.

As it was, he took each situation as he found it. He'd hated killing the Yuuzhan Vong, but the situation hadn't suggested or allowed for any alternative other than the death or capture of his family. It may have been a bad choice, but at the time it was the only one he was capable of making.

He tried to untangle himself from this internal dialogue, but the more he tried, the more frustrated he became, and he was on the verge of admitting failure anyway when something changed around him.

He came back, bringing the near world into focus, and found everything off but emergency lights.

"Dear me!" C-3PO moaned. "I knew it!"

"Threepio?"

"Master Jacen! You're conscious!"

"What's going on, Threepio? How long have we been powered down?"

"Ever since that mass came out of hyperspace," C-3PO said. "I wanted to help, but Captain Solo was quite unpleasant."

"I'm sure it's not you he was mad at, Threepio," Jacen assured the droid. "I'll go see what's going on."

"Look there," his father was saying as Jacen entered the cockpit.

"I see," Leia breathed. "Yuuzhan Vong."

Jacen studied the long-range scanner readouts. "They're attacking that freighter?" he asked.

"No," Han said. "They ain't attacking it, kid. They're escorting it."

"Escorting? Where are we?"

"One jump from the Cha Raaba system," Han replied.

"Cha Raaba? That's where Ylesia is, right?"

"Kid gets a gold epaulet," Han murmured.

"And Ylesia is where the Peace Brigade is headquartered," Leia added. "So that ship—"

"Supplies for the Brigade and the Vong," Han concluded. "Couldn't have figured it better myself. Looks like Lando was right, only if the Peace Brigade is moving stuff inside Yuuzhan Vong space, someone must be moving it to them from *outside*."

"Well, we have to stop them!" Leia said.

"What?" Jacen asked. "Why? They haven't attacked us. They don't even see us."

"True enough," Han said. "Gives us a nice advantage."

"But—I thought this mission was about setting up networks for refugees and intelligence. No one said anything about taking the fight to the enemy."

"Hey, Jacen," Han said, "it's not as if we're going out of our way to harass collaborationist shipping, though why the thought of doing so should upset you I can't imagine. But there they are, and here *we* are—"

"Can we just disable them?" Jacen asked.

"Jacen," Han said, turning to face him, his eyebrows lifting. "Jacen, in case you didn't notice, there's a *war* on. Now, I know you've gotten all mystical on me lately, and I'm trying to be understanding, but if you expect the rest of us to go along with your philosophy of the day, think again. You stick with the Force and let me deal with this. Anyway, for all you know that freighter could be full of slaves and sacrifices. You really want to leave them to the mercy of the Vong?"

"I don't feel anything like that in the Force," Jacen said firmly.

"Jacen," Leia chimed in. "You know I respect what you're trying to do, but you have to understand something—"

"I understand," Jacen interrupted. "I understand that you told me this mission was about something I could get on board with, and now in the middle of the flight you're changing the coordinates. I'm not trying to tell you what to believe. But when you brought *me* along on this trip—"

"When I *brought* you along on this trip," Han roared, "I never said you could be *captain*, and I didn't tell you this is a democracy. Jacen, I love you. But sit down, shut up, and do as you're told."

Jacen was so stunned by his father's anger that it did not, at that moment, even occur to him to continue the argument.

"Great," Han said. "So here's what we're going to do. We're going to take out that Yuuzhan Vong escort, and then we're going to make the freighter an offer."

"Offer?" Leia said.

"Yep. We'll offer not to blow her open if she surrenders quietly." He checked his panel. "Power in five minutes. Jacen, get down to the turbolaser."

Jacen hesitated, a painful, sickening knot growing in his gut. "Okay."

"And I want you to use it if needed."

"I will. Sir." And with that he stalked out of the cockpit.

FIFTEEN

The villip squirmed, stretching itself to its limits in an attempt to portray the fine mass of tendrils that composed the living headdress of Master Tjulan Kwaad. It did not entirely succeed, but did so sufficiently well that Nen Yim was able to tell that the senior master of her domain was agitated.

"Why disturb me over such a question?" Tjulan Kwaad asked. "You have access to the Qang qahsa, do you not?"

"I do indeed, Master Kwaad," Nen Yim replied. "However, the qahsa does not grant a mere adept entry to protocols beyond the fifth cortex."

"Nor should it. Adepts are not ready for such secrets. Especially adepts such as yourself. You and your deceased master disgraced our domain."

"That is true," Nen Yim said carefully. "However, Warmaster Tsavong Lah chose to pardon me and . . . reward me with a chance to further serve the glorious Yun-Yuuzhan. I should think my domain would do as much."

"Do not presume what your domain would do," Tjulan Kwaad replied testily. "Even the Yim crèche would not do as much. The warmaster is a warrior, covered in glory and more than ample *as* a warrior. But he is not a shaper, and he does not know how dangerous your heresies are."

"Those were the heresies of my master, not mine," Nen Yim lied.

"Yet you did not report her."

Yun-Harla aid me, Nen Yim prayed. The mistress of trickery loved lies as much as Yun-Yammka loved battle. "How could discipline be maintained if every adept felt free to question her master?"

107

"You could have reported her to *me*," Tjulan Kwaad roared. "You owe fealty to me as lord of your domain. Mezhan Kwaad was as much my subordinate as you. That you neglected that relationship will never be forgotten!"

"My judgment failed, Master. That does not change the fact that this ship is dying, and I need your help."

"Each of us begins to die the instant we are born. Our ships are no different. That is existence, Adept." He spoke her title as if it hurt his mouth to do so.

Undeterred by his ire, Nen Yim pressed on. "Master, is it not true that the Yuuzhan Vong need every breath of every one of us to complete the task of conquering the infidels?"

The master laughed harshly and without a trace of real humor. "Look around at the misfits on your ship, and you will know the answer. Were they worthy, they would be at the point of our talons."

"An arm must drive the talons," Nen Yim replied. "A heart must pump the blood to nourish the muscles that propel the arm."

"Phahg. A metaphor is a preening lie."

"Yes, Master." Her experiments had yielded mostly frustration. She had been able—without resort to ancient protocols—to coax neurons into reproduction and shape ganglia that could perform many of the operations of the brain. She could probably, given time, shape an entirely new brain, but as she'd explained to her initiate, Suung, that would not solve the problem. She needed to regenerate the old brain, complete with its memories and eccentricities. Anything else she did only delayed the inevitable. Further, any master who examined her work would know instantly that she had been practicing heresy, and then her efforts to save the worldship would end quite decisively. She had hoped that the knowledge in the vast Qang qahsa library rikyams of the shapers would yield a helpful protocol at some cortex beyond her access, but if a master of her own domain would not help her, no one would.

"I thank you for your time, Master Tjulan Kwaad."

"Do not disturb me again." The villip smoothed back into its normal shape.

She sat for a time, tendrils bunched in despair, until her novice entered.

"How may I serve you today, Adept?" Suung Aruh asked.

Nen Yim did not spare him a glance. "The freezing of the arm has further diseased the maw luur. Take the other students and floss the recham forteps with saline jetters."

"It will be done," Suung replied. He turned to leave, but then hesitated. "Adept?" he said.

"What is it?"

"I believe you can save the *Baanu Miir*. I believe the gods are with you. And I thank you for tending to my education. I did not know how ignorant I was. Now I have some measure of it."

Nen Yim's sight clouded, the protective membrane over her eyes reacting to sudden intense emotion as it did to light irritation. She wondered briefly if anyone knew why such dissimilar things should provoke the same reflex. If it *was* known, she had never heard it. Perhaps that knowledge, too, was beyond the fifth cortex.

"The gods will save us or they will not, Initiate," she replied at last. "It is not to me you should direct your confidence."

"Yes, Adept," he said, in a subdued voice.

She regarded him. "Your progress has been quite satisfactory, Suung Aruh. In the hands of a master you could be shaped into a most useful adept."

"Thank you, Adept," Suung replied, trying to hide a look of surprised gratification. "I go now to my task."

As he left, she noticed the villip pulsing for attention. Wondering what new sarcoma was gnawing at the fabric of her life, she rose and stroked it.

It was Master Tjulan Kwaad again.

"Master," she acknowledged.

"I have reconsidered, Adept. I am unswayed by your arguments, but I feel it foolish to leave you unsupervised lest you bring more shame to us all. I have dispatched a master to govern you. He will arrive within two days. Obey him well."

The villip cleared before she could answer. She stood staring at it as a beast stares at the wound that is killing it.

It hadn't occurred to her that Tjulan Kwaad would *send* a master, only that he might find the protocol and transmit it to her. A master, here, would see what she had done, and know.

Perhaps the new master would save *Baanu Miir*, and that was good. But Adept Nen Yim would soon embrace death.

SIXTEEN

The interrogation chamber was a bleak, washed-out yellow room on the third floor of a building painted entirely in the same color. A sickly sweet scent like burned sugar and hair blended with ammonia seemed to ooze from the flaking duraplast, and the sickly light of ancient argon arc fixtures blanched any real color that entered the building.

Brought in in stun cuffs, Anakin and Tahiri had been hauled through a lower floor seething with judicials, prisoners, and clerks to this nearly abandoned area of the building. There the two Jedi had been separated and placed in different rooms. He could still feel Tahiri's presence, of course, and not far away, which was comforting.

"We have witnesses now who substantiate the charge of murder," the judicial with the bruised eye—Lieutenant Themion, as it turned out—informed him.

"Right. They killed the Rodian," Anakin said.

"I'm talking now about the man *you* killed."

"We didn't kill anyone," Anakin protested. "We saw someone in trouble—"

"A Jedi, like yourself."

"Yes. We were trying to help him when the Peace Brigaders starting blasting at us."

"The way I hear it, *you* attacked them."

"My friend drew her weapon, yes," Anakin replied. "They were murdering the Rodian."

"Then you charged them, fought, and shot one with a blaster."

"No!" Anakin said. "How many times do I have to tell

you this? One of them shot at me, missed, and hit the other guy. I didn't kill anyone, and neither did my friend."

"We have witnesses who saw it differently."

"You mean the other Peace Brigaders, don't you?"

"And some of the vagrants in the crowd."

That took Anakin aback. "Why . . . why would any of them say that?" he wondered.

"Maybe because it's true," Themion suggested.

"No, it's not true. They're lying, too. Maybe the Peace Brigade forced them to." *Or maybe you did, Lieutenant Themion.*

"Let's back up," Themion said. "You saw the Rodian struggling with the Peace Brigaders. Rodians are a vile, murderous lot. Did it ever occur to you that maybe he had *done* something? That the officers of the Peace Brigade were just doing their duty?"

"The Peace Brigade is a collaborationist organization," Anakin said hotly. "They sell us out to the Yuuzhan Vong."

"The Peace Brigade is a *registered* organization," Themion informed him. "They are licensed to make arrests, and to deal with those who resist arrest." He scratched his chin. "They are certainly entitled to defend themselves against offworld, troublemaking Jedi," he added.

Uh-oh, Anakin thought. So his suspicion had been correct. The police and the Peace Brigade were in this together.

"Am I entitled to an advocate?" Anakin asked.

"One has been assigned you."

"When can we meet?"

"Not until your trial, of course."

"You mean my sentencing."

The officer smiled. "It might go easier on you if you tell us the rest. Who sent you. Which ship is yours. Your name."

"I want to see the ambassador from Coruscant."

"Yeah? I'm afraid I don't have that comm ID handy. If you want to call someone on your ship, and have *them* contact the ambassador, that's fine."

Right. Then they'll get Corran, too.

"No, thanks," Anakin said.

The officer stepped forward quickly and slapped him so hard his head rang.

Tahiri, wherever she was, felt it. She responded in the Force in one of those rare, clear-as-transparisteel moments.

Anakin! And pain, and fear, and anger.

"Tahiri!" Anakin shouted. "No!"

"Your friend has already confessed," Themion said. "She was stubborn, too." He hit Anakin again. This time Anakin faded a little from the blow to reduce the impact, but it still hurt.

Somewhere near, a storm was gathering.

"Don't hit me again," Anakin said sternly.

Themion misunderstood. "Aw, does that hurt, little Jedi? Try this." He pulled a stun baton from his belt.

"Really," Anakin said.

Themion raised the weapon. At the same moment, the door wrenched open with a squeal of metal. Tahiri stood there, a blaster in one hand.

"Do-ro'ik vong pratte!" she shouted.

Themion, open-mouthed, turned to face her and she hit him with a Force blast that threw him three meters. He would have gone much farther, but the jaundiced wall stopped him with prejudice, and he collapsed, groaning.

"I warned you," Anakin said.

Tahiri rushed to his side. "Are you all right?" she asked. "I felt them hitting you."

"I'm fine," Anakin said, rising from the chair. Unknown to the officer, he'd already unlocked his stun cuffs using the Force; now he shucked them from his wrists.

"You're not fine," Tahiri said, touching the side of his head. He winced. "You see?" she said. She turned back toward Themion, who was trying to rise. "You smelly Jawa, I'm going to—"

"You're going to put the stun cuffs on him and that's *all*," Anakin said.

"He deserves worse. He's a liar and a coward who beats helpless people." Her eyes narrowed.

"Stay out of my mind, you stinking Jedi," Themion snarled.

"Give me the blaster, Tahiri."

She handed it to Anakin without looking.

"Now," Anakin said. "You let her put these cuffs on you, or I'll let her do whatever she wants."

Themion let her. Then Anakin leaned around the doorway. A blaster bolt greeted him—down the hall, another judicial was rushing forward.

The shot missed, and he ducked the next one. He felt another surge in the Force, and the judicial went flying into the corridor wall. The impact knocked his senses out of him.

"I think we'd better leave," Tahiri said, from behind him.

"I think you're right," Anakin replied. He knelt and took the guard's blaster and dialed it down to the lowest setting. He took the stun baton, too.

"After we find our lightsabers," Tahiri said.

"*If* we can find them," Anakin cautioned. "They took mine somewhere downstairs. Or at least I think so."

They reached the turbolift with a minimum of effort.

"Be ready when we reach the bottom floor," Anakin said. "They're sure to be ready for us. One of these guys must have called down by now."

Tahiri nodded, an unsettling smile on her face.

"Tahiri?"

"Yes."

"Beware of anger."

"I'm not angry," she said. "Just ready."

Anakin eyed her dubiously, but they didn't have time to go over it now. "Stand against the sides of the lift. They may shoot before it even opens."

She did as he suggested. A moment later, the doors sighed open.

No sizzling bolts of energy greeted them. Instead they were met by laughter and shouts of encouragement. Puzzled, Anakin peeked around the lift door.

Two judicials stood in a ring formed by their comrades. They were swinging clumsily at one another with lightsabers. One was Anakin's, the other Tahiri's.

"Use the Force!" someone hooted, as the man wielding Anakin's violet blade accidentally sliced a desk in half.

It took only a minor suggestion that they weren't there for Anakin and Tahiri to walk out of the lift and around the edge of the excited crowd. Apparently, either no one upstairs *had* called down or—more likely—no one here had bothered to answer the call. In any event, everyone in the building seemed completely engrossed in the "duel."

"Keep cool, Tahiri," Anakin said as they drew near the door to the outside. "I have an idea."

The fellow holding Anakin's lightsaber made a clumsy jab at the other judicial, who replied with an equally inept circular parry. Anakin took that opportunity to use the Force to wrench his weapon from the officer's hands—it looked as if the parry had disarmed him. The lightsaber flew high in the air, sending everyone in its possible trajectory scurrying away. It struck the argon arc fixture in the ceiling, then continued on to strike the power grid node on the other side of the room. The room plunged into darkness, save for the two lightsabers, both of which suddenly vanished.

On the street, Tahiri burst into laughter.

"Don't laugh," Anakin said. "Run!"

"I'm just thinking we probably saved their lives," Tahiri replied. "The way they were going, they would have lost at least a hand or two. If—" She stopped as Anakin abruptly halted.

"What?" Tahiri asked.

"Maybe running is the second-best idea," Anakin said, pointing at the police airspeeder parked in front of the station.

The two jumped into the rusty orange vehicle. It had an old-fashioned computer input, and it took Anakin only a few seconds to slice into the security system. Just as a mob of officers burst onto the street, he bypassed the code and started the speeder. He throttled it up to full as he turned the corner and climbed, ignoring the craft's artificially frantic warning that he was not in an authorized traffic lane.

A few blaster bolts seared by, along with a number of obscenities. Then the judicial ward was behind them.

* * *

By the time they reached the spaceport, Anakin and Tahiri had picked up a respectable tail and were starting to dodge long-range fire. For that reason, when Anakin saw the *Lucre*'s cargo port open, he drove the nimble craft directly into it, nearly clipping a very surprised Corran Horn while doing so.

"Sithspit!" the older Jedi shouted. "What do you think—"

"Close the landing ramp, Corran! Close it now!"

"What? What have you—"

Several bolts fizzling against the bulkhead cut Corran short. On reflex he slapped the close mechanism, carefully not showing himself through the port.

"I take it we need to fly?" Corran said as Anakin and Tahiri dismounted the speeder. *What have you done now, Anakin?*

"Might not be a bad idea," Anakin replied. He was trying not to sound cocky, and failing.

"I'll be very interested to hear why," Corran snapped.

"Fly now," Anakin said, heading for the cockpit. "I'll explain later."

"Explain *while*," Corran said as they settled behind the controls.

"Right," Anakin said as the engines begin to whine to life. "It started when we felt a Jedi in trouble . . ."

"You're right; it can wait," Corran decided. Hearing the story was probably only going to make him angrier, a distraction he didn't need right now. "And *I'm* flying. You calculate a series of jumps, at least three, and close together."

"To where?"

"Anywhere. No, strike that. Not back toward the *Errant Venture*. Coreward. We'll find the *Venture* later."

"Okay," Anakin said. "Working on solutions now."

"And hang on. Tahiri, you strapped in?"

"Yes, sir."

Corran rose on repulsors and kicked the engines violently into light. The *Lucre* sliced through the murky clouds, where Corran steepened their angle, watching his sensor readouts, wondering how long it would take the Eriaduans to scramble their fighters, trying desperately to remember what he knew of their planetary defense from his days in CorSec.

Soon enough, both questions were answered: not long and not nearly enough, respectively. As several heavily armed interceptors closed from several sides, he cleared his throat.

"Any time now, Anakin."

"Hang on," Anakin replied. "I have three jumps. I'm rechecking the last bit."

"No time. Lay it in and let's go."

The transport's shields trembled beneath a terrific blow. The port opaqued.

"Wow!" Anakin said. "What—?"

"That was no interceptor," Corran said grimly. "That was a planetary defense laser. Are we laid in?"

"Sort of . . ."

"Great." Corran broke atmosphere, engaged the hyperdrive, and the stars sleeted out of existence.

The first jump took them no more than half a light-year, and Corran had time to see that one of the interceptors had correctly guessed their vector before they jumped again, seconds later. The second jump was longer, followed immediately by a third. It was hard to tell, but it looked as if they lost their tail on that one.

"How long is this jump, Anakin?"

"A few hours."

"Great. Then why don't you explain to me, in great detail, why you were joyriding on a judicial speeder. And do *not* leave out the part that explains why people were shooting at *me*, and why you two disobeyed my direct order."

"I understand why you did it," Corran said when the two had finished relating their story. "But you shouldn't have."

"Why?" Tahiri demanded. "Wouldn't you have done the same?"

Corran hesitated fractionally. "No. I felt Kelbis Nu, too, but so dimly I couldn't figure out where he was. But even if I'd known, I have both of you to think of. As you should have been thinking of me. Anakin, you've always been impulsive—"

"This was my fault," Tahiri interrupted.

"Yes. Emphatically, *yes*. But Anakin set the example. Didn't either of you learn anything on Yavin Four?"

"Yes," Tahiri said. "I learned that the Jedi can count on no one but ourselves."

"Really? Your dad is no Jedi, Talon Karrde is no Jedi, nor were the people under his command who died trying to rescue you."

"Well, no one was going to rescue Kelbis," Anakin pointed out.

"Including you."

"But we might have. We had to try."

Corran looked at them both tiredly.

"This isn't over," he said. "When we get back to the *Errant Venture,* we're going to have this talk again, with Kam and Tionne and anyone else I think of who might be able to get a word past this youthful, idiotic self-confidence of yours. But for the moment—you say Kelbis said something about Yag'Dhul?"

"His last word," Anakin said. "It took a lot out of him to say even that. He really wanted me to know something. I think Yag'Dhul may be in danger."

Corran's eyes narrowed, reflecting a sudden, plunging-stomach suspicion. "Anakin, *where* is this jump taking us?"

"You said Coreward," Anakin replied innocently.

"Tell me we aren't going to pop out in the Yag'Dhul system."

"We aren't going to pop out in the Yag'Dhul system," Anakin told him.

"Good," Corran said, relieved.

"We're going to come out really near it, though," Anakin added.

"Why you—" Corran held back a series of specifically Corellian words he that *really* wanted to use. But Tahiri was only fourteen. Would he make it through Valin's and Jysella's teenage years without turning to the dark side?

Probably not. "How close?" he said, trying to sound not quite as irritated as he was.

"One jump. I thought you'd at least like to check it out."

"Anakin! Supplies! We were just supposed to get supplies, not mount a search-and-rescue–recon mission!" He buried his face in his hands. "Now I understand those pitying looks Solusar was giving me before we left."

Corran wished Mirax were here. She knew how to deal with this kind of thing. "How long before realspace?"

"Another five minutes."

"Terrific. Now listen to me very carefully. I am the captain of this vessel. From now on you don't even visit the 'fresher without my say-so, either of you. You will follow my orders. That means, by the way, that you do not imagine or guess at my orders, but actually wait until you hear them."

"I *was* following orders," Anakin protested. "You said to jump Coreward."

"Don't insult us both, Anakin. You're better than that."

"Yes, Captain."

"Good." Corran settled himself before the controls and awaited the reversion to sublight speeds.

They reentered realspace with a pockmarked asteroid nearly filling their field of vision. Corran swore and decelerated, cutting hard toward the nearest horizon of the rock. A jagged crater edge loomed, and he knew they weren't going to make the angle. Desperately he switched on the repulsorlift.

The *Lucre* squealed a metallic protest as the field bounced them none too gently away from the asteroid. Corran let out his breath and killed their motion relative to the planetoid until he could get his bearings.

A good thing, too, because in the surrounding space he made out hundreds of asteroids, densely packed. It would take a good deal of care to fly out of it unscathed.

"You could have warned me about the asteroid field," Corran told Anakin.

"I would have if there had been one," Anakin said in a strange voice.

"It wasn't on the charts?"

"It's still not," Anakin said. "Look at the sensor readings."

Corran did, and swore again as everything snapped into focus. Aside from the cratered stone he'd nearly hit coming out of hyperspace, the rest of the objects near enough to see had the organic but all-too-familiar lines of ships grown from yorik coral.

"This is a Yuuzhan Vong fleet," Anakin said.

SEVENTEEN

"I've located the *Errant Venture*," Luke said. "Not far from Clak'dor. We'll be there in a day or so."

Mara nodded. "Good," she said shortly.

"How are you feeling?"

Mara shot him a dirty look. "Skywalker, why do you ask questions you know the answer to? I feel overweight. My ankles feel as if I have stun cuffs permanently fastened to them. I'm always nauseated. Nobody told me I would get nauseated again. I thought that part was over early on."

"So did I," Luke replied. He pressed his lips together. He sensed more than mere irritation behind Mara's words. There was a kind of defensiveness about her outburst. "Is there something you want to tell me?" he asked gently.

"If I *wanted* to tell you, I would, wouldn't I?"

"Not if you thought it might upset me," Luke said.

"You've got me. I hate that shirt. In fact, I think you're a crummy dresser, period."

"You bought me this shirt," Luke reminded her. "Mara, are you sick again? Have you come out of remission?"

Mara studied her fingernails. "Cilghal's keeping tabs on that," she said, still with that underlying air of defiance.

"And?"

Mara's face pinched tight. "The disease isn't present in our child."

"Is it active in you again?" Luke demanded.

Mara watched the starfield for several long minutes. "Maybe," she admitted. "Maybe."

* * *

As predicted, they found the *Errant Venture* about one standard day later. The Star Destroyer opened a berth for them, and he navigated the *Jade Shadow* in without incident.

A small crowd awaited Luke, Mara, and Cilghal. Booster Terrik, captain and owner of the *Errant Venture,* stood in front, a great gundark of a human with an impressive, well-tended beard and curling mustachios. Just behind him and to the side were three more humans, two in Jedi robes. Luke recognized Kam Solusar by his sure stance, haunted features, and receding blond hair. His wife, Tionne, was as unmistakable; her hair was a silver river cascading down her shoulders. The third human was another woman, clad in a dun jumpsuit, her black-glass hair cut in a bob: Mirax Terrik Horn, Booster's daughter and sometimes business partner. She was married to Corran Horn, who was conspicuous by his absence.

Behind them were some thirty-odd youngsters of at least seven species. This was what remained of the academy on Yavin 4, the praxeum that had trained almost a hundred Jedi. Now Yavin 4 was occupied by the Yuuzhan Vong, the temple that had housed his students destroyed. With half the galaxy hunting for Jedi gifts to present to the Yuuzhan Vong warmaster, the only safe place for the moment was no place. For months, Booster had been jumping randomly about the galaxy to keep the students hidden.

Two others were missing as well, Luke noticed. Anakin Solo and Tahiri Veila. Knowing Anakin, that was a bad sign. Luke made a mental note to ask after him as soon as the pleasantries were over.

"Look there," Booster growled, as Luke and Mara descended the landing ramp. "There's the man who made the once mighty and terribly feared Booster Terrik into a glorified baby-sitter. I ought to space you right now, Jedi."

"I can't tell you how grateful I am," Luke said. Though he knew Booster meant well, he didn't have the energy or inclination for banter at the moment.

"You ought to be. Jedi brats." He mussed the hair of a young boy with brown hair, then the girl next to him. "With some notable exceptions, of course," he amended.

"You're funny, Grandpa," the boy said. Then he turned his brown eyes toward the *Jade Shadow* and Luke and Mara. "Hello, Masters."

"Hello, Valin," Luke replied. "I hope you've been staying out of trouble and concentrating on your lessons."

"I have, Master Skywalker. I promise."

"And the rest of you?" Luke directed his gaze over the assembled students.

In return he got a chorus of assents and barely bridled enthusiasm.

"Well, that's good, then. Kam, Tionne, Mirax. Good to see you."

There was a round of clasping and hugs, and then a moment of awkward silence.

"I guess we need to talk," Luke said at last. "I need to fill you all in on a few things."

"That's all very well," Mirax said, "but Mara looks tired."

"I'm okay," Mara disagreed.

Mirax shook her head. "I've had two kids. I know that look. Let me take you someplace where you can freshen up, and let the rest of them have their conference. Luke doesn't need you for that, does he?"

"I guess not." She shot Luke a look, and he knew what it meant. *My health concerns are private. You will not speak of them.*

He nodded to let her know he understood.

Out loud, what he said was, "If you're tired, go with Mirax. If I leave something out, you can fill them in later."

Mara smiled wanly. "Put on a little weight and everyone treats you like an invalid."

"You'll see how long *that* lasts after the big event," Mirax said. "When Baby Skywalker has a little accident, everyone will magically think you're plenty strong and capable."

"Boy. And I thought this was the best part."

"Yep," Mirax said. "That's exactly what I'm telling you. Come along now. I've got a comfy couch with your name on it."

"I'll come with you, too, if you don't mind," Cilghal said.

"Of course," Mirax replied. "The more the merrier."

They sat around Booster's circular conference table, absorbing the news.

"Do you really think you would have been arrested?" Kam asked, folding the fingers of both hands together into one very large fist.

"I honestly don't know," Luke replied. "Hamner thinks the whole thing was a ploy engineered to get me away from Coruscant. He may be right. Borsk Fey'lya has never been one of our strongest supporters, but I can't see him thinking that arresting me would solve any of his problems. In fact, I think we narrowly escaped an insurrection *because* he ordered my arrest."

"Last I heard," Booster said, "the senate was divided over the Jedi question. Maybe it's tipped, and Fey'lya was just being the politician he is."

"Maybe," Luke agreed. "In a way, it doesn't matter. What does matter is what we do now."

"And that is?"

"Right now, Han, Leia, Jacen, and a number of other allies are out there creating a network to help Jedi or whoever else needs to escape from danger zones—to get us in and out of Yuuzhan Vong and Vong-sympathetic space as safely as possible. I have no doubt that in time, that network will be in place. But when that day comes, we need a terminus—a planet that only we know about, that only we can find. We can't just keep hopping around the galaxy—we have to have a home base to plan and act from. If Han and Leia are creating a great river, we need a sea for it to flow into."

"Well, that sounds good to me," Terrik said. "I certainly don't want *all* of you robe-wearing freeloaders on my ship. You have someplace in mind?"

"Frankly, no. I was hoping for some suggestions."

"The Maw installation," Kam said.

"We're already using that," Luke said, "but the Maw is pretty well known. Almost impossible to navigate in, but well known. Any number of collaborators could at least point the Yuuzhan Vong there, and we still don't know the limits of their technology. We're risking a base there, a safe house, but I won't place the future hope of the Jedi in that exposed a position."

"If there were another cluster of black holes like the Maw . . . ," Tionne began.

"Well, there is," Booster said. "Or at least a place like it. Worse, actually."

"Where?"

"Think. What makes the Maw such a nightmare? All those mass shadows, butted up against each other. Gravity bending space and time so much that almost no hyperspace route is a safe one. There's another place like that."

Kam nodded. "The Deep Core," he said. "Terrik, you're crazy."

"You're the one who suggested the Maw," Booster pointed out.

"Yes, but we know how to get in and out of the Maw."

"Somebody *found* the way," Booster said.

"Right. Somebody crazy."

"Kyp found it, too," Luke said. "Using the Force. If Kyp could do it at the Maw, we can do it in the Core. It just won't be easy."

"A world of our own," Tionne lilted. "A Jedi world, safe for the children. It's a worthy goal."

"Worth a song or two, wouldn't you say?" Booster asked.

Tionne, well known for her ballads, nodded and enigmatically smiled.

Not so enigmatic to Kam. His eyes went very wide. "Us?" he said.

His wife continued smiling. "The students will have Luke, at least until Mara gives birth, and I suspect for a bit after. And they will have Corran when he returns. We have been too long sedentary, Kam. *You* have. This will be good for us."

Booster bellowed laughter. "I suspect we've found your madman, Solusar."

Kam set his shoulders uncomfortably. "Yes, perhaps you have," he acknowledged.

"Speaking of Corran," Luke said, after smaller versions of Booster's laughter had wandered around the table, "where is he? I didn't see Anakin either."

"Boy was getting deck fever," Booster said. "He went with Corran for supplies."

"They took Tahiri with them?"

"I don't know about that," Booster said.

"He did," Kam said.

Booster's eyes narrowed in anger. "Without asking my permission? Who's captain here, anyway? When that Cor-Sec whelp my daughter married gets back, I'm going to teach him who is, that's for sure."

"I'm sure Corran knew what he was doing," Luke said.

"Oh, I wouldn't go that far," Kam averred. "He took Anakin and Tahiri, together? No, I doubt he has any idea whatsoever what he's doing."

EIGHTEEN

The *Lucre* was a Codru-Ji sword dancer gone mad, gyring, whirling across a stage of plasma bursts and coralskippers flying as thick as swarming insects.

"Twenty kilometers down, another thousand to go before clearing the fleet," Corran said coldly.

Anakin didn't answer as the *Lucre* dropped into a sudden, hard-out sprint, a bid to close that impossible gap.

It wasn't going to happen. Coralskippers contracted around the ship in a sphere, and the shields flared with the effort of absorbing the energy of the constant plasma bombardment. All too soon, the shields failed, and the next round of hits were to the drive.

"So long," Corran said. Then the *Lucre* was an expanding fury of superheated helium and metal fragments.

"Wow," Tahiri breathed. Her voice sounded tinny in the helmet of Anakin's vac suit. "That didn't take long."

"No," Anakin said. It had only been minutes since they set the ship off on its preprogrammed suicide course and launched themselves from the hatch under cover of a barrage of laser and missile fire. In the five minutes it had taken them to reach the asteroid's surface, the *Lucre*'s brief solo career had begun and ended.

"No gawking," Corran said. "There's a fissure over there. Let's move toward that. They might get the bright idea to search here at any moment."

Tahiri took a step in the desired direction and was suddenly floating away from the surface. She yelped, flailing her arms.

Corran caught her foot, and her momentum pulled him

off his feet. Anakin grabbed them both with the Force and brought them back to the asteroid's surface.

"Don't walk," Corran advised. "The gravity here is negligible, just enough to give your inner ear a sense of up and down. Don't let it fool you—the escape velocity of this rock is about five kilometers an hour, if that. Pull yourselves along." He maneuvered himself so his body was parallel to the surface and began doing just that, grasping at the uneven stone. Tahiri and Anakin followed his example, as silly as it felt. Anakin glanced often at the space around them, but none of the Yuuzhan Vong ships seemed to be moving in their direction.

They reached the fissure, a cleft that dropped slantwise into the asteroid for about twenty meters. Because of the angle, at the bottom of it they could see only a narrow slice of starscape. That was good, because it meant only a small slice of the starscape could see *them*.

"Now what? Anakin asked.

"Now we wait." Corran carefully shrugged off the metal case he'd worn like a backpack. "With the survival kit, we can hold out for maybe three days. Hopefully the fleet will move out before then, and we can activate the emergency beacon. Given considerably more luck, a ship will happen by and pick us up."

"That's a lot of luck," Anakin remarked.

"Well, if nothing else, maybe this will teach you that luck isn't the bottomless well you seem to think it is," Corran said.

"We might have tried to run for it," Anakin said peevishly.

"You saw what happened."

"I can fly better than a computer."

"Not that much better," Corran said.

"But now we're stuck here. This fleet must be the danger Kelbis Nu was trying to warn us about. If we wait for it to leave, it'll be too late to warn Yag'Dhul."

"Well, you have a blaster and a lightsaber," Corran said dryly. "Given your opinion of yourself, you might as well take on the fleet with those."

Anakin felt Corran's sarcasm like a physical blow, and it stung. "I'm sorry," he said. "I thought I was doing the right thing."

"No doubt," Corran replied.

"Captain Horn," Tahiri said suddenly, "if it weren't for Anakin trying to do the right thing, your kids would be Yuuzhan Vong captives right now. In fact, along with me and the rest of the candidates, they would basically *be* Yuuzhan Vong. He got us out of that; he'll get us out of this."

Corran was silent for a moment. "You know I'm grateful for what you did on Yavin Four, Anakin. Tahiri's right. But I'm afraid you learned the wrong lesson there, and Tahiri along with you. You can't stroll up to *every* reactor going supercritical and walk away again. You aren't immortal, and you aren't invincible. So far your quick thinking and strength in the Force have just barely managed to counterbalance your recklessness. But one day, the fraction is going to tip on the other side of the line. Maybe it already has. If you don't come to terms with that, you're going to get a nasty surprise."

Anakin thought of Chewie, of Daeshara'cor, of Vua Rapuung, the Yuuzhan Vong who had saved his life. All dead now. "Everyone gets a nasty surprise someday," he said. "I'd rather get it standing up than lying down."

"Getting killed isn't the only danger, Anakin. You rely heavily on the Force. It informs your every action. Just now you pulled Tahiri and me back to the surface of the asteroid with it, when you might have done so with your hand."

"And I might have drifted off with you. It was easier, more certain."

"And you made that decision reflexively, without thinking. In emergency situations, in battle, you make a lot of decisions like that. If you make the wrong one—"

"I'll go to the dark side," Anakin said. "So I keep hearing."

"Being cavalier about it won't help."

"Captain Horn, I've thought about the dark side for most of my life. My mother named me after the man who became Darth Vader. The Emperor touched me through her womb.

Every night I had nightmares that ended with me in my grandfather's armor. With all due respect, I think I've probably thought a lot more about the dark side than anyone I know."

"Probably. Inoculation doesn't make you immune."

"It does in medicine," Anakin said.

"I'm guilty of a bad analogy then. I do *not* stand corrected on the point."

"This is going to be a fun three days," Tahiri said.

A standard day passed, though of course they only knew that by their chronometers. The asteroid wheeled slowly, about once every four hours. Anakin spent much of his time watching the fleet through the narrow window the fissure left them, trying to estimate how many ships there were. With electrobinoculars, he managed to reckon at least four capital ship analogs and as many as thirty smaller warcraft. That wasn't counting coralskippers, of which about one-third were at any given time flying patrol. The rest remained docked to their larger brethren.

Anakin drew his lightsaber and closed his eyes, concentrating, trying to feel the Yuuzhan Vong ships through the blade's lambent heart. They were there, a faint presence, with none of the clarity offered by the Force. On the other hand, the Force offered nothing at all where the Yuuzhan Vong were concerned.

"You *can* feel them," Corran's voice burred.

Anakin turned. Corran was pulling himself gingerly along the fissure wall.

"Yeah. A little."

"I wonder if we can get our hands on a few more of—what did you call them?"

"Lambents."

On Yavin 4, the crystal in Anakin's lightsaber had been destroyed by a close brush with the singularity of a dovin basal. Pretending to be a slave, working the fields that grew various sorts of Yuuzhan Vong greenware, he'd been assigned to work a field of lambents. The plants produced small living crystals that the Yuuzhan Vong used for hand torches and valence inputs. The crystals were controlled via a telepathic bond formed when the crystals were harvested. Anakin had bonded with a lambent and used it to rebuild his lightsaber, with the unexpected result that he could now occasionally sense the Yuuzhan Vong and their living servants. It had given him the edge he needed to survive Yavin 4 and rescue Tahiri.

"Right, lambents. If we could build more lightsabers like yours, it could be a big help to us."

"I don't know. Uncle Luke examined mine. He couldn't get the lambent to react to him at all when he turned the lightsaber on."

"Because it's bonded to you?"

"I don't think so," Anakin replied. "The Yuuzhan Vong use lambents attuned to other Vong. You'd think my lambent would react to other humans, since I attuned it. Anyway, to get more, we'd have to stage a raid on some Yuuzhan Vong ag planet. That would probably be too aggressive, for Jedi." He fought and failed to keep an ironic tone from the statement.

Corran had reached him now. The mirrored faceplate of the vac suit still gave back only stars, but he could feel the older man's serious expression.

"Anakin, switch to a private channel."

"Hey!" Tahiri broadcast, from somewhere.

"I need to talk to Anakin alone," Corran said. "It won't take long."

"Better not. It's spooky enough out here without you guys getting all secretive on me."

They changed frequencies. "Look, Anakin," Corran began. "I was a little hard on you back there. But I want you to understand that it's not just about you. You may not know it, but all of the younger Jedi and a lot of the older ones look up to you. The buzz is you're the next Luke Skywalker, at the very least."

"I don't encourage those rumors," Anakin said. "I don't like them."

"I believe that. It's also irrelevant. They're starting to

emulate you. Tahiri, back on Eriadu and on Yavin Four—classic Anakin. On Yavin Four, Sannah and my son, Valin, were trying to be like you when they pulled their foolish stunt. All the candidates want to be like you, but the fact is, most of them *can't*. They don't have the raw strength or the talent to pull themselves out of the kind of scrapes you get into. Part of being a Jedi is setting an example."

"I know that," Anakin said.

"And believe it or not, you can still learn a thing or two from your elders."

"I know that, too, Corran. I'm sorry if I've been disrespectful." He paused. "And I'm sorry I led Valin into danger. I didn't mean to. It never occurred to me that he would follow me."

"But he did," Corran said gently. "He's lucky you were there to get him out of it. As Tahiri was lucky on Eriadu."

"Yeah. Corran?"

"Yes?"

Anakin deliberated a moment before continuing. "About Tahiri."

"You're worried about her."

"Yes."

"Want to explain why?"

Anakin almost did, but then he shook his head. "I want to think about it some more. And I want to talk to her."

Corran chuckled softly. "Well, we've got nothing but time. I'm sure you'll find an opportunity soon enough. Just give me the sign if you want me to switch channels."

"Thanks. And Corran?"

"Yes?"

"I do respect you. But you flew with Rogue Squadron. Weren't you ever the least bit reckless?"

Corran's mirrored face stared back at him. "Yes," he said. "And one day, hopefully, you'll be able to understand something about what it cost me."

It didn't take long for Tahiri to come over, curious as to what he and Corran had been discussing.

"Why are they just sitting there?" she asked, waving a gloved hand at the visible stripe of stars and ships above them.

"Any number of reasons," Anakin replied. "They may be waiting for more ships, or for some sign from their gods."

"Yeah." She stepped forward a little too hard and bounced up. She steadied herself against the slanting stone. "Are we going to make it through this?" she asked.

"Yes," Anakin said, without hesitation.

"I thought so." She nevertheless sounded a little scared.

"Come here," he said.

She moved until they could touch.

"Switch off your comm and touch your helmet to mine." It's not that he didn't trust Corran not to listen, but after all, the man had been in espionage most of his life.

Tahiri did as he said, and their helmets met with a soft thunk. He couldn't see her face, but he could imagine it there, centimeters from his own. He could almost see her eyes.

"What's the big secret?" she asked. Coming through two layers of alloy, her voice sounded distant and metallic.

"Are you okay?" he asked.

"Sure."

"Do we need to talk about what happened back on Eriadu?"

She didn't answer.

Anakin hesitantly pushed on. "That was a Yuuzhan Vong battle cry. When you broke in to rescue me."

"I know. It just sort of . . . came out. Anakin, all of the words they put in me are still there. The other stuff faded, or most of it. But their language—I still hear it. Sometimes I think in it."

"It, um, worries me."

"It shouldn't. I'm okay."

He wound up his courage a little tighter. "I should have told you this a while back," he said. "I waited because you already had enough to worry about, after we got off Yavin Four."

"What?"

"I had a vision about you. At least I think it was a vision."

"Go on."

"You were grown up. You were, umm, scarred up and tattooed like Tsavong Lah. You were Jedi, but dark. I could feel the darkness radiating from you."

"Oh."

"It worried me."

"And you didn't tell me this? You didn't think I should know?"

"When you killed the shaper, I saw the look in your eyes. The look *she* had."

"By she you mean me, of course. The she I might have been if you hadn't rescued me."

"Something like that."

"You don't think ... you don't *still* think that could happen to me? That I could end up like the me in your vision? How could I? You saved me from them, stopped them before they finished."

"I thought so. Think so. But when you came through that door speaking Yuuzhan Vong—"

"It's nothing," Tahiri insisted. "It's just words. And I would never hurt you."

That rang strange. "Who said anything about you hurting me?" Anakin asked.

"I just assumed, in your vision, I was threatening you."

"No," he said, a little suspicious but not willing to push it. Had she had a vision, too? She somehow didn't sound surprised at his. "No," he continued, "it was like I was looking through someone else's eyes, not my own. I don't think I was there. But whoever was—you said something about them being the last. Just before you killed them."

"Anakin, I'll never join the Yuuzhan Vong. Believe it." Even through two helmets, her voice rang with utter conviction.

"Okay," he said. "I just wanted to tell you. I thought you ought to know."

"Thanks. Thanks for not keeping me in the dark."

"You're welcome."

Their helmets were still touching, and she didn't say anything else. He was glad he couldn't see her face, because he would have had to look away.

And yet he *wished* he could see it.

Her gloved hand came up slowly. He took it and felt something almost like an electric jolt. They stood that way for a long time, until Anakin felt suddenly very . . . awkward.

He was about to let go when the asteroid suddenly began to vibrate, a faint tactile buzz coming from everywhere. At the same time, Anakin felt weight, dragging him not toward the surface of the asteroid, but against the wall of the fissure.

"What?" He suddenly thought to switch his comm back on.

". . . under acceleration!" Corran was shouting.

It took only an instant for the implications of that to sink in. Then Anakin flicked on his lightsaber. The blade limned the stone around them in purple light.

Anakin sliced through the stone, five strokes that set a chunk of nickel-steel floating to butt against the new "down" of the fissure wall.

The stone went down only about twenty centimeters. Below that was yorik coral.

"This is a ship, too!" Corran shouted.

To prove him correct, the g forces continued to mount.

NINETEEN

Jaina was awakened by a blaring horn and the arrhythmic thumping of running feet. She sat up, trying to remember where she was.

The walls, ceiling, and floor were of blue-black ice. She'd been sleeping in her flight suit inside a thermoskin. Right, she had it now. Kyp's hideout.

The other two people sleeping in the chamber—a human female named Yara and a disheveled Bothan whose name she had forgotten—were clambering to their feet. Jaina shrugged on her parka and followed them into the corridor and down to the command center.

Kyp was there, calmly giving orders. He saw Jaina and smiled, and she felt that funny little twist in her stomach again.

"Good morning," Kyp said. "Sleep well?"

"Not bad, considering my bed was a block of ice," she replied. "What's going on?"

"Yuuzhan Vong recon just popped into the system. Not much of an outfit, but I don't want them to find us here. If we hurry, we can jet out the back way before they're any the wiser." He locked his gaze on her. "That means I'm going to have to ask for your decision—now. If you won't take this to someone in the military, I'll have to do it alone. I'll never convince them, but I have to try."

His sincerity and urgency burned fiercely in the Force. Jaina remembered the column of sunfire, creeping toward the Yuuzhan Vong weapon. It wasn't as if Kyp didn't have proof. She at least owed his evidence a hearing, didn't she?

"I'll go to Rogue Squadron with it," she said. "It's the

only place I know where I might still be welcome, and Colonel Darklighter will know what to do. But I'll need your data."

"Packed up and ready to go. And I'm going with you, just to make sure you get there."

"That might not be a good idea. If Uncle Luke isn't safe on Coruscant, I can't imagine you would be."

"Or you, for that matter," Kyp added. "After all, you were last seen fleeing with them. I was hoping you could arrange a rendezvous someplace else."

Jaina hesitated. "We could try that—I could send a message to Colonel Darklighter. But what if the Yuuzhan Vong or the Peace Brigade traces the communication?"

"You're a smart young woman. I'm sure you can think of someplace you and Darklighter know that you can refer to obliquely."

"Sure, probably."

Kyp's grin expanded again. "Good." He jerked his head in the direction of the bay. "I took the liberty of refueling your X-wing and giving it the once-over. I'm afraid there's no time for you to give it a personal inspection. We've gotta haul jets."

"Okay," Jaina said, "but if I flame out from a cracked nacelle, I'm holding you responsible."

"Don't worry. I prefer my friends uncooked. Especially my more attractive ones."

"Boy, you've been practicing that flattery stuff, haven't you?" Jaina shot back. "I've already agreed to help you. No need to pour frill syrup on honeycrust."

"I wasn't," he replied, smiling that annoying smile again.

They reached the X-wings in silence, where Kyp's people were already arrayed. There were more than a dozen and one, now, and she recognized few of them. They all had a certain raggedness to them, a look of almost never sleeping. They had eyes as hard and glinting as Corusca gems, and they looked at Kyp as if he were some Master of old.

"All right," Kyp told them. "We want to fly quiet this time. Most of you know we seeded a moon of the sixth planet with a signal emitter. They'll go there first and find nothing but a wayward probe. Keeping the planet between us and them will allow us a sunward course. By the time we need to change our vector, the solar radiation ought to cloak us from their long-range sensors. Then we put the sun behind us and make the jump. Any questions?"

There were none, only a swelling sense of pride and confidence. Jaina tried to shrug it off—these weren't *her* feelings, after all. But it was infectious.

"Great," Kyp said. "As soon as we're out, I'll trigger the thermal charges. They won't find a thing, and we can always dig in here again."

They cleared the planet without incident, keeping comm silence until they were well around the primary. There, Kyp peeled off from his wing and came alongside Jaina. He signaled for her to switch to a private channel.

"Ready?" he asked, when she'd made the switch.

"I didn't think we had reached the node."

"The Dozen are headed to another hiding hole. We're heading Coreward. We split up here."

Jaina nodded. "Just give me the jump, so I can lay it in."

"Coming," Kyp said.

They made the jump, and then another. After that they had a long realspace jaunt through another uninhabited system.

"Jaina?"

"Still here," she said. Kyp was only about ten meters away. He had his cockpit light on, so she could see his face through the transparisteel.

"Why did Luke send you? Really?"

"I didn't lie to you. He's trying to pull the Jedi back together." She paused. "He also wanted to know what you were up to."

"That's very paternal of him," Kyp remarked. "Almost as paternal as planting a tracer in my ship last time I was on Coruscant."

"You found—" She suddenly recognized that Kyp had been nudging her very subtly in the Force.

"Don't ever do that," she snapped.

"I do what I must," Kyp replied. "I guessed there was a tracer. I couldn't find it. Must be something new. I had to trick you into confirming it, though, and I respected your intelligence enough to believe you wouldn't fall for such a simple ruse without a nudge. I do apologize, but then, you did come to spy on me."

"If you think that, you don't know much about me," Jaina replied. She glared across the empty space at him.

"Perhaps that's true. But you didn't willingly tell me about the tracer."

"That's not my secret to give out."

"Neither are mine. Do you understand?"

Jaina thought about that a moment, then nodded. "Understood."

"Okay."

"No, not okay. I'm still not happy with you, Kyp. I don't think I like who you've become."

"I've become what I need to be. What your uncle Luke was in the war against the Empire."

"Boy, you must love your mirror."

"No. I'm not saying I like what I've become either, Jaina. Your uncle Luke eventually went to the dark side—"

"Hey," Jaina snapped. "At least he fought it. You spent what, a *week* training to be a Jedi before the dark side seduced you?"

Kyp laughed easily. "Something like that."

"And you blew up a planet, right? If it hadn't been for Master Skywalker speaking for you, you'd be in prison to this day, if not dead. And my father—"

"I know what I owe Han," Kyp said. "I won't forget it. I haven't even begun paying off that debt."

"Or the one to Uncle Luke. But that doesn't stop you from bad-mouthing him all over the galaxy, does it? It doesn't stop you from undermining him as a leader."

"Any time Luke is ready to be a leader again, I'm ready to follow him," Kyp said.

"Riiight. Just so long as he tells you to do things you already want to and doesn't tell you to do anything you don't want to."

"You've just described what a real leader does."

"Yeah? And that's what you are, aren't you? A leader. I see the way your squadron looks at you. You like it too much. I doubt very much you would give that up, whatever course of action Master Skywalker might lead us on."

"Jaina," Kyp said, after a moment, "I won't say you don't have a few good points there. Maybe I am addicted to this now. That doesn't mean it shouldn't be done. Every day, thousands of living, breathing beings are sacrificed to the Yuuzhan Vong gods. There's a pit on Dantooine. I've seen it. It's almost two kilometers across and full of bones. And the slaves, what they make the slaves do . . ."

He stopped, and she felt waves of anger, pity, and grief lap over her. "The Vong obliterate whole worlds, and yes, I know I did that once, but I'm not crazy enough to think it was *right*. The Vong think it's a holy obligation. Maybe Master Skywalker is right to urge a passive role. Maybe that's what the Force really asks of us. But I don't believe it. Luke Skywalker risked everything in *his* war, the war against the Empire. Everything, including the peril of turning to the dark side as his father did. That was his war, Jaina. *That* was his war. This one is ours. Luke wants to protect us from ourselves. I say we're all grown up. The old Jedi order died with the Old Republic. Then there was Luke, and only Luke, and a lot of fumbling to re-create the Jedi from what little he knew of them. He did the best he could, and he made mistakes. I was one of them. His generation of Jedi was put together like a rickety space scow, but from it something new has emerged. It's not the old Jedi order, nor should it be."

His eyes burned across the space between them like quasars. "We, Jaina, are the new Jedi order. And this is *our* war."

TWENTY

The *Millennium Falcon* was purring, and the controls felt just right in Han's hands. Better than they had felt in a very long time, as a matter of fact. Oh, the coralskippers tried their best. They swooped in close, firing their molten projectiles and skittering away from return fire like a school of particularly ugly fish. The larger craft—about the size of the *Falcon* itself—kept a steady fire of its own weapons, releasing whole flights of grutchins. But today was not a lucky day for the Yuuzhan Vong, at least not so far.

Han whooped and turned tight, scraping so close to the transport analog that one of the pursuing coralskippers, already singed by laser fire, smacked right into it.

In his peripheral vision, he saw another skip flame out, drilled by turbolasers.

"Kid can shoot," Han told his copilot.

"He's your son," Leia said. Her voice surprised him. For a nanosecond he'd forgotten it was her there, expecting to find Chewie instead.

And the odd thing? He didn't feel the gullet-sucking sorrow he usually did. A little wistful, maybe, a little melancholy. A little happiness, too, to have his wife beside him. He'd nearly wrecked that, hadn't he?

He blinked as a volley of Yuuzhan Vong ordnance found his shields when they shouldn't have.

"Like I said, *Han*—" Leia sputtered.

He'd built some distance from the largest Yuuzhan Vong vessel. Now he turned and built g's toward it. "Concussion missiles when I tell you."

"Han?"

141

The Yuuzhan Vong ship loomed closer and closer, and Han grinned out of the side of his mouth.

"Yeah, sweetheart?"

"You've noticed we're going to hit that thing?"

Han held course.

Leia nearly shrieked because the alternating smooth and striated pattern of yorik coral filled nearly the entire viewport. At the last instant Han nosed up slightly to miss by a few tens of centimeters.

"Missiles, now!" Han said.

The missiles detonated just behind them, a full spread. The Yuuzhan Vong ship broke in half.

"Noticed I'm going to hit *what* thing?" Han asked innocently.

"Have you lost it?" Leia exclaimed. "What do you think, that you're twenty again?"

"It ain't the years—"

She smiled, leaned over, and kissed him. "As I've said before, you have your moments. I always knew you were a scoundrel at heart."

"Me?" The exaggerated innocence that had once come so naturally felt suddenly right again.

The rest of the Yuuzhan Vong ships went out like Hapan paper lamps caught in a high wind, and Jacen shot them into star food. Without the yammosk on the larger ship to coordinate them, the skips were less than dexterous.

"Speaking of scoundrels," Han said, tapping on the comm unit.

"Hailing the freighter *Tinmolok*."

The hail was answered immediately. "Yes, yes. Do not shoot! We are unarmed! We are Etti! We are not Yuuzhan Vong!"

"So you say," Han said easily. "I can see that you're taking cargo into occupied space."

"Relief only! Food for the native populace!"

"Oh, really? Well, now, that I've got to see. I'm coming alongside."

"No, no, I . . ."

"No problem. Just glad to be able to help."

"Please, Captain, may I ask who you are?"

Han leaned back and clasped the back of his head in his hands. "You, sir, are speaking to the proud captain of the, ah—" He glanced at Leia. "—*Princess of Blood*. Prepare to be boarded."

Leia rolled her eyes.

"This is piracy," the Etti captain—one Swori Mdimu—grumbled as Han and Jacen took possession of the crew's sidearms.

"That's good," Han told him. "I thought I was going to have to write it down for you, so you'd know what happened. Though for the record, it's actually privateering. See, *pirates* steal from anyone. They're greedy, and they just don't care who they hijack. Privateers, on the other hand, only attack ships allied with a certain fleet. In this case, I'm choosing for my targets any lowlife gutless and stupid enough to supply the Yuuzhan Vong or the Peace Brigade, or any other collaborationist scum, with anything whatever."

"I told you—"

"Look," Han said. "In about five minutes, I'm going to see your cargo. If it's just a bunch of food that the Yuuzhan Vong are buying for their captives out of the goodness of their sweet, tattooed hearts, I'll let you go, with apologies. But if I find you're carrying weapons and ordnance, or any other sort of war matériel, I'm going to smack you around. And if you have *captives* . . . Well, you have an imagination. Use it."

"No!" the captain said. "No captives. It's as you said. Weapons for the Peace Brigade. Not my idea! I have an employer. I need this job. Please don't kill me and my crew."

"Quit your whining. I'm not killing anybody, this time. I'm setting you adrift in one of your shuttles."

"Thank you. Thank you!"

"Here's how you thank me," Han said. "You tell anyone who'll listen that we're out here. Any ship delivering to a Yuuzhan Vong–occupied system is *mine*. And next time, I may not take prisoners. You get me?"

"I get you," Swori Mdimu said.

"Great. My, ah, *buddy* here is going to put you all in stun cuffs now. I'm going to have a look at your cargo. If there are any surprises waiting for me, better tell me now."

"There—there are two Yuuzhan Vong guards. They will be alerted."

"No kidding?" Han said. "Okay, so we're cuffing you *and* locking you up. Then the two of us will take care of these guards."

"Two of you?" the Etti said incredulously. "Against Yuu-zhan Vong?"

"Hey, don't worry. You want us to lose, right? But if we don't, I'll be back, and we need to have a little talk about who exactly your employer is."

Once the prisoners were secure, Han started off down a corridor.

"Da—ah, Captain?" Jacen said. "Cargo hold's the other way."

"That's right," Han told him.

"What're you . . . ?"

"Just stay here. If the Yuuzhan Vong come up, give a yell. I'll be on the bridge."

Han returned from the bridge a little later, and the two of them went to the cargo access axis. At the first set of locks, they found two Yuuzhan Vong guards, collapsed near the door. Their faces were masses of purple—not from their own scarification, but from the capillaries that had burst beneath their skin.

"You killed them," Jacen said dully, hardly believing it. "You sealed off the compartment and let the air out."

Han glanced at his son. "Right on all but one count. They aren't dead."

Jacen frowned and knelt to search for some sign of life, since with the Yuuzhan Vong the Force could not help him. One of the two stirred at his touch, and he jumped back.

"See?" Han said, a sure note of satisfaction tinting his voice. "I just dropped the pressure until *they* did. There are surveillance cams in here."

"Oh."

"Better cuff 'em, unless you want to fight 'em. I thought things would go smoother this way."

"Dad, what if there had been captives in here?"

"Then I would have *seen* them on the surveillance. Jacen, give the old man some credit."

"Permission to speak freely, Captain."

Han sighed. "Go ahead, son."

"Dad, I don't like this. Maybe you think being a pirate is okay, but—"

"Privateer," Han corrected.

"You really think there's a moral difference?"

"If there's ever a moral difference in being on one side instead of the other in a war, yes. Doesn't your all-knowing Force tell you that?"

"I don't know what the Force wants. That's exactly the problem."

"Yeah?" Han said sarcastically. "You knew what to do when you found your mother with her legs half cut off. Fortunately. Or do you think it was wrong to save her life?"

Jacen reddened. "That's not fair."

"Fair?" Han threw his hands up. "Kids these days. Fair."

"Dad, I know the Yuuzhan Vong are a darkness that must be fought. But aggression—that's not my way. Setting up Uncle Luke's great river, that I know I can do. This . . ."

"And you thought we were going to be able to carry out Luke's grand scheme without ever getting our hands dirty? You heard them back at the Maw—we need ships, we need supplies and weapons, we need *money*." Han tapped up the ship's manifest on the captain's datapad and whistled. "And now we have all three. Three E-wings, right out of dry dock. Lommite, about two hundred kilos. Enough rations to feed a small army." He glanced back up at Jacen. "Not to mention that the Peace Brigade doesn't get any of this stuff. C'mere. I want to see something."

They made their way through the crated supplies until they came to those the manifest designated as weapons. Han worked the seal on one until it popped open.

"Well, how do you like that?" Han remarked.

"Emperor's bones," Jacen breathed.

The crate contained not blasters, stun batons, or grenades, but Yuuzhan Vong amphistaffs.

"Looks like our Brigade buddies are making the transition away from the evils of technology," Han said. "Wonder if they've started scarring themselves yet?" He looked significantly at Jacen. "You still don't think this was worthwhile?"

Jacen stared at the hibernating weapon-beasts.

"It's done, now," he allowed.

Han shook his head. "I don't think so. I want to find out who is sending this stuff. Those amphistaffs were grown somewhere. Where? Duro? Obroa-skai?"

"You told the captain of this ship you would continue hijacking ships bound for Yuuzhan Vong space. Was that the truth?"

"It was. I've been trying to explain why."

"It's a bad idea."

"Well, maybe. But like I told you earlier, I'm the captain."

"It's not that simple for me."

"No? Then here's something real simple. We're taking this freighter and its cargo back to the Maw. When we're done, you're free to take one of these E-wings to Luke and sit the rest of the war out meditating or whatnot. Become a nurse or something. I don't care. But if you're going to keep this up, I don't want you on my ship, son or not."

Jacen didn't answer, but his face went all stony. It was times like this that Han occasionally wished he had just a little of that Force ability to feel what others felt, because Jacen was a blank slate to him more often than not.

As his son vanished around the corner, Han realized exactly what he had said, and memory suddenly jolted through him with the force of vision. He saw himself with Leia in the cockpit of the *Falcon* the day they'd met, right after escaping the Death Star. "I ain't in this for your revolution," he'd told her. Not much later he'd told Luke much the same thing, dodging out of the fight against the Death Star for what seemed all of the right reasons, not the least of which that it was hopeless. *That* Han Solo had had a pretty weak grip on the idea of a worthy cause.

Somehow, things had gotten turned around. Not front to back, but in a weirder way. Ultimately it was because he just didn't understand the kid, and the kid hadn't a clue about Han.

Anakin he could understand. He used the Force in exactly the way Han would, if he had the ability. Jacen had always been more like Leia, and in the last year or so the resemblance had only grown stronger.

But here, suddenly, in the least flattering way he could imagine, the Solo genes were finally showing.

"Don't go, son," Han murmured, but there was no one to hear him but the sleeping weapons.

TWENTY-ONE

Corran flicked on his lightsaber and began helping Anakin cut into the ridge on the Yuuzhan Vong ship. Tahiri got the idea and joined them. Together, they sawed a hole deep into the ridge before Anakin's knees began to buckle from his rapidly increasing mass.

Suddenly a chunk of the ship broke free and fell inward, pushed by the same acceleration that was about to kill the three Jedi. Atmosphere blew out, curtains of ice crystals sparkling in the starlight as Corran leapt through the gap, pulling Tahiri with him. Anakin followed.

Normal weight returned instantly as they entered the ship, probably due to the same gravity-bending dovin basals that drove the craft.

Anakin looked around him to see where they were.

In the mingled glow of their lightsabers, Anakin made out a dark grotto, walls haphazardly patched with luminescence. Even as he watched, however, the light faded as the bitter cold and vacuum that slunk in with the Jedi killed whatever plant or creature manufactured it. The chamber's function was difficult to determine. The roof was very low, no more than a meter and a half, and it rambled on for a considerable distance. Black columns or tubes ran from floor to ceiling every two meters or so. The columns bulged in the middle, and Anakin thought they were pulsing faintly.

Corran gestured for the two younger Jedi to touch helmets with him.

"Someone will show up to check the hull breach soon," he told them. "We need to be ready."

"I'm ready," Tahiri said. "Really ready. This is a lot better than sitting on some old rock, waiting for them to find us."

Anakin sensed a bit of annoyance from the older Jedi as Corran went on with his analysis. "I'm guessing this section, whatever it is, is sealed off, else there would still be air whistling through. We need to find the lock."

"Too late for that," Anakin said as his lambent lisped a faint warning. "We've already got company coming. Close."

"How can you tell?"

"I feel them."

Corran nodded. "May the Force be with you," he told them. Then he moved off to crouch near one of the pillars.

Light appeared toward the far end of the chamber: six lambents like the one in Anakin's sword. In their light he saw six shadowed bipeds stepping through a typical Yuuzhan Vong dilating lock. He took deep breaths, relaxing his muscles one by one, preparing for the fight.

Closer, he saw they wore rust-colored formfitting suits—creatures really, of course, probably some vacuum-hardy variant of the ooglith cloaker. Their faces were visible, however, through transparent masks. To Anakin's surprise, only two of them revealed the facial scars of warriors. Two others had the more delicate tattoos he had come to associate with shapers. Indeed, their cloakers bulged conspicuously around their heads, doubtless due to the tendril-bearing creatures they wore as headdresses. The remaining pair had the look of workers or perhaps slaves.

The two warriors set themselves in guard stances while the shapers examined the hole.

Anakin felt rather than saw Corran creep forward, not toward the group of Yuuzhan Vong, but toward the door they had entered through.

Moving carefully but as quickly as he could, Anakin followed, tapping Tahiri on the shoulder to get her attention.

Come on, he suggested in the Force, hoping she got the sense of it.

She did. The three crept through the darkness behind the repair party. In the vacuum, their feet made no sound at all.

They had almost reached the lock when Anakin felt the tingle of approach behind him. He turned in time to see a warrior loom up silently, amphistaff arcing toward Anakin's head.

Anakin leapt back at the last instant, nearly letting the weapon graze him. He flicked his lightsaber on, and it blazed to life. The warrior's eyes went wide with surprise.

He didn't know what he was facing, Anakin guessed.

Whatever his feelings, the warrior didn't hesitate long. He renewed his attack, spearing with the sharp end of the weapon. When Anakin caught the attack in a circular parry and pressed to bind, the staff suddenly went limp, escaping his net of light. It came flicking in an arc toward his face, now semirigid.

Anakin launched himself forward and under the attack. As he passed by the warrior's right side, he lifted his weapon parallel to the floor in a cut across his opponent's face. The energy blade sliced through the mask, and the warrior fell back, flailing, air and blood mingling and freezing in a mass around the cut.

The other warrior was battling Corran, while Tahiri tried to work the lock.

Corran's dual-phase weapon moved in tightly controlled arcs, always where it needed to be. That fight was nearing its end, too. Corran had stripped a long patch of cloaker from his enemy's arm. It was already healing, but vacuum and frostbite had done their damage; the arm hung uselessly. Corran parried a flurry of increasingly wilder and more desperate attacks. Taking the last in a parry that pushed his opponent's staff high above their heads, he then turned his point down and drove it into the warrior's exposed armpit. The blade sank deep, but the warrior still brought his weapon down, cracking solidly against Corran's head. Both men fell away, Corran with his hands to his helmet, the Yuuzhan Vong writhing in death throes.

Anakin spun to face their remaining enemies, but none was moving toward them. *Not warriors,* he thought. *But still dangerous,* he amended, remembering the deadly tools on the shaper Mezhan Kwaad's hands. Still, he ought to feel them approaching, if they tried.

Anakin knelt by Corran. The amphistaff had dented the helmet of the vac suit, but worse, a crack had formed between the metal and the transparisteel—he could tell by the rime of frost forming on it. Corran was already struggling for consciousness.

Tahiri was still working at the lock. Anakin pressed his gloved hand over the crack, wishing he had a patch, but those were in the emergency pack, on the other side of the room past the Yuuzhan Vong. By the time he went there and got back—assuming he didn't have to stop and fight—Corran would be dead.

He increased the feed of Corran's oxygen in hopes of keeping the pressure high enough to prevent his blood boiling.

Pale light fell across them, and he looked up to see that Tahiri had finally cycled the lock. He dragged Corran through, and within seconds the smaller chamber beyond was pressurized. They passed through the inner lock more easily and into another corridor, this one still illuminated by the phosphorescent fungi.

Anakin quickly worked Corran's helmet off. The older man was red-faced and had a nasty bump on his head, but otherwise seemed to be in pretty good shape. Within a minute he was standing, albeit shakily.

"Thanks, Anakin, Tahiri. I owe you both." His head jerked this way and that. "We need to keep moving," he said. "A ship this size could have a hundred warriors on it."

"I've never been so glad to be wrong," Corran admitted later. In under an hour they had defeated the remaining five warriors on the ship and rounded up and incarcerated the rest of the less military Yuuzhan Vong. Now the three Jedi sat in the control room, or what passed for it.

The ship—if by ship one meant the available living space—was actually quite small. The bulk of the vessel was the concealing stone of the asteroid and vast caverns of greenware that none of them could even guess the function of.

"We were lucky," Corran said. "If we'd been most places on the surface, we would have had to cut through fifty meters of rock. As it was, we were on the cooling fin—at least that's my guess as to what it was."

"This must be some sort of scout ship," Anakin guessed.

"Or a surveillance craft," Corran said. "At the moment, that's not the most important question. We need to know three things, fast." He ticked them off on his fingers. "One: does the rest of the fleet know we've captured it? Two: where is it going? Three: can we fly it?"

"Tahiri?" Anakin said.

Tahiri had settled into the chair facing what Anakin knew from experience to be a bank of indicators—embedded lumens, several villips, patches of varying texture and color that were probably manual controls. The real key to flying the craft rested in the loose cap Tahiri held in her lap. Called a cognition hood, it established a telepathic link between pilot and ship.

"I can fly it," she said softly.

Corran grimaced. "Why not let me try it? We still don't know what hidden dangers using that thing might have."

"I've flown one before," Tahiri said, "On Yavin Four."

"It has to be her," Anakin said. "She speaks and thinks in the language, for one thing. Since the scientists have my tizowyrm, she's the only one of us who can. And . . ." He trailed off.

"They changed my brain," Tahiri said bluntly. "I can fly it. You can't, Captain Horn."

Corran sighed. "I don't like it, but you might as well give it a try. At this point I have to admit you two have a lot more practical knowledge than I do when it comes to Yuuzhan Vong technology."

Tahiri nodded and placed the cap over her short golden hair. It writhed and contracted to fit. Her eyes clouded, and sweat started on her brow. Her breath chopped raggedly.

"Take it off," Corran said.

"No, wait," Tahiri said. "It was just a little different that time. I can handle it. I'm adjusting." Her brow furrowed in concentration. "The ship's name is *Stalking Moon*. A hyperdrive jump has been laid in. It's coming up in about five minutes."

Two organisms suddenly waggled to life, and between them appeared a hologram, showing something that might have been a map, complete with unfamiliar icons. One, shaped like a three-pointed star, was highlighted in red and moving rapidly. A few of the others were moving as well.

"That's the fleet," she said. "The fast-moving thing is us." Her head turned toward them, though her eyes were hidden by the hood. "I don't think anyone is following us."

"Can you tell where the jump is taking us?"

Tahiri shook her head. "There's a designation. It translates to something like 'next prey to feel our talons and glory.'"

"Yag'Dhul?" Anakin speculated.

"We'll see soon enough," Corran replied. "If so, this ship may have been sent ahead to make tactical maps or something. We may be the first of the fleet to arrive. Anakin, you may get your chance to warn Yag'Dhul."

"True," Anakin said. "If the—who lives at Yag'Dhul, anyway?"

"The Givin," Corran said.

"The Givin don't blow us out of the sky. We are, after all, in a Yuuzhan Vong ship."

"Well, there is that," Corran said. "But we have a better chance there than staying here. If Yag'Dhul is where we're going. We're headed back to a Yuuzhan Vong base, for all we know."

"You want me to try and stop the jump?" Tahiri asked.

Anakin watched Corran consider that. Then the older Jedi shook his head in the negative.

"No," he said. "We're in this deep. Might as well see what the bottom looks like."

TWENTY-TWO

It was hard to read a Mon Calamarian. With their bulging, fishlike eyes and wide lips, they looked, to the untrained human eye, perpetually surprised or amused. They lacked the same complex facial muscles that humans had evolved for nonverbal communication, their species being possessed of another set of semiotic tools for that purpose.

Nonetheless, Mara somehow saw the horror on Cilghal's face when the healer entered the medical chamber Booster had allowed her to set up.

"Oh, no," Cilghal murmured. Her partially webbed digits fluttered in agitation. "Please, Mara, recline." She indicated an adjustable medical bed.

"No problem," Mara said. Her knees had gone flimsy on the short walk over from her quarters. Her mental image of herself had morphed into a huge bloated thing balanced on ridiculous, straw-thin legs.

What she saw in Cilghal's clinical mirror fit no image of herself at all, past or present. Her eyes were sunken into gray pits, their emerald color faded to a sickly yellow. Her cheeks were hollow, as if she hadn't eaten in days. Her skin was so pale the vessels stood out like topographic maps of a river delta on Dagobah.

What a beauty, Mara thought. *I could dance in Jabba's palace again, if I could dance. Of course, I'd attract a different type of admirer than I did last time . . .*

Wait'll Luke sees this. He's going to have a meltdown. Unwilling to run the risk that some slicer could trace a HoloNet communication back to the *Errant Venture,* Luke had taken his X-wing out to contact several eminent physicians and transmit Mara's latest test results. He'd been gone three days.

"I need to know what it means, Cilghal."

"How do you feel?"

"Hot, cold. Nauseated. As if nanoprobes are trying to carve my eyes out from behind with microscopic vibroblades."

The healer nodded and placed her webbed hands so gently on Mara's abdomen that it might have been sheets of flimsiplast that floated there.

"Three days ago, when you went into meditation, how did you feel?" Cilghal asked.

"Sick. I already knew it was coming back. I thought if I was alone, in total concentration and without distraction, I might be able to control it like I did before."

"This is not like before," Cilghal said. "Not at all. The rate of molecular mutation has increased fivefold. It's much worse than before you began taking the tears. It might be because so many of your body's resources are tied up in the pregnancy; it might be because the serum weakened your ability to fight without it." She closed her eyes, and Mara felt the Force in motion, within and about her. "It's like dark ink, staining your cells. Spreading."

"The baby," Mara demanded. "Tell me about my son."

"The Force burns bright in him. The darkness hasn't reached there. Something keeps it at bay."

"Yes!" Mara whispered, clenching her fists.

Cilghal's eyes wobbled together so her gaze met Mara's. "It's you, isn't it?" the healer said. "You're putting everything into keeping the disease from entering your womb."

"I can't let it," Mara said. "I can't."

"Mara," the healer said, "you are declining at a terrifying rate."

"I only have to last until the birth," Mara pointed out. "Then I can start taking the tears again."

"At this rate, I'm not sure you will survive the birth," Cilghal told her. "Even if we induce it, or do it surgically. You're already that weak."

"I don't *lose*," Mara told her ferociously. "I'll be strong enough when the time comes. It can't be much longer, can it?"

"You aren't listening to me," Cilghal said. "You could die."

"I *am* listening to you," Mara replied. "It's just that what you're telling me doesn't change anything. I'm going to have this baby, and he's going to be healthy. I'm not going back on the serum. I've come through tougher things than this, Cilghal."

"Then let me help you. Let me lend you some of my strength."

Mara hesitated. "I'll report every day for monitoring and whatever healing you can accomplish. Is there anything else I can do?"

"More than once a day," Cilghal said. "I can strengthen the power of your body to fight. I can cleanse it of some toxins. I can fight the symptoms. But the disease itself . . . there's nothing. No, I can think of nothing else to do." Despair and failure seemed to drift from the healer.

"I need your help, Cilghal," Mara said. "Don't give up on me yet."

"I would never, Mara."

"Good. I need to eat, but I'm not hungry, and I can't keep anything down. I'm sure you can help me with that, right?"

"That I can help with," Cilghal replied.

"It's one thing at a time, old friend," Mara said. "Every parsec begins with a centimeter."

Cilghal nodded and went off to gather some things from storage. Mara lay back, suddenly dizzy, wishing she felt half of the confidence she espoused.

TWENTY-THREE

Master Kae Kwaad was as lean as one of Nen Yim's shaping fingers. He walked with an odd limp and a strange twist to his shoulders. His headdress was a ropy, unkempt mess. He wore a masquer to conceal his real face, a fashion among the Praetorite Vong but not common among shapers of any domain for decades. The masquer portrayed young, clear features, with scarlet-tinted yellow eyes. His real age was difficult to determine, though his skin had the smoothness of relative youth.

"Ah, my adept," Kae said as Nen Yim made the genuflection of greeting. "My willing adept."

Nen Yim tried to keep her expression neutral, but she heard something in his voice that suggested a leer behind his masquer. And the way his eyes traveled over her—what sort of master was this? Masters were above the carnal, beyond it.

No, she remembered. That was what was taught, but her old master Mezhan Kwaad's downfall had had much to do with her forbidden affair with a warrior. Masters were *supposed* to be lustless. Supposing it did not make it so.

The master brought up the seven shaping fingers of his left hand and touched them to her chin. To her distraction, the fingers seemed cramped, or paralyzed. "Yes," he murmured. "A very talented adept, I'm told." He noticed her regarding his hand. "Ah," he mused. "My hands are quite dead, you see. They died some years ago. I do not know why, and the other masters did not deign to replace them."

"That is unfortunate, Master."

He chucked her under the chin. "But you will be my hands, my dear—what was your name?"

"Nen Yim, Master."

He nodded sagely. "Yim. Yim Yim Yim." He clubbed his twisted, dead hands together. His eyes were open but seemed to see nothing. "Yim," he concluded.

Yun-Yuuzhan, what part of you was he? she wondered, quills of disgust pricking up her spine.

"I do not like that name," Kae Kwaad said in a sudden, angry burst. "It offends me."

"It is my name, Master."

"No." Wiry muscles quivered in his arms, as if he were on the verge of attacking her. "No," he repeated more calmly. "Tsup shall be your name. Nen Tsup."

Nen Yim stiffened further. Tsup was the name of no crèche or domain she had ever heard of. It was, however, an antique word for the sorts of slave who tended their masters in unseemly ways. The word itself was so obscene it was rarely used anymore.

"Come, then," the master said, with an air of detachment. "Acquaint me with my demesne."

"Yes, Master Kae Kwaad."

Feeling ill, Nen Yim led him through the moldering halls of the worldship to the shapers' quarters, through a tremoring hall that had begun to have periodic spasms, past her own quarters to the master's apartments, which had stood empty since before her coming to *Baanu Miir*. Five slaves staggered behind them, nearly buckling beneath the weight of enormous transport envelopers.

When the opening dilated, the master stood, staring into space.

"Where am I?" he asked, after a time.

"Your quarters, Master."

"Quarters? What, by the gods, are you talking about? Where *am* I?"

"On the *Baanu Miir*, Master Kae Kwaad."

"Well, where is *it*?" he screeched. "The coordinates. The exact location. Must I repeat myself?"

Nen Yim found herself twisting her fingers together, like a terrified crècheling. She stopped it immediately. "I do not know, Master. I can discover it."

"Do so!" His eyes narrowed. "Who *are* you?"

"Your adept, Nen Yim."

A crafty look came over his face. "I do not like that name. Use the one I gave you."

"Nen Tsup," she said softly.

He blinked, slowly, then snorted. "What a vulgar little thing you are." He sneered. "Hurry. Find out where we are. And then we shall shape something, yes? It will amuse us."

"Master, I wish to speak to you about the ship's rikyam, when you have the time."

"Time? What is that? It is nothing. The brain will die. You do not confuse me with your talk, Adept. No, you do not confuse or amuse or titillate me, though you think it. Yun-Harla herself could not have me! Flattering yourself. Trying to trick me. Get out of my sight."

When she was alone, Nen Yim sank down into a crouch and softly beat the heels of her hands against her head.

He is mad, she thought. *Mad and crippled. Tjulan Kwaad sent him to taunt me, nothing more.*

Beneath her feet, she noticed, a patch of the inner hull was rotting.

A day passed without her seeing him, but when Nen Yim entered her laboratory, there was the twisted, demented Kae Kwaad. He'd somehow unsealed the dermal shelf where her experiments were hidden and was stroking her personal qahsa with the carapace of his right hand. She hadn't tried particularly hard to hide anything, reasoning that doing so was wasted effort. Her modifications to the ship were ample evidence of her heresy. Hiding the experiments would only delay the inevitable.

"I like this," Kae Kwaad said, waving at her tissue samples. "I like the colors." He smiled vaguely and pointed his useless digits to his eyes. "They trickle in here, don't they? After that they don't get out. They just talk and whistle, wriggle and curl." He scratched one dead hand absently against the other.

"Tell me what you're doing, Adept," he said.

"Master, I'm only doing my best to heal the ship. If I have

strained protocol, it was only because I thought it best for the Yuuzhan Vong."

"*Strained* it? Strained it?" He laughed, an unpleasant scratching sound. Then, as abruptly, he folded down onto one of the slowly shifting benches and placed his head between his hands.

"I requested a master because I do not have access to protocol records above the fifth cortex," Nen Yim went on. "I had no answer to the rikyam's dilemma, so I sought one."

"And now you have a master." Kae Kwaad chortled. "And now we shall shape."

"Perhaps Master Kae Kwaad would like to review the damage to the spiral arm."

"Perhaps the master would have his adept listen instead of speak. Today we are shaping. Recall the protocol of Hon Akua."

Nen Yim stared at him. "We are to form a grutchin? But the fleet is replete with grutchins."

"Inferior grutchins. Your generation! In your haste to make them stronger, faster, tougher, you have forgotten the most important aspect of shaping! The essence!"

"What is that, Master?"

"*Form.* Have you ever seen a perfect grutchin, Adept?"

"I . . . do not know, Master."

"You haven't! You have *not*! In the mind of Yun-Yuuzhan is a perfect grutchin. It has never been seen by Yuuzhan Vong except in the protocols—never in living form. You and I, Adept, will incarnate the grutchin in the mind of Yun-Yuuzhan. It shall be perfect in form and proportion, precise in hue. When we are done, Yun-Yuuzhan will know us for true shapers, who create in his image."

"But the rikyam—"

"The rikyam? How can you even think of such a mundane matter when we are to embark upon *this*? Once we have created the perfect grutchin, do you really expect Yun-Yuuzhan—or those simpletons Yun-Harla or Yun-Ne'Shel—will deny us anything? Now we must work!"

It was soon after this that Nen Yim began to seriously consider the murder of Master Kae Kwaad.

PART THREE

DESCENT

TWENTY-FOUR

Leia found Jacen where he had been for the last several days—tinkering with one of the captured E-wings. Since they had taken the freighter, he had hardly said a word to anyone, and on their return to the Maw he had thrown himself into the project of fitting the fighter with augmented shields and readying her for extended flight. Han had been almost as sullen. Her husband was tough, but there was only so much loss that even Han Solo could take. It had been good to see something of his old cocky, arrogant self reemerge, though she wasn't going to admit that to him aloud.

But Han's good humor had been short-lived. His fight with Jacen and the following silence had managed to leak most of the fuel from his engines.

Jacen glanced down at her from near the astromech housing, but didn't say anything.

"Jacen," Leia said, "could I talk to you, please? Or do you intend never to speak to me again?"

Jacen gazed down again. "What's there to talk about? I think you and Dad have presented your point of view from pretty much every angle there is, and I think you know mine."

"It must be nice to be so sure about everything," Leia told him.

Jacen uttered a short, guttural laugh. "Yeah," he replied, "must be."

That had a raw sound to it that bothered Leia. How could someone so young sound so cynical? Especially Jacen, whose ideals had always been lofty ones. Of course, she knew better than anyone that most cynics were crash-burned idealists. Was Jacen that hurt?

It made what she had come to say all the harder, but she had to say it.

"Anyway," she said, taking the plunge, "you're wrong. There *is* another angle to look at this from."

"And what would that be?" Jacen asked. She didn't know whether he sounded more like Han or herself in that moment of caustic sarcasm, and she wasn't sure which would make her angrier.

"Jacen, would you knock off the rebellious teen act for just a minute? And maybe consider for just a second that the entire galaxy doesn't spin around you and your moral decisions?"

Jacen continued to stare stonily at her, but he lifted his shoulders lightly, as if accepting yet another onerous burden. "I can try that," he said. "What have I missed?"

"You've missed that your father needs you, that's what. That I need you."

"That's not fair," Jacen said. "I don't want to be a pirate, so you'll try emotional blackmail?"

"Is that what you call it? Jacen, maybe we weren't the best of parents. Maybe we weren't around as much as we could have been, and maybe this is your way of paying us back. But if your only interpretation of 'your father needs you' is that I'm trying to manipulate you, then I've been a far worse mother than I ever dreamed. If that's all you see, by all means, go. I wouldn't want you on those terms."

"Mom, I—" His voice went strange, and with a sudden start she saw he had tears in his eyes.

"Oh, Jacen—" she began.

"No, Mom, it's all right." He clambered down from the craft and wiped at his eyes. "I deserved that."

"I didn't come here to hurt you. I'm not even sure I came here to persuade you to stay with us. I just wanted to try to explain why your father is acting the way he is. Jacen, your dad is always proud of you even when he doesn't understand you, which is most of the time. He's always tried to be supportive of your decision to become a Jedi Knight, even though the farther you step into that world the farther you go from him. You're more a part of Luke's universe than you are of his, and his biggest fear is that you're ashamed of him, or somehow think him less because of what he is, because he can never be or even fully understand what you're becoming. Deep down he knows he's losing you a little more each day, and that soon enough you'll be strangers. This little spat of yours has only served to confirm that for him."

"He told you all of this?"

"Of course not. Han doesn't talk about things like that. But I know him, Jacen."

"You're right, then."

Leia frowned, a little confused by this sudden turnabout. "About what?"

"You're right—I hadn't quite seen things from that vector. Thanks. Thanks for telling me."

She reached to embrace him, and to her relief, he folded willingly into her arms.

"How could he ever think I was ashamed of him?" Jacen whispered.

They parted, and Jacen looked at her through tear-sparkled eyes. "This is one of the hardest things I've ever had to do," he said.

Leia's heart felt like neutronium. "You're still going?" she asked.

He shook his head. "I decided to stay with you guys two days ago."

"What?"

"Dad was right. Or part of what he said was right. I made a commitment when I came out here with you. I'm holding to that commitment. And with me along, we're more likely to be able to hijack these ships without hurting anyone. I'll be able to tell if there are captives on board. Turning my back on this whole thing feels worse than being a part of it. I still don't like it, but I'll do it. I won't fight Dad anymore."

"Then why have you been working on the E-wing?"

Jacen shrugged. "It was something to do other than sit

around waiting to get into another fight. Somebody can use it. That's why we took it, right?"

"Right," Leia assented.

"So when do we head back out?"

"Soon. The captain of the freighter gave up some interesting information. They came via Wayland, which is where they picked up the weapons, but most of the cargo originated on Kuat."

"Kuat?"

"Yes," Leia said. "Of course, we don't know exactly who sent the supplies—the company name they gave was a shell, and we haven't worked back to who's really the source of the funds, but we will."

"Jaina thought there was something rotten about the senator from Kuat, Viqi Shesh, when they met back on Duro. You don't think . . . ?"

"I don't trust Viqi Shesh as far as an Ewok could throw her," Leia said. "But it's still too early to make accusations." She paused. "By the way, there's something else you should know—there's news from Coruscant. Chief Fey'lya ordered Luke's arrest."

"You're kidding. He really made good on that threat?"

"Maybe, or maybe it was just a more elaborate bluff. Luke and Mara didn't take any chances, though. They left before the arrest could be made and joined up with Booster." Her voice softened. "So you see, there are other things you *could* be doing."

"Now you're trying to change my mind again?"

"No," Leia said firmly.

"Fine," Jacen answered. "What else did you learn from the captain?"

"That there will be another ship along in a few days—a freighter full of captives."

Jacen tried on a little smile. "Well, I'd better finish up with this E-wing today, then, if the *Princess of Blood* is going to be there to meet it."

"Don't *you* start that nonsense, too. Just because you're going with us doesn't mean you have to indulge every stupid thing your father comes up with, you know," Leia said.

"No, you're right to the core, Mom. We Solo men have to stick together. And I kinda like the name. I've been thinking about something to paint on the side—"

"This conversation is now over," Leia said, as seriously as she could. But she felt she could breathe freely again for the first time in several days, as if her lungs were suddenly twice the size they had been.

"Let me tell Dad, huh?" Jacen said.

"You've got it." With a lighter step, she went to make her own preparations.

TWENTY-FIVE

The reversion to realspace was different in the Yuuzhan Vong ship, somehow. Slower, maybe. Anakin made a mental note to try to discover whether that was merely perceptual or real. If the latter, were the alien ships more vulnerable during reversion? It would be worth knowing.

"Well?" Corran said, studying the changed star chart. "Where are we? Are we surrounded again?"

Beneath the hood, Tahiri turned her head this way and that, as if looking for something.

"Nothing that I see," she said. "There are plenty of ships in the system—most of them around that planet with three moons—but none of them look like Yuuzhan Vong yorik coral. And none of them seems to be paying attention to us."

"Interesting," Corran mused. "Three moons, eh? Is there a space station near that planet?"

"That could be what that is," Tahiri said.

"From your description, this likely *is* the Yag'Dhul system. The Givin have pretty good detection equipment. I wonder if this ship somehow dampens the hyperwave shock during reversion? Or if it's fully cloaked?"

"I'll ask the ship if you want," Tahiri said.

"Do that."

After a brief pause, Tahiri shook her head. "It doesn't know, or I'm not asking the right question. But it doesn't detect any probes locked on us."

"Maybe that's why the slower reversion," Anakin speculated.

"You noticed that too, huh?" Corran said. He rubbed his hands together. "Well, at least we didn't jump straight from a supernova into a neutron star. Though I suspect we don't have a lot of time here. Tahiri, any sense of what this ship was supposed to do once here?"

This time Tahiri nodded in the affirmative. "Yes. We're supposed to scent the readiness of the enemy."

"So it *is* a scout ship," Anakin said.

"Which means the main fleet will be expecting intelligence from us," Corran concluded. "The question is, how long will they wait before deciding something has gone wrong? Tahiri, can you fake a message? Stall them a little?"

Tahiri shook her head. "No. I'd have to use a villip, which means they would see my face."

Anakin watched Corran ponder that unhappily for a few seconds. "There are always the prisoners," he told the older Jedi.

"I realize that," Corran said, "though I doubt we can hope for their cooperation. It's worth a try, though. Meantime, we have to make contact with Yag'Dhul. Any ideas there?"

"The warmaster had a villip modified to broadcast on our frequencies," Anakin said.

"True. Can you do that?"

"No," Anakin confessed.

"Tahiri?"

"The ship doesn't know how to, and neither do I. We can fire a remote villip at a ship if it gets near enough."

Corran barked a phrase of laughter. "Which would certainly be interpreted as an attack. That's a last-ditch option. Anything else?"

"Sure," Anakin said. "I can modify the emergency beacon in the survival pack and run it through one of our wrist comm units."

"Do it, then," Corran told him. "Meanwhile, I'll interrogate prisoners while Tahiri keeps an eye on surrounding space and an ear up for queries from the fleet. Anakin, be back here in half an hour."

Corran surveyed the prisoners. The prison was makeshift—there probably was a real one someplace, but Corran hadn't wanted to waste the time looking for it. Using medical tape from the survival pack, Corran had fastened the living captives to the walls of the corridor leading to the helm, where he could keep an eye on them.

He studied the shapers first. They both had headdresses that looked like squirming masses of snakes. One had a hand that resembled some sort of sea creature, except that the fingers had tool attachments: pincers, a knife, and so on. Tahiri had insisted that the shapers needed to be strip-searched, and Corran had agreed to a hasty one. The search had produced several dubious organisms that had been placed in another chamber some distance away.

The remaining survivors Anakin and Tahiri had identified as members of the Shamed caste—workers who maintained the more unpleasant functions of the ship.

He didn't see anything in any of their eyes he thought he could work with—no fear or uncertainty, just a nearly uniform and haughty anger. Still, with a species you didn't know, it was hard to tell what facial expressions meant.

"Do any of you speak Basic?" he asked.

One of the shapers lifted his head, his orange-limned eyes fierce. "I speak your infidel tongue. It tastes like the waste excretions of an ill vhlor on my tongue, but I can speak it. Please, ask me something so I may deny it to you."

Not too promising. "We infidels don't normally sample the waste excretions of ill animals, so I don't fully understand the reference," Corran said. "I suppose that such delicacies are reserved for the Chosen."

"It's not possible for you to mock me," the shaper said softly.

"Sure it is. You may be dense enough not to recognize it, but I can certainly mock you."

"What do you want with me, infidel?"

"What's your name?"

"I am Kotaa of the glorious Domain Zun-qin," he replied.

"Who was designated to make contact with the fleet once this ship was in the Yag'Dhul system, Kotaa Zun-qin? What was he supposed to say?"

"He will say nothing. You killed him. The warriors are in

charge of this mission, of course. And do not think I will aid you in any scheme to defraud my people, *Jeedai*. Our fleet is poised to strike, as you must know, and strike it will."

Corran's eyes narrowed—not at Kotaa's words, but at something he had caught from the corner of his eye when the shaper had said the word *Jeedai*.

"I don't suppose you want to tell me when they will strike if they don't hear from us?"

"I would be happy to vivisect you," the shaper offered. "So that your death might offer the Yuuzhan Vong knowledge and thus have meaning. I am inclined to do you no other favor."

"I'll keep that in mind," Corran said. "I don't get an offer like that every day. Every other day, maybe . . ." He turned away from the shaper and looked more closely at the others. "Anyone else care to insult me?"

"I alone am able to mutter in your tuneless language," Kotaa Zun-qin said.

"That's fine," Corran said. "I have a translator." He approached one of the Shamed Ones. This was a smallish female, her only identifying marks a trio of poorly healed puckered burns on each cheek. He cut her free of the med tape binding her to the bulkhead. The shaper yammered something at the Shamed One in Yuuzhan Vong, and she answered tersely.

Corran pulled his blaster and motioned for the Shamed One to go ahead of him. Together they went up the corridor and into the control room.

"What's going on, Tahiri?" Corran asked.

"Not much. We're still not noticed, so far as I can tell, and no more Yuuzhan Vong ships have jumped."

"No news is good news. Can you talk to one of the Vong for me?"

"Yuuzhan Vong," Tahiri corrected.

"Whatever. Can you translate?"

"Sure," she said cheerfully, removing the control mask from her head.

When the Shamed One saw Tahiri's scars, her eyes widened, and she gabbled something in her own language.

"What did she say?" Corran asked. He really hated having to rely on secondhand information. He hated having *no* information even more.

"She noticed my scars," Tahiri explained. "She asked if I am the Jedi-who-was-shaped."

"She's heard of you?"

"I guess so."

Very, very interesting, Corran thought. Unless this one was actually at Yavin—and what would the odds of that be?—word was getting around, even among the Shamed Ones. Maybe especially among the Shamed Ones.

"Ask her name," Corran instructed.

"It's Taan," Tahiri said after consulting with the Yuuzhan Vong.

"Tell Taan I saw her make a strange face when the shaper called me a Jedi," Corran said. "Ask her what that meant."

Tahiri conversed with the Shamed One briefly, then turned her green eyes up to Corran.

"She wants to know if it's true what they say about the Jedi."

"What do they say?"

"That the Jedi are the salvation of the Shamed Ones."

Corran considered that. "She thinks of you as something special, doesn't she?"

Tahiri's cheeks pinkened. "Apparently the story of what happened on Yavin Four is a popular one among the Shamed Ones. Or a version of the story, anyway."

"Really. Can you get the short version from her? And be sure not to correct her if her story conflicts with the facts."

Looking a bit puzzled, Tahiri asked the question and received a lengthy answer. She translated it for Corran verbatim, in pieces.

"The Jedi have powers that no Yuuzhan Vong has. We know the warriors, the shapers, and the intendants are jealous of these powers. Some even fear them. At first we feared the Jedi, too, for they were infidels and dangerous foes. But on Yavin Four, two Jedi came. They came to redeem Vua Rapuung, once a mighty warrior who was marked with Shame by the shaper Mezhan Kwaad. One of the Jedi had been captured by this same shaper, and another became the comrade of Vua Rapuung. Together, side by side, the Shamed One and the Jedi defeated the shaper and redeemed Vua Rapuung. He died as no other warrior has died, saluting an infidel. The gods not only permitted this, they must have aided it. Now many say that perhaps the high castes do not know the will of the gods as well as they say, or perhaps they are hiding our redemption from us. Perhaps Shamed Ones are not shamed because it was ordained. Perhaps the Shamed Ones are not shamed because the gods hate them. Perhaps instead, our status is imposed on us by the high castes so they will have hands to do the least and most onerous of tasks, so they may live lives of glory and not debase themselves with the mundane. Perhaps the Jedi are our salvation. The legend of Vua Rapuung and the Jedi suggests it, and is often told."

"Wow," Corran said, when the recitation was done. "Are you sure you got all of that right?"

"Pretty sure," Tahiri said. "I might have used a different word here and there, but it still comes out to the same thing."

"Ask her if *she* believes this."

Again, his query was translated and asked.

"She wasn't sure. Now that she sees our might, she thinks it may be so."

"Ask her if she is willing to work with us, as Vua Rapuung did."

More unintelligible chatter; then Tahiri grinned. "She says she will help us, if there is anything someone as humble as she can do."

"There is something we can try, at least," Corran said. "It may not work, but it should be better than nothing."

Anakin returned to the helm, lugging the communication device he had patched together from the beacon and his comlink. He found Corran and Tahiri with a Yuuzhan Vong of the Shamed caste. The Shamed One was talking to a villip. The villip had modeled itself to the massively scarred visage of a warrior.

"What—" he began, but Corran cut him off with a severe look and a finger held to his lip. Anakin took the hint—the villip might pick up his extraneous sound and transmit it, as well. He chewed his lips restlessly. The face on the villip scowled and barked, hissed, and finally, more calmly, seemed to give a series of instructions. Then the villip relaxed into its normal, neutral form.

Corran glanced at Tahiri. "Well?" he demanded.

"I think it went pretty well," she said.

"*What* went pretty well?" Anakin asked.

"Our friend here just spun off quite a tale," Corran told him, nodding at the Yuuzhan Vong. "She told the commander of the fleet that when they came out of hyperspace, something went wrong. She didn't know what, because she is merely a Shamed One. She was tending the grutchin larvae, located near the primary dovin basal, and felt a weird jolt. When she didn't receive any orders for a time, she went to see what was needed of her and found the whole crew dead, in fact, hardly recognizable, pasted all over the bulkheads."

Anakin pursed his lips and then chopped his head forward. "I like it," he said. "That leaves a couple of possibilities for the commander to think about. Either she's lying, and there's been a revolt on board the ship, or she's telling the truth. If she's telling the truth, they'll know that what she described was the result of a complete failure of the dovin basal's ability to negate inertia—except right at the base of the basal. After that, they have to decide if the *Stalking Moon* ran into something natural—I dunno, a quantum black hole that made the basal recoil, something like that— or some superweapon the Givin have in place to wreck unwanted ships."

Corran nodded. "Glad you approve," he said sarcastically. But beneath his tone Anakin sensed a cool admiration that made him feel suddenly self-conscious.

"You ever consider a career in covert security?" the older Jedi asked. "Anyway, yes, that's basically what I was thinking. Even if they think option one is the case—"

"Revolt?" Tahiri said doubtfully. "I don't think so. Even

if they could conceive of Shamed Ones killing warriors and shapers, they wouldn't *want* to admit it. Do you know what would happen to the commander who let something like that happen on his watch?"

"As I was saying," Corran went on, a little testily, "even if they consider one, they have to consider the others before they bring a whole fleet here or even a second ship. They're trying to explain to Taan how to relay the telemetry of the sensing nodules, and she's pretending to cooperate. So. Let's hope they're for real and we have a bit of time. Anakin, you were successful?"

"Yes. The signal isn't that strong, so it may take a few moments to tune."

"Get started, then."

Anakin nodded and set to work. "Why Yag'Dhul, do you think?" he asked Corran, as he fiddled with the gain, focusing on the distant hum of hyperwave noise from farther insystem. "I mean, if they want Coruscant, they already have Duro to stage from."

"They're closing their back door. Yag'Dhul sits on the intersection of the Rimma Trade Route and the Corellian Trade Spine. It also gives them a clean shot at Thyferra."

"Oh!" Tahiri said. "Bacta!"

"Right. If they control bacta production, they control the health of everyone in the galaxy. Or maybe it's a ruse—the New Republic puts a lot of ships and matériel at Thyferra, and the Yuuzhan Vong try to take Fondor again or push on to a less-defended Coruscant from Duro. Either way, holding Yag'Dhul gives them a lot more options."

Anakin had a steady feedback response. "All right," he said. "We're ready."

"Hail the planetary defense force," Corran said. He closed his eyes, concentrating. "Try . . ." He reeled off a quadratic equation, then smiled wearily. "It might not be right, but it ought to get their attention."

"Hailing, Captain," Anakin said.

Five minutes later, there was still no response. Anakin modulated the wave form, sharpened the gain, and repeated.

"It ought to be working," Anakin muttered. "Unless they're deaf."

"Or unless their attention is focused elsewhere," Corran mused.

"What do you mean?" Anakin asked. "Why wouldn't they be watching their borders?"

"You don't see any ships or even probes in this region, do you? The Yuuzhan Vong have softened up other worlds with internal conflict and other methods of espionage. They may already have agents here."

"Or maybe they've already poisoned Yag'Dhul, like they did Belkadan."

"Too slow. Word would get out," Corran said.

"Unless they use something we haven't seen yet," Tahiri pointed out. "That's what shapers do, you know, come up with new things."

Corran nodded. "They do seem to keep condensing weapons out of nebular gas," he allowed. "But—"

Their speculation was cut off by a whine and sputter from Anakin's rewired comm unit. Behind a sleet of gravitic interference, the naturally armored figure of a Givin glowered at them with empty eyes. More than anything his—her?—face resembled a large human skull that had been melted, allowed to sag, and re-form.

"Yag'Dhul primary bastion to unidentified ship," the Givin said. "You have used an outdated and illegal hail code. However, your ship conforms to the configuration of a Yuuzhan Vong reconnaissance vessel." Then the mouth slit clattered something unidentifiable.

To Anakin, anyway. Tahiri gave a little gasp of horror.

"What did he say?" Corran demanded.

Tahiri turned her aventurine gaze on the other two Jedi. "It's Yuuzhan Vong. He said, 'Welcome. We've been expecting you.' "

TWENTY-SIX

Wedge Antilles pinched his face in a scowl. Unlike some other things about him, time had only made his glare more impressive. Jaina felt it brush her and shivered, though she knew she wasn't its intended target. That would be Kyp, seated between her and Gavin at the roughly finished wooden table.

"General Antilles—" she began, but then the full weight of his anger *did* fall on her, stopping her cold.

"You should have told us he would be here, Lieutenant Solo," Wedge said, his voice as soft and tense as the wire on Tionne's lute. "It was less than honest, and far less than I expect of you."

Beyond the rustic stone walls of the hilltop garden and its topiary canopy, the sun jeweled the Silver Sea with noontime light, and the fields that rolled up to the shore breathed of bristing blooms and balmgrass. A herd of stumpy, gracile-necked fecklen whirred and boomed their displeasure at a family of hopping squalls. The sky was blue, with no hint of vapor. After the cramped quarters of an X-wing, a ranch on Chandrila was the best meeting place Jaina could have imagined. More practically, it was also a place where it was easy to see one's enemy coming and speak freely, with only minimal fear that unwanted ears might hear. That was especially true because the estate was owned by a trusted relative of Gavin Darklighter's wife, Sera.

But that lovely world all but vanished for Jaina, replaced by Wedge's eyes, those verdant polished spheres that had seen so much combat and tragedy, that had looked kindly on her as a child. Wedge, who had fought alongside her father and mother and her uncle Luke from the very beginning. To have him glare at her like this was . . . very difficult.

She felt a sudden, comforting presence, and for a minute accepted it, grasped for it even. She needed every reassurance she could get. Then she recognized it as Kyp's touch. That was the last thing in the universe she needed right now, comforting or not.

Get back, Kyp.

She swallowed and addressed Wedge again. "General, I apologize, but I didn't think you would meet with me if you knew Kyp was involved. Neither did Colonel Darklighter."

Antilles now turned his ire toward Gavin. "You were in on this too, Gavin?"

"She could have hidden Durron's connection from both of us, Wedge, simply by not bringing him along when she met with me. She didn't. She was up front with me. I advised her to do things this way because I know you and—more to the point—I thought there was every possibility that my call to you was monitored. There are plenty of people who would love to make a present of Kyp Durron to the Yuuzhan Vong. You want to blame someone, blame me."

General Antilles chewed at that, didn't seem to like it, and swallowed it anyway. He glanced back up at Kyp. "Durron, I don't like you," he said. "The very best thing you are is a murderer. The very worst—"

"Wait a moment, General," Kyp interrupted. "You know what I was going through back then. Han Solo and Master Skywalker forgave me and brought me back into the fold. I had hoped that you could, too."

"You don't deserve their forgiveness," Wedge shot back. "Look how you've repaid them. Luke you denounce and deride, and as for Han, you've roped his daughter into a politically precarious position, if not something far worse."

"General," Kyp said quietly, "I'm sorry about Qwi Xux. I've told you that before. At the time I thought what I did was for the best. She had information in her head that could have brought the New Republic to its knees."

"You leave her out of this," Antilles warned. "You don't

even so much as speak her name, or I'll blast you where you stand."

"General," Jaina said desperately, "please. Whatever you may think of Kyp, he's discovered something important. Something that threatens us all."

"Fine," Antilles said, sitting back and brusquely waving his hand. "You have evidence of this danger? Let me see it. The sooner this is over with, the sooner I can find some clean air to breathe."

The four of them watched in silence as Kyp replayed the holo Jaina had seen last beneath the frozen surface of an unnamed world. When it was over, the silence continued for some time. It was Wedge who broke it.

"Emperor's black bones," he muttered.

"That was my reaction," Gavin replied. "Now you understand why I thought you should see this."

"Yes. I suppose I do." Wedge straightened and knitted his hands together. He looked at Jaina. "You've seen this for yourself?"

"No," Jaina admitted. "I've seen this same holo. But it's pretty clear what it is."

Wedge rubbed his forehead. "No," he said, "it's not unambiguous. It could be a fueling device, for instance."

Kyp cleared his throat. "General Antilles, may I speak?"

"Go ahead," Wedge said, grimacing.

"It may be a fueling device, of course. That doesn't mean it isn't a weapon. If that ship can manipulate gravity at that scale, only fools wouldn't understand its military implications. Whatever you might say about the Yuuzhan Vong, they aren't fools."

"No," Wedge said. "No, they aren't. But until we see it used militarily—"

"It would be too late then, General," Kyp burst out, leaping to his feet.

"Shut up and sit down," Wedge snapped. "Let me finish what I was saying."

Kyp's lips remained pressed tight, and for an instant Jaina caught a glimpse of something she didn't understand. It passed quickly.

Kyp sat down.

"You're done, Durron? Good. What I was saying was, until we have real evidence that this is a military weapon, we can't go to the senate with this. Maybe not even then."

"Why?" Jaina asked.

"Because they won't do anything," Wedge replied. "At least not right away. And senate security is leakier than a gas siever. The Yuuzhan Vong would know within hours that we're aware of their superweapon. Hours after that, their officials would assure Borsk Fey'lya that it's either harmless, or something meant only to be used in their own defense. They'll reiterate that they have no designs on the rest of our systems so long as we comply with their demands."

"You mean like turning anyone with Jedi training over to them," Jaina interjected.

"Right. Which brings up my final point in this round." He looked straight at Kyp. "When they consider the source, a lot of senators would rather trust the Yuuzhan Vong than Kyp Durron."

Kyp bore that silently. Jaina couldn't.

"Your pardon, General, but that's absolutely insane. Kyp's been out there fighting while the senate has dithered, caved to Yuuzhan Vong demands, and ordered the arrest of Master Skywalker. If anyone isn't to be trusted, it's Fey'lya and the senate."

She braced for another salvo from Wedge, but he smiled gently instead. "Solo, that's what I just said."

"It is?"

"More or less. Understand this, though—I know you don't care for Chief Fey'lya. I don't either. But he isn't a traitor and he's not stupid. He doesn't think the Yuuzhan Vong will keep their word any more than you or I do. But he *is* a politician, and he thinks he can play that game better than they can. Everything he's doing is aimed at buying time, and he's right. Time is what we need, to understand Yuuzhan Vong technology, to digest their tactics, to strengthen our own forces. Fey'lya will never order a strike while the

Yuuzhan Vong are quiescent. He'll maintain the illusion of truce as long as he can."

"So you're saying there will be no military mission to take this thing out?" Gavin said, outraged.

"No official mission, no," Wedge replied.

"Then what *are* we going to do?" Jaina asked.

"Whatever we do," Wedge said, "there will be repercussions. Anyone involved in this could easily end up in the same escape pod as Luke."

"Wouldn't that be a shame," Gavin drawled. "Rogue Squadron has resigned from the New Republic before. We can do it again."

"Rogue Squadron can't handle that," Wedge said, waving at the frozen holo of the ship and its trail of starfire. "Can it, Durron?"

Kyp nodded reluctantly. "The Yuuzhan Vong have the Sernpidal system locked up tight. It will take real muscle to get in there. But if we take out that thing, we also take out their major shipyard. You want to buy time, General? That could buy you quite a lot."

"I see that, Durron. But I'm just a retired adviser to Rogue Squadron. I don't have the power to send a fleet."

"General, with all respect," Jaina said, "you may not have the official power, but you have the influence."

Wedge folded his arms and regarded her for a long moment. "Solo, do you believe this? Do you believe what Durron has shown us?"

Jaina felt the weight of that question pressing her toward the planet's core. *This is why Kyp wanted me here,* she reflected. *They trust me.*

"Yes," she said. "I believe him."

The general hesitated another few seconds, then held up his hands in surrender. "Gavin, I don't have to ask where you stand on this."

"No, sir, General. I saw that thing when they were growing it, when there was plenty of time to destroy it. I had to sit around while my information was all but ignored, and now we have something to deal with that we may not be able to stop at all. But Rogue Squadron will give it its best shot."

"Volunteers only," Wedge warned.

"Of course. As if that will make a difference."

Wedge grinned wryly. "I understand, but the point has to be made. As I said, I want everyone to understand the political as well as the mortal danger inherent in this."

"Understood."

"Very well. I'm going to contact Admiral Kre'fey. I think he will be extremely interested in this situation. If that falls through, well, we'll go from there." He turned to Kyp. "I want you to understand something, Durron. You will not be in control of this mission, nor will you be at liberty to command your gang of pilots unsupervised. We'll need every ship we can get, but not if that means the chance of an unpleasant surprise from a bunch of undisciplined hotshots."

"If my pilots were undisciplined, General, they would not be alive," Kyp replied. "But if you're making my participation dependent on following orders, that's fine with me—so long as I'm involved in the decision-making process. They are my pilots—I owe them a voice."

"A voice you'll get," Wedge replied, his own speech strained. "But for the duration of this mission, you will submit to authority."

Kyp nodded fractionally. "As you say, General."

Antilles rose, nodding at Gavin and Jaina. "Colonel, Lieutenant. I'll speak to you later."

That's the problem with trying to hide from a Jedi, Jaina thought. Through the spirate leaves of the tintolive trees grappling with the hillside, she could see Kyp, dressed in Jedi robes, walking up the flagstone steps to the small pavilion she had found in her search for solitude. The afternoon had brought puffs of cloud with it to wander shadows across the plain below. A lone, distant peak was crowned with darkness and lightning, a reminder that not all water vapor was so peaceful. Behind her, the centuries-old villa rambled across the ridgetop, a maze of gardens, orchards, and cool stone halls. Her mother had once described a family estate on Alderaan. Jaina imagined it had been much like this.

"Hello, Kyp." She sighed as he came around an immaculately groomed stand of some sort of feather-leafed tree with bark scored into diamond patterns.

"You're avoiding me," he said.

"You noticed."

"Mind telling me why?"

"Because I know you're going to ask me to fly with you, and I can't." *And because you're hiding something from me.* But she didn't want to give that last up to him just yet.

Kyp leaned his shoulder against the nearest tree. "Why not?" he wondered. "Not that I was going to ask." His voice was gentle, jovial, and he grinned suddenly at something he must have seen on her face.

"What's got you so amused?" Jaina asked.

"You looked . . . surprised. It's fetching."

"I fetch nothing," she snapped. "It's just *you*. You're all over the grid. One minute you're as touchy and surly as a feral bantha, the next you're the meditative Jedi Master, the dear friend, the sensitive fellow. Who are you, Kyp?"

"Who are you, Jaina?"

"Oh, no. Don't start that with me."

"The questions you ask condition the answers you get," he said with a small shrug.

"Okay, okay. So you didn't come to ask me to fly with you."

"No, you were right about that," Kyp admitted, absently scratching his left ear. "I intended to ask."

"So you've asked and I can't. For a lot of reasons. Not the least of which is that I'm still a member of Rogue Squadron, and they'll be in the same battle."

"As you say, asked and answered. But I have a more important request."

"Get to it, then."

Kyp straightened and clasped his hands loosely together. His features took on an unusual gravity. Behind him, in the middle distance, a flock of avians with quicksilver wings rose toward the sky. A moment later, when the mutter of thunder that had startled the flock reached her ears, Kyp was still hesitating.

"I'd like you to be my apprentice."

"You're kidding."

"Not in the slightest. You've interrupted your Jedi training. I think you should take it up again. I think you will bring something very special to the order."

"Yeah? And why wouldn't I go back to Aunt Mara, then?"

"Because she's unavailable. Besides, you don't agree with her. You have much more in common with me."

"In a Sarlacc's belly."

"Whatever. But you know it's true." He paused. "You're trying too hard, and maybe it was too early for me to ask. I like you, Jaina, and I value what you are and what you could be. Keep it in mind. I'll leave you to the peace you sought." He turned to go.

He was almost out of sight when she leaned forward and called out to him.

"Wait."

He turned slowly.

"I . . . uh, I'll think about it. Probably not for long, but yeah, I'll think about it."

"Good," he replied. "That makes me happy."

"Yeah, well, don't get too happy," she said.

She didn't watch him go. Instead she turned her face out to the vista.

I'm blushing! She berated herself. *How ridiculous.*

But she didn't feel *merely* ridiculous. She felt . . .

No. Forget it.

So she turned her thoughts outward, to space above, to her brothers and her parents, wondering how they were, what they were doing, hoping they were well.

And to the coming battle.

TWENTY-SEVEN

"Chalk up another one for the *Princess of Blood*," Han said, lifting a mug of something the bartender had called Corellian ale—and which was certainly anything but. "That's what? Our fifth cargo?"

"Losing count already, Dad?" Jacen asked, sipping his own dubious concoction.

Around them, the cantina was color and sound, motion and emotion. Even without consciously using the Force, Jacen felt mired in swirling drunkenness, avarice, secret sorrows, and public appetites.

Harsh Tatooine light lanced into the cantina through two windows facing out into the street. Above, various species mingled on a second-story balcony that circumscribed the round central room. In the center of the dusty floor of yellowish tiles, a Dressellian slung drinks from within a circular, red-topped counter.

Near Han and Jacen, ten bovine Gran clad in matching umber jumpsuits clustered together around a table too small for them. They whispered in their sonorous tongue, casting occasional three-eyed glances at two rodentlike Chadra-Fan squinting across another table at a Dug and arguing in loud tones over a hand of sabacc.

"You aren't going all meditative Jedi on me again, are you?" his father asked, with that little quirk in his mouth.

"No," Jacen answered solemnly. "I'm all pirate. I pillage; therefore I am."

"That's the spirit." Han cocked an eyebrow quizzically. "Really? No lectures for the old man?"

"None at all. It's not like we're keeping what we take. It's being put to good use."

Han sighed. Jacen thought it sounded a little mournful. "Yeah," he said. "That's true. Look, son, I've been thinking—after this war is over, we're going to have bills to pay. The senate has had most of my assets seized, and who knows if we'll ever see them again." He put his elbows on the table and steepled his fingers. "So—"

"Dad! No!" Jacen said. "If we're aiding the resistance, that's one thing. But if we keep more than operating expenses, we really *are* pirates."

"Right, sure, but just a *little* off the top wouldn't make much of a difference, would it? In the long run?"

Jacen stared, horrified at his father's sincere gaze—until the elder Solo winked, and he got it.

"You were having me on."

"Just checking, kid. Making sure you really were still my son Jacen."

"I am that—whoever he is, that's me."

Han looked down at the table. "Yeah. And . . . uh, whoever he is, I'm, uh, very proud of him."

"Thanks, Dad," Jacen said. He wanted, suddenly, to give his father a hug, but the newest cantina at Mos Eisley spaceport probably wasn't the best place to do that.

"Anyway," Han said. His gaze shifted about uncomfortably, then needled out someplace past Jacen. "There we go," he said. "The rest of our dinner party."

Jacen didn't turn. One thing he'd learned around his father—if there were only two of you in a place like this, it was best if you weren't both looking in the same direction.

"Well, well," a profound bass boomed behind them. "Han Solo. And if I make my guess, one of his spawn."

"Hello, Shalo. How are things?"

"I don't believe it. The great Han Solo actually knows my name. I told you I was sending Terya."

"I have a good memory," Han replied. "And Terya is a Rodian." He glanced around the cantina. "Looking good. How's business?"

Shalo finally moved into Jacen's field of vision. He was

human and surprisingly small to have such a deep voice. Bald, craggy-nosed, about his dad's age.

"Not bad," Shalo said. "The Yuuzhan Vong snubbed their flat noses at Tatooine, so we're the center of commerce out here on the Rim, these days."

"Uh-huh. That's pretty convenient for you, I guess. I hear you're giving even Chalmun's some competition."

"Yeah, well, times change. Business changes. My drinks are cheaper."

Han jerked a thumb toward the man. "Last time I saw Shalo here he was a petty thug at the bottom of Durga the Hutt's food chain."

"That was a long time ago."

"Sure. And after that you worked for Hirth, out of Abregado-rae. That went sour, too, didn't it? Then you got involved with the Hutts again, and they sent you here to manage one of their operations. Come to think of it, I guess the occupation of Nal Hutta is the best thing that ever happened to you, huh, Shalo? Now the operation's all yours."

"It ain't been bad. Solo, you got a point? I'm a busy man. I've heard you're back in business, so to speak. You have something you want moved?"

"Not exactly, Shalo. I need a little information."

"So long as you're willing to pay for it."

"Sure," Han said. "Like you said, I'm back in business now." He passed a hundred credits across the table toward Shalo. "Gesture of good faith," he said.

"Okay. What do you want to know?"

"There's a certain shipping concern. I think you know the one I mean—has certain *occupational* interests?"

"I can't say I know what you're talking about. There are lots of shipping firms."

Han leaned forward a little. "But this one—ah, c'mon, Shalo. Who do you sell all your slaves to?"

"Slaves? I'm not in that business, Solo."

"You disappoint me, Shalo."

Shalo smiled and shook his head. "No, you disappoint *me,* Solo. I guess everyone gets old. Now your son pays the price."

Han looked at Jacen in mock surprise. "You're picking up the tab, son?"

"My boss doesn't pay me that well," Jacen replied.

Han looked at Shalo. "I guess now we don't know what *you* mean, Shalo."

"I mean there's no bounty in the galaxy higher than the one on your boy, here, and I'm collecting it." He raised his hand and dropped it.

Nothing happened. Puzzled, he repeated the signal frantically.

A bright green shaft of light suddenly appeared, jutting out of the tabletop. It terminated a centimeter from Shalo's throat.

"Urk," Shalo said.

"Please don't move," Jacen requested sincerely.

"You get 'em all, Karrde?" Han called into the silence that now ruled the cantina. He kept his eyes focused on Shalo.

"Shada has it under control," a cultured voice came back. "We'll be right there. I'd like to make sure all of my people are in position."

Jacen couldn't glance around, but he felt a number of newcomers enter the cantina.

"Take your time," Han called back. "I was just having a chat with my old buddy Shalo."

"You're crazy, Solo," Shalo said.

"Now, is that polite? Listen, Shalo. I can wipe out you and your whole petty operation if I want—or you can cooperate. I . . ." Han smiled and shook a finger. "You know—I *did* know about your employees with the blaster rifles. So did my colleagues. One of them—do you know Shada D'ukal? She can be very disarming."

"D'ukal is here?"

"I love the way you say my name," a woman's voice said from just behind Jacen. She stepped into view.

Shada D'ukal was a strikingly handsome woman in perhaps her late forties with long black hair streaked liberally with pure white. The man next to her was a good match to her with his silver-streaked hair and impeccable goatee.

"Captain Karrde," Han said, standing. "I'm so glad you could make it. Shada, good to see you again. You've both met my son Jacen."

Karrde stroked his goatee and studied the offered seat with mock suspicion. "Oh, well," he said at last. "If I can't trust a scoundrel and a pirate, who can I trust?"

"Hey, I trusted you."

"A good thing, too," Shada said. "Two of the sharpers were assassin droids."

"Shalo, I'm impressed."

The two newcomers sat down. "Hello, Jacen," Shada said. "I'm a little surprised to see you here."

"You're not the only one," Jacen replied.

"It's the Solo blood," Han opined. "It comes with the looks. So how's things with you two?"

"Things are going well enough on our end," Karrde said. "I think I can meet whatever needs you have. But first, I have a little present for you."

"Hey?" Shalo said. "Could you please have your Jedi get that thing away from my throat?"

Han raised both brows skyward. "Oh, you mean *this* Jedi? My eldest son? The one you were going to turn in for the biggest bounty in the galaxy?"

"I wouldn't have actually *done* it," Shalo explained. "I was going to try to extort protection from you, that's all."

"Yeah, right. You're slime, Shalo. You give the Hutts a good name. And now you're going to give *me* something."

"Wh-what?"

"What I *asked* for, you vac-head."

"Oh. The shipping company."

Han nodded. "That's right, the shipping company."

"Berths fifteen through eighteen. It's all I can tell you."

Han leveled a finger. "Shalo . . ."

"Hey, it's not like they have a name and a logo. They just come and pick 'em up."

"The slaves?" Jacen asked. "What do you suppose happens to them?"

"I don't know. I don't ask questions."

"You know where they go," Jacen accused.

"I deny that."

Jacen caught something then, in the Force.

"Hey, Dad?"

"In a minute, son." Han jerked his chin toward Shalo. "Let him deny it," he said. "It doesn't matter. We'll check out your story, Shalo, and if it turns out you're lying to us—"

"Yeah, yeah, you'll be back, I know."

"No. Oh, no. You're going *with* us. But for right now, I'm going to turn you over to this nice lady here, okay? I need to talk to my other friends."

Shalo turned to see the "nice" lady and blanched when his eyes fell on a towering, white-furred, heavily fanged humanoid. The beast hissed and spat something that might have been a language.

"No, H'sishi," Karrde said gently, apparently answering. "You can't eat him. Yet."

Shalo's face was nearly as white as the Togorian's fur as she led him off.

"Now," Han said, "what's my surprise?"

Karrde smiled. "I had my slicer look into those ships you've been hitting, the ones coming out of Kuat. It took some doing, even for him. The funds for the ships were washed so many times they ought to be random molecules by now. But in the end, it looks like the allocation can be traced back to the office of Kuat Photonics."

"Kuat Photonics?" Jacen asked.

"A privately held corporation." Karrde handed Han a data card. "A list of the owners."

"Would Viqi Shesh be on that list?" Jacen asked.

Karrde studied him. "You expect her to be?"

"We had some trouble with her at Duro," Jacen said. "It was just a feeling."

"Sorry to disappoint you," Karrde said. "Not under that name."

"Maybe you could check the names?" Jacen asked. "See if they're legitimate?"

Karrde laughed sardonically and looked at Han. "Is that the Solo sense of humor, or is he serious?"

"I take that to mean no," Jacen said dryly.

"What he means is," Han explained, "it would take a long time—a *very* long time—and probably get us nowhere. Meanwhile, we'd be there instead of here, where we can actually stop the ships. If Shesh is behind this, we'll hurt her more out here than on Coruscant."

"The old man has it right," Karrde said. "The tracks my slicer found are faint to begin with. They could be easily erased."

"But we might find proof," Jacen argued. "Real proof."

"Maybe," Han said. "Maybe at berths fifteen through eighteen."

"Are we going to hit them?" Shada asked.

"Hit them? No. They'll be easier pickings in space."

"Shouldn't we at least check them out?" Jacen said.

Shada nodded. "I'll have look."

Jacen straightened. "Mind if I tag along?"

"I do," Han said. "Or didn't you get that part about the bounty on your head?"

"Jealous, Solo?" Karrde asked Han.

"How's that?"

"Well, your son is pulling down easily three times what you were ever worth."

"Inflation. In Imperial credits it works out about the same. And don't distract me—Jacen goes back to the *Falcon*."

"Oh, no. You aren't my captain on the ground, Dad."

"Where did you pick up *that* nonsense?" Han growled.

"You wanted me to help with this business—I'm helping. If Shada will have me, I'm going with her."

"A lady never minds the escort of a handsome gentleman. Especially one with Jedi powers."

Han threw up his hands. "Fine. I give up. But you can make that two handsome escorts, because I'm not letting my son out of my sight. I know this slagheap too well."

Karrde's eyes narrowed, suddenly, and he drew his blaster. "This is, for the moment, an academic conversation, my friends."

"Why?" Jacen asked.

His answer came as blasterfire.

TWENTY-EIGHT

Nom Anor, alone in his sleeping chamber, prodded the gablith masquer that gave him the appearance of a Givin, and it peeled off. A little more reluctantly, he coaxed the communication gnullith-villip hybrid from his throat. The sleeping quarters were always pressurized, no matter what, so he ought to be safe. Even Givin could not stand exposure to hard vacuum indefinitely.

Posing as a Givin had more unique challenges than any role he had assumed before, their language not the least. When speaking to one another, they expressed themselves in phrases that more resembled calculus than grammar, though of course the two had much in common. Even with the tizowyrm to translate for him, Nom Anor still often tripped on the language. For that reason alone, many of the Givin knew who and what he really was—it was only with the help of his local agents that he managed to remain disguised to the rest.

This he disliked. Long experience had taught him that Nom Anor could count only on Nom Anor. And if he were discovered by the wrong people . . .

He put the gnullith-villip back on. Why take chances?

Noting the time on the ridiculously complex Givin chronometer, he withdrew the box that housed his villip and prepared to stroke it to life. He found it already pulsing for attention, and in a few moments he regarded a facsimile of Commander Qurang Lah's face.

"The *Stalking Moon* is in this system?" Nom Anor asked the warrior.

Qurang Lah's features twisted into a glare.

"Your perfect plan develops clots of blood," he growled.

"You mean the Rodian Jedi?" Nom Anor asked. "Our agents on Eriadu have dealt with him."

"Yes? And the infidel ship that jumped into the midst of my fleet?"

Nom Anor didn't blink. He couldn't. It had rapidly become clear, working with Qurang Lah, that the warrior harbored a deep resentment toward him. This was not unexpected, but it was not trivial, either. Nom Anor had no warriors loyal to him; he had to rely on Qurang Lah to place his fleet and troops when the time came. There would come a moment when Nom Anor was truly vulnerable, and at that moment, Qurang Lah might hold the key to his survival.

That, to Nom Anor's mind, was the only flaw in his plan, whatever trouble Qurang Lah thought he foresaw.

"Your fleet is on a major shipping route," the executor said. "The possibility of a chance meeting with an infidel ship was known to us. I'm certain you destroyed it."

"Almost instantly. But now we have lost contact with the *Stalking Moon*."

That was an unpleasant surprise. "Perhaps they've merely experienced disorientation after leaving hyperspace. The cloaking shadow it wears is prone to complications."

"And perhaps your 'allies' were waiting for her and *destroyed* her as she reverted."

"That's not possible," Nom Anor said. Or was it? The Givin were stranger even than the humans, much harder to read. Had he miscalculated so badly?

No. This was a minor setback, nothing more. The plan was good.

"We have some hours, yet," Nom Anor assured the warleader. "I shall discover what troubles, if any, the *Stalking Moon* is having and report promptly back to you."

"See you do," Qurang Lah snapped.

Non Anor's expression soured as the villip calmed. If something had happened to the advance ship, could he still convince his Givin allies to perform their act of sabotage?

Of course he could.

But he smelled Jedi in this somewhere, beyond the lone Rodian who had identified Nom Anor as Yuuzhan Vong when visiting Yag'Dhul Station. It had been easy enough to have him tracked and murdered, and his Peace Brigade contacts on Eriadu assured him that the Rodian had never had a chance to communicate to anyone else.

But then the Peace Brigade had been known to lie before, when they thought it made for better groveling, and the Jedi had the power to send thought without words.

Nom Anor sat and composed his ideas carefully. If there were Jedi here, what would they do?

He had to be ready for them when they came. He *would* be. And perhaps, added to the conquest of Yag'Dhul, Givin slaves, and the threat to the source of bacta in the nearby Thyferra system, he would have another jewel or two to hand Tsavong Lah.

TWENTY-NINE

Luke gripped Mara's hand and tried to keep his tears at bay, tried to make his mind still, free of pain, fear, and grief.

"Cut it out, Luke," Mara said. "You're giving me the creeps." Her voice was a dry croak, barely louder than the stridulations of larval tlikist.

Luke took a shuddering breath and tried to smile. "Sorry," he said. "Not one of my better days."

"It's got to be better than mine," Mara said.

Her hand in his felt papery and hot. He gripped it harder, feeling the disease beneath. It was in furious motion, mutating at rates that medical science had once considered impossible. The only still point in her body was that place where their child floated. Somehow, even now, when her skin had gone blotchy and her hair was falling out, when the chain reaction that was fast approaching meltdown raged in her flesh, she still kept their child safe.

"Maybe—maybe it's time to let Cilghal induce labor," he said.

"No." Mara's voice cracked on the word, but it was the loudest noise she had made in days. Her eyelids dropped over her pale orbs. "I told you," she whispered. "I can feel it's wrong. If I do that, we'll both die."

"How can you know that?"

"How can you ask? I *know*. The Force."

"But this is killing you, Mara," he said. The words sounded as if someone else were saying them, like an unknown language.

"No. Really? I would never . . . have . . . guessed."

He felt her fluttering toward unconsciousness again.

"Mara?"

"Still . . . here."

Luke glanced at the sleeping form of Cilghal on a nearby cot. The healer worked night and day, using the Force to slow the progress of the disease. The results were hardly noticeable. Only Mara had ever been able to control it, but her terrific will was too focused now.

"Mara," he said softly. "Mara, you have to let me in."

"I can manage, Luke."

"Mara, my love . . . no games this time. You want to do this your way, and I respect that. Now you have to respect me. That's my child, too—and you, you're the best part of my world. Let me help."

"Selfish," Mara said.

"Yes, maybe," Luke admitted.

"Meant me," Mara corrected. "Help our child."

Luke reached into her, then, into the maelstrom. He felt how truly feeble her life was. Her pain racked his body; her dark fevers gnawed at the fringes of his brain. It was overwhelming, and the most profound sensation of hopelessness he had ever felt shuddered through him.

No. I'm not here to take her pain. I'm here to add my strength. He knew it, but it felt beyond his control. There was too much, coming too fast. He pushed at it, forcing it away, trying to flow a river of vigor into her, but she wasn't there to receive it, to use it as only her body knew how. He was at the mercy of her disease as much as she was.

He heard a noise and realized he had cried out.

Calm. I am calm. I bring calm with me, and tranquility. I am tranquility.

But the sickness laughed at him. Starbursts of images and sensation exploded everywhere. He saw Palpatine's leering face, saw his own, younger features through a veneer of hatred. He was a child on the street, cold and lonely.

All negative feelings, all fears and hates and greeds. Only the worst of Mara was here, where the disease had its way.

He fought the despair, but it pooled in his feet and slowly, slowly filled him up, sap climbing inside a tree.

He knew in that moment he could never save her. Mara was lost to him, forever.

THIRTY

"Oh, Sithspawn," Corran swore.

"The Givin are in league with the Yuuzhan Vong?" Anakin said doubtfully. "The Givin build *ships*. The Yuuzhan Vong *hate* technology."

"Yeah, but their real estate isn't all that promising," Corran said. "Maybe they figure that if they cooperate, the Yuuzhan Vong won't bother 'em much."

"I don't understand," Tahiri said.

"Yag'Dhul has three moons," Corran explained. "The tidal forces are so strong that at times and places the atmosphere itself gets rolled back, exposing the surface to space. The Givin actually evolved to survive in vacuum for short periods of time. What would the Yuuzhan Vong want with a planet like that? The location, yes, because it's strategic for purposes of their conquest. But they probably wouldn't settle the planet."

"I think they're waiting for a reply," Anakin noticed, gesturing at the tiny image of the Givin.

"Tahiri, tell them in Yuuzhan Vong we're having some minor difficulties, and we'll be back in touch in a moment."

"Sure." She said something into the comm unit. Then she looked back up. "They want to know why we aren't using the villip. They have theirs with them."

"Brother. This gets worse and worse." Corran stared at the row of villips. One was pulsing slightly. Was that it?

"Tell them it's none of their business," he said. "Make it sound like we're mad about something. No—wait. Tell them—tell them the sound of them speaking the Yuuzhan Vong language so poorly is insulting to us. Tell them we'll speak the infidel language, Basic, and that the commander is about to speak to them."

Tahiri did so, after which Corran took up the comm unit. Keeping the visual off, he tried to remember the cadence of Shedao Shai's accented Basic, back when he had dueled with the man.

Here goes nothing. He started to open his mouth, then quickly changed his mind. "Tahiri, Anakin—give me a name. A credible name."

"Hul," Anakin said. "It's a warrior's name."

Corran nodded, flicked the comm back on. "This is Commander Hul Lah," he snarled. "Is everything prepared?"

"All is in readiness, Commander," the Givin answered. "The defense grid will fail in 15.08357462 standard hours. You may bring your fleet from hyperspace then."

Corran blinked. Something about that . . .

"There is no suspicion, then?" he asked.

"None. The Body Calculus is completely unaware of our vector with you. The failure of the defense grid and long-range communications will seem accidental. Only when you take possession of our system will the truth be known. We have hidden our factors carefully."

"Commendable. We will verify this, of course, but you may rest assured that if you are telling the truth, the glorious Yuuzhan Vong will honor our agreement with you."

"Thank you, Commander."

"Hul Lah, out."

Corran pursed his lips thoughtfully. "Those guys aren't the government," he said. "Or at least, not all of it. It's just some faction."

"Let's contact the real government, then," Anakin suggested. "Let 'em know what's going on before their defense grid fails."

"That's a problem," Corran said. "We don't know anything about who we just dealt with. It might be the local chapter of the Peace Brigade, or it might be a faction in the Body Calculus. Either way, the odds of contacting the wrong people are way too high."

"Maybe we should just get out of here and alert the New Republic military, then," Anakin suggested.

"It's an idea, but it will lose us Yag'Dhul. There's no way to get a fleet here in fifteen hours. If the Givin had their own fleet scrambled, there might be a chance of holding the Yuuzhan Vong off long enough for a New Republic force to arrive, assuming the Senatorial Oversight Committee releases them to do so. No, we've got to get the attention of the right people, before the defense grid goes down."

"Umm," Anakin mused.

"What? Out with it."

"Well, I have an idea, but you aren't going to like it."

"I'll take anything I can get right now. Talk."

"We attack Yag'Dhul before the grid goes down. Whoever comes out to stop us, that's who we want to talk to."

"I don't like it," Corran said.

"I didn't think you would."

"I don't like it, but it will work. Anakin, calculate a jump that will put us as close as safely possible to Yag'Dhul—or better, the space station. Tahiri, can you figure out how to lay it in?"

"Sure. All I have to do is see it in my mind."

"Let's get cracking, then. I want to do this before common sense sets in."

They reverted two hundred kilometers from the orbit of Yag'Dhul's farthest moon, a short distance from the military station that Booster Terrik had once commanded. Corran had fond memories of the place, because it reminded him of his early days with Mirax. It felt strange to be attacking it.

The station, which had been Rogue Squadron's base during the Bacta War, was now part of an expanding Givin military-industrial complex. Unhappy with having their system being used as a battleground by foreign forces, they had demanded and been ceded the station a few years after the truce with the Imperial Remnant. It now protected their shipyard.

"I'll bet they'll notice us," Anakin remarked, watching

through a transparency that Tahiri had opened up to give them a view of surrounding space. "Hyperwave dampeners or not, rocks this size don't just appear out of nowhere."

"Unless the grid is already down," Corran replied.

"Oh, I don't think it is," Tahiri said. "Or at least, that would be a big coincidence. Twenty somethings are on their way."

"Twenty what?" Corran asked. "Starfighters, corvettes, capital ships?"

"I don't know," Tahiri replied. "I don't know a lot about ships."

"Well, how big are they?"

Tahiri didn't answer for a few moments. "I'm not sure how to read that," she said. "They're sort of clusters of spindly rods. Three engines each. Real fast."

"Starfighters? How far away?"

"Fifteen phons and closing."

"What's a phon?" Anakin asked.

"I don't have any idea," Tahiri replied. "They just implanted the language, not conversion charts."

"Bring her around, thirty degrees starboard," Corran said.

"Starboard?"

"To your right! Your right hand!"

"Don't get touchy, Captain Horn," Tahiri said. "I'm doing my best, but I'm not a pilot! And I can't tell if I've turned fifteen degrees or not."

A dull thud echoed through the ship. Tahiri gasped.

"What was that?"

"That hurt!" Tahiri said. "Something just blew up part of us."

"Are they hailing?"

"I—" She broke off again as several more impacts rocked the ship. The last one was very loud.

"That broke the skin," Tahiri said. "We're losing air. I'm going to shoot back."

"Don't shoot back," Corran said. "Do you hear me, Tahiri? Do not shoot back."

"The ship wants to," she wailed. "It's hurt."

"Don't let it."

"They're hailing," Anakin said. "Standard frequency."

"Answer, then, fast. Tahiri—turn away from those ships and run as fast as you can."

"They're a lot faster."

"Well, use the dovin basal to absorb their shots, if you can figure out how to do that."

"The ship is doing it already," she replied. "It's just not very good at it."

"Not a warship," Corran muttered. "Anakin?"

"Something's wrong with the transponder," Anakin said.

"Well, fix it!"

"I'm trying."

"Tahiri, can you take evasive action?"

"I'm evading as much as I can. But this is a really big ship, and they're really fast."

Another staggered series of blasts ripped along the side of the *Stalking Moon*, and now Corran could see their antagonists, flitting about in admirably swift craft. He didn't recognize the design, but the Givin were known for quality if not quantity in shipbuilding. A good quarter of the racing yachts in the galaxy were built in the Yag'Dhul system.

Corran glanced at Anakin. The boy—no, the young man—was working calmly at the cobbled-together communications device, one lock of hair falling in his face. He didn't look like someone who feared death in the slightest. Probably he didn't. Taan, the Shamed One, was as impassive and quiet as she had been since her conversation with the distant Yuuzhan Vong commander.

The ship jerked and shuddered, and somewhere near, Corran heard the sound of air screaming out into vacuum. A smell like vaporized rancor swirled into the chamber.

"We're dying," Tahiri said dully. "Let me shoot back. Please."

"No."

"Got it!" Anakin said.

"Give me that!" Corran grunted. "Make sure the visual is on, this time."

The Givin who appeared on the tiny screen didn't waste

any time with polite mathematical greetings. "Yuuzhan Vong ship, this is Dodecian Illiet. You will stand down and surrender or be destroyed."

"Dodecian Illiet," Corran replied, "this is the captain of the Yuuzhan Vong vessel *Stalking Moon*. We surrender."

The Givin didn't blink—he couldn't—nor could his exoskeletal face register any other emotion Corran recognized. But he still gave the impression of vast surprise.

"You are not Yuuzhan Vong," the Givin said.

"It's a long story," Corran replied. "We did not intend to attack you, only to get your attention."

The Givin paused, listening to someone off-screen, then turned his empty eyes back to Corran.

"Our attention you have, Corran Horn. Prepare to be boarded."

THIRTY-ONE

"Shalo was smarter than I thought," Han snarled as he drew his blaster. "He had backup for his backup."

Jacen tried to pick apart the action. Karrde had placed people strategically within the cantina—both in the balcony and on the floor—to disarm Shalo's men, and then set up a cordon outside. That outer ring of protection was now under attack by a third group. A very numerous third group. Karrde's people outside were already down or had retreated within the building.

"Help me with this table," Han said.

Jacen grabbed one edge and helped his father drag it to one of the windows. Several bolts seared by their heads as they barricaded the opening, bringing with them plumes of ubiquitous Tatooine dust.

"This planet always was bad luck," the elder Solo grumbled. He lifted his blaster and fired a couple of shots over the edge of the table without looking.

"Good thing you have the situation completely in control," Jacen remarked.

"Hey, no plan is perfect. Did you get a look at who they were?"

"Peace Brigade, I'm pretty sure."

"I'm getting tired of those guys. Shalo set us up."

"Imagine that, one of your old buddies setting you up."

"Well, there's been worse," Han said. "You ready?"

"Ready for what?"

"I give it about six seconds before they start lobbing grenades in here. We do *not* want to stay here. On three?"

"Three it is."

"Karrde?" Han sang out.

"Busy," Karrde replied, firing through the doorway.

"Give us some cover."

"You got it."

"One, two—hey!"

On two Jacen ignited his lightsaber and bounded to his feet. He was immediately forced to deflect three blaster bolts in quick succession. His father popped up behind him, nailing one of his assailants with the first shot.

"That building across the street," Han said. "Go!"

Fire rained down from the rooftops as they raced across the sunburned ground. Jacen deflected the more accurate shots while his father blazed away. Jacen slashed open the closed door of the trinket shop directly across the street, and the two men ducked in. A veritable barrage shredded the door frame behind them.

"They can throw grenades in here, too, you know," Jacen remarked.

"Sure, but now we have 'em in a crossfire."

"My door!" shrieked the Toydarian merchant behind them.

"Sorry about that," Jacen told the merchant.

"Sorry? Sorry won't—eep!"

A concussion grenade bounced through the door, and the Toydarian flitted for cover.

"See?" Jacen said. He gave the bomb a telekinetic swat that sent it back out the door.

His father seemed to have predicted the trend. What was left of one of the cantina windows blew out with a billow of flame.

"Karrde!" Han shouted, firing wildly at anything moving on the street.

Han was interrupted by the Gamorrean who came blazing around the edge of the door. The being's close-range fire missed, but the butt of his weapon didn't when he dealt the Corellian an uppercut that lifted him off his feet. His father's body knocked Jacen off-balance, and before he could recover, the Gamorrean, squealing and snorking, wrapped his thick limbs around Jacen's body and slammed him into the nearest wall. The Jedi's lightsaber went flying.

Stunned, Jacen boxed his attacker's ears, but if there was any effect, he didn't notice it. He tried to focus on retrieving his lightsaber, but in all of the confusion he couldn't be sure where it was.

He felt the Gamorrean, though, felt his heart hammering in his chest. He could easily reach out in the Force and . . .

No. He would die first.

And that was coming up fast, because he couldn't breathe. He beat feebly at his attacker's head as outside the twin suns seemed to be going out.

Then he was falling, slumping against the wall and covered with ceramic statuettes of Sand People and Jawas falling from the shelves above. The Gamorrean had turned back to Han, who had just clobbered it over the head with some sort of larger stone statue. His father's eyes were widening in surprise at the fact that the Gamorrean hadn't collapsed, but only gotten madder.

"You're a thickheaded son-of—" he began, but then had to duck a powerful right.

"Look," Han said, dancing back from the Gamorrean, "you don't know who you're dealing with. If you just go ahead and surrender, I'll go easy on you." He looked suddenly past his enraged opponent to Jacen.

"That's right, Jacen. Use your lightsaber!"

Jacen was still trying to find his feet, much less his lightsaber. *What's he talking about?*

The Gamorrean turned, though, and Han hit him over the head again, holding the statue in both hands. This time it broke. The Gamorrean, looking puzzled, collapsed.

"You okay, son?" Han asked.

"Yeah. A little woozy."

Han hefted the half of the statue that remained in his hands, then proffered it to Jacen. "Here, a little souvenir."

Jacen turned it over in his hands and uttered a small laugh. Very small, because it hurt his stressed—perhaps cracked—ribs.

Han, meanwhile, was rooting for his blaster, one eye on the door.

"I should have known that old smuggler wouldn't sit still to be blown up," Han muttered.

Looking past his father, through the dust and smoke, Jacen could make out a pair of figures on the rooftop—Karrde and Shada. They had just finished the snipers there and were now using the high ground to clear the streets. The job was almost done.

About fifteen minutes later, Jacen and Han met outside with Karrde and his people. By some minor miracle, none of them had been killed, though several would be in bacta tanks for a while.

"I'd say Tatooine isn't going to be one of your safe houses," Karrde remarked. "I also suggest we get off this ball of rock before the Brigade convinces the spaceport to impound our ships, if they haven't already."

"I wouldn't worry too much about that," Han said. "The Darklighter family still has some clout, and we're at their dock. Still, it would probably be best to get out of here." He shook his head in disgust. "What a waste of time this was. Now that they know we're here, we'll never find out anything about their operation."

"Oh, I wouldn't say that," Jacen said.

"What do you mean?"

"We've still got Shalo, right?"

"Unless H'sishi was ambushed on the way back to my ship."

"I got something from him, something he was hiding. I tried to tell you."

"What?"

"I'm not sure. But he was expecting something. Something big."

Shalo was a good deal more subdued during his second interview, and much more cooperative.

"A convoy is stopping off here," he admitted. "Day after tomorrow. On its way to Ylesia."

"What's the cargo?"

"Oh, you know, cargo."

"No, I don't know," Han said. "Please, enlighten me."

"Spice, weapons, maybe a few, uh . . . a few slaves."

"Sacrifices for the Yuuzhan Vong, you mean. You're quite a piece of work, Shalo."

"I'm a businessman, Solo."

"Sure. Tell you what, once we're done with this convoy, we'll drop you off someplace where you can get nice and cozy with your new business partners. Nal Hutta, maybe."

Tsavong Lah regarded the strange creature before him. It looked like some shaper's fevered joke, with its short, ruffled feathers, spindly limbs, and cochlear antennae. It blinked luminous, slanted eyes at him and stretched its ridiculously wide mouth to speak.

"Greetings, Warmaster," it said.

The warmaster considered her for another moment before deigning to answer.

"The deception-sect priests and the haar vhinic tell me you have yielded much useful information concerning the infidels. You seem to have been most observant during your captivity."

"I would do more," Vergere said boldly.

"So I am also told. You have information regarding the ship that has been harassing our infidel lackeys." As he spoke, a pair of villips projected an image of a matte-black ship, lens-shaped, with odd projections.

"I know the ship," Vergere replied.

"And why would you speak this only to me?" the warmaster rumbled.

"Because," Vergere said, "I think the identity of this ship would be of particular interest to you, and because I believe you would prefer to have this information discreetly."

"You presume much about me, familiar-of-a-dead-priestess."

"If I presume incorrectly, I am prepared to embrace punishment."

Tsavong Lah gave her an abbreviated nod of approval.

"Waste no more of my time," he said. "Say what you came to say."

"I know the ship because it is the one from which I escaped," Vergere told him. "It is the *Millennium Falcon,* and its captain is named Han Solo."

"Solo?" Tsavong Lah felt a surge of rage at the name, and his vua'sa foot-claws clacked restlessly against the deck.

"Solo," the creature said. "Father of Anakin Solo, who caused the late distress at Yavin Four, or so I'm told. Father of *Jacen* Solo."

Tsavong Lah reared to his full height. "You were correct, familiar. This *is* of interest."

"Find the *Millennium Falcon,* Warmaster, and you will find Jacen Solo. I believe he is aboard her. If he is not, once you have his father, he will not be long in arriving. It is the way these infidels think."

"Indeed," the warmaster replied, a vast satisfaction rising in his blood. "And the *Jeedai* are most particularly weak in that respect."

THIRTY-TWO

Admiral Traest Kre'fey seated himself in the tactical chamber room of his flagship, the *Ralroost*. His violet eyes were sternly set, but Jaina nevertheless felt a brief but tangible impulse to stroke his fur, which was whiter than the wastes of Hoth. Contrasted with his black flight suit, it positively shone.

It was a feeling that evaporated immediately when the dignified Bothan began to speak.

"I've reviewed all of the information presented me," he said. "General Antilles, is there anything missing? Any other little surprises?"

"No, Admiral," Wedge replied. He glanced aside at Kyp. "Not that I know of."

"Well," the admiral mused. "Who would have guessed that the Yuuzhan Vong were another pack of superweapon aficionados. I thought we were done with that when we were done with the Empire."

"Apparently not," Gavin Darklighter said dryly. "I share General Antilles's distrust of Kyp Durron, but—"

"*This* I'm getting tired of." Kyp grunted and stood. "If you will excuse me, I'll go destroy it myself—with my lightsaber if I have to. This isn't worth the bother."

"Oh, Kyp, sit down and let Colonel Darklighter finish," Jaina snapped.

"Yes, why don't you do that?" Admiral Kre'fey said dryly. "And in the meantime, why don't you credit me with the brains to sort things out for myself, without the benefit of your posturing? Believe it or not, Master Durron, I can sympathize with you to a certain extent. Like yourself, I've found it more productive to fight the Yuuzhan Vong in my own way, without bureaucratic shackles. It has made me quite as unpopular as you are."

Kyp dropped his head fractionally. "Your pardon, Admiral. I'm an admirer of yours; I'll make no secret of that. If I could have found you, I would have proposed alliance long ago. But about one thing you are mistaken. While the New Republic may have little use for either of us, you are still better liked in most quarters, as present company demonstrates."

"Well, son," the admiral said, "I suspect that in great measure that is a burrow you've buried yourself in. Don't expect anyone else to dig you out."

Kyp merely nodded and returned to his seat.

"Admiral," Gavin said, "may I continue?"

"Please."

"I was saying that Durron and his Dozen-or-so went to what must have been desperate lengths to get this information. You remember, Admiral—we were there *before* the Yuuzhan Vong buttoned down the system as tightly as they could. What he got out of that is the clearest proof we're going to get that the Yuuzhan Vong are priming something very dangerous indeed. It's my opinion that we ought to do something about it."

"General Antilles?"

Wedge clicked his tongue. "I agree," he said.

"As do I," the Bothan concurred. "You see, Master Durron, what another moment of silence would have cost you? Nothing at all."

"I understand, Admiral. My apologies."

"Very well. I've been looking for a good target to take out, and this will do nicely. The nice thing about super-weapons is that they are usually big, and this one seems no exception. I should think we will be able to hit it."

"Hitting it will be the very least of our worries," Gavin said. "From what Kyp said, the Yuuzhan Vong have pretty much mapped all the safe hyperspace jumps near the weapon and have them effectively blockaded. Since Sernpidal is also one of their major shipyards, and since the Yuuzhan Vong haven't started any new offensives lately, we can expect a pretty warm reception."

"I'm sure that's so, Colonel Darklighter. However, I have information that perhaps you do not. Sernpidal is one of the several parts of occupied territory that has been of interest to me in the past months. I've watched it—from somewhat a greater distance and with a good deal more caution than Master Durron, but I have watched traffic to and from it. In the last week, a large number of ships have departed Sernpidal. I was unable to determine where they were bound."

"A new push?"

"Possibly they are merely reinforcing their borders with new ships," Kre'fey said. "Or perhaps they are preparing the way for this superweapon of theirs. I should hasten to point out that nothing nearly the size of the weapon has been observed leaving, so it is presumably still there."

"But maybe not for long, if the Yuuzhan Vong are about to renew their Coreward advance," Wedge mused. "Maybe the whole peace-for-Jedi deal was an even greater ruse than we suspected—not just to get rid of the Jedi, but to give them the time to finish growing that thing."

"We're agreed, then, the sooner we act the better," Kre'fey said.

"Sure," Gavin said. "But getting *in*—"

"I have an idea about that," the Bothan said. "If I may."

"Of course, Admiral."

"When Colonel Darklighter and I last entered the Sernpidal system, we were able to evade the Yuuzhan Vong defenses because when Sernpidal was destroyed, the redistribution of the planet's mass opened up new hyperspace entry and exit points in the resulting asteroid field. The Yuuzhan Vong couldn't risk jumping into the asteroids after us because they hadn't calculated the positions of those points. By now, they must have accounted for all such locations. Master Durron, what enabled you to enter the system after those shifts were accounted for by the Yuuzhan Vong?"

"The Force, Admiral, is a powerful ally. I've had some experience with using the Force to read gravitic fields. We awaited our opportunity, and we got it when they tested their weapon. The size of the gravitic anomaly shifted the gravitic profile of the asteroid belt enough for us to risk a jump."

"And we may now assume they have countered that possibility."

"It seems likely."

"What I propose, then, is this. I know where I can procure an old *Immobilizer*-class Interdictor. She's not much to look at. She was hulled in battle and left adrift, where she was largely gutted by scavengers. Two of her mass-shadow generators are intact, however. I'd begun restoring her, but it's a dauntingly expensive task. She's got no life support, half her armor is gone, and she lacks engines. However, I could fit her with a hyperdrive and shields quite easily. We could then tow her where we need her."

"Oh, I like this," Wedge said, rubbing his hands together. "It's crazy—begging the Admiral's pardon—but—"

"You're going too fast for me, Admiral, General," Jaina said.

"We jump the Interdictor into one of the blockaded coordinates," Kre'fey explained. "No crew, with rudimentary automation. The instant it arrives, its shields go up and the gravity wells go on."

"And it lasts about half a minute, if that," Jaina replied.

"Which is plenty," Wedge explained. "The gravitic fluctuation will shift things enough to move the safe entry point. We should be able to calculate where to. Two seconds after we send the Interdictor, we start piling starfighters through. Hopefully the difference in location will be great enough that we'll miss whatever nasty surprise they have waiting for the next ship to attempt a deep-space jump."

"Exactly, General," Kre'fey said.

"That'll work," Gavin said. "At least, I think it will."

"It will get us in where they aren't expecting us," Wedge said. "More, we can't ask for."

"It will be enough," Kyp said excitedly. "It will do." The rogue Jedi stood. "I am prepared to place my people under your command, Admiral, for the duration of this mission. I'm sure you'll put us to good use."

"I'm sure I will, Master Durron. We should begin coordinating now. In two days' time, the Yuuzhan Vong will discover that someone in this galaxy still has teeth. Strong, sharp ones. Let's reconvene in three hours' time to discuss the specifics. For now we're adjourned."

THIRTY-THREE

"I really wasn't designed for this," C-3PO said, for something to the power of a hundredth time. "The waiting is really the worst of all."

Han checked the console, saw nothing again, laced his hands behind his head, and leaned back. "That so, Goldenrod," he said. "Personally, I think it would be worse to have our hull blown open by proton torpedoes."

"Well, yes," C-3PO admitted, "that might be—"

"Or lose power and life support and drift forever in the cold dark of space."

"Oh, how horribly vivid. That certainly doesn't appeal—"

"Or worse yet, what if we're captured? They'll give us to the Yuuzhan Vong for sacrifice. Just think what the Vong would do to *you*, Threepio. They wouldn't do it fast, not given how much they hate droids. They'd do it slow, keep you aware for every second of the terrible—"

"Captain Solo?" C-3PO interrupted plaintively.

"Yeah, Threepio?"

"I've reconsidered. Waiting isn't so bad after all. Why, for all I care, we can wait forever."

"Don't let him get to you," Leia said from the copilot's chair, her eyes closed. "Everything will be fine."

"Oh, thank you, Princess," C-3PO said. "It *is* nice to be reassured, from time to time."

"You're welcome, Threepio. It's the least I can do, considering we'll probably be vaporized in this next exchange. I'd rather you went comfortably."

"Vaporized?" C-3PO gasped. "I—I believe I'll see if

Master Jacen needs some help with—with whatever he's doing."

"You do that, Goldenrod," Han replied. C-3PO clanked off, making worried noises.

"That was mean, Princess," Han remarked. "I like this side of you."

"I was trying to sleep."

"Well, *I* can be quiet."

"No, that's okay. I'm awake, now. What's going on?"

"Not much. Karrde showed up a while back, with four ships. Should be more than enough, given the size of the convoy Shalo described."

"When do we expect them?"

"Any time now. An hour from now or ten."

She nodded and sat up sleepily. "You got my son a little banged up down on Tatooine," she accused.

"Well, he's not the first and he won't be the last to take a bruise or two on that forsaken planet." His cocky tone relented a little. "I didn't think I was putting him in real danger."

"No, I understand," Leia said softly. "Being a mother creeps up on me sometimes. It's a shame it didn't creep up on me more often when they were little."

Han took her hand. "We didn't have the luxury to be perfect parents," he told her. "Whatever that is. The thing is—they turned out okay."

"I know. That isn't the issue. Han, they won't ever be little again. It's over. Even Anakin is almost grown, and I missed so much of it. And Jaina—"

"There's nothing wrong with Jaina she won't outgrow."

Leia shook her head. "I don't know. She can be so bitter sometimes, and I really can't blame her. For all of her toughness, she's also fragile." She patted him on the shoulder. "Like someone else I know."

"Ah, carbon sluff," Han said. "I ain't breakable. You ought to know that by now."

"We're all breakable, Han."

"Huh."

"But I digress. I don't think it was a bad thing to take Jacen down there. You two seem . . . better for it."

Han shrugged. "What you said—about missing so much time when they were little. Maybe I, uh . . . feel a little of that. Maybe I sort of like having him around, working with him. When he's not going all moral on me, at least." He patted her on the shoulder. "Like someone else I know."

Leia shot him a fond smile disguised as a sarcastic smirk. She quickly let it relax. "Have you told *him* that, Han?"

"Nah. It might go to his head. I figure with that Force stuff he sort of knows anyway."

"You above all people should know that sometimes those most sensitive to the Force can be the most clueless about people."

"Well, you have a good point there," Han replied. "Sometimes I think—"

Suddenly ships began reverting to sublight.

"Heavy freighters," Han said, sitting up. "There's our convoy. Get ready, *Princess of Blood*."

"You've always known how to flatter a girl, Han."

"That escort," Han muttered after a little more study. "Two capital ships. I don't like it."

"You don't think a heavy escort makes sense?" Leia asked. "They know we've been intercepting their shipping. They don't know about Karrde. Two capital ships and the starfighters they can carry would be plenty to deal with the *Falcon*."

Han shot her a hurt look.

"Hey, I'm just being realistic," Leia said.

"So am I. You're right. Two capital ships seems like overkill."

"Let's back off, then," Leia said. "There'll be other convoys."

"The freighters. Scan them."

"Ouch," Leia said. "Nasty thought."

"Yeah. I have lots of those."

"Well, they look clean. I don't think they're hiding a fleet.

There is an odd radiation signature from that last cargo pod. Looks incidental, though."

"What's going on up there?" Jacen called from the laser turret.

"Your father is having second thoughts," Leia called back down.

"Huh? I'm just being a little cautious," Han said.

Leia frowned. "Seriously, Han. If you have misgivings, let's get out of here."

Han sighed. "I just don't like it. Maybe I'm getting old." He leaned forward and tapped on the comm unit. He and Karrde had a limited-range tight-beam system set up that was unlikely to attract attention.

Karrde appeared a few seconds later.

"Doesn't smell good, does it?" Karrde said.

"You read my mind. It's like they're trying *too* hard to look well prepared. If that makes any sense."

"It doesn't, but I know what you mean. Maybe we should let this one pass."

"Han—" Leia interrupted.

"Just a minute," he said. "Okay, Karrde, maybe—"

"*Han!*"

"Hello!" Karrde said. "Well, at least we haven't completely lost it. Yet."

"Huh?" Han stared where Leia's finger was pointed. A Yuuzhan Vong frigate had just dropped out of hyperspace, along with an interdictor like the one they had run into earlier. As he watched, coralskippers were already detaching.

"Well," Han remarked. "Things get more interesting all the time, don't they?"

THIRTY-FOUR

"Looks like it was built for children," Tahiri commented as the three humans were escorted through Yag'Dhul Station.

"Rebels built it during the war with the Empire," Corran informed her. "I've heard it said that they made it small to give stormtroopers a hard time if they ever invaded."

"What's all that on the walls?" Every square centimeter seemed to be covered with fractal patterns and notation in some sort of script. Now and then something seemed vaguely familiar, more often not.

"Givin decorative motifs, I'd guess. Rogue Squadron sure didn't paint this stuff."

"Looks mathematical," Anakin said.

The four Givin guards, who might have cleared things up, either didn't speak Basic or had no desire to talk. Soon enough, however, they were gently pressed into the largest room Anakin had seen thus far. It still wasn't very big, but tactical stations and a bank of holoprojectors with various views of the surrounding space made it somehow comforting after the Yuuzhan Vong ship. This was tech he was familiar with.

The Givin waiting for them was not as comforting. His exoskeleton had been painted with many of the same symbols Anakin had seen on the walls. Anakin guessed him to be the same one who had demanded their surrender.

"Dodecian Illiet, I presume," Corran said.

The Givin rose. He spoke in oddly clattering Basic. It sounded somehow more mechanical than it had over the comm.

"I am he," he replied.

"Have I had the pleasure? You seem to know my name."

"We made it our business to know who was in our space. You were among those waging war against Ysanne Isard from here."

"We had the permission of your government when we were here."

"Another spring tide cubed, another government," the Givin replied. "I did not recognize you myself—soft-bodied creatures are difficult for us to distinguish between, except at the rudest scale. Our computer system compared voice and facial records and estimated your identity at a 98.2 percent probability. I confess, I was uncomfortable with such a high margin of error, but when I addressed you your reaction seemed to confirm the probability. Are you indeed he?"

"I am Corran Horn, yes," Corran replied. "Any grievance you have against Rogue Squadron is mine. It does not adhere to these two."

"The only grievance against you is entering our system and apparently beginning an attack run on our station. That, however, is a rather severe charge."

"I apologize again," Corran said. "I hope it was noted that we did not fire on you, even when fired upon."

"It is so noted and numerated. I shall be happy to hear you balance the equation before us."

Anakin couldn't feel a trace of deception in the dodecian, and he was trying. That seemed a good sign, at least.

"I think these are the right guys, Corran."

Corran shot him a cautioning glance, but addressed his next sentence to the Givin.

"We've come to warn you, Dodecian Illiet, that a Yuu-zhan Vong fleet is preparing an invasion of this system. The ship we were piloting was a scout ship we captured. It was designed to come here unnoticed and contact some faction of your own people. This faction has apparently arranged for your defensive grid to collapse shortly, to facilitate the invasion."

The Givin absorbed this silently, though Anakin got the impression he was also listening to someone else, commenting on what Corran was saying.

"Explain in detail," the Givin finally said.

"There's not much time—"

"You leave us with too many unknown factors. More detail."

Corran laid it all out, starting from their jump into the Yuuzhan Vong fleet, ending with their surrender. The Givin asked few questions, seeming content mostly to listen. When Corran was finished, the dodecian rapped his fingers against the table. They sounded almost as if they were made of ceramic.

"You are Jedi," he said at last. "The Yuuzhan Vong seek you."

"Yes."

"Perhaps you tell me this only to save yourselves."

"If you don't believe me, double-check your defensive grid."

"It is being done," the Givin replied.

"You'll have proof enough when the Yuuzhan Vong show up," Tahiri blurted.

"True," the Givin said, apparently not caring which of the humans it was speaking to. "But even so, what use have they for our system?"

"We think they wish to stage a strike at Thyferra, and perhaps then the Core."

"Ah. So they have the same use for our system that you did, Corran Horn."

"Umm . . . yes."

"And perhaps as little impact on our way of life."

"You think so? And yet these Givin I first spoke to were collaborating with the Yuuzhan Vong for some reason."

"Yes, that is of concern," the dodecian said. "Our politics are . . . complex, and needn't concern you. However, though such collusion with the Yuuzhan Vong might have been designed to upset the Coalition of Factors, there is still no reason to suspect that the Yuuzhan Vong actually pose a threat to our species."

"But," Anakin said, "they pose a threat to this station, and to your shipyards. The Yuuzhan Vong hate all technology."

"Then perhaps we will hide the ships until they have gone."

"Consider," Corran said. "Since I was last here you've taken pains to integrate with the economy of the New Republic. You crewed this station, as I understand it, so your system would no longer be a battleground for foreign powers. You expanded your shipbuilding capabilities. Will you risk sacrificing that?"

"We certainly risk it if we engage the Yuuzhan Vong in combat. From what we understand, they can be quite formidable."

Tahiri abruptly interrupted. "If you don't fight them, you'll be slaves," she said. Her voice had gone low and weird, as it had when she thought she was a Yuuzhan Vong, back on Yavin 4.

"There is no reason to suspect that."

Tahiri laughed. "I was a Yuuzhan Vong captive. I've seen what they do. Don't you get it? Right, they may be staging a strike on Thyferra from here. They may have ten reasons for being here. But I can tell you what one of them is."

"Explain," the Givin said.

"You. Your species. The Yuuzhan Vong make every tool they use from living things. They believe life was given to them by the gods to shape. You think they aren't interested in ready-made sentient beings who can survive in vacuum? The things they could make with you! They'll blow up this station and blast your ships and cities into ions. Then they'll take you and give you to their shapers. That will be the end of your complicated politics, Dodecian."

"Emperor's bones, she's right," Anakin said.

The Givin was silent for a half minute. "You really think this is true?" he asked at last.

"If you let them in without a fight, you've got no chance," Tahiri assured him.

The Givin paused again, and again Anakin got the impression he was listening to some far-off voice.

"It is confirmed," the dodecian said. "The defensive grid has been sabotaged. Fortunately, it can be remedied."

"Does that mean you'll fight?" Corran asked.

"I do not know. That decision does not lie with me. But we have taken into account all you said."

"Let me contact Coruscant," Corran said. "I can try to get more ships here, though I can't promise anything."

"I will enter that request," the Givin said.

"Another thing. What have you done with the Yuuzhan Vong we took captive?"

"They are being questioned, to verify or dispute your story."

"But Taan—" Tahiri began.

"Will be fine," Corran said, cutting her off.

"The prisoner will not be harmed," the dodecian confirmed. "Now. If you will accompany my aide, you will be provided with quarters and repast fit for your species."

"Are we prisoners?"

"I would prefer you did not think of yourselves as such. You have been allowed to retain your Jedi weapons. But I would also prefer you remain confined to the quarters we assign you. The station is delicate. Were there to be violence of any sort, it could well suffer explosive decompression."

"I understand," Corran said stiffly.

Anakin did, too. It was a polite threat. Try to escape— suck vacuum. That was an equation it didn't take a Givin to understand.

"That is well," the dodecian replied.

Anakin caught something, then, from the dodecian, something so tangible it almost formed words. If it were put into words, it would go something like, *We have Jedi to bargain with. That also is a factor.*

THIRTY-FIVE

Though his mind and mood sped through an astonishing array of transmogrifications, the perfect-grutchin idea some-how remained fixed firmly in the faltering brain of Master Kae Kwaad. Nen Yim and all of her apprentices were pulled even from standard maintenance and set to the task of weeding through grutchin germ plasm in search of "perfect" structures, incubating larvae and discarding those that dis-played any slight deviation of form or color that Kae Kwaad detected. During this time, the master became ever more of-fensive, at one point demanding that Nen Yim work in a state of complete undress. At another, he forced Suung to get down on hands and knees and act as his stool, a task fit only for a slave.

Nen Yim considered the inventory of toxins that one might accidentally ingest or accidents that might befall one in the business of shaping. Her plans began to form themselves.

Ona Shai gripped her hands into fists behind her back and shot Nen Yim a deep glare.

"The capillaries of the maw luur are belching half-digested wastes in the Toohi sector," the prefect complained. "Many Shamed Ones have sickened from the fumes and cannot perform their tasks to full efficiency. A few have died."

"That is regrettable," Nen Yim replied. "However, I am uncertain why you discuss it with me."

"Because your master will not admit me or speak to me via villip," the prefect snarled.

"I am his adept. I can do nothing without his leave."

"When you were the head shaper, things got done," Ona Shai said. "Since this master has arrived, conditions have only gotten worse."

"If I agreed with that, I wouldn't be at liberty to say so," Nen Yim told her.

"I don't ask you to gossip with me as if we were a pair of slaves," the prefect snapped. "I'm asking you to intercede, to place my words in the master's ear. To release *you*, at least—or even Suung Aruh—to tend to this problem with the maw luur."

"I will certainly mention your concern."

Ona Shai nodded tersely and turned her back on Nen Yim. She could see the ridged muscles of the prefect's back, as tight as the tendon-rigging of a landing sail. She also noticed that she had recently sacrificed three fingers to the gods.

"This ship must last another year, at least, Adept. If it does, some of our habitants may survive to be offloaded onto a new worldship."

"I will speak to the master," Nen Yim replied. "I can do no more."

Ona Shai dropped her head. "Disgraced we may be, Nen Yim," she murmured. "But the gods cannot intend for us to die out here, so near the glory of conquest, able to see our new worlds but not to ever touch them. Death is nothing, but the ignominy . . ."

"I shall speak to him," Nen Yim repeated.

Her path back to the shapers' quarters was a crowded one. The Toohi sector was not the only dispossessed part of the ship; the Phuur arm had become unlivably cold toward the tip. With nowhere else to go, Shamed Ones and slave refugees crowded the halls. Their rustle of conversation quieted where she passed, but behind her it began again, with an angrier note to it. Once or twice, she was certain she heard the word *Jeedai*, and felt a quiver run along her spine.

Tsavong Lah had killed nearly every slave and Shamed One who had been at Yavin 4, yet still somehow the legend of the *Jeedai* had spread even here.

Was this yet another thing she would take the blame for?

She found Kae Kwaad where she often did, clucking over the grutchin larvae, his useless hands drawn up onto his knees. He did not even glance at Nen Yim as she entered.

"I've spoken to the prefect," she said. "Ona Shai urges that we turn at least some attention to the functioning of the ship. Toohi sector is now experiencing noxious fumes."

"That's interesting," Kae Kwaad said thoughtfully. He pointed at one of the larvae, indistinguishable from the rest. "This one will have to be destroyed. Its color is off."

"Indeed," Nen Yim said.

"See to it," Kae Kwaad said. "I must rest now."

"You should speak to the prefect," Nen Yim pressed.

"What would a master shaper have to say to the likes of her?" Kwaad sneered. "You have spoken to her. It is enough."

Nen Yim watched him go, then despondently turned her attention to the larva. She was carrying it toward the orifice, to feed it to the maw luur, when she suddenly understood that she was no longer considering the death of Kae Kwaad, but was committed to it. Not only that, but she had chosen the method of his death.

Grutchins were used to breach the hulls of infidel ships and contained an acid powerful enough to eat through metal alloys. A single bite from one would be sufficient to end the life of her miserable master.

So instead of destroying the pupa, she worked her own shaping on it. She removed neurons from the tiny brain of the grutchin, and with the protocol of Qah imprinted a simple series of reflexes keyed to the scent signature of Kae Kwaad, which she obtained from skin cells shed in his quarters. As a failsafe, she made the triggering of the reflexes dependent on a word she herself would utter.

When the grutchins had matured, she would speak the name Mezhan, and Kae Kwaad would die, her new master slain symbolically by her old.

When she was finished, Nen Yim slept, and for the first time since Kae Kwaad had come aboard the *Baanu Miir,* her sleep was peaceful and dreamless.

*   *   *

A ket later, the pupae began to molt.

When he saw the small but adult beasts, Kae Kwaad began to shriek incoherently and sank into what appeared to be a deep depression. Calmly, Nen Yim bore his ranting and whims, waiting until the end of the day, when the initiates had been dismissed.

"I want all of the initiates killed," Kae Kwaad said quietly. "They are plotting against me."

"I am sure they are not," Nen Yim told him. "They have worked diligently. It is only their training that is at fault, and I am to blame for that."

Why was she trying to reason with him, even now? She eyed the grutchins, an arm's length away. She and Kae Kwaad were alone now. She need only speak the word.

She had taken the breath for it when he spoke again.

"No, Nen Tsup, seductive Nen Tsup, perhaps I am to blame. It is my hands, you see. They are not as steady as once they were." She noticed that he spoke with a sort of glacial slowness, and his eyes had a peculiar look to them. "My thoughts are drops of blood," he whispered. "Pooling at my feet. My every thought is a sacrifice."

Nen Yim hesitated. It was as if, far in the distance, she saw a door dilate open, with strange light beyond. She kept the word in her throat and moved nearer, near enough that their bodies were touching. His glazed eyes met hers, and she endured as he caressed her with those stunted hands.

How is it you were not sacrificed to the gods, Kae Kwaad? she wondered. *How is it you live to shame your domain and species?*

For an instant his eyes changed, sparked, as if he knew what she was thinking, as if they were in on the same joke and only pretending to act their roles.

It was gone very quickly.

"Master," she asked, "why is it you do not replace your hands?"

He looked down at them. "My hands. Yes, they should be replaced. But it is denied me. Only another master can access that protocol, and none will do it. They are all against me, you know."

"I know," she whispered, leaning her mouth near his ear. "And yet," she said, lowering her voice even farther, "you *are* a master. You could do it yourself."

"I haven't the hands to make hands."

"But *I* do, Master Kae Kwaad. I do."

"And you would have to learn the protocol," Kae Kwaad replied. "And you are forbidden it."

Now her lips were touching his ear. "I might do much that is forbidden, Master," she said.

He turned to look at her. She saw nothing behind his eyes, now, and it suddenly occurred to her that he might be worse than mad; he might be using one of the ancient, forbidden toxins that induced stupor. Such a self-indulgence . . . *would be exactly like this being,* she finished.

He hit her, then, a backhand that shattered one of her teeth and sent her spinning to the ground with the taste of blood in her mouth. She lay there, expecting him to follow the attack, ready to speak the word. This was her last chance; if she hesitated longer, he would have the grutchins destroyed because he thought them somehow imperfect.

He kept looking at her with that same vague expression, as if he had never moved his hand, never touched her.

"Fetch the Qang qahsa villip," he said quietly. "I shall give you access. You shall shape me new hands. The perfect grutchin will not escape us."

A trembling, diminutive triumph quivered in Nen Yim's breast. She nurtured it with caution. Much could still go wrong, but she had found a chance, at least, to save the worldship. Though she wished she could bathe her body in acid to erase Kae Kwaad's touch, he had agreed to give her the thing she needed most.

As she went to find the villip, she promised herself that whatever else happened, whether she saved the ship or failed, whether she was executed for heresy or not, this wretched, pathetic thing whose touch had polluted her would die before she did.

PART FOUR

REBIRTH

THIRTY-SIX

Realspace greeted Jaina with an actinic flare and a shock wave that bucked her X-wing violently. She flinched instinctively, closing her eyes against the glare, the memory of impaired sight still imprinted on her nervous system.

Have some sense, girl, she thought, forcing them back open. *You're in enemy territory!*

And about to smack into an asteroid, the same one the coralskipper Gavin Darklighter had just drilled had exploded against. She yawed hard to port to avoid an identical fate.

"Heads up, Sticks," Gavin's voice crackled in her ear. "Rogues, form up. We've got plenty of company on the way."

"As ordered, Lead," Jaina said, weaving her way through the irregular bits of shattered planet that stretched as far as her sensors could make out.

Starboard and above her horizon, the yellow star at the heart of the system was half eclipsed by the outstretched arms of the distant gravitic weapon. Nearer and dead ahead was the more immediate target of Rogue Squadron—the cordon where Kre'fey's stripped-down Interdictor had sacrificed itself. Its shields had already collapsed, and its mass-shadow generators were random ions; but an expanding cloud of superheated gas marked clearly where it had been. Wedge had added one thing to the Bothan admiral's already good idea—he'd rigged the reactor to go supercritical when the shields reached 12 percent.

There was no knowing how many Yuuzhan Vong ships it had taken with it. However many it had, there were plenty left coming through the drifting planetary shards, and they were the business of Rogue Squadron. Calculations had shown that the temporary shift in gravitic stresses in the system would give them a very small window of opportunity—not big enough to risk Kre'fey's larger ships on, but plenty big enough to sneak the Rogues and Kyp's Dozen through. The Dozen were headed straight for the weapon to scout out whatever forces were guarding the thing. The Rogues' job was to clean out the Yuuzhan Vong nested around the stable hyperspace entry, which was the only way in for the *Ralroost*—and for the Yuuzhan Vong forces at the perimeter of the system. The Rogues had to gain control of it.

"I make something big at the target coordinates," Gavin informed them. "Might be a ship; might be a battle station. Designate Wampa. One-flight, we'll take that. Two and Three, keep those skips off us."

Jaina double-clicked to acknowledge, and peeled off with Three-flight, lining up off Twelve's port wing. She felt a brief sadness, remembering that she had once flown wing for Anni Capstan, back when she first joined the squadron. Anni had died at the Battle of Ithor. Twelve was a stranger, a Duros named Lensi. Jaina had met him in the final briefing.

"Turn two hundred thirty-one to twenty-three," Alinn Varth, leader of Jaina's flight, ordered. "We'll take that bunch."

Jaina acknowledged and did as ordered, seeing as she did so a flight of eight skips in pyramid formation, coming in fast. The space around was relatively clear of asteroids now, reflecting the low mass-density that made the area safe for jumping into and out of. Jaina felt exposed.

"Only two to one," Lensi said. "Not bad."

"Don't get cocky, Twelve," Varth snapped. "This is just the first course."

"As ordered," Twelve responded. Then he rolled, firing splinter shots at extreme range. Jaina stayed with him, but held her fire until they were closer in. The skips began firing all at once; Jaina jinked the stick and cut a hard corkscrew turn. The plasma globs went by without even singing. Now behind the skip that had fired at her, she got a targeting lock on it and began spraying it with underpowered shots. The skip produced a void and began absorbing them, but in doing so lost some of its mobility and taxed its power. When the shots started getting through, Jaina switched to a full-power quad burst.

To her surprise, the anomaly gobbled that, too.

Sithspawn. "Watch it, Twelve," Jaina said. "They're on to the bait and switch. They're letting the splinter shots in early."

"Acknowledged. Let me dust that off your tail, Eleven."

A quick glance showed Jaina she had indeed picked up an admirer. She yanked her stick back, hard, but the skip followed. Her shield took a hit.

Twelve dropped in behind the skip while Jaina put her X-wing through a series of convoluted maneuvers. The skip hung right in there.

"Grounded for too long," she muttered.

Then the tagalong flared and tumbled, trailing plasma.

"Thanks, Twelve," she said.

"Not a problem."

Jaina dropped and rolled down to target another coral-skipper. Like the previous one, this one started letting the splinters through early.

"We can learn, too," she said under her breath. She kept up the spray, fired quad lasers, then fired again on full power. Three glowing holes appeared in the skip. It continued along its vector, no longer firing. Jaina wasted no more time on it, but found Twelve and dropped back to his port.

"Let's get that stray," Twelve said.

"Negative, Twelve," Nine's voice crackled. "Re-form. We can't get them all, and we can't afford to let them separate us for any length of time."

"As ordered," Twelve acknowledged.

Four more skips were coming in. *If we don't get this door open soon*, Jaina thought, *we'll never get it open at all.*

A sudden harsh crackle quivered Jaina's eardrums. Then

Gavin's voice. "I've lost Three," he said. "Deuce, take my back. I'm going in."

Jaina gritted her teeth, wishing she could see what was going on at Wampa, but she had her own problems. Three skips came up on her port. She hated to do it, but after a little splinter fire she switched to proton torpedoes. A void appeared to catch the deadly missile, and as programmed the warhead detonated before it could be sucked in. The bonus was that the explosion was near enough to take out all three Yuuzhan Vong fighters.

That's right, boys. Keep coming like that.

Then it occurred to her they were probably encouraging her to waste the torps. After all, they were never going to take out that monster down in the shipwomb with lasers.

But of course, they couldn't take it out at all if they died here. One thing at a time.

The *Falcon* bounced on the expanding plume of vaporized coral her lasers had just coaxed out of the interdictor. Han's view of the massive ship broadened, and also allowed the fifteen or so coralskippers on his tail a shot at the *Falcon* without danger of hitting their mother ship. Cursing, Han dived low again and quickly encountered the major problem with that, one he had never encountered while using similar tactics against Imperial Star Destroyers.

The Yuuzhan Vong ship opened a void. If Han's reflexes had been a single twitch slower, they would have smacked right into it, and he didn't want to find out what that would do. He hit the repulsors and bounced again, intentionally this time, hurling the *Millennium Falcon* into a tight arc that quickly became a circle. The skips followed—in time for half of them to run into a new explosion, this one from a concussion missile.

"That's better," he grunted.

"We're doomed," C-3PO noted.

"Lock it down. We've seen a lot worse than this."

"Might I point out—"

"No."

The quad lasers were pounding steadily, Jacen and Leia doing their part. A gratifying number of skips had already succumbed to his family's efforts, but they weren't the problem. The big ships were the problem, especially the Interdictor.

Only the *Falcon* had a shot at it. Karrde's ships were fighting for their lives against the two Peace Brigade vessels and the Yuuzhan Vong frigate analog.

"Han Solo," he muttered, "suckered into the most obvious pirate trap imaginable. I'll never live it down."

"I'll add that to the list of other things you'll never live down," his wife's voice said over the open intercom.

"Yeah, well, you'd better hope I *do* live this one down, sweetheart."

"Dad?" Jacen said. "Did I ever mention this whole pirate thing was a bad idea?"

"Why no, son, you—Wow!"

His exclamation was comment on the jet of plasma the interdictor had just released. Its diameter was greater than that of the *Falcon*, spearing up like a solar flare. He avoided it by a turn so sharp that even with the inertial compensators at 98 percent, the g's sent blood rushing from his head.

Behind him, he heard a loud clattering sound as C-3PO smacked into a bulkhead. Again.

"Okay," Han muttered. "Time for a change in strategy. Threepio, quit fooling around and haul yourself up here. I need you."

The golden droid's head peeped around the corner. "You need *me*? I would be happy to be of service, Captain Solo, but I don't see how a protocol droid could be of help. Unless you want me to transmit our surrender, which I must say seems like a bad idea, even when you consider the alternative."

"That's not it," Han said, weaving through a cloud of fresh skips. "Earlier, we noticed an odd radiation signature from one of those cargo pods. Figure out what it is."

"Sir, I really don't see—"

"It's that or you start working on your surrender speech."

C-3PO moved to the sensor readout. "I'm quite sure I don't know what I'm doing. Nevertheless, I hasten to be of service. Oh, why didn't I stay with Master Luke?"

THIRTY-SEVEN

"This is driving me crazy," Tahiri fussed. "Not knowing. For all we can tell, the Yuuzhan Vong have already taken over the entire system."

"I think there are a few hundred Jedi proverbs about patience," Corran said. "Though they all elude me just this moment. Try to follow Anakin's example." He paused. "I can't believe I just said that."

Anakin hardly paid attention to his companions. He was mostly beyond the plain, boxy room they were "guests" in, riding the Force out through the reaches of the Yag'Dhul system. He brushed the intricate, mathematical beauty of the tides of the planet and its three moons, felt the straining of Yag'Dhul's atmosphere toward space. He heard the whispering of millions of Givin minds in the corridors of their hermetically sealed cities. He touched a billion shards of stone and ice that had never cohered into planets, biding their time until the sun finally caught them in its fiery noose.

And he felt *them*, the Yuuzhan Vong. Not in the Force exactly, but through the telepathic lambent incorporated in his lightsaber. The feeling was akin to a faint, staticky comm signal—but it was unmistakable.

"They're here," he said.

"Who?" Corran asked.

"The Yuuzhan Vong. They're in the system. I can't tell anything else, nothing about how many or how—" He choked off as something new, strong, and terrible struck him in the Force. He gasped, and tears welled in his eyes, spilling down his cheeks.

"What?" Tahiri said. "What's wrong?"

"Mara," Anakin managed. "Don't you feel it? Aunt Mara is dying. And Uncle Luke . . ." He sprang up from his cross-legged position. "We have to get out of here. Now." He drew his lightsaber.

"Anakin, we can't," Corran said. "The dodecian wasn't kidding when he threatened to decompress the station. The Givin can survive in vacuum, remember?"

"We have to do something," Anakin said hotly.

"Anakin, dying on Yag'Dhul Station won't help Mara. We have to keep our heads."

"I won't just sit here and wait for them to come for us. We can't leave it up to the Givin to decide whether we live or die."

"I say we escape," Tahiri said. "All we need is another ship."

"As long as you're wishing for the unlikely," Corran said, "why not at least wish for vac suits first. That way we would at least stand a chance of reaching the imaginary ship we're going to steal."

"You used this place as a base once," Anakin reminded him. "Don't you know where they would keep vac suits?"

"Well, I've considered that, of course, but I don't see any reason the Givin would still have those around. Or that they would be in the same place they were twenty years ago."

"We could use the Force, make one of the guards take us to them," Tahiri said.

"Absolutely not," Corran said with a frown. "You're not going to the dark side on my watch. Do it on Luke's."

"What, then?" Anakin asked.

"Consider also that the odds this room is being monitored are extraordinarily high," Corran said.

"Since when did a Corellian ever care about odds?" Anakin muttered.

"Fine. No odds. They *are* listening to us. Count on it."

Anakin knotted his fingers in frustration. "Then I hope they hear me when I point out how ridiculous this is. We came here to warn them, and this is how they repay us?"

"Anakin, look at it from their point of view. We came

here in a Yuuzhan Vong vessel and acted as if we were going to attack their station. Now we claim a huge fleet is on the way to conquer their planet, and further we accuse them of having at least one faction collaborating with the Yuuzhan Vong. It would be hard for me to swallow."

"Well, they have their proof by now."

"There is that," Corran admitted. "You can't tell how close the Yuuzhan Vong are?"

Anakin shook his head. "No. It's not like that."

As if on cue, a deep tremor ran through the station.

"But if I had to guess," Anakin went on, "I would say they were really, really close."

"Right," Corran said. "We have to get out of here."

"Haven't we just been saying that?" Tahiri complained.

"The difference is, now *I'm* saying it," Corran replied. Unhitching his lightsaber, he went to the door.

It wasn't locked, and there were no guards outside.

"Interesting," Corran said, as the station trembled again.

Struck by a sudden suspicion, Anakin reached out in the Force once more, this time narrowing his focus to the station itself. To his relief, his suspicions were not confirmed. The Givin hadn't abandoned the station and them with it.

In fact, at that moment, two Givin carrying blaster rifles entered through the hatch at the end of the hallway.

"Jedi," one said, in clipped Basic. "You will come with us."

"We can take them," Anakin said, very low.

"Probably," Corran acknowledged. "But we aren't going to. Not yet, anyway." He smiled at the Givin. "Lead on," he said.

They passed several more Givin in the hallways, all in a rush, none seeming inclined to notice them. When they reached the command center they found it in a flurry of activity and eerily silent. The viewscreen depicted several large Yuuzhan Vong ships firing globs of plasma.

Dodecian Illiet glanced up at them as they entered.

"It would appear you were correct," he said tightly. "Congratulations."

"It would have been nice to hear that a few hours ago," Corran said.

"No doubt. You three will want vacuum suits. When the Yuuzhan Vong board, we will empty the station of air."

"Aren't you fighting back?"

"We are, but this station has limited firepower. Our shields will not hold much longer, and our fleet is assembling to protect Yag'Dhul. We can expect no help from them. The Yuuzhan Vong force is indeed quite formidable. I expect we have very little chance of victory."

"Don't be so hopelessly optimistic," Corran said.

"Perhaps I misphrased, somehow," the Givin said. "I did not mean to imply optimism on my part."

"I was being sarcastic," Corran said. "Never mind. Where are the vac suits?"

The dodecian gestured at another Givin. "In the old storage lockers at what you may remember as designated ring one-C of the docking area. My subordinate will take you to them in case your memory fails. I regret your position in all of this. I regret further that an attempt was made to bargain with your lives."

"They didn't bite?"

"On the contrary," Illiet said. "I reached a settlement with them. They promised to spare our station if you were turned over to them."

"Then why . . . ?"

"I did not believe their promise," the dodecian said. "Go. There is a small ship at docking port twelve, berth thirteen, if it has not already been destroyed. I grant you use of it. The rest of our vessels were used to evacuate unnecessary personnel before the attack commenced."

"Thank you," Corran said.

"Thank you for your efforts on our behalf," the Givin replied. He looked back at the tactical readouts. "You should hurry." He didn't look back up.

THIRTY-EIGHT

Nen Yim bathed in a sea of knowledge. Protocols glistened and swirled in the depths, revealing the foundations and endless permutations of life in intimate and splendid detail. Beneath the cognition hood her expression was one of awe and wonder, and for the moment she was the eager, maze-eyed young woman she had been only a few cycles before, loving and in love with the art of shaping, with knowledge itself.

She had long since passed the fifth cortex into the realm of the masters. Here were the living designs for the dovin basals, the thought-seeds of yorik coral, and yes, the protocols governing the creation of master hands. These she passed, navigating the shoals and depths with her questions, steering with her determination.

She found the germ of the worldships and swam through its thick skin. Parts she had seen before, of course—the outline of the recham forteps, the pattern of the osmotic membranes of the endocrine cloisters—but these were only components. She had never seen the profound logic of the vessels laid out holistically. Her grasp of the organic relationships between organs had been based mostly on deduction, and she found it instructive to observe where she had been right and where wrong.

At the center of it, at the outer limits of the seventh and final cortex, she found, at last, the brain. Its making uncoiled for her. She opened herself in turn and absorbed the information, let it fill the places her vaa-tumor had burned a place for. Strands of amino acid sequences flowed by like twisting rivers, pooling in her enhanced memory. Neurons divided, splitting and scrolling into million-branched ganglia that further folded into cortical coils. Subsystems nomic and autonomic explained themselves as the developmental process continued, finally settling into stability, maintenance, reorganization, stasis.

And in the end, when it had all come and gone, when her own brain strained at the rush of knowing, she understood at last.

The ship was doomed. The rikyam would die, and there was no protocol to stop it. Wonder dimmed in her, and the vast living library around her suddenly stood revealed to her not so much as a storehouse, but as a prison. Or a mausoleum, for though it created the impression of being alive, everything in the great Qang qahsa was desiccated, sterile, unchanging. There was nothing new here. If the protocols truly came from the gods, the gods had not seen fit to add anything to the sum of Yuuzhan Vong knowledge in a thousand years.

But that was impossible. Since the invasion of the infidel galaxy, new protocols had been handed down from the gods to Supreme Overlord Shimrra and thence to the shapers. The gods had been generous, especially in doling out weapons. Where had that knowledge gone?

That thought stirred something in the Qang qahsa, as if it had been waiting for someone to think it. The seventh cortex faded from her consciousness, leaving her adrift in peace and dark, more confused than ever.

There is nothing beyond the seventh cortex, she thought. I have moved to a place the gods have not yet filled.

If there were gods. Mezhan Kwaad had denied them. Perhaps . . .

But even as she renewed her doubt, something changed in the void. Like a light in the distance, or a tunnel opening.

And then she beheld something that could not be there.

An eighth cortex.

With renewed hope she moved toward it.

The membrane resisted her, filling her with pain that etched along her every nerve ending.

This place is forbidden, even to masters, the qahsa told

her. It was the first time it had spoken to her in something resembling language, the first time she felt its ancient sentience notice her. She recoiled. *Who may come here if not master shapers?*

Return, the voice said.

I cannot, she answered. Breathing hard, Nen Yim ignored the voice of the qahsa and pushed forward with her mind, accepting the pain, making it a part of herself. The agony grew, burning away her thought, but she held to her purpose, made it an animal thing that pain only fed and could never quiet.

Her heart beat unevenly, and her breath chopped. She tasted blood. Beyond the cognition hood, she was distantly aware that her body was arching in tendon-ripping spasms.

Open! she shrieked. *Open to me, Nen Yim! Open or kill me!*

And suddenly, like waters parting before swimming hands, the eighth cortex opened.

She looked within, and all hope vanished. She collapsed into her grief and was lost.

Light filtering through her open eyes woke her. A sour smell cloyed in her nostrils, and she realized that it was her own congealed blood. She tried to move and found her body almost paralyzed with pain.

Standing over her, grinning, was Kae Kwaad.

"What did you see, little Nen Tsup?" he asked gently. "Did you see it all? Are you satisfied, now?"

"You knew," she said.

"Of course I knew."

She looked groggily around. They were in the shaper laboratory.

"Mezhan," she said.

Nothing happened, except that Kae Kwaad grinned more broadly. "I suspect that word was supposed to trigger something. The grutchin you altered, perhaps? I took the precaution of destroying it."

Something about Master Kwaad's speech seemed very different. Wrong.

"Clean yourself up, Adept," the master said softly. "We have a journey before us, you and I."

"Where?" she managed to ask, through lips her own teeth must have gnashed and torn.

"Why to see *him*, of course. Supreme Overlord Shimrra. He is waiting for you."

THIRTY-NINE

"Eleven, you've got two on your tail."

"Thanks, Ten," Jaina answered, "but tell me something I don't already know." She jiggled the etheric rudder, watching the trails of superhot gases whip soundlessly past. Off to starboard, she caught a glimpse of the battle at Wampa, but the flashing lasers and long plumes of incandescence didn't tell her anything except that *someone* was still trying to cook the rock.

She took a hit. The starfield tumbled crazily, and her cockpit was suddenly hotter than the midday double suns on Tatooine. Sparks crackled across her console, and every hair on her body stood at attention.

My engines are gone, she thought. *I'm dead.*

Interestingly, the thought did nothing to frighten her. Her only regret was that she wouldn't get to see the big show at the end.

"Captain Solo, the Yuuzhan Vong ship is hailing us," C-3PO shouted excitedly. "They must have a modified villip on board."

"You tell them I'm a little too busy shooting down their ships to answer them," Han replied, flipping the *Millennium Falcon* ninety degrees to squeeze thinwise through a tightly formed wedge of skips.

"They seem quite eager to communicate," C-3PO persisted.

"Well, tell them we'll call back." He'd been forced away from the interdictor by seemingly endless swarms of coral-skippers. Now the monstrous ship was following them, trying to establish the dovin basal equivalent of a tractor lock. In desperation, Han drove for the freighters, figuring he could at least use them as shields.

He hadn't had time to check on Karrde lately, though the barked commands over the open channel told him the information broker was still alive, at least.

He made the largest of the freighters, dodging its insignificant defensive lasers with ease, and once there looped around to face his pursuit, a determined snarl on his face.

He blinked. There was nothing there. Not a single coralskipper had followed him.

"Sir," C-3PO said, "the commander of the Yuuzhan Vong warship *Sunulok* has called his ships back. If we do not answer his hail, he will commence hostilities in sixty seconds."

Han checked his sensor display. The coralskippers had retreated to the vicinity of the interdictor, which was now at a stop relative to the *Falcon.* He estimated he was outside of the *Sunulok*'s tractor range—barely.

He eased back half a klick, to see what would happen. The ships didn't budge, though he noticed Karrde hadn't had any such reprieve. Off to his port, that battle raged on. It looked like Karrde was losing.

"Better let me talk to 'em, Threepio," Han said. "I don't think letting them speak to a droid is going to make them any happier."

"Indubitably, sir."

Keeping a careful eye on both the viewport and sensor displays, Han keyed on the comm.

"*Sunulok,* this is *Princess of Blood.* You ready to surrender, yet?"

The Yuuzhan Vong were not.

"This is Warmaster Tsavong Lah. You waste my time with nonsense," the warmaster grated.

"Hey, you called me. What do you want?"

"You deny me visual, skulking coward," he said. "But it avails you nothing. You are Han Solo, and your vessel is the *Millennium Falcon.*"

Well, I wonder who he bought that information from?

Han thought. *So much for the anonymity of piracy.* "You're callin' *me* a coward?" Han exploded. "You're the scum who had his underlings cut my wife."

"She was not worthy to fight me. Neither was your *Jeedai* son."

"Listen, scars-for-brains, I couldn't care less how you explain your weak knees and yellow belly. We had a good fight going here. You want to finish it, or you want to call it quits? Either way is fine by me."

"Jacen Solo is with you. I want him. Alive. When I have him, you're free to go."

"Oh, sure. I'll just put him in an escape pod and send him over."

"Dad?" Jacen's voice came up from the intrasystem channel. "Dad, maybe it's not a bad idea. If I can get him to duel me . . ."

Han ignored Jacen and turned to C-3PO. "You got a read on that radiation signature yet?"

"Yes, sir, but I'm afraid it's not very helpful. It's very low grade—the cargo pod contains liquid hydrogen enriched with tritium."

"Cheap reactor fuel," Han grumbled. "Industrial waste. I was hoping for a cargo of ion mines, or something."

"I'm sorry, sir," C-3PO said.

"Infidel," Tsavong Lah roared. "There is no sign you are preparing an escape pod."

Han's jaw dropped. "This guy doesn't have any sense of humor at all. He really thinks . . ."

Well, let him think it, then. He opened the channel for a reply. "Just give me a sec, will you? He is my son, after all."

"You have two minutes."

Han chewed his lip, thinking furiously.

Leia called up from below. "Han, couldn't you put a concussion missile in the escape pod?"

"Nah, they'll catch that," he said. "Waste of a missile we'll probably need."

"It's got to be me, Dad," Jacen said. "I'm going back there."

"Oh, no you're not." Han swung on C-3PO. "Jettison

both escape pods. Now. *Right* now. Aim them both at the Vong ship."

"Sir, I'm not sure which—"

"There," Han said, pointing. He cut the engines back in and began creeping back toward the freighter and the Yuuzhan Vong ship it nearly eclipsed. Two escape pods suddenly went tumbling across his field of vision.

"Hopefully, it'll take 'em a few seconds to figure out there's no one on board," Han said. He fired his forward lasers. "Goldenrod, take a deep breath. If this doesn't work . . ."

"But, sir, I don't *breathe*, of course I—oh, no!"

Anakin, Tahiri, and Corran followed the Givin through the cramped corridors of the Yag'Dhul space station, their footing upset by ever-more-violent explosions.

"Do you have any idea where we're going?" Anakin asked Corran.

"The basic layout hasn't changed that much," Corran said. "We're headed down toward the berths."

"Yes. Going to the berths," the Givin said helpfully.

They reached an axis a few moments later and piled into the turbolift, which, at the Givin's command, whirred them down toward the anterior berths. Power flickered, and the lift jarred to a halt, only to start again a moment later when the lights came back on, albeit dimmed.

"I'll be sorry to see this place go," Corran murmured.

Anakin caught a thread of wistfulness in that, something like he got from his father now and then. Almost . . . almost as if Corran wished he were younger again.

Which was ridiculous. The older you got, the more people took you seriously. Anakin was very much sick of being treated like a kid, especially by people who knew less than him.

Mara . . . Mara had treated him more like an adult. And Mara was dying, and there was nothing he could do. He almost wished the turbolift would open to a bunch of Yuuzhan Vong, so he'd at least have someone to . . .

That's not a wish, he realized. *That's the lambent.*

"Guys," he said quietly, "you'd better activate your lightsabers."

At least Corran didn't ask questions, this time. He just did it.

The door whisked open, and there they were. Six Yuuzhan Vong with amphistaffs.

"Me first," Corran said, leaping out, lightsaber blazing. Tahiri was a blur, and Anakin right behind her when he realized he only counted five Yuuzhan Vong warriors outside.

But the lambent said six.

He spun—almost in time. The Givin struck him across the bridge of the nose with a tightly balled fist, propelling him from the turbolift into the enemy-filled room beyond. His body struck Corran in the back of the knees. Surprised, the ex-CorSec Jedi still managed a shoulder roll, though Anakin caught a bright glimpse of pain from him as an amphistaff struck a glancing blow. Head ringing, Anakin brought his radiant weapon up in a high parry he knew he had to make, felt the sharp thwack of a staff across it. Still aware of the danger at his back, he then threw himself to the side. He rolled up to see Tahiri doing a high, Force-aided flip to land in a protective stance beside Corran. Anakin rose and threw the most powerful telekinetic blast he could at the group of Yuuzhan Vong.

If they had been any other species, it would have pasted them to the wall. Instead, two fell and the other three staggered as if in a high wind. Tahiri, unable to affect them at all, found another solution; a stack of cylinders in the corner suddenly flew into the already off-balance warriors, sending the rest of them down. Only the Givin, who had stepped back from the action, kept his feet, and he was laughing, a harsh, very un-Givinlike laugh.

From side corridors, eight more Yuuzhan Vong filed into the far side of the room from where the Jedi now stood against a bulkhead, lightsabers bristling out like quills.

The Givin reached up, touched the side of his nose, and something oozed off, revealing the Yuuzhan Vong beneath.

"A good effort, for infidels," he said, taking an amphistaff proffered by one of the newcomers. He looked squarely at

Anakin. "Not the Solo the warmaster wishes most, though after Yavin Four your worth has risen immeasurably."

"I don't know you," Anakin said.

"No. But your mother and I have met. I am Nom Anor, and you may consider yourself my captive."

"We'd rather not jump to that conclusion, if you don't mind," Corran said.

"The odds are against you."

"You must not know much about Corellians," Corran said.

"Don't be tiresome. You three have earned respect. If you were not infidels, I might even call you warriors."

"I can't say the same for you," Corran said. "What about it, Nom Anor? Me and you, man to man."

"Duel you as you dueled Shedao Shai? And if I win, the rest of you would surrender?"

"No. But you could prove you aren't afraid to face me."

"Sadly, my duty to my people forces me to decline your offer," Nom Anor said.

Tahiri suddenly began shouting in Yuuzhan Vong. The warriors looked at her, first puzzled, then angry. One turned and spat something at Nom Anor.

"What did you say?" Anakin asked.

"The warriors with him don't speak Basic, and they don't have tizowyrms. They didn't realize that Nom Anor was turning down a challenge. I told them you were the slayer of Shedao Shai."

"Good going, Tahiri. Now what?" Corran asked.

"The head warrior of this bunch—Shok Choka—wants to take up the challenge."

"Tell him I accept," Corran said.

"No," Anakin said. "Tell him *I* accept. Tell him I slew many warriors on Yavin Four. Tell him I fought with Vua Rapuung. Tell him I demand my right to combat, or I will carry their names as cowards to the gods."

Nom Anor was shouting himself hoarse in Yuuzhan Vong, but the warriors seemed to have almost forgotten he existed. It would have been funny if the situation hadn't been so deadly.

As Tahiri translated, Anakin stepped out, lightsaber blazing. The other warriors fell back, forming a ring. Shok Choka stepped into it.

FORTY

When Jaina's engines came back on-line and she realized she wasn't going to die—at least not right away—she was, naturally, grateful. When, an instant later, Two and Ten dusted the skips off her tail, she was ecstatic. She proved this by frying the two skips hanging tight on Nine.

But the best part was watching Wampa blow. It came apart in eight symmetrical plates billowing outward on a ball of fire. The wave of charged particles blew over her at lightspeed, nearly—but not quite—generating enough static to drown out Gavin's fierce cry of exultation.

After that, the Rogues cleaned up the remaining skips—without their war coordinator, apparently on Wampa, they weren't that much trouble. What was left of Rogue Squadron re-formed.

They'd lost Three and Four, and Eight was hobbling along on one damaged engine.

"Dozen, how's it going down there?" Gavin asked.

Kyp's voice came through a steady throb of gravitic distortion.

". . . lost five starfighters. Can . . . hurry, or you'll miss the party."

"Hang in there, Dozen, we're on our way."

And then, another beautiful sight. The *Ralroost*, reverting to realspace in all her glory, followed by two corvettes and a heavy cruiser.

"Kre'fey here," the admiral's voice boomed. "Congratulation, Rogues. Excellent work. If you don't mind, we'll clear a path to target prime now."

"Admiral," Gavin replied. "We don't mind at all."

Trailing the *Ralroost,* Jaina turned her nose sunward and dived.

"We're going to hit!" C-3PO squealed.

"That's the general idea, Professor," Han said. The *Falcon* bumped into the side of the freighter module—two quick shots from the forward laser had cut it adrift. Now he engaged the *Millennium Falcon*'s main engines and cranked them to full. The cargo pod lurched into motion, aimed straight at the Yuuzhan Vong Interdictor. The *Falcon* rattled like a metal bearing in a vorth cage, but Han held her nose steady.

"What in blazes is going on up there?" Leia shouted over her the intercom.

"Just keep a lookout for skips. We'll be seeing them pretty quickly."

He was right—it didn't take the *Sunulok* long to figure out he was up to something. Coralskippers came howling in, blazing away at both the cargo pod and the *Falcon.* The trembling of the *Falcon* took on a different tone, now, as plasma bursts ate her shields. But the deciding factor for Han was the sudden bloom along the outbound rim of the freighter module. He turned the *Falcon*'s nose up and *flew.*

"I hope you know what you're doing," Leia said.

"Relax, sweetheart," Han said, though he felt anything but relaxed. His hands had a death grip on the controls as he tried to coax more speed from his great bird.

Then something stopped them, hard. The interdictor had finally gotten its lock. Han blanched and tried the repulsorlifts, glad he hadn't told C-3PO what he was doing so the droid could quote him the odds.

He was stuck. He could only watch now.

The tanker module was still hurtling toward the *Sunulok* too fast for the huge vessel to dodge without a hyperspace jump, but it was coming apart under the steady fire of the smaller ships. Han watched as its liquid contents continued, undeterred, spreading in a bizarre funnel-profile wave toward the Yuuzhan Vong ship.

"I don't understand, sir," said C-3PO, in a hopeless and

subdued voice. "What could liquid hydrogen possibly do against—"

"Watch and learn, Threepio," Han said. Then, under his breath, "At least I hope." He fired three of his six remaining concussion missiles. "Leia, Jacen. Target the Interdictor, full power. Give her everything you've got."

"But the hydrogen won't burn without oxygen," C-3PO said.

"Sure won't," Han replied.

The lasers lanced out just ahead of the missiles. At about the same moment, the *Falcon*'s shields went down and the skips started taking her apart.

And then everything broke loose.

Shok Choka was big, even for a Yuuzhan Vong warrior. Each ear had three large chevrons cut from it, and a mounded scar ran from his chin, sliced through his lips, and continued along the ridge of his skull. He held his amphistaff behind his back, the hand grasping it a little lower than his waist. He locked his amber gaze on Anakin's ice-blue eyes. His knees were bent, and though he was perfectly still, he somehow projected corybantic motion.

Anakin cut his lightsaber off and held it loosely at his side. He began to circle the warrior slowly in a relaxed, almost contemptuous manner. Calm flowed through him. Shok Choka followed him with his predator gaze.

Anakin stopped, smiled faintly, then stepped into the warrior's range.

The Yuuzhan Vong moved almost faster than vision could process, the rigid amphistaff chopping down. Anakin's saber burred on, and he raised it in a wide, high block. Choka, anticipating that, arrested the slash and instead lunged in to spear Anakin in the throat. Anakin retreated, dropped his parry, again low and wide, as if he were defending for two people instead of one. That placed Choka's weapon so far out of line he couldn't make the third parry, but instead had to flip back toward Anakin and Tahiri. His still-live blade, slashing wildly, scored a meter-long cut through the bulkhead that only just missed Corran.

Stamping and howling, Shok Choka came on. Anakin blocked a powerful blow that carried his blade into the bulkhead for a second time in a long, elliptical slash. He ducked a vicious jab that spanged into the wall and rolled forward, past Shok Choka's stamping feet and back out into the center of the room. Even as he stood, the warrior was renewing his attack.

Now, suddenly, Anakin tightened his defense, so that rather than pushing the Yuuzhan Vong's blows as far away from him as he could, they were missing him by centimeters. Still smiling, he fell into the counterrhythm of the dance, the amphistaff whipping and whirling, spearing and slashing.

The warrior suddenly dropped and swept Anakin's feet from under him, something the young Jedi hadn't seen coming at all. He thudded to the floor awkwardly and threw his blade up to catch the inevitable downward blow, but the staff whipped around and cut his shoulder, the deadly poisonous head slapping against the floor centimeters from his arm. Anakin caught the amphistaff with his left hand and with his right, lifting from a prostrate position, drove his weapon through the knee joint of Shok Choka's armor. The warrior grunted and aimed a powerful punch with his left fist toward Anakin's head, but Anakin wasn't there. Releasing the amphistaff, ignoring the cut in his hand grabbing it had caused, he bounded up and was suddenly standing above the warrior, who had overcommitted to the punch. In the split second while Shok Choka decided whether to tumble forward or attempt to regain his balance, Anakin cut his head off.

Before the body could hit the floor, Anakin bounded toward his friends. Corran had already seen the plan, and with a single swipe of his own blade finished cutting the bulge-sided triangle Anakin had begun in the bulkhead with his "wild" parries. The other Yuuzhan Vong, stunned by the death of their war captain, hesitated an instant too long. One got a parting shot at Anakin, the last of the three to duck through the small opening. Several somethings cracked against the metal bulkhead—thud bugs, probably.

Then he was through, turning a corner in the corridor be-hind Tahiri, and they were all running as fast as they could manage. They passed through a pneumatic bulkhead. Ana-kin slashed the controls as it sighed closed. He caught a glimpse of a Yuuzhan Vong face turning the corner, and a second later heard a thud on the other side of the door, then several more. Glancing back over his shoulder as he con-tinued to run, he didn't see it open.

"You did that on purpose!" Corran accused. "I thought at first you were just fighting sloppy."

"We need to find berth thirteen!" Anakin gasped.

"On it," Corran shouted back. "This way."

"How far do we have to go? Because—" Tahiri began to ask.

"Just keep running," Anakin urged.

"—because my ears are popping," she finished.

Anakin realized that his were, too, and that he was a lot more winded than he ought to be.

"Sithspawn," Corran said. "The Givin have opened the station to space. We'll never make it to berth thirteen." He stopped, looked around. "Wait a minute," he said. "Follow me."

He led them down a side corridor, where he paused.

"They've changed the designations," he muttered, "but I think this is it." He keyed a door open.

"We *might* make it to the ship," Anakin shouted, fol-lowing him into the room beyond. It was wall-to-wall storage lockers.

Corran sounded as if he were across a space twice as large when he replied. "No way. We're not even to the docking ring." As he spoke, he began cutting though the locks on the lockers with his lightsaber.

"Check the unlocked ones, you two," Corran ordered. "We're looking for vac suits. This is the sector Illiet told us to go to."

Anakin did, feeling the air grow thinner and colder as he did so. Most were empty. "But what if Illiet was in with Nom Anor?"

"I doubt it. If he was, why such an unwieldy trap? Nom

Anor must have contacted the other Yuuzhan Vong to meet him, to get him off the station. Hah!" He yanked a large vac suit from one of the lockers. "Look at this thing," he said. "It must be twenty years old."

The next locker turned up an airpack, but no suit. Neither did the next few, and Tahiri was starting to giggle with hypoxia. Anakin felt symptoms himself.

"Okay, that's it," Corran said. "You two. Get in there." He pointed to one of the large lockers.

"Why?" Anakin asked.

"Just do as I say. This one time, please, without questions, just do what I tell you to."

It seemed funny that Corran was shouting at him again. Part of Anakin knew that was a bad sign.

He grabbed Tahiri's hand and pulled her into the locker. Corran shoved the airpack in behind them.

"Minimum feed to keep you alive. Remember the locker is probably leaky." He swayed on his feet, seeming to nearly collapse. "I'll be back. There's another set of lockers down the hall."

He slammed the locker door, and they were in total darkness. Anakin felt around for the feed valve, and soon a small hiss escaped the airpack. He turned it up until his dizziness subsided.

"What if he doesn't have enough strength to get the suit on?" Tahiri said. "What if it's leaky?"

"Don't think about it," Anakin said. "We can only wait now."

"The walls are getting cold," she said.

They'll get a lot colder before it's over, Anakin thought. *Unless the Yuuzhan Vong light the station up and blow it to atoms. Either way it won't be long before we don't care anymore.* Maybe Corran was right. Maybe his luck had finally run out.

"Don't worry, Tahiri," Anakin said, contrary to what he was thinking. "Corran's been out of more scrapes than the two of us put together. He'll be back."

FORTY-ONE

The space around the *Sunulok* birthed stars. That's what it looked like, anyway, and in astrophysical fact that was more or less what was happening.

The cloud of boiling liquid hydrogen had enveloped most of the Interdictor, and wherever a laser beam or concussion missile pierced that gauzy haze an unbearably bright pin-prick of light erupted, then quickly blossomed larger before suddenly going out.

"Keep firing, you two," Han told his wife and son, adding the forward guns to the mix.

"I see it, but I don't believe it," Jacen said. A constellation of the expanding and deflating suns burned around the *Sunulok*, now, so brightly they almost couldn't see it, and Han laughed aloud, though the coralskippers were still pounding the *Falcon*. The dovin basals' grip on the *Falcon* suddenly relaxed, and the laser beams were lancing through the hydrogen cloud to burn clots off the Yuuzhan Vong ship itself. Targeting the cluster of dovin basals, Han launched his last spread of concussion missiles and then threw the *Falcon* back into drive.

He punched up Karrde's comm channel. "Hey," he said, "the interdictor is out of commission, but I can't say for how long. If I were you I'd go to lightspeed."

"That's the most beautiful thing I've heard in a long time," Karrde replied. "I'm gone."

"Keep those skips back until we hit hyperspace," Han told Leia and Jacen.

"Can do," Jacen called back up.

Behind them, Han was gratified to see plasma boiling

from the *Sunulok*. A few minutes later, they'd left the Interdictor—and the rest of their enemies—light-years behind.

Jaina saw Ten shredded against an asteroid, and pressed her lips tight in anger. She hadn't known the Twi'lek in the pilot's seat, but he'd been part of her flight, and he'd saved her life at least twice in this fight.

What's worse, Alinn Varth, Three-flight leader, had been dropping in to take out the coralskipper on Ten's tail, and ended up flying straight through the burning debris as it skipped off the intervening rock. Jaina watched in horror as her leader's X-wing vanished, haloed in inferno.

But Varth came out the other side, banking, three skips on her tail. Jaina dropped down like a bird of prey, spraying the lead skip, then launching one of her remaining three proton torps. The resulting explosion cracked two of the fighters and sent the third spinning aimlessly.

"Thanks, Twelve," Varth gasped.

"You okay, Nine?"

"Negative. I've lost guns and short-range sensors."

Gavin heard. "Fall back, Nine."

"Colonel—"

"Fall back. That's an order."

"Yes, sir," Varth said. "As ordered, sir."

"It's just us," Lensi said, for once not sounding brash.

"It'll be just me, if you don't watch it," Jaina replied. "You've got two coming down."

"Got 'em. Thanks, Sticks."

The weapon was *huge* now that they were closing on it. *Maybe it's not fully alive yet,* she hoped.

Kre'fey had been as good as his word; the *Ralroost* and her companions had cut through the defense perimeter around the weapon that had so successfully kept Kyp's squadron at bay, leaving the faintly glowing hulks of two Yuuzhan Vong capital ship analogs to mark the way in. Now they were setting up for the run on the gravitic weapon, and roles had reversed. This wasn't the fabled Death Star; if the Yuuzhan Vong ship had a weak point, it was unknown to the motley forces attacking it. In Kyp's holo, the huge iris in the center of the thing had seemed to project the gravity field, so that was number one priority, and when taking out something you didn't understand, honking gobs of fire-power was always the safest bet. The *Ralroost* had the guns—it was up to the starfighters to see she had a chance to use them.

There were two more large ships in the system; One had moved between Kre'fey's flotilla and the weapon; the other was hanging back, presumably to control the ample swarms of coralskippers that were still massing against them.

"Seven," she heard Gavin say, "break off and take lead with Eleven and Twelve."

"Mind if I cut in?" a new voice asked.

"Wedge?" Gavin said. "You're sure you want to do this, what with your arthritis and all? How'd you slip your nurse?"

"Told her I was going to take a steam bath," the aging general quipped. "What've you got for me?"

"Good to have you, General. Gives us two full flights. Take Seven, Eleven, and Twelve. Guys, you are now designated Two-flight."

"I copy, One Leader," Jaina said. She could hardly believe it. She was flying with Wedge Antilles!

"Good enough," Wedge said. "Tighten up, Two-flight. Looks like we have some business up ahead."

The next wave of skips hit them and hit them hard, fighting with a sort of desperation that Jaina hadn't yet seen in the Yuuzhan Vong. They came in clusters, three flying as shields for a fourth. Jaina needled them at long range with her lasers, determined not to waste another proton torpedo if she didn't have to.

"I don't like this," Wedge said. "They aren't maneuvering. They're just coming head-on."

"Makes them easy pickings," Lensi said. From the corner of her eye, Jaina saw one of his targets flare out.

"Too easy, Twelve," Wedge said.

One of Jaina's targets tumbled out of formation, its cockpit a fused mass of coral.

"Two-flight, break!" Wedge suddenly shouted. Even as he did so, the cover skips broke, and their undamaged charges accelerated through the gap. They weren't firing weapons, and they weren't throwing out voids.

Jaina jerked her stick up, and the skip rose to meet her.

"I'm going to hit!" Seven screamed, before his channel went dead.

The voids slowed the skips down. When they weren't using them, they were incredibly maneuverable. Jaina's climb was as tight as she could get it, but the skip was matching her, still coming on, still at the bottom of her field of vision, clearly determined to ram her. Meanwhile, the remaining two skips that had flown shield for it were trying to pick up her tail. She had nowhere to go, and if she brought her weapons in line to fire, she'd meet her enemy head-on, as Seven had just presumably done.

Suddenly a quad burst of lasers from above her imaginary horizon cut the skip in half. Jaina didn't have time to see who her rescuer was. She jammed the stick down and starboard, skimming by the wreckage of the coralskipper and shaking the two behind her.

Except the two behind her were already gone.

"You're clean, Jaina," Kyp's voice informed her. "General Antilles, permission to fly what's left of my Dozen with you."

"Granted, Durron. I'll take what I can get, now."

The *Ralroost* and its escorts had taken a lot of hits in the first wave of suicides, but once the tactic was understood, the remaining starfighters fanned out and picked off the determined skips far in advance. The Yuuzhan Vong that made it through their runs intact ended up behind them, where collision was much less effective. They still had their weapons, of course, and it made Jaina more than a little nervous to have so many live enemies at her back, but target prime was just ahead, and she had a job to do.

The *Ralroost* opened up on the galaxy-shaped ship. Red streamers of plasma lanced out from the curved tips of the Yuuzhan Vong weapon, but the destroyer's shields handled the fire easily.

"I don't get it," Jaina said. "Why use conventional weapons? Why aren't they using the gravity weapon?"

"It's our lucky day," Kyp said. "It must be off-line."

Multiple proton concussions blossomed at the axis of the Yuuzhan Vong weapon, rendering it a dull-red glowing mass.

"Jaina, behind you!"

Kyp's warning came too late. Twin bursts of plasma sheared through her shields and into her ion engines. A quick babble from her astromech told her that if she didn't shut down in fifteen seconds, the whole mess was going supercritical. She'd lost a stabilizer, too, and the ship was spinning crazily.

And she still had a tail. Kyp got one of them, but the other just kept coming.

This is it.

The Yuuzhan Vong superweapon filled most of her gyrating vision, now. Grimly, she did her best to aim for it, then shut down. Maybe she could skip off it with repulsors. If not, at least she would put another ding in the thing.

But then something in the huge craft made a very big bang, and all she saw was inferno.

"Corran's been gone a long time," Tahiri whispered.

"Not so long," Anakin replied. "Only about five minutes."

"Seems longer." He felt her shiver, probably from the biting cold. In fact, the only part of Anakin that wasn't freezing was the strip along his side where he was pressed against the younger Jedi.

"There has to be something we can do," she said. "If we can yank Massassi trees out of the ground with the Force, surely we can—"

"What? Pull a bunch of oxygen molecules up here from Yag'Dhul, seal up the station, and repressurize it?"

"Hey, at least I'm trying to think of *something*."

"So am I," Anakin said, his voice rising a little. "If you have an idea, let's hear it."

"You know very well I don't have an idea," Tahiri snapped back. "You'd feel it if I did."

"Tahiri—"

"Oh, just shut up."

Anakin suddenly understood. Tahiri was frightened, as frightened as he had ever known her to be.

"I'm scared, too, Tahiri."

"No, you're not. You're never scared. Even when you *are*, you aren't by normal standards."

"I was scared when I thought I'd lost you on Yavin Four."

She was silent, and Anakin lost his read on her, but he suddenly felt her shoulders quivering and knew she was crying.

Reluctantly, he reached his arm around her.

"I'm sorry," she sobbed. "I got you into this. Corran's right—I keep thinking I can be like you, and I'm not. You always win, and I always screw up. If it weren't for me, you'd be back on the *Errant Venture* right now."

"But I'd rather be here with you," he said.

He couldn't see her face turn toward him or see the widening emeralds of her eyes, but he knew they were there.

"Don't say things like that," she murmured. "I know you think I'm still a little kid. I—"

She stopped, very suddenly, when he found her face with his fingers. Her cheek was smooth and cold. He found a stray lock of hair across her eyebrow and traced lightly over the raised scars on her forehead.

Anakin rarely did things he didn't know he was going to do. But it had never occurred to him that he was going to kiss Tahiri until his lips were already touching hers. They were cold, and she pulled back.

"Oh," she said.

"Oh?"

"*That* was a surprise."

"Sorry."

"No—c'mere." She took his face in both hands and pressed her lips against his. It wasn't a big kiss, but it was sweet and warm, and it jolted through him like ten g forces.

"Your timing is perfect," she breathed. "Wait until we're doomed to give me my first kiss."

"Mine, too," he said, his face warming despite the cold. "Umm . . ."

"How was it?" Tahiri said, answering his unverbalized question. "Kind of weird." She kissed him again. "Nice."

She took his hand and put her cheek against his. "If we survive, we'll have to figure this out, you know," she said.

"Yeah."

"I mean, I'm not the kind of girl who'll kiss just anyone on a first-time-to-be-stuck-in-a-locker-on-an-airless-space-station."

"Might be simpler if we don't make it," Anakin remarked.

"Yeah. Are you sorry?"

"No. No, not even a little."

"Good."

"So let's survive," Anakin said, "so we get a chance to figure this out, okay? Do you think you can manage a hibernation trance? Our air will last a lot longer that way."

"I'm not sure. I've never done it."

"I'll help. Just clear your mind—"

"Maybe you don't know very much about girls. You just *kissed* me, and now you want me to clear my mind? It's like there's a tribe of Ewoks dancing in there."

He squeezed her hand. "C'mon. Try."

Something clanked outside.

"Did you hear that?" Tahiri whispered.

"Yeah. But how? There shouldn't be any air to carry the sound." He reached for his lightsaber.

Something started working at the locker door. It swung open, and Corran was crouched there, an expression of extreme concern on his face. He still had a vac suit on, but without the helmet.

"You're okay," he breathed.

"We're okay," Anakin acknowledged. "Where did the air come from?" He started crawling out of the cramped space.

"I remembered there was a modular backup system. I was afraid the Givin had taken it out, but they haven't. I sealed up the room and pumped air in. It probably won't last long, so get into those, quick." He gestured toward a pair of smaller vac suits.

As they were scrambling into them, Corran shot Anakin a peculiar look.

"What?" Anakin said.

"Should I have left you two unchaperoned?"

Vaping Moffs! Does it show? Anakin wondered.

Just once, he wished most of the people he knew weren't Jedi.

"You fools," Nom Anor hissed at the three warriors. "First you let them slip from your claws, now you cannot find them again? You are a disgrace to the Yuuzhan Vong."

He stood next to where the ship the warriors had come on was connected to the infidel space station by an oqa membrane, speaking through the gnullith-villip hybrid in his throat. He disliked having to command through the thing, for it distorted his voice somewhat, lessening its effectiveness.

The new leader of the warriors, Qau Lah, threw a withering glare his way. "The infidels opened their station to space. We were forced to obtain ooglith cloakers, as you know, since you wear one yourself. We *will* find them." He lifted his chin and bared his teeth. "Besides, it is the Yuuzhan Vong who does not accept challenge from a worthy opponent who disgraces his people."

Nom Anor narrowed his eyes, then chopped his hand in a gesture of command. "Go. Find them."

As they turned, he lifted the infidel blaster he had secreted in his sash. It made him feel vaguely sick to handle it, but he had learned to do all sorts of distasteful things lately.

He shot Qau Lah in the back of the head from a meter away, then the warrior next to him. The third managed to raise his amphistaff before the blaster burned a hole through his face.

That was three. Cursing to himself, Nom Anor started off to find the rest of the warriors who had seen him with the Jedi, to make certain none of them would carry report of what they had seen back to Qurang Lah.

FORTY-TWO

"What happened back there, exactly?" Leia asked.

"Hand me that," Han said, gesturing toward his tools.

The *Falcon* had made five quick jumps with no sign of pursuit. Now they were headed for the Maw, but Han wasn't waiting for the facilities there to begin his repairs. The second he thought they were safe, he'd begun tending to his baby.

Leia handed him the demagnetizer.

"Not that," Han said. "*That.*" He pointed just as vaguely. "The thingie."

"*Which* thingie?"

"The hydrospanner."

She handed it to him, rolling her eyes. "I'm not gonna sprout fur, you know," she said. "I'm not going that far."

"I don't know," Han replied dubiously. "I knew this woman once, real pretty. Hit fifty and grew a mustache."

"*Han.* The *Sunulok*?"

"Ask your son. He's the one with the education."

Jacen turned from his own work on the power core. "I'm pretty sure I get it," he said.

His mother looked up at him. "Do tell."

"The cargo tanker was full of liquid hydrogen, right?"

"That far I got."

"Dad dumped it all over the *Sunulok,* and we fired into it. That didn't do anything, except the *Sunulok* produced voids to swallow our shots. They started swallowing hydrogen as well."

"And choked on it? What?"

"The voids are like quantum black holes. You reach

266

the event horizon—which in this case is more or less microscopic—and gravity becomes nearly infinite. Which means acceleration does, too. When a concussion missile hits one, for instance, the matter in it is instantly compressed into neutrons and then, *blip*, singularity. Just like a black hole. And like black holes, if you dump in too much matter at once, it has to queue up to get in. It starts compressing *outside* the event horizon, so on the way in it undergoes fusion."

"And the black holes swallow most of the energy," Leia said.

"Exactly. The light we saw was only a fraction of the energy being produced, the part that escaped. Most of it went into the singularity. We know from experience that disappearing energy taxes the dovin basals, right? In a few seconds the *Sunulok*'s voids swallowed dozens of hydrogen fusion explosions. It shut them down."

"Looks like *all* of your education wasn't a waste," Han remarked.

"Wow," Leia said. "That could be a good countermeasure against those voids."

"Not really," Han said. "It would only work if the hydrogen density was like it was—it was still semiliquid. In another few seconds, it would have dispersed enough that it wouldn't have done anything. If the *Sunulok* had been moving, they would have whipped through it in a second. No, we had the perfect setup, and since I'm pretty sure the *Sunulok* survived, the Vong probably won't let that happen again. Nice thought, though."

Jacen was about to add something else when the Force blindsided him with agony. He must have cried out, because both of his parents looked at him at once.

"What is it, Jacen?" Leia asked.

"It's Aunt Mara," he replied shakily. "Something bad is happening to Aunt Mara."

Aunt Mara! Jaina felt the pain and despair hit her like the heavy end of a hammer. She shook her head, not sure where she was. Had she blacked out?

Stars tumbled by, and her astromech chirped frantically.

Oh, right. She'd been flying into the Yuuzhan Vong super-weapon, when it exploded.

Aunt Mara! The spike in the Force was fading, but the impression remained of Mara unraveling like a rotten phil-fiber.

Jaina balled her fists in frustration. Mara was hundreds of parsecs away, and here she was in a dead ship.

I can't help her now, Jaina thought. *Got to help myself first.*

She and her astromech managed to kill the tumble, but they were still without engines. Far behind her she could make out the wink of laserfire through a cloud of gas that must be the debris of the Yuuzhan Vong weapon.

We did it!

She was drifting sunward, but was outside of the asteroid field and in no obvious or immediate danger. At least she didn't think so until she noticed, ahead of her, a heart-shaped chunk of yorik coral. A *big* hunk.

After a few missed beats of her own heart, however, she saw it wasn't under power. In fact, what it looked like more than anything was a dovin basal. Alone, unattached to a ship.

"You think it's flotsam?" she asked the droid.

It whistled a noncommittal reply. It was too busy to care about space junk.

Curious, Jaina adjusted her sensors, and noticed something else strange. The dovin basal had a twin, about a hundred klicks away, in the same orbit. Inward, toward the primary, another pair—and another, and another. It was a sort of corridor of dovin basals stretching from the Yuuzhan Vong superweapon almost to the star in the center of the Sernpidal system.

"Oh, no," she said. "No, Kyp, you didn't. Not even you would . . ."

No, of course he would. And he had made her part of it. And she had brought in Rogue Squadron.

She wanted to throw up. If she hadn't been in a sealed cockpit with limited room to do so, she probably would have.

The astromech informed her that it had managed to rig a new antenna. Jaina opened a channel.

"Rogue Leader, you out there?"

Static, and then Gavin Darklighter's voice. "Jaina? Jaina, thank goodness you're alive."

"Copy, Rogue Leader. Can you send somebody to pick me up?"

"Absolutely. We're finished here."

"Colonel Darklighter, you might want to come yourself. There's something here I think you should see."

FORTY-THREE

Luke.

Luke awoke to his name and found Mara's hand on his arm. Her eyes were clear, and her lips were quivering as if she were trying to speak.

"Mara," he murmured. "Mara." He had more to say, but he couldn't get it out. *I love you. Don't die.*

Her head inclined, very slightly. He took her hand and felt the pulse there, stronger than it had been in days, but irregular.

Now. We have to do it now.

"Do what? Mara, I don't understand."

Now. Her eyes closed again, and her pulse dropped away.

"No! Mara!"

When Darth Vader had suddenly realized that he had a daughter as well as a son, Luke had felt a desperation that was the palest reflection of this. He'd hurled himself at the black-armored figure that was his father, battering him with his lightsaber until he cut Vader's arm off. In doing so Luke had taken a decisive step toward the dark side.

Now, though his body did not move, he hurled himself at Mara's disease with the same blind, desperate fury, battering against it with the Force, trying to shatter the slippery, mutable compounds of which it was made. The electrifying strength of anguish drove him on, and the fact that he was trying to do the impossible meant nothing. He clenched his fists until the veins stood out on his arms, attacking something he couldn't see.

That wasn't there to see.

No. Luke, no. Not this way.

Luke fell away, trembling. "How then?" he shouted, maybe at Mara, maybe at the universe itself.

"Luke!" Cilghal was standing in the doorway. "I felt—"

"She wants me to do something, Cilghal," Luke snarled. "She diverted some of her energy to wake me, and a little more to stop me from . . . What does she know, Cilghal?"

"I don't know, Luke," Cilghal said. "But you've been telling your students attack is not the answer. Trust yourself—you're right. You need to calm yourself."

A retort got hung just inside of his throat. How could Cilghal possibly understand?

But she was right, of course. It was easy to remain calm when nothing upsetting was happening.

"I know," he admitted, his breathing evening out. "But I *know* I have to do something. Now, or she'll die."

"Let me try," Cilghal said. "Maybe I can understand what she wants."

"No. It has to be me. I know that."

He calmed himself further, sloughing off his darkening emotions, cleansing himself with deep, slow breaths. Only when he felt truly centered did he reach out toward Mara again, probing her gently through the Force rather than attacking her disease.

Attack is not the answer.

But she was so far gone. There was nothing to defend, except . . .

And suddenly, he thought he understood. One part of Mara was well—better than well, free of all disease. *That's* where he needed to be, not waging warfare, but strengthening, defending from the one fortress that still stood.

He reached out again, this time as lightly as one of Mara's caresses, into the place where their child rested, and there he found his wife, wrapped around the baby like a dura-steel wall.

"Let me in, Mara," he said aloud. "You have to let me in." He laid his hand on her arm, squeezing gently. "Let me in."

Skywalker?

"It's me. I think I understand, now. I'll do what I can. But you have to let me in."

The wall wavered, but held. Had he guessed wrong? Had she herself already forgotten, her memory erased by the pain?

"I love you, Mara. Please."

He trembled, still touching her arm. He couldn't force her. He wouldn't if he could.

Come on, Luke.

The gate opened, and he felt another pulse, another life. He reached for his son.

The child stirred, as if recognizing his father's touch. He reached back, and Luke felt little tickling thoughts, like waking laughter and amazement. It was a voice both familiar and infinitely strange. It was a voice becoming real.

"I love you. I love you both," he breathed. "Take my strength."

He and Mara joined like fingers twining, and like a tiny third hand, the unborn child linked with them as well. A human child. His child. Mara's child.

The mutual grip grew stronger, but it wasn't the desperate strength of combat or the raging power of a storm. It was a calm, enduring, and at the same time fallible, mortal embrace—the embrace of family long separated.

They mingled, each with the other, until Luke felt his identity blur, and he began to dream.

He saw a young boy with hair of pale red-gold, tracing lines in the sand. He saw an older boy, kneeling by a river course, rubbing a smooth, round stone between his fingers and smiling. The same boy, perhaps ten years old, wrestling with a young Wookiee.

He saw himself, holding the boy, watching glowing lines of traffic move through the sky of some strange world—like Coruscant, but not Coruscant.

He did not see Mara, though he looked, and that brought a new note of discord to his thoughts.

Always in motion is the future, Yoda had once told him. Still, he reached farther, searching for Mara, farther along that uncertain, shifting path. The boy grew older; he was at the helm of a starship of strange design . . .

All futures exist in the Force, a familiar, impossible voice suddenly said. *You do not choose the future so much as it chooses you. Do not look for answers there.*

"Ben?" Luke croaked, stunned. It couldn't be Ben, of course. That time was long gone, and his old Master was truly one with the Force, unreachable, and yet . . .

But it didn't matter whether it was Ben, the Force, or a part of Luke himself that had just spoken. It only mattered that he had glimpsed what might be, and only the tiniest part of that, but it was only what *might* be. He couldn't let it concern him—now was not the time for searching or speculation, for both were active manifestations of doubt, and he could afford no doubt right now. Doubt was more deadly than the Yuuzhan Vong disease. It was the only real limitation a Jedi had.

He let the images slide away, and felt again only the moment, three hearts beating, three minds becoming one.

Hi there, Luke. Glad to have you back, Mara seemed to say. And then they were expanding, extending outward in every direction, like a galaxy being born. Like anything being born. Like life itself.

FORTY-FOUR

"Wow," Anakin said, when he saw the ship waiting for them in berth thirteen. They'd squeaked by two groups of ooglith-cloaked Yuuzhan Vong prowling the halls, apparently still searching for them, and had expected a fight when they reached the ship—if the ship was even still there. It was, and the Yuuzhan Vong weren't.

"Maybe Nom Anor and his bunch got caught when the air went out," Corran speculated.

"Wow," Anakin repeated.

"Don't gawk," Corran said. "We don't have time for it. It may take us some time to figure out how to work this thing. There is still a fleet out there, remember?"

"Right," Anakin said. "Sorry."

But it was hard not to be impressed. The Givin ship was simple, elegant, nearly all engine, about the size of a light transport. A bundle of spindly cylinders protruding from a relatively enormous engine torus made up the core of the ion drive, though three more extended on booms from the side of the main assembly. These last weren't fixed, either, but could be maneuvered in a complete sphere. Forward of that was the hyperdrive assembly, and almost as an afterthought, it seemed, a crew section and cockpit that was nearly all transparisteel.

On board they found that only the sleeping compartment could be pressurized. The life support unit was thus commensurately underpowered, so they remained in their suits. The controls were a complete mystery until Corran pointed out they were laid out mathematically according to Ju

Simma's theorem. Once that was understood, the ship was weird to operate, but not particularly difficult.

Corran took the controls and unlocked the docking bolts.

"Here we go," he said. "The pitiful laser this thing has won't be of much use in a fight, so we're just going to run, unless anyone else has a better suggestion."

"But the station—" Tahiri began.

"Is doomed. And the best hope for the Givin is reinforcements from Coruscant."

"I was thinking about Taan."

"I'm sorry," Corran said. "But the Yuuzhan Vong will probably retrieve her. If she's lucky . . . Anyway, we're out of this, just as soon as I can get us out. Let's see, where would the inertial compensator be?"

Anakin pointed to a logarithmically scaled input. "I'm guessing that's it."

"We'll see. Strap in and hang on. I hope this thing has the legs it advertises."

It did. Anakin could barely restrain a whoop when they blew out of the dock. If he had been flying, he wouldn't have been able to keep it in.

"An A-wing couldn't touch this thing," he said.

"It's not all about speed," Corran said.

"If you're running, it is," Anakin replied reasonably, as they streaked past a patrol of coralskippers. They turned late, like a herd of startled banthas, and began pursuit. Within a minute the skips must have been under top acceleration, but they looked almost as if they were standing still.

As Anakin studied the sensor readouts from the copilot's station and began calculating a series of jumps, he began to feel less cheery.

"We've got some ahead of us, closing. Heavy cruiser analogs, two of them."

"We'll see how well the Givin build shields, then," Corran replied.

Minutes later, Corran was juking and jinking through

heavy fire. The shields held admirably well, but as predicted, the laser was useless. Corran cut the ship onto a course perpendicular to Yag'Dhul's ecliptic plane, fighting for enough distance from the planet and its three massive moons for a safe jump, but they ran into trouble there, too, in the form of more Yuuzhan Vong ships.

"Thick as gluttonbugs," Corran remarked.

"I can lay in a short jump," Anakin said.

"In an unfamiliar ship? Very dangerous."

"What choice do we have?" Anakin replied.

In response, Corran turned back toward Yag'Dhul, diving toward the thick of the fighting, where the delicate-looking Givin ships were taking on twice their number of Yuuzhan Vong vessels. To Anakin, it didn't look like a very good place to be. "We should jump," Anakin repeated.

"Anakin, I was flying when you were nothing more than a fight brewing between Han and Leia. Before that, even. Give me credit for knowing a thing or two."

"Yes, sir."

"Program the jump, just in case. But we're not going to try it unless we run out of options."

They whipped through the Yuuzhan Vong perimeter, shaving as near the big ships as Corran dared—which was pretty near—and dancing evasively through skips. Anakin took potshots with the laser, and though he never managed to get through the void defenses the ships generated, it still felt better than doing nothing.

"We're going to make it," Corran said. "The ships up front are too busy to—" He broke off as every single Yuuzhan Vong ship ahead of them suddenly turned and began accelerating in their direction.

"Sithspawn!" Corran sputtered, pulling up hard to avoid a coralskipper that appeared intent on taking them out with its own mass.

It dodged by them, not even bothering to fire. In utter confusion, Anakin watched the rest of the Yuuzhan Vong fleet race past them, out toward interstellar space.

"The ones farther out are jumping," he reported, studying the sensor readouts. "They're running. I don't get it.

What could the Givin have done to light their jets like that?"

"It's not the Givin," Corran replied, his voice edged with astonished relief. "It's something else."

"Recalled?" Nom Anor spat, staring incredulously down at the villip and its portrait of Qurang Lah. "But we are near victory! Their defenses crumble."

"Meanwhile, an infidel fleet desecrates and obliterates our primary shipwomb."

"Impossible," Nom Anor said. "Their ridiculous senate could not possibly have approved of such a strike without my knowing. Even if the military launched such a campaign without senate approval, my sources would have informed me."

The commander snarled a sort of smile. "It would appear, Executor, that Yun-Harla has abandoned you. Opinion is that you are perhaps not as clever and useful as you make yourself out to be. You have been outmaneuvered by the infidels. They set a trap, and you led us into it for them."

"Absurd. If there is an attack on the shipwomb, it is unrelated to this mission."

"Not unrelated at all, since you had us commit our reserves for this battle. Had they remained at the shipwomb, they would have been sufficient to repel the infidels. As it is, we have only a narrow chance of reaching the battle in time to salvage anything."

"Then let us remain here. We have now demonstrated to the infidels that we intend to continue our conquest of their galaxy—unless we finish here, we will have nothing to show for that tactical loss."

Qurang Lah showed his sharpened teeth. "The loss is yours, Executor," he said. "You may be sure that the warmaster will hear a most complete version of how you've bungled this entire business." His eyes narrowed. "Let me speak to Shok Choka."

Nom Anor kept his face impassive. "He was slain by the *Jeedai*. All of your men were."

The commander's face pulled into an incredulous frown. "All of them? And yet you made it safely back to your ship?"

"I was separated from your warriors and the *Jeedai* when the Givin emptied their station of atmosphere."

Qurang Lah held his stare for another moment. "Yes," he said softly. "The warmaster will hear much from me."

Before Nom Anor could begin another rebuttal, the villip cleared, leaving him to pace the decks of his ship in frustration.

Not to mention trepidation.

FORTY-FIVE

Jaina climbed out of her X-wing wearily, feeling far older than her eighteen years. She wanted to get in bed, turn the lights out, and stay there.

She wanted Jacen, and Anakin, and her mother and father. She wanted to hear C-3PO going on inanely, and she wanted to see Aunt Mara, to find out what was wrong with her.

What she got instead was Kyp Durron, climbing out of his starfighter, a grin smearing across his face as he walked toward her.

In a way, he would do.

She watched him come, with that stupid smile, until he was close enough. Then she slapped him, hard.

His smile faded, but otherwise he didn't react.

"You *knew*," she said. "You knew, and you lied, and you made *me* a part of it."

The other pilots, in the middle of postbattle jubilation, were starting to stare.

"What are you talking about?" Lensi asked. Jaina had seen the Duros coming from the corner of her vision.

"Tell him, Kyp. Tell him what his friends died for. Tell them that thing we just paid so dearly to blow up wasn't a superweapon. That it wasn't a weapon at all."

Kyp straightened and folded his arms. "Everything the Vong possess is a weapon," he said.

"B-but the footage we saw in briefing," Lensi stammered. "I *saw* what it did. It pulled fire out of Sernpidal's sun."

"No," Jaina said. "That's what it looked like, but that's not what happened. The Yuuzhan Vong set up a relay system of hundreds of dovin basals, hung in a long corridor all the way to the sun. It was just a big, unwieldy linear accelerator, a way to get hydrogen and helium to use in their shipbuilding, or something. But a giant gravitic weapon? No. Kyp made that up, to get us here."

While talking to Lensi, she hadn't taken her gaze off Kyp's face. Nor did she now.

"What was it, Kyp? What did we just blow up? Or do you even know?"

"I know," Kyp said. "It was a worldship, a new one. If it's any comfort, it wasn't finished, and there probably weren't many Vong aboard."

"Then why did you want it blown up? Why did you lie?" Lensi asked.

Kyp's face hardened. "The Yuuzhan Vong have destroyed, conquered, and raped our planets. They enslave civilian populations, and they sacrifice our citizens by the thousands. But until today, the only Vong we've hurt are those who come against us—the warriors. I wanted to hit them where they live, to let them know their civilians aren't sacrosanct if ours aren't."

"Then why an *empty* worldship?" Jaina asked. "Why not just pick a full one and blow it up, Kyp? You can't tell me *you* would be squeamish about that."

"You're wrong about that, Jaina, and I think you know it," Kyp said. "But sure, from what I've managed to find out we could have probably blasted one of their older ships. But that wouldn't have really hurt them. This does. Their worldships are dying, and a lot of them aren't in good enough shape to make it anywhere they can let people off. This one would have been hyperdrive capable, and it could have housed the populations of many of their smaller worldships. Now they have to choose between letting their children die in space or expending military resources to move them to conquered planets. Either way, it only helps us fight them—and it sends a message."

"Yeah, right," Jaina snapped. "It sends the message that we're not any better than they are."

"*We* were here first. It's *our* galaxy. If they had come peacefully, we would have given them the space they needed." He lifted his chin and raised his voice to address everyone in the room. "You should all be proud of what you did today. You fought against terrible odds and you won. You struck a blow against the Vong, and a good one. This was for Sernpidal, for Ithor, for Duro, for Dubrillion, for Garqi—for every planet the Vong have despoiled."

To Jaina's utter astonishment, he got cheers. Not from everyone—she saw Gavin and Wedge across the room, their faces tight and angry. But *nearly* everyone.

"Ask them, Jaina. You don't really have a homeworld. You were raised all over the galaxy. Most of these people know what it's like to have had a home, and too many of them know what it's like to lose one, thanks to the Yuuzhan Vong. You think they mind evening the score a little?"

"I think you owed us the truth. Maybe we would have decided to help you if you had been straight with us."

"And maybe you wouldn't have. As long as you thought it was a superweapon, you were ready to go. But we've set them back here more than the destruction of any weapon. By the time they grow another one—"

"—their children start dying. Right. I get that. Bravo, Kyp. Well done. Except you used *me*. You made *me* tell your lie, and now the blood of every Yuuzhan Vong child who suffocates in space is on *my* hands, too."

"There's more to this universe than Jaina Solo, believe it or not," Kyp said, very quietly. "I'm sorry you feel used, and I wish I hadn't had to lie to you. But I did have to. You wouldn't have helped me otherwise."

"And I'll never help you again," Jaina said. "You can count on it. If you were dying of thirst on Tatooine, I wouldn't even spit on you." And with that she left, found the stateroom she had been assigned, turned out the lights, and wept.

The next day, with Gavin Darklighter's permission, she left to find the *Errant Venture*.

FORTY-SIX

"It's a weird thing," Corran said, as the *Errant Venture* grew larger through the transparisteel lozenge of the Givin ship.

"What's that?" Anakin asked.

"Being happy to see my father-in-law's ship."

"Ah." Anakin tried to smile, but he couldn't. He'd been searching for Aunt Mara in the Force. The results were ambiguous—at times he thought he had her, but at other times it didn't seem like her at all. The feeling that she was dying had scarred his mind, and deep in his gut he feared she was already dead and his occasional sense of contact was merely a residual imprint of her living self.

He turned to go back and wake Tahiri and found her standing only a meter or so away. She gave him a brief smile.

"Uh . . . hi," he said.

"Hi," Tahiri replied. Her eyes refused to settle on his for long, but he could feel her uncertainty matching his own. "Looks like we're almost there," she pointed out unnecessarily.

"Yeah." Why did his fingers feel like hammers and his legs like spongy pillars? This was *Tahiri*.

"And we can finally get out of these things for good," Tahiri went on. "I never want to wear a vac suit again as long as I live."

"Right. Me either." The suits had made a recurrence of what had happened in the locker on Yag'Dhul Station impossible. What would happen when they were in shirtsleeves again?

It was a nearly terrifying thought.

"You think Mara's okay?"

Anakin shook his head. "No."

"She will be. She has to be."

"Yeah." A long, awkward silence followed as they drew near the *Errant Venture*. Corran was busily trying to prove they were who he said they were—despite the fact that they weren't in the same ship they'd left in—so he could get clearance to enter the docking bay.

"Hey, Anakin?" Tahiri asked.

"Yeah?"

"What's going on? You've hardly said two words to me since we left Yag'Dhul."

"We were kind of busy, and I . . . I'm worried about Aunt Mara."

"Uh-huh. Look, have you changed your mind?"

"About what?"

"About . . . you know. Are you sorry now? I mean, we were about to die and everything. It's perfectly understandable, because we've been best friends for so long, but maybe now you're thinking I'm too young, and remembering all the trouble I've gotten you into, and, well, maybe we ought to just forget . . ." Her green eyes did meet his then, with a sort of ionic jolt.

"Tahiri . . ."

"Right. I get it. No harm done."

"Tahiri, I haven't changed my mind. I'm not sorry at all. I don't know exactly what it all means, and we *are* young, both of us. But I don't regret kissing you. And, um . . . it wasn't just because I thought we were dying."

"Yeah?"

"Yeah."

"Well, okay then."

He was trying to decide what to say next without totally messing up the situation, when a staggering pain suddenly jolted through him.

"Aunt Mara!" he gasped. "Aunt Mara!" Another blinding wave of agony made his knees buckle.

*   *   *

The instant they were docked, Anakin bolted from the ship, pushing past the Jedi students who had come out to greet them, running as fast as he could toward the medical lab. In the turbolift, the worst agony yet ripped through him so powerfully that he was forced to block himself off from it before he fainted.

Outside the medical facility he found Mirax, Booster, Valin, Jysella, and half a dozen other people jittering around. When Anakin burst onto the scene, all eyes turned toward him.

"Aunt Mara!" he gasped. "What's wrong with Aunt Mara?"

Mirax embraced him. "Mara is fine," she said. "Where in space have *you* been? Is Corran with you?"

Anakin brushed off the question. "But the pain . . ." he began.

"It's normal," Mirax replied. "Corran?"

"Corran's fine," Anakin said. "He'll be right here. Mirax, I felt her dying."

"She was. Now she's not. Somehow, in the Force, she and Luke . . . We don't know how. But the Yuuzhan Vong disease is gone. Completely."

"Then the pain—"

"Natural. Hideous, overwhelming, but natural. Believe me, I've experienced it twice."

"You mean . . . ?"

A few moments later the door sighed open. Cilghal stood there, looking very, very tired.

"You can come in now," she said. "A few at a time, please."

Anakin and Mirax went in first.

Mara still looked sick. Her face was sallow, and sweat sheened her brow. But she was smiling, her jade eyes filled with an unfamiliar sort of happiness. Luke knelt at the bedside, holding her hand.

"Luke, Mara," Mirax said. "Look who I've brought."

"Anakin!" Luke said. "You're okay! Are Corran and Tahiri with you?"

"Yeah," Anakin said absently, his attention fixed on the small bundle in the crook of Mara's arm. He stepped closer.

Small dark eyes glanced vaguely in his direction, passing over him as if he didn't exist.

"Wow," he breathed.

"Hello, Anakin," Mara said weakly. "I knew you'd be here."

"I thought you were . . . Can I come closer?"

"Sure."

Anakin stared down at the newborn. "Are they all that ugly?" he blurted.

"You'll want to rephrase that," Mara said, "after what I just went through. Think in the general direction of antonyms."

"I mean, he's—"

"His name is Ben," Luke said.

"He's beautiful. In the Force, and . . . But he's all sort of squinched and wrinkly."

"Just like you were," Mara said.

"And you're really okay?"

"I've never, ever been better," Mara told him. "Everything is perfect." She looked down at her child. "Perfect." As weary as it was, her smile had enough wattage to light all of Coruscant.

FORTY-SEVEN

Nen Yim walked with bowed head through the labyrinthine corridors of the great ship. Sculpted pylons of ancient but living bone raised the vast ceilings, and choirs of rainbow qaana hummed hymns to the gods through their chitinous mandibles. Rare paaloc incense—forbidden to all but the highest of the high—remembered the ancient homeworld of the Yuuzhan Vong to the hindmost recesses of her brain.

Kae Kwaad slunk beside her, strangely subdued.

In the center of the vast chamber, they came to a raised dais of pulsing, fibrous hau polyps, and atop it, shrouded in darkness and translucent lamina, reclined an enormous figure. Only his eyes were clearly visible, glowing maa'it implants that shifted through the colors of the spectrum. Other than that was only an irregular shadow that sent shivers of worship aching through her body. For a terrible moment she believed she had been brought into the very presence of Yun-Yuuzhan himself.

Kae Kwaad prostrated himself. "I have brought her, Dread Shimrra."

The eyes burned into her, but it was long, tremulous heartbeats before the figure spoke.

"Would you look upon me, Adept?" he said, his whispered voice surely as majestic and terrible as that of the god he resembled. "Would you look upon me and die?"

Nen Yim supplicated. "I would if you wish it, Dread Lord."

"You are a heretic, Nen Yim. Bred of heretics."

"I have done what I thought I must for the Yuuzhan Vong. I am prepared to die for my transgressions."

Shimrra made a noise, then—a rustling, vaporous noise that she only gradually recognized as laughter.

"You have seen the eighth cortex."

"I have gazed within it, Lord."

"And what did you see there? Speak."

"I saw . . . the end. The end of the protocols. The end of the secrets. Besides those few marvels the gods have gifted us with since our arrival at the infidel galaxy, the store of our knowledge is nearly exhausted."

"So it is," Shimrra acknowledged. "You alone of all shapers know this." Something that was not a natural hand gestured at Kae Kwaad from the shadows. "Onimi. Reveal yourself."

"Yes, Dread Lord." Kae Kwaad—no, *Onimi*—capered, then. With a twist, the dead shaper hands dropped from his wrists, revealing ordinary Yuuzhan Vong digits. He stripped off the masquer that hid his face, and bile rose in Nen Yim's throat at what she saw there.

The man she had thought a master shaper was deformed. Not scarred or modified as sacrifice to the gods, but misshapen as one born cursed by them. One eye lolled lower on his face than the other, and part of his skull was oddly distended. His mouth was a twisted slash. His long, lean limbs twitched with a sort of mad delight.

"Onimi is my jester," Shimrra murmured. "He amuses me. Sometimes he is useful. I sent him to watch you and fetch you."

"You see, my sweet Nen Tsup?" Onimi crowed. "You see?"

But Nen Yim did *not* see. She did not see at all.

"Silence, Onimi. Prostrate yourself and be silent."

The jester flattened himself against the coral deck and whimpered like a fearful beast.

"Yun-Yuuzhan shaped the universe from his own body," Shimrra intoned, his voice now modulated like a sacred chant. "In the days following his great shaping, he was weak, and in that time Yun-Harla tricked him into giving her some of those secrets. These she passed to her hand-maiden, Yun-Ne'Shel, and thence to me. I am the gateway of that knowledge. But Yun-Yuuzhan never gave up all of his secrets. Many he still holds for us, free of Yun-Harla's deceptions. They await us. I have seen it in a vision."

"I still do not understand, Dread Lord. The eighth cortex—"

"Silence!" The voice raised suddenly to a mind-numbing rumble, and Nen Yim found herself as prostrate as Onimi. She prepared herself for death.

But surprisingly, when he resumed, Shimrra's voice was again mild. "In my vision, Nen Yim, you were raised to the rank of master. In my vision, you quested for the knowledge that Yun-Yuuzhan holds out. He offers it, but he demands sacrifice and labor to obtain it. He requires that you pursue your heresy."

Nen Yim, afraid to speak, lay quiet, slowly understanding that she was not to die after all.

"The other shapers are the dupes of Yun-Harla," Shimrra went on. "They shall not know of this. You will labor here, with me. You will have the resources and assistants my household provides. Together with me, you will bring the deepest secrets of shaping forth from the waking mind of Yun-Yuuzhan, and before that unleashed knowledge, the infidels will fall." He paused. "Now, you may speak."

Nen Yim composed herself. "Dread Lord, the inhabitants of the worldship *Baanu Miir*—"

"They are nothing. They are dead. They might have been spared but for the infidels, who desecrated our shipwomb and destroyed the new worldship there. It is nothing. They were the old. The shapers are the old. You are on the new path, the most sacred of all, Master Nen Yim. Forget what has gone before."

They are nothing. The infidels had killed them, everyone on *Baanu Miir*, on every worldship too old and worn to achieve faster than lightspeed. In her heart, at that moment, Nen Yim felt a hard rage and made a solemn vow. Up until now, the infidels had been an interesting problem to her, almost an abstraction. Now they were her enemies in the deepest sense. Now she would work to bring about their annihilation.

And behind that quiet rage, quickly overwhelming it, overwhelming even the godlike presence of Shimrra, rose a strange, dark glee.

Now my shaping truly begins, she thought. *And the universe shall tremble at what I create.*

EPILOGUE

Luke warily regarded the holographic image of Borsk Fey'lya, chief of the New Republic.

"So you're saying I'm free to return to Coruscant?" the Jedi Master asked the cream-colored Bothan's diminutive image.

"If you wish," Fey'lya replied. "I want you to understand that the original order for your arrest came from the senate, not from me. It took some time, but I have exerted the pressure necessary to have it rescinded."

"I appreciate that, Chief. But I seem to remember that it was *you* who threatened me with arrest a few months ago. How can I be certain that this isn't just a trick to lure me back?"

"In point of fact," Fey'lya said, "I hope you *don't* come back."

"Why is that?"

"Don't take me for a fool, Master Skywalker. I am aware of at least some of your activities. It is perhaps possible that some of them are . . . useful. However, there are still elements in the senate—powerful elements—who cite you and your Jedi as the cause behind the Yuuzhan Vong breaking their truce. Now, you and I know—whatever I may have said before of political necessity—that the truce was broken because the Yuuzhan Vong very simply want every world in our galaxy. But, though I've made the arrest go away, I still am not in a position to actually sanction your rogue activities."

"In other words, you want deniability."

"I *have* deniability, Master Skywalker. I want to keep it

that way, for the time being." He paused. "In time, things may change."

"I think I understand you, Chief," Luke said. *In time we Jedi may be your only hope.*

"Good. In that case, I'll bid you good day—or night, whichever it is, wherever you are. And, Master Skywalker?"

"Yes, Chief Fey'lya?"

"I hope things go well with the birth of your child."

"As a matter of fact, I now have a son," Luke said.

"My deepest congratulations to you and your wife," Fey'lya said.

"Thank you," Luke replied. "May the Force be with you."

The Bothan nodded gravely, and his image wavered out.

"How could you be so calm with that preening Hutt-drool?" Mara asked. She was half reclining on the bed, Ben sleeping—finally!—in her arms.

Luke shrugged. "It would have been the easy path to show him anger. After all, his actions nearly cost me everything." He sat on the bed next to her, and she nestled under his arm. He looked down at his son.

"But we're okay. He's not worth the pain of anger. Besides, if we can mend skyhooks instead of crashing them, we should."

"You're such a softy, Skywalker," she said, but nestled deeper into his arms, so he could reach all the way around her.

"You had another communication while I was in the 'fresher," she said.

"I was just getting to that. It was Kam. He and Tionne think they've found the planet we're looking for. And they send their congratulations."

"So they're headed back here?"

"Yep."

"Wow. And the *Falcon* showed up yesterday. When Jaina gets here, it'll be a real reunion."

"Yeah." Luke touched the tiny, perfect digits of Ben's hand. "And guess who'll be the center of attention? That's you, fellah." He cocked his head. "He looks like you today."

"He looks healthy," Mara said softly. "After that, he could look like a Dug for all I care."

"You did it, Mara," he whispered, kissing her cheek.

"*We* did it, Luke."

"Now I only want to know one thing," Luke said.

"That being?"

"How long before we get to sleep through the night again?"

Mara snorted and patted his hand fondly. "If this one is anything like the Solo kids, I'd say at least another twenty years."

Something in Ben's gray eyes seemed to agree.